On his sprint to the jeep, Raul saw three enemy aerospace fighters flash by to the south on high-speed runs. He clambered into the vehicle, which started with a desperate lunge to get where it was going before a passing pilot decided it made a nice stationary target.

They raced eastward, toward the BattleMech hangars. Ahead of him, just taking to the air, Raul saw the Yellow Jacket that Blaire had called for Tassa Kay. She would be on the field as well. He might never hear about Dieron, he suddenly realized. And as a strafing fighter tore up the road in front of them with its nose-mounted autocannon, Raul quickly came to realize something more important about live combat.

He might never hear about anything again. Ever.

A CALL TO
ARMS

A BATTLETECH® NOVEL

Loren L. Coleman

A ROC BOOK

ROC
Published by New American Library, a division of
Penguin Putnam Inc., 375 Hudson Street,
New York, New York 10014, U.S.A.
Penguin Books Ltd, 80 Strand,
London WC2R ORL, England
Penguin Books Australia Ltd, 250 Camberwell Road,
Camberwell, Victoria 3124, Australia
Penguin Books Canada Ltd, 10 Alcorn Avenue,
Toronto, Ontario, Canada M4V 3B2
Penguin Books (N.Z.) Ltd, Cnr Rosedale and Airborne Roads,
Albany, Auckland 1310, New Zealand

Penguin Books Ltd, Registered Offices:
Harmondsworth, Middlesex, England

First published by Roc, an imprint of New American Library,
a division of Penguin Putnam Inc.

First Printing, February 2003
10 9 8 7 6 5 4 3 2 1

Cover design by Ray Lundgren

 REGISTERED TRADEMARK—MARCA REGISTRADA

Printed in the United States of America

PUBLISHER'S NOTE
This is a work of fiction. Names, characters, places, and incidents either are
the product of the author's imagination or are used fictitiously, and any
resemblance to actual persons, living or dead, business establishments,
events, or locales is entirely coincidental.

For Janna Silverstein,
who immersed herself in the *BattleTech* universe
and helped make a good book better.

ACKNOWLEDGMENTS

Writing this novel came as something of a relief. It proved to me (and others) that *BattleTech* would continue. From the uncertain times when FASA first announced that it would close its doors until now, there was always that fear that the novel *Endgame* would indeed be the proverbial "it." Finis. Rest in print.

It's so great to see that you can't keep a good universe down. *BattleTech*'s saga will continue under the *MechWarrior* title, and it is important to me to note that this novel, *A Call To Arms,* would never have happened without contributions from the following:

Jordan and Dawne Weisman, Mort Weisman, and Maya Smith, for their support and hard work behind the scenes at WizKids Games. Also Sharon and Mike Mulvihill, Pam, Scott, and others who continue to help take the company and its various universes to new heights.

My agent, Don Maass, who worked very hard with the new company. My editor, Janna Silverstein, who worked very hard with an opinionated author.

Michael Stackpole, who's always available for brainstorming or answering the odd question and who dispenses his hard-won advice freely. And special thanks to Randall and Tara Bills—Randall for his continued support and friendship, and Tara, for putting up with the two of us in the same room.

Also I'd like to thank Oystein Tvedten, again, for the very cool maps, and Bones, Warner, Chris, and Herb, for their direct contributions.

Love to my family, Heather, Talon, Conner, and Alexia. Your support is still what makes this all worthwhile.

Of course, I have to mention Rumor, Ranger, and

Chaos, who help lower my stress level just when I need a good lap-warmer, and then keep me from getting complacent just when I need a hairball on my chair. And now there is the dog, Loki, who still can't figure out why the other three don't want to play. They're cats! Leave them alone.

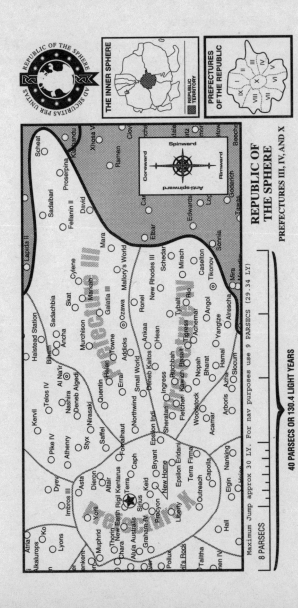

REPUBLIC OF THE SPHERE
AND SECURITAS PER UNITAS

THE INNER SPHERE

REPUBLIC
TERRITORY

PREFECTURES
OF THE REPUBLIC

REPUBLIC OF
THE SPHERE
PREFECTURES III, IV, AND X

Spinward

Coreward   Rimward

Anti-spinward

40 PARSECS OR 130.4 LIGHT YEARS

Maximum Jump approx 30 LY. For nav purposes use 9 PARSECS (29.34 LY)

8 PARSECS

Prolog

(Two Years Before the Blackout)

Program 12: Highlake Basin
Achernar
Prefecture IV, The Republic
26 October 3130

Sporadic artillery *cr-umped* along Raul Ortega's rear-ward flank: twenty-pounders. They stomped large craters through the crusted, cracked-mud surface of Achernar's Highlake Basin, scuffed blackened earth and embers of burning grasses into the air, and occasionally kicked over an infantry position, forcing survivors to scurry like armored ants reforming injured lines.

Those bright, orange-tipped flashes shattered the deepening twilight and cast brief shadows forward of Raul's *Legionnaire* as he stalked the fifty-ton BattleMech into the no-man's-land separating his forces from Charal DePriest's. From three stories up, his cockpit placed as a head on the humanoid-style war machine, Raul stared out through a ferroglass shield to study the battlefield. Armored vehicles drove and dodged through the killing zone, their autocannons and machine guns stitching the air with white-hot tracers. Ruby laserfire splashed armor into molten puddles. Flights of missiles arced up on fiery plumes, falling over into hard-hitting showers that blasted into the ancient lakebed and ripped open armor and flesh where they found it.

Two gutted APV's, both of them Charal's, burned at the edge of the dry lake basin, roiling black, greasy smoke into a charcoal sky.

He felt a loose smile—the one Major Blaire called Raul's *kay-det* grin—creep over his face. Those two vehicles didn't make up for his lost Marksman, a blackened husk left at the foot of the Taibek Hills, but with a bit of luck Charal would have failed to deploy her own battlesuit infantry and that would put the other MechWarrior-cadet at a disadvantage.

After two hours in the hot seat, muscles strained and sore and his hands sweat-slick on the simulator's well-worn controls, Raul didn't mind asking for a touch of luck.

"Charlie-one through six: advance and engage," Raul commanded his carefully hoarded infantry. The Cavalier-suited warriors leapt out of hiding from jagged-edged craters or spilled from his two Saxon transports. A few bounded up on thrusters. Most swarmed forward in short, erratic sprints. Raul could hope that one squad might actually make a battlefield capture, but if nothing else, he decided, they would draw fire away from him.

It wasn't soon enough, though. A particle projector cannon scorched the air just over his *Legionnaire's* left shoulder. Raul ducked away reflexively. He stutter-stepped his BattleMech several cautious paces to the right where a JES Tactical Missile Carrier fell under his sights, branded in enemy-red on the head's up display.

He checked his ammunition reserves in a glance—down, but not critically low—and set his crosshairs over the *Jessie's* dark outline. The *Legionnaire's* targeting computer painted a shadow-reticle to the right of the hovercraft, adjusting for relative motion. Raul corrected his aim, swinging over the BattleMech's arm to lead the JES Carrier by several meters, and then pulled into his only weapons trigger.

His rotary autocannon spit out a long tongue of fire

and fifty-mil rounds tipped with depleted uranium. The slugs punched into the hovercraft's right side missile launcher, chewing through simulated armor as the vehicle slewed sideways. A weakened support arm twisted under the launcher's weight, buckled, and dropped the boxlike launcher into the full stream of hot, angry metal. Missiles ruptured, their solid fuel boosters catching fire and cooking off several warheads before the tank crew could dump the ruined ammunition, and the launcher disintegrated into a blossom of fire.

The explosion rocked the hovercraft up on its skirt and spilled away the supporting cushion of air. The *Jessie* tipped up and over, coming down on the overhead launcher, which discharged in a sympathetic detonation. Armor panels bulged on all sides, then burst apart. A gout of fire shot into the sky, thick and tall, glowing yellow-orange at the center and simply darkening to a nimbus of red wisps at the edge. It looked . . . minimal.

Fake.

Raul's smile slid away. Cheap fire effects always ruined the explosion in his opinion, reminding him that his battle wasn't exactly real. Fire should dance and cavort, cheering his temporary victory.

It was one of only a few flaws in the Mark III simulators used by Achernar's training command. Usually, he lost himself within the simulation without problem. The cockpit swayed with each step his *Legionnaire* took, hitched hard when a trio of missiles slammed into his left leg, and the simulator threw him forward against the five-point restraining harness every time the BattleMech's cockpit took a direct hit. It also dumped heat through small vents near his feet when he stressed the fusion reactor. All reinforced the illusion—the lie—that he controlled an actual BattleMech—except for the fire.

Not that he'd let simplified effects distract him from beating Charal DePriest. Charal had more formal training, raised in a family of long military traditions. Raul pushed forward with determination and a measure of raw talent detected in the academy admissions testing. They had long since left the other cadets far behind. Challenging each other for the number-one spot, academic and practical standings too close to call for several months now, their good-natured rivalry had turned serious. It was more than a game today—more than a routine training procedure in Achernar's Reserve Training Corps. This was his final exam. Graduation.

Today's simulated battle decided who picked up the vaunted billet in Achernar's militia, commanding one of The Republic's rare BattleMechs, and who finished a law enforcement degree looking forward to commanding a desk for two years before learning how to write parking citations.

Enemy icons cluttered Raul's head's up display, laser-projected across the upper third of his cockpit's ferroglass shield. Their short tag lines of information tangled in among IFF codes for his own skirmishers. In his mind, the coded tags resolved into two forces of similar troops, spread out over the dry lake basin. Armored vehicles chewed up the ground with belted treads and knobby tires. Hovercraft glided along with deadly menace like wolves among sheep. If Raul held an edge it was in raw firepower, although Charal DePriest made up for that with superior mobility.

More than made up for it, in fact, as a green-haloed square on his HUD burst in a flare of emerald light. At a glance he read that a squad of Charal's hoverbikes had overpowered and destroyed his remaining Demon tank.

Raul cursed his luck for drawing Program 12, the Highlake Basin, and then cursed himself for not anticipating Charal's early move out of the Taibek Mountains, the jagged edge of the northwest horizon. Swallowing back the dry, metallic taste of his anger, he dialed in the frequency for his computer-controlled vehicle commanders.

"Alpha group, spread nor-nor'west. Beta, spread nor'east."

These were his two primary battle group formations of heavy armor. By cupping them around Charal's advance forces, supporting his infantry drive, Raul hoped to fold the enemy into a pincer. If nothing else, he might be able to thin out the middle of the field, allowing him to push through and finally come to grips with his opponent.

"Delta group," he called up his reserve line of armored vehicles, holding defensive positions behind him, "shake out into a skirmishing wedge."

The HUD's chaos of icons thinned, but not so much that he would get an easy push through at Charal DePriest. He'd have to fight his way through, which was exactly what Charal wanted of him. The entire confrontation so far, she'd commanded from a support position while he always stalked the forward edge of battle. She waited for him to soften up his defenses on her stinging probes—waited for him to make a mistake. The first MechWarrior to fall wouldn't end the scenario, no matter how far ahead he (or she) might be.

It would give the other commander free reign to leisurely destroy the opposing, computer-generated force down to the last digital man.

As if summoned by that dark thought, a pair of SM1 Destroyers glided out of the enemy pack, hunting him. Raul pulled back behind the defensive line he'd set with four Joust-701s, counting on the threat of their large lasers to hold back the *Sims*. He knew better than to close with an SM1's 'Mech-killing twelve centimeter bore, and Charal knew enough not to challenge an entrenched line. The *Sims* fell back, their drive fans pushing them on toward better prey, and Raul stalked northwest to mirror the sudden movement of Charal's *Legionnaire*.

She'd make the first mistake, and he'd be there to catch her. He allowed for no other possibility.

Being a MechWarrior was all Raul had dreamed of as a teen, whether sitting with his father through their seventh screening of an *Immortal Warrior* holovid or in his school studies of The Republic's military history. It didn't matter that there were no longer any wars to fight. To him, the Word of Blake Jihad was ancient history. Devlin Stone's Reformation and the resulting birth of The Republic of the Sphere had required some fighting, but not much compared to the previous four hundred years of Succession Wars and the Clan invasion. And even Stone's last battle had been fought nearly two decades before, bringing an end to the Capellan Crusades and peace to the Inner Sphere.

The allure of being a MechWarrior, though, was one that refused to pale, and had become almost legendary with the widespread arms reduction. It spoke to Raul in the reverent way people referred to Devlin Stone's Knights of the Sphere. With the intense coverage of the gladiator 'Mechs on the game world of Solaris VII. Even in the way his classmates looked at him now; only a cadet and MechWarrior-candidate but, in their minds, a future officer, knight, legate or prefect.

Raul had promises to keep, and no one was going to stand in the way of that dream. He searched through his cockpit's ferroglass shield for a new target.

Charal DePriest found him first.

A storm of tracers skipped off Raul's cockpit shield and then drifted down over the *Legionnaire's* torso as Charal reached out from long range to walk a line of destruction from head to hip joint. Ferroglass cracked into the legs of two long spiderwebs, barely holding up under the assault. The simulator trembled violently, shaking Raul against his five-point harness—hard enough to leave deep bruises across his shoulders and abdomen. His neurohelmet slammed back against the seat's headrest, cracking one of the support posts.

The *Legionnaire's* massive gyroscopic stabilizers relied on Raul's own sense of equilibrium, linked through the pilot's neurohelmet. Shaken, Raul blinked back a wave of dizziness and the sensation of sudden vertigo as his BattleMech balanced on uncertain footing.

Recognizing the uneasy sway of his *Legionnaire,* Raul spread out both of the 'Mech's arms for balance and throttled into a slower walk to recover the stricken avatar. Icons danced over his HUD, demanding his attention. But Major Blaire had taught them that it was always better to do something immediate and constructive in a live-fire situation than debate overlong on the exact right thing to do. Raul was an attentive student.

"Alpha group, hard press." His order might buy him some time if Charal had to deal with a sudden advance.

His own reticle tracked across the cracked shield, painted by a targeting laser, but for the distance Raul switched over to his infrared monitor and full computer imaging. Charal was on the move, but he bracketed her in a long pull of autocannon fire before ever looking at his HUD for more information. Raul spent several hundred rounds on empty air but several hundred more into the outline of Charal's *Legionnaire*. His return fire chipped away armor from its arms and upper chest, rocking it back but not doing enough damage to knock Charal off her feet.

Static whispered into Raul's ears as a transmission burst from his computer-controlled subofficers crackled over the speakers built into his neurohelmet. "Alpha group," the voice identified itself. "We're through, sir."

For a brief second Raul thought that his armor group had decided to desert him. That would be a new twist coming out of the computer's limited programming. Then, shaking off the last of his dizziness, he caught on that elements of Alpha formation had penetrated to the rearward lines on this flank.

Raul was behind her!

His head's up display painted the same picture as he spent several critical seconds in study. Charal's brief move forward, coupled with his return push of battlesuit infantry and armor, had opened up the field between them so that both *Legionnaires* faced off over open ground. Her western flank was in chaos, cut off from their commander by a narrow line of his own troops. She had two . . . looked like three armored vehicles left in the immediate area that might be able to reach her side.

"Beta group, smash forward. Tie them up. Alpha, hold your line. Delta, reinforce Alpha." Raul rattled off his commands with a confidence born of immediate need. If only he could wait for his reserve infantry in Delta to move up, he might be able to capture Charal's BattleMech—and wouldn't that be a fine cap to his RTC record?

Throttling into a forward run, Raul pushed his *Legionnaire* ahead at better than one hundred kilometers per hour. Charal was already backpedaling, realizing her exposed position, but not soon enough. Sporadic fire from her rotary autocannon pecked and pockmarked his armor, hammering away barely a ton of protection from his *Legionnaire's* lower legs and torso.

"Lance 701," he called for the quad of Jousts that had held off the SM1 Destroyers earlier, "detach from Delta." He'd need them to help put Charal down quickly. "Advance at flank speed, engage enemy *Legionnaire*."

At the Jousts' eighty-six kph top speed, Raul left the tracked vehicles behind quickly. They only needed to reach a fair distance, though, to bring their missile racks and extended-range lasers against her 'Mech, or, if need be, any of the supporting armor Charal had left to her.

As if realizing her error, and that she would never get free in time, Charal DePriest waited with two armored vehicles pulled in at her flanks. The computer tagged them as VV1 Rangers, anti-infantry vehicles—hardly the forces one would draw on to hold off a BattleMech.

Caution whispered at the back of Raul's mind and he slowed his pace, throttling down to seventy kph, buying himself crucial seconds. A MechWarrior did not push a losing position, not a MechWarrior trained under Major Isaac Blaire. 'Mechs were too rare—too expensive—to risk them with a cavalier attitude. Raul had taken hits on his evals for that, and to see Charal suddenly hold the line when everything he saw would have him screaming *run* gave him a long pause.

But there was nothing new to see. Her flanking forces had yet to break free of his two-pronged assault, and except for the VV1's she had a single Scimitar combat hovercraft and what now looked like a squad of Purifier armored infantry.

Not enough. Not nearly enough against his quad of Jousts, and Charal knew it. She had something else in mind.

He learned what a moment later.

"Alpha group. Enemy has disengaged."

The report sounded too good to be true, that Charal was abandoning the battlefield, especially when Beta and Delta echoed the same situation a split-second later. Then the first flight of LRMs saturated the dead *lakebed* around his position, geysering earth and blackened rock into the air. A dozen scattered missiles slammed into his BattleMech's upper body, blasting away armor. The explosions echoed into his cockpit, filling his ears with a stuttering roar.

Raul's alarms screamed from multiple targeting system locks. Other than Charal's small trio, the nearest vehicle was still nearly a half kilometer away—a JES Strategic Missile Carrier packing along its four racks of long-ranged missiles. *Big Jess* launched a second, full spread of missiles just before it exploded under the concentrated fire of what looked like Raul's entire Beta formation.

Charal's armored forces had disengaged all right. They were completely disregarding Raul's troops, falling back through his lines no matter the cost to rendezvous on her position and concentrate on one single target: Raul's *Legionnaire*.

She had pulled him right into a massive trap!

"Alpha, Beta, Delta, defend my position!" Raul's voice held a frantic edge to it, one he never would have used in command of real troops. "Lance 701, full assault on enemy *Legionnaire*."

Their lasers were already stabbing out at the 'Mech as Charal advanced now behind a makeshift screen of the two Rangers and Scimitar. Purifier battlesuit troops leapt forward on tiny jets, and on Raul's far right one of the SM1 'Mech-killers broke free and sped into the killing ground after him as well.

Missiles churned up the lakebed again. Several rained down on his *Legionnaire's* shoulders, caused him to stumble forward while Charal's rotary pummeled him with fifty-mil rounds. Her autocannon slugs struck all over his armor like hundreds of tiny hammers, each one tolling a death knell.

Raul ran through the storm of hot metal, blinking away the tracers' ghostly afterimage and keeping his finger down on the firing stud of his own rotary autocannon. His only salvation was to take her down first. Take her down, and then mop up her computer-controlled forces as his armored vehicles hit them point-blank from behind. His stream of non-stop autocannon fire cut through her BattleMech's right arm but failed to make it deep enough into her side to silence the rotary.

A Cavalier battlesuit trooper leapt for her, but she smashed it out of the air with a backhanded swat. One of Raul's Jousts cut a molten wound directly over the reactor shielding of Charal's *Legionnaire,* and on his thermal imaging screen her heat level blossomed to a critical level, but not enough to slow down her rapid-cycling barrages.

A second of Charal's JES Strategics lumbered into range—on Raul's left this time—launching flight after flight of missiles, which hammered down around him until the entire planet of Achernar appeared to be shaking itself apart. Charal held up her deadly, cutting assault from the front while the Rangers split apart and, with the Scimitar, hit him on three sides simultaneously. An inferno of laser fire and the Rangers' stinging miniguns hammered into him, shaking the massive BattleMech beyond the capability of its gyroscope or its pilot to compensate.

Raul had time for one last burst of fire from his autocannon. Then he stumbled. He fell first to his knees, sliding along in a pose of subjugation, then facedown into the earth, the impact rattling his teeth together. The ferroglass shield caved in, its digital picture dropping out large shards that would—in a real battle—ricochet through the cockpit on dangerous, even deadly, paths.

He tasted blood, and his vision swam through a murky

haze. Fighting for his final hold on consciousness, Raul levered one of the *Legionnaire's* arms beneath it and pushed against the planet. His shattered cockpit shield scraped free of the baked mud, he looked up over one of the speeding Rangers to see Charal also fighting her way back to her feet. His final burst had cut into her gyro housing, knocking the leviathan over but not out.

"Still . . . time . . ." Raul told himself, fighting to get his legs under him. His bitten tongue throbbed with each word.

The fury of missiles and autocannon fire had abated, the calm at the eye of a storm. He heard a light scrabbling, like steel-toed mice nesting inside his *Legionnaire's* armor, and worry stabbed up from the dark memories of his training but it took an extra moment for the source to register. The Purifiers! Charal's infantry had crawled up from the ground, hooking footholds into his joints and ruined armor, searching for deep wounds to tear into or—worse—his cockpit hatch.

Raul's heads-up display blinked and stuttered, occasionally wiped itself with gray-snow static, but it looked as if two of his Jousts were now out of commission. Through his shattered ferroglass shield he saw a ruby lance slice deep into Charal's left leg. It did not keep her from pulling back to a solid stance. The simulator's speakers banged a deep, metal echo into his ears—the sound of infantry on his outer hatch. Swallowing against the taste of blood, and his own worry of failure, Raul braced himself up into a three-point crouch and drew his targeting crosshairs over the center of Charal's 'Mech. His targeting computer locked onto a bleeding-thermal wound, the reticle burning a golden bull's-eye over her reactor.

Gambling for one last shot, Raul thumbed the firing stud.

And the simulator's screens went blank.

No video image of Highlake Basin. No enemy 'Mech or vehicles. No friendlies, either. He wanted to believe that his final shot had gone off and burst through her reactor shielding, tried to talk himself into it, but as a hand slapped the simulator's outside shell and began to crank open the heavy door, he knew. His ears still ringing from the loud sound effects of battle, Raul heard the cheers and clapping of the RTC cadet corps, saluting the victor and the newest MechWarrior in Achernar's militia.

Charal DePriest.

1

The Job

San Marino Spaceport
Achernar
11 February 3133

Customs Security Officer Raul Ortega glanced up from his handheld noteputer, distracted. The spaceport's underground service area bustled with a sudden burst of frenetic activity that only came with the arrival of a new DropShip to Achernar.

Dozens of tram-haulers crawled along electric tracks, flatbeds stacked high with colorful plastic crates and large, metal shipping containers stenciled from dozens of different worlds. A trio of LoaderMechs stomped along beside the haulers. The Loaders' high, hunched shoulders nearly scraped against the tunnel ceiling and the high-pitched whirr of their flywheel batteries stressed toward fingernails-on-slate with each heavy step. On the far outside of the wide corridor moved foot traffic as cargo handlers and shipping agents fought against a flood of able-bodied spacemen heading into River's End, Achernar's capital, on shore leave.

Thick air carried the warm tastes of ozone and sweat and cheap cologne.

Raul stood just outside the trunk corridor in one of

many warehousing routes, waiting in the company of
Lord Erik Sandoval-Groell for the industrial parade to
pass. The young noble glared at the interruption, arms
crossed, one hand tapping an impatient rhythm. "Everything is in order," Sandoval said loudly, trying to hurry
Raul along.

Erik Sandoval wore an officer's uniform and the captain's bars of his honorary rank, both privileges granted
him by his uncle, Duke Aaron Sandoval, The Republic's
Lord Governor of Prefecture IV. He shaved the sides of
his head for the traditional topknot of a Sandoval dynasty scion, braiding what was left back into a short, dark
queue. The youngblood had eyes of heavy amber, which
burned softly with an inner fire. Only three or four centimeters taller than Raul's medium one-seventy, he carried
the extra height with shoulders back and proud chin thrust
forward as if it conveyed some sort of extra superiority.

"I do have other business to complete today."

Apparently Sandoval had conveniently forgotten that
he had flagged down Raul's cart, interrupting the CSO's
call to Docking Pad Seven. Raul wanted to put the short
attitude down to the prerogative of an off-world noble,
or the frustration of an officer with bureaucracy. Erik
Sandoval-Groell was both. But Sandoval had also been
on Achernar long enough to allow for some social graces,
and his local command was part of the problem with any
red tape delays and he damn well knew it.

Sandoval either wasn't likable, or simply wasn't trying
to be.

But Raul nodded politely, returned to the noteputer
he cradled in his right hand. He paged down through
manifest logs, comparing his noteputer's glowing green
screen to the hardcopy pages Sandoval had pressed on
him. He traced a set of serial numbers to three large-
class lasers stockpiled in one of the spaceport's secure
warehouses. And there was more. One hundred ten tons
of armor composite. Fifteen tons of various munitions.
A Mydron eighty-millimeter autocannon.

"It's all restricted-access." He paged back up the list of serial numbers. "Why do you need all this?"

"I need it because I have the permits which say that I can have it. I only require your local release." Reminded that he *did,* in fact, require local release, Sandoval relented somewhat. "I'm leading my people into the Tanager Testing Range on a live-fire exercise."

His people.

Nausea clutched lightly at Raul's insides, and he worked to keep his revulsion from showing inside his dark, near-black eyes. Sandoval meant the Swordsworn, one of several factions that had cropped up in the Republic since the Blackout. The Swordsworn openly swore their fealty to Erik's uncle, believing that Exarch Redburn had abandoned Prefecture IV in his worries for other sectors within The Republic of the Sphere. Erik Sandoval wore his loyalty brazenly with the small patch sewn over his uniform's left breast pocket—a longsword cleaving across planetary dawn. The thought of The Republic breaking down into "us" and "them," into *his* people and *Raul's* people, left a sour taste at the back of Raul's throat that he hadn't known since attending Charal DePriest's commissioning ceremony two years back.

A sarcastic reply would have gone a long way to clearing his palate, scoring cheap points off the visiting noble. It might also have been a solid step toward that new career his fiancée occasionally asked after.

A LoaderMech swung out of its lane, saving Raul from a heated reply by barging through a gap in pedestrian traffic in an attempt to cut the corner and move ahead of a slower-moving tram. It carried a flanged barrel in its forked pincers, swaying dangerously close to the two men as it tried to squeeze in between them and the pair of electric carts parked nearby. Raul stiff-armed Sandoval back into the wall—perhaps a bit rougher than he needed to—then yanked off his black service cap, using it to flag down the LoaderMech's driver.

The LoaderMech rocked to a halt in midstep. A look of guilt flashed over the Loader driver's face as he identified the silver badge sewn onto the right front pocket of Raul's black uniform, quite clearly a Customs Security Officer. There was no chance for conversation, not with the driver encased in ferroglass and plugged against the high-pitched whine of the Loader's flywheel-battery conversion. He offered Raul a sheepish shrug and cocky grin, the half-serious apology of a man who knew the worst Raul could do was take down the Loader's serial and generate a letter of warning.

Raul waved the man through with a frustrated slash, standing aside as the bulky Loader finally squeezed past and still made it ahead of the tram. The distraction had given him the moment he'd needed to regain his composure. He tucked his hat brim into his belt at the small of his back, combed his curly, dark hair back with long fingers, and turned again to Erik Sandoval-Groell.

"My apologies, Lord Sandoval." Raul smoothed the words over, meaning them about as much as the Loader-Mech driver had meant his guilty shrug. Perhaps a little more. Eric Sandoval wasn't the enemy. "I'll get someone on your request right away," he said, performing some quick input into his noteputer.

The young noble straightened his uniform, glaring. "Your supervisor told me that you would handle this." Sandoval's tone somehow carried the full weight of his authority as well as that of Raul's boss. "Personally."

A tight smile strained at the corners of Raul's mouth. "Personally," he agreed, resigning himself to another twelve-hour day. He fought to keep the irritation from coloring his dark brown eyes any blacker. "If you will send some men to"—he checked his screen—"warehouse alcove one-twelve, I'll meet them there as soon as I'm done with my emergency call to Docking Pad Seven. All right?"

The pinched expression on Sandoval's face didn't say it was all right. But it was hard to argue when Raul had basically conceded the point *and* had played an "emergency" trump.

"I'll send some of my people over," Sandoval promised. "I'll also be talking to Superintendent Rossiter, you may be certain."

Raul snagged his service cap from the small of his back and tugged it on smartly. He nodded a respectful salute to Erik Sandoval-Groell. "Sir," he said, skimping a bit on the title but maintaining a professional manner even when his inner sense of decorum agreed that Sandoval deserved little more than flat competency.

Eric Sandoval returned to his cart and shifted it into gear, leaving Raul free to climb back into his own battery powered vehicle. Merging into the trunk corridor, Raul steered carefully around pedestrian and LoaderMech traffic and tried to set aside his frustrations. He didn't worry too much about what his boss would say. Carl Rossiter was a reasonable man stuck with an unreasonable job these days, and Raul's call to Pad Seven *was* an emergency—of sorts—in the manner that it came directly from the office of Achernar's military legate, Brion Stempres. If it came down to who deserved Raul's attention first, the CSO would bank on Achernar's ranking military officer, Stempres' friendship with the Sandovals notwithstanding.

The drive to Pad Seven wasn't so long that Raul had time to worry after Erik Sandoval or whatever critiques he might bring to his supervisor, so instead he lost himself in an old Customs game, reading the shipping stencil prefixes on large containers and trying to identify the world from which they came. Many of them were easy, shipped in from other worlds in Prefecture IV: Tikonov and Tigress, Rio, Yangtze, and Ronel. Others tested his knowledge. M3A was Mara, of The Republic's Prefecture III. Denebola, D9B8, was actually the governing capital of Prefecture VIII but a rare trading partner with Achernar. He pegged another container originating from VIII, SM8, but couldn't place it between Syrma or Summer. He filed a mental note to look it up later.

True challenges came from outside The Republic, of course. Centered at the core of the Inner Sphere, with mankind's birthworld of Terra cradled in its middle, The Republic had long enjoyed decent trading relations with most other major powers: House Kurita's Draconis Combine, the mercantile Sea Foxes. In the few months before the Blackout, the Senate's new Free Trade Agreement had opened up a floodgate of shipping coming in from the hundreds of worlds belonging to the Lyran Commonwealth. Even now the gauntlet crest of House Steiner was not an uncommon sight in the service corridors. And here was a prefix from deep inside the balkanized Free Worlds League. And there . . .

The sword-and-sunburst crest of House Davion's Federated Suns. A device very similar to the one adopted by Aaron Sandoval and the Swordsworn.

So much for the game.

That the Swordsworn insignia borrowed so heavily from the Davion crest was not surprising. The Sandoval dynasty had deep roots in the Federated Suns, with other family lines still governing many worlds along the Davion-Kurita border. Aaron Sandoval came from a long tradition of powerful rulers, most of them jealous of their own position and ready to defend it, their worlds, and nation with armies under their complete domination.

It was because of such military-political dynasties, in fact, that the legendary Star League fell and the Inner Sphere suffered through three hundred years of Succession Wars, the Clan invasion, and then the Word of Blake Jihad. Abolishing such violent nationalism was the very reason behind Devlin Stone's creation of The Republic of the Sphere. His incentives inspired large measures of the population to relocate until many Republic worlds held a mixture of races and cultures, blending them together, easing the tensions of old rivalries. His plan worked.

For two generations.

Raul swerved his cart out of traffic at Docking Pad Three, catching sight of a black Customs Security uniform and the harried face of CSO Palos Montgomery near the wide-open, and empty, bay. Officer Palos stood before a small crowd of dockhands and suits—union reps, was Raul's guess—holding back their questions and outbursts with upraised hands.

Setting the brake on his cart but leaving it idling, Raul waved Palos over. His friend's normally gaunt face looked positively drawn and haggard today, and his green eyes were bloodshot from long hours.

Palos held himself up on the cart's battery compartment cover. "Thanks, Raul. I needed a break from that."

"Shouldn't you be coming off night shift?"

His friend laughed, a weak chuckle that died prematurely. "Oh, yeah. I'm looking at sixteen hours today, but what you gonna do?"

What indeed? The Blackout caused by the crash of nearly every Hyperpulse Generator in The Republic—perhaps over the entire Inner Sphere—had left each world isolated as they had never been in the long history of Humanity's spread among the stars. Customs was just one agency being forced to pick up the slack, and no amount of overtime was going to appease a population discovering its fear of the dark.

"What's the problem?" Raul asked, nodding his commiseration. "Where's the DropShip that was due on Pad Three?" By his memory, that vessel should have been down yesterday. But there was something from his morning brief . . . "Is it still having . . . drive failure?"

Palos nodded. "Yeah. That's the problem exactly. And it's my problem until we get that egg dropped down and opened up. The crew claims to be on top of it. They just want to be sure about not plummeting down through the atmosphere."

Raul dismissed such problems with an airy wave. "Bah. Dropping without a drive flare isn't the problem."

"No?"

Raul grinned. "Huh-uh. It's that sudden stop at the very bottom."

Fourteen hours on the job, a touch of dark humor was just what Palos needed. He smiled, briefly. "Thanks. That just leaves hourly waves of shipping agents and long-shoreman reps to deal with."

"Tell them you heard the problem might be fixed. Tell them to give you a couple hours while you leave to go get a revised ETA. Then clock out and hand it to day shift."

Palos smiled fully this time. "You going to cover that?" he asked.

Raul shrugged, looking forward to a sixteen-hour day himself now. Jessica would have to wait on dinner. "If I can't, I'll get someone to handle it. Go."

He nodded his friend on his way, moved his cart along the corridor and filed a mental reminder to check on the wayward DropShip as soon as possible. He shrugged uncomfortably. With luck, his fiancée would be working late at the hospital. It would save them from another discussion over the problems—her viewpoint—of performance-based citizenship. As Jessica Searcy liked to put it, in medical terms, the Sandovals and the Sword-sworn were only symptoms of an ailment that had begun to exhibit even before the near-total collapse of the HPG network. The loss of interstellar communications, like the loss of a social antibiotic, simply allowed the sickness to fester and spread.

She could very well be right, Raul knew. It wasn't just the pro-Sandoval population. Achernar also had a small faction of supporters for Kal Radick and his Steel Wolves, and by all reports Ronel was dealing with inde-pendent raiders as well as a pro-Combine faction calling itself the Dragon's Fury. Shots had already been fired between factions. And Ronel, like Achernar, *had* a work-ing HPG. Two worlds among the twenty-five systems of Prefecture IV that did. Or, which at least were on speak-ing terms. How was it on a world completely cut off from everything, brought only shipboard rumor and a few hardspooled communiqués with each passing JumpShip?

The word brought last week via JumpShip was not good, suggesting that several worlds of The Republic were under full assault. But by the schisms growing from within or some outside force? Raul didn't know.

The air around Docking Pad Seven was stifling and smelled of hot metalwork, still bleeding waste heat left over from the DropShip's settling burn. The tunnels under Achernar's San Marino spaceport had been excavated during the peaceful years of Devlin Stone's reign, with landing pads able to accommodate up to the largest DropShip class. These docking pads lowered on thick, myomer trunks—the same artificial muscle system used to animate BattleMechs, only on a grander scale—to bring cargo doors below ground level. Ventilation was the only problem, requiring electrical motors and short-term tolerance to the residue heat from drive flares. Knowing how severe the weather on Achernar could get, running hot or stormy depending on the season, Raul was grateful for the underground service corridors.

Just now Pad Seven accommodated a popular Union-class merchant conversion. The lower fourth of the spheroid vessel nested down into the service area, enough to gain access to its three cargo bays. Raul's badge—double-checked against his identification—gained him unrestricted access to the secure landing facility. He drove his cart into the bay and straight up the secondary loading ramp, pulling aside once for a burdened LoaderMech and once more to edge past a crowd of spaceport technicians who had bluffed or bribed their way through security to see the same thing that had originally pulled Raul into the warrens today.

It was a BattleMech.

The bay smelled of grease and the must and dust from cargos loaded on a dozen different worlds. A cavernous space, once designed to hold two lances of BattleMechs, only two 'Mech alcoves with gantry support remained in this merchant conversion. One was webbed over with netting and charged-myomer restraints, tying down two stories worth of stacked crates. The other held a 'Mech. It squatted back on thick, reverse-canted legs. Unlike the box-jointed *Legionnaire* Raul had once trained on, this machine was designed with lean, purposeful lines and was rare to Prefecture IV. To Raul's knowledge it was only found in lance strength among the Northwind Highlander Regiments.

A *Ryoken II*. And a modified one at that.

Raul left his cart parked safely off to one side. Tucking his service cap away into his belt, he strolled slowly over to a gathering of uniforms and spaceport suits, eyes only for the BattleMech. Part of his RTC cadet days had included training on standard BattleMech configurations and visual identification of weapons systems. Refresher courses during his twice-yearly reserves duty had kept him up to date.

The *Ryoken II* was based on higher-level technology, developed by the Clans during their centuries-long exile from the Inner Sphere. Having left as saviors, members of Kerensky's Star League army, the Clans came back as conquerors and were barely held in check. Such technology had been co-opted into The Republic's small military when Devlin Stone accepted a sampling of Clan population after the Jihad.

Normally the *Ryoken II* fielded four long-barreled X-class light autocannons with twin missile launchers beefing up its shoulderline. This *Ryoken* had traded away long-ranged missiles for beefy, short-ranged six-packs. Two small barrels tucked into the chest would be some type of medium-class lasers, but there was no mistaking the wide bore and high-energy flashing of the remaining two weapons. Particle projector cannons, the hardest hitting weapon for its range that any MechWarrior could want.

"Now who's this?" someone asked from the center of the nearby meeting. The voice was feminine, but hardly soft. "Some new vapor-brained appointee here to tell me that he only has the best interests of all in mind?" The offhand insult wasn't nearly so attention grabbing as the casual way with which she tossed it out.

Raul pulled his attention away from the redesigned 'Mech, mentally kicking himself for not making a more politic approach. Uniforms outnumbered suits by two-to-one in the small gathering, though now Raul noticed that there were DropShip officers present as well as the military reps he'd expected. Holding the center of the pack as if ready to take on all-comers was a strikingly beautiful woman. She had dark red hair and green, predatory eyes which sized him up in a glance. Wearing nothing more complicated than a standard utility jumpsuit, she had unbuttoned it down to the top swells of her breasts, showing off a touch of cleavage and a faceted crystal necklace charm wrapped in three golden bands. Compact and confident, everything about her screamed *MechWarrior* to Raul in a way he had only imagined from holovids.

"You have something to contribute?" she asked. "Or did we wait around for an hour just so you can check out my hardware?" Raul wasn't so certain she was speaking about the BattleMech.

Still, an entire morning spent in the company of military officers and shipping clerks could set anyone on edge, and after Erik Sandoval he didn't imagine anyone else getting as deeply under his skin. "You are?"

"I am bloody annoyed." Her eyes flashed dangerously, and this time Raul caught a hint of Germanic accent in her voice. Lyran? "I am tired of being told where I can and can not take *my* 'Mech. That's who I am."

Her 'Mech? So possessive . . . was this machine in private ownership? If so, no wonder her arrival set off a confrontation. "Are you being denied visitation to Achernar?"

One of the suits stepped in a split second ahead of a shipboard officer. "As we tried to explain to Ms. Kay, we are only trying our best to decide whose jurisdiction most adequately—"

"That is restricted military technology," a line captain piped in, trumping the suit and ship's officer both. He shared many of Raul's Latino features, including the swarthy skin which came in so handy on Achernar, but he was taller and much more slender. "Legate Stempres demands that it be held by secure forces."

Raul saw the building outbursts rising to the lips of several nearby people, and cut them all off with a raised hand and a calm "Hold." The first rule of any negotiation, especially one that you want to deal with quickly and cleanly, was to pare the argument down to its primary opponents. "Ms . . . Kay? You own the *Ryoken*? It is your property?"

"Master of the obvious."

Raul let her blunt manner slide. "Captain Norgales," he read the nameplate pinned over the line officer's breast pocket, "you are here to represent Legate Stempres, correct?" And maybe even Erik Sandoval, by association. Raul barely let the other man nod and start to speak before cutting past the spaceport clerk and roping the ship's officer into the conversation. "And your position here is, what?"

"Ship's Second Officer Thomas. Captain Grey wants me to make certain that Tassa Kay is given full consideration, and that her . . . property . . . is not removed for any destination without her approval."

Tassa Kay. Raul had her full name now, and a problem he could deal with quickly. "Second Officer Thomas, you can assure your captain that no one will remove the BattleMech without giving him proper notice. Until the 'Mech walks out the cargo bay door, it's still his cargo and under his orders." Thomas seemed obliged to wait and see that for himself, but Raul nodded curtly. "Thank you, Shipman." He looked around. "And thank the rest of you for your time and effort here. I'll speak with MechWarrior Kay and Captain Norgales now, please."

The suits were the only ones to leave without muttered protests, happy to wash their hands of the issue and land it fully in the lap of Customs. Ship's Officer Thomas pulled his supporters to one side of the bay, giving Raul some privacy. The line officer nodded his own subordinates aside.

"Divide and conquer gets you only so far," Tassa Kay said, though a touch less harsh than the moment before. In her eyes, Raul thought he might have climbed up a notch. A flush warmed the back of his neck.

"Mr. Ortega," Norgales began much more civilly this

time. "Legate Stempres wants to make his concerns very
clear. With the trouble on Ronel, and elsewhere, the arrival of a privately owned BattleMech is not a small
matter."

"He wants it under his own personal lock and key,"
Tassa added. She shook her hair back over her shoulder,
and Raul watched it fall back in a graceful shimmer.
"Not going to happen."

Neutral, Raul warned himself. Stay neutral. "It is standard procedure to secure such equipment in Customs
lockup here at the San Marino," he reminded Norgales.
"And Customs is not under the Legate's authority. We're
civilian law enforcement."

Norgales shrugged his indifference over the semantics.
"But a request from Achernar's military leader, on a
military matter . . ."

Raul knew where Norgales was heading. If the Legate's weight didn't sway a CSO's opinion, it would certainly land upstairs on his boss, or even on the Director
of Customs herself. Raul needed an unassailable position
if he were to deny such a request. More than his general
attraction to the visiting MechWarrior. "MechWarrior
Kay." He struggled to find placating words, knew they'd
be useless against the growing fury which creased her
brow. He decided to ask the question outright. "Do you
have any mitigating circumstance which suggests your
property would be better protected under Customs
authority?"

"No. Not as such." Tassa pursed her lips in thought,
obviously debating something with herself. With a rueful
shake of her head, and a suspicious glance toward Norgales, she reached inside the deep neck of her jumpsuit
and pulled out a folded piece of paper that she handed
to Raul Ortega.

The folded document still held the heat of Tassa Kay's
body, warm to the touch and smelling ever so faintly of
jasmine. A verifax, the CSO noted, seeing the edge of a
hologram woven into the fibers. All but impossible to
forge. Opening the first fold, the hologram shone forth

like a beacon—and a gut punch to Raul's stomach. It was a sword, driven point-down through a novastar and surrounded by ten tiny suns—one for each Prefecture of the Republic.

The official seal of the Exarch.

If there were any doubts those were erased by the signature of Exarch Damien Redburn, written in a tight military scrawl just above the hologram. Raul opened the next two folds with greater care, almost reverence. The verifax message was as short as it was compelling, and definitely in keeping with the manner of the Exarch.

Please extend to the bearer, Tassa Kay, all possible courtesy. She has earned the gratitude of this Republic. Damien Redburn.

Raul swallowed dryly, and looked at Tassa Kay with new eyes. Her anger and frustration were still apparent, but also he noticed a slight air of amusement about her. The way her lips tipped up in one corner, and the jaunty set of her shoulders. A cat, toying with two mice. Or even a spider, which had just invited two flies into her parlor.

Well, one of those flies was happy to see the fangs behind her . . . well . . . not-so-honeyed words. Still, Raul had wanted to help Tassa out, and she had handed him ample justification for any decision he cared to make. Legate Sempres certainly couldn't argue with the Exarch, who was both the civilian *and* military leader of The Republic. He passed the verifax over to Captain Norgales and waved Second Officer Thomas back into the fold.

"Customs takes charge of MechWarrior Kay's *Ryoken*," he told Thomas, but never straying his eyes too far from Tassa. "It will be held at our remote station here at the San Marino," he backed Tassa Kay's impending outburst down with a shake of his head, "for the additional security offered by the presence of local militia. Customs will retain authority. Captain Norgales?"

Norgales didn't look at all happy, but he carefully handed Tassa Kay back her verifax and nodded.

Raul smiled tightly. "Good enough. Second Officer Thomas, if you'll get the appropriate noteputer forms, I'll attach my authorization. Good afternoon," he said to Norgales. And to Tassa, "Good luck." Raul stepped away from the two of them, knowing it was always best to distance one's self from any difficult negotiation as soon as possible. Let the decision stand on its own—no discussion of the merits.

He occupied himself instead with another look over the *Ryoken II,* walking directly up to its berth, standing in the overhang of the BattleMech's forward-thrust cockpit. The upper legs had an extra-wide flare of armor near the back—something he hadn't noticed before. If he didn't know better—

"So tell me what you see."

Tassa Kay stood just behind his left shoulder. Raul hadn't heard her approach, which seemed impossible given her forceful presence. He felt it weighing against him now, radiating a subliminal warmth. He swallowed against a knot in his throat.

"*Ryoken II,* obviously," he said. "Six-packs swapped in for the usual longshots, medium lasers over the top— I'm guessing extended-range—and PPCs at the waist. It must run hotter than an inferno round in combat, but its damage profile would be equally severe. And unless I'm mistaken, you've added jumpjet ports. The chassis can't support so much modification, though." He considered, hedged. "Unless you *also* lightened up your armor profile by using ferrofibrous material." All in all, it sounded like a military evaluation right out of the book.

Tassa must have thought so as well. "You don't talk like a cop," she said, almost accusing him. She stepped around to his side, where she could see his face.

"Republic Guard, Achernar Second Militia," he admitted. Then, "Reservist."

"Great Father, more weekend warriors." The oath

slipped out quickly, but didn't seem to be a personal slight so much as a general observation. "No offense," Tassa offered. "I should not be surprised, after Dieron."

For the second time since meeting her, Raul was actually able to forget—for a moment—the physical pull he felt. "You came here from Dieron?" That was one of the worlds where heavy fighting had supposedly occurred. A hundred questions sprung to mind. One fought its way to the fore. "What happened?"

Tassa looked down at her shoulder, as if staring through her jumpsuit fabric to the Exarch's verifax. "It was . . ." She seemed uncertain of the words. Her eyes glanced back to Raul, head still cocked down. "It was messy."

"Meaning you aren't going to tell me?"

"Not right now," Tassa agreed. "But I owe you. You buy me a drink sometime, and maybe I'll talk about it. Maybe." She raised an eyebrow, turned on her heel and started away.

Raul smiled, laughing at himself, at his obviously male reaction to Tassa Kay's every move. A shadow of guilt darkened his thoughts as he remembered Jessica and the dinner date he was going to break tonight, but not so upsetting that he couldn't make one more stab. "How long are you going to be on Achernar?" he called after her.

Tassa Kay never looked back. "As long as it takes."

A cryptic remark, but somehow very much in keeping with the MechWarrior's entire person. Raul watched until she left the cargo bay, and then with one more glance at the *Ryoken*, went to find Ship's Officer Thomas. He still had a job to finish here, and more on his plate with Erik Sandoval's request and several reports to file with his Superintendent concerning both events.

And with those priorities, and the memory of Tassa Kay still large in his mind, Raul let slip one more small job. One he would remember, and see to eventually, but too late.

2

Predators

Steel Wolf JumpShip **Star Hunter**
Zenith Jumppoint, Tigress
Prefecture IV, The Republic
15 February 3133

Star Colonel Torrent forced an expression of calm confidence as the Steel Wolves' JumpShip *Star Hunter* counted down from its final warning, preparing to jump between stars. Muted, metallic tones clocked each second. The bridge crew's excitement and the nervous energy of his two companions washed against him in wave after wave of raw emotion. Torrent felt each one break against his resolve, shattering into a spray of smaller, more manageable worries. Standing firm against the undertow, he let the strains of interstellar travel and his coming mission wash through his body until they bled down into the diamond plate decking and dispersed.

A warrior showed no weakness.

"Fifteen seconds," Captain Thule Nygren announced over the JumpShip's 1MC circuit, his gravelly voice echoing through the long, wasp-bodied vessel and likely though each of the four DropShips being carried by the *Star Hunter*. He spent a glance toward Torrent and the other two Steel Wolf warriors. All three stood on the bridge observation platform, leaning forward with hands locked tight on the upper rail, levering their upper body strength against the JumpShip's null gravity. He was obviously debating whether or not he should offer them seats again, or perhaps insist that they accept them this time.

Torrent shook his head ever so slightly, brown eyes hard with resolve. The captain shrugged his own concerns aside.

"Off by thirty thousand klicks or more," Star Captain Nikola Demos offered from her place next to Torrent, making a wager on the accuracy of the jump. Her dark hair glistened like the wing feathers of a raven. Her midnight blue eyes glanced between her colonel and Star Commander Yulri. She shuffled forward, hooked her feet under the lower rail, which ran only ten centimeters above the deck. "Anyone care to risk their first take of *isorla*?" she asked, putting her own battle spoils at risk.

Captain Nygren made a face at the idea of any Clan warrior, even a Bloodnamed one, making book on his crew's competence. Torrent saw it, and knew that only decorum kept the man quiet. Nikola, like Torrent, was a Steel Wolf rising star—she in the tactics of armored vehicles, and he a MechWarrior. It was not wise to come up against a *ristar* too often, especially on the downhill side of one's career. It would also be improper for Torrent to accept the wager, but he caught the eye of Star Commander Yulri and gave him a commanding nod.

"Aff," Yulri agreed to the wager on Torrent's behalf. "Done."

And the *Star Hunter* jumped.

Having stored up massive amounts of energy while laying at the Tigress system zenith, the Odyssey-class JumpShip now poured all it had through the Kearny-Fuchida drive at its core. The KF field burst outward, wrapping itself about the *Star Hunter* and its DropShip payload, isolating the vessels from time and space as the drive tore a hole through reality and briefly connected two star systems. A JumpShip could leap up to thirty light years at a jump. The entire event lasted only a matter of seconds in real time, during which the vessel was no longer a part of the natural universe. Subjectively, by shipboard time, it was instantaneous. Or it was supposed to be.

It never felt that way to Torrent. He sensed the Kearny-Fuchida field unfold, rushing up from behind and roiling over his earlier determination. It caught the large man in between breaths, and the dying hiss of his last exhalation echoed inside his ears, falling and rising and then falling again.

Sweat beaded over Torrent's shaved head as time stood still around him. Drops fell away, swept forward by the field's current, spattering against JumpShip's forward view screen where Tigress' sun shone as nothing more than an exceptionally bright star. Where each bead of sweat struck it ate away a pinprick of reality. Those added up until great holes of nothingness pockmarked the frozen tableau, and finally Torrent stared forward into a veil of pitch-black.

Far in the distance, a single point of extremely bright light pierced the abyss. It hung there, motionless for a moment, and then suddenly rushed up at him growing into a blue-white sun far larger than it should be as seen from either a zenith or nadir jump point. Torrent recalled why. For this B-type star, DropShip travel time from a standard jump point would have been somewhere on the order of one hundred days. Not exactly a surprise strike. Fortunately such systems inside The Republic tended to be so exactly modeled, down to the smallest gravity fluctuation, that JumpShips could make fairly safe use of non-standard jump points deep within the system's gravity well.

The *Star Hunter*'s crew had calculated a null gravity point in between the one inhabited planet and its moon, Ahir al Nahr. That would cut reaction time down to twenty-four hours.

Or so the local defenders would believe.

Reality snapped back into place with a violent shudder

and the metallic groan of the *Star Hunter*'s gravity-stressed hull. Nikola slumped forward ever so slightly, but straightened up again before anyone besides Torrent likely noticed. Yulri lost his footing and drifted up from the deck, shaking away a sudden attack of vertigo. The JumpShip crew fell to their tasks with a new fury, shifting in between various workstations, confirming the vessel's position and making the usual round of damage control checks.

Captain Nygren ordered the station-keeping drive fired. A dull roar vibrated up through the deckplates and gravity returned at point-two Gs. Yulri sagged back to the deck, getting his feet beneath him.

Torrent smoothed one broad hand back over his shaven pate, wiping away a light sheen of sweat, which he brushed against the side of his uniform. On the viewscreen, the blue-white sun swung out of view as the ship turned. A large, dark body replaced it.

Achernar.

"Star Commander Yulri." Torrent's deep voice betrayed nothing of his own strained nerves. He swallowed down the dryness in his throat, washing away the memory of the jump. "See after the *Lupus*."

Dismayed by his show of weakness, Yulri nodded at the bridge deck. "Aff, Star Colonel."

Nikola waited until the access door was dogged shut after their comrade. "They say that everyone suffers some degree of TDS." Transit Disorientation Syndrome. Bad cases could not even think about jumping, not unless they wanted to spend several days afterward in sickbay.

"*They* would be wrong." Torrent glanced at the sealed door. "Yulri is of the Carns Bloodname house. They never adapted well to space travel. Inferior genes."

"Not like us, quiaff?"

Torrent remembered her slouch, saw the white-knuckle grip she still held on the observation rail. He smiled, skinning tight lips back from white, white teeth. "Aff," he agreed. "Not like us."

Then, with a show of his own adaptation, Torrent shoved himself off the rail, gliding backward in the low gravity as if falling away from the observation platform. When his rear foot touched the deck he spun lightly and lunged for the door, caught the handhold and reanchored himself in a standing position. He undogged the door with his left hand, sliding back the rocker-bar with one smooth pull. Metal creaked and popped, and the door swung open.

Before he exited the bridge, however, Torrent first caught Thule Nygren's attention with an upraised chin. "Captain. What is our exact position?"

Although Torrent still lacked his own Bloodname, Nygren remained properly respectful to Achernar's mission commander. Torrent's victory would also win honor for him and his crew. "We are thirty-seven thousand eight hundred klicks and change inside the orbit of Ahir al Nahr, two point seven degrees above the ecliptic ray drawn between Achernar and its sun." He could not help the touch of pride, reporting, "We are only *eighteen thousand* klicks off our intended jump station." A hair-breadth, considering the large numbers involved in space flight.

Nikola Demos gave them both a fake smile, taking her lost wager in good form. Torrent laughed, once, loud and deep, sketched a salute to Captain Nygren, and then squeezed through the narrow hatch.

He was well aware of the stares he drew in his wake—from the bridge personnel, from crewmen he passed in the ship's corridors—and the hopes and desires which chased after him. His impressive size had little to do with it, though filled out at two hundred ten centimeters he so obviously carried the blood of Elementals, the Clans' genetically augmented infantry, in his veins. Everyone, even Bloodnamed officers, paid deference to him because of his heritage. Rather than feed his vanity it only fueled his drive to succeed. That, too, was part and parcel to his legacy.

Torrent was canister-born and sibko-trained, raised in full Clan tradition, and heir to a Kerensky Bloodname. His earliest memories were of lessons on his personal history as a child of the iron wombs, and the expectations that went hand-in-fist with being *trueborn*. Raised in a military crèche, he excelled in physical training and showed an early disposition for command. His academic training included a great deal of history, learning of others who had come before, being inspired by their accomplishments.

No other Bloodname legacy carried as much prestige among the trueborn as his. It was General Aleksandr Kerensky who had led his Star League followers from the Inner Sphere so many centuries ago, founding the Clan homeworlds. He and his son, Nicholas, were the great fathers of Clan society. Nicholas used martial law and strict adherence to a eugenics program in his vision to create a great warrior race: Battlesuit infantry of terrifying size, pilots with supernatural instincts, Mech-Warriors.

When the Clans finally returned, promising themselves that they would bring order to the Inner Sphere, the latter half of that invasion was led by a Kerensky descendent. And during the Jihad, it was Katya Kerensky who found in Devlin Stone a worthy leader to follow, later bringing with her a large slice of Clan Wolf to help form the Republic of the Sphere.

The descendents of those Clan warriors had kept to their traditions, even inside The Republic. Now Torrent, of the Kerensky Bloodname house, was pledged to help Galaxy Commander Kal Radick bring the Steel Wolves back into the fold of their parent Clan. Such an accomplishment would win Torrent much honor, to be recorded in the military file stored on his codex. That only left the winning of a Bloodname in ritual combat to ensure him a place in the Steel Wolves' breeding program. His DNA would be selected to raise entire sibkos of cadets, even after his death. The scientists offered him an immortality the kind of which all Clan warriors dreamt.

And it was time to begin inspiring the next generation of Kerensky descendents.

The *Star Hunter*'s docking waist ringed the vessel at midship, a circular corridor that connected each of the vessel's four docking hardpoints. Torrent approached the open floor hatch, which dropped a ladder down near the *Lupus'* gantry, stepped over the access, and then caught hold of the nearby ladder when a familiar face looked up from below his feet. Star Colonel Colton Fetladral blocked his descent.

"Up on the bridge again?" Fetladral asked. "Harassing our good Captain Nygren?"

Colton Fetladral owned ten years on Torrent, with mocha-dark skin and ebony hair running toward a premature iron gray at the temples. At thirty-eight Fetladral was old by Clan standards, but his earning a Bloodname and rising to the rank of Star Colonel—commanding one of the three Steel Wolf clusters—had already earned him a place in the breeding programs. Chances were better than good that if anything happened to Kal Radick, Colton Fetladral would rise to command of the Steel Wolves.

Torrent's chances were good, and he was coming up fast behind Fetladral.

"I go where the action is," Torrent said with a shrug that strained the shoulder seams of his utility uniform. "During a jump, that is on the JumpShip bridge."

Fetladral nodded. "And did you win your wager with Star Captain Demos?"

"Yulri talks too much."

"Do not blame him. I pressed. And what warrior should not be proud of his commander, quiaff?" Fetladral moved aside.

Releasing his hold on the ladder, Torrent dropped down through the final hatch with knees bent to absorb his landing. A hand reached up to him and he caught it, accepting the anchor. Fetladral reigned in his colleague until both men were comfortably braced at the bottom of the ladder. Fetladral wore gray utilities with razor-sharp military creases, same as Torrent, but his were smudged and stained with grease from working with his technicians. Such work was beneath Fetladral's station, but unavoidable if he wanted to be ready for his part of the coming offensive.

"So," the older officer asked again, "did you win?"

Torrent frowned at his hand, now smudged with the same red grease that Fetladral wore. It smelled of sharp oil and metal. Common packing grease for myomer. "Star Colonel Fetladral. Have you known me to lose?"

Fetladral's wolfish smile faltered, reminded of his recent loss to Torrent in the bidding for Achernar. Torrent had pledged to Kal Radick's plan with fewer resources, by Clan tradition winning him the right to the Steel Wolves' primary target and first choice among the faction's military. "As yet I have not, Star Colonel Torrent. This time, however, you may have bid below the cutdown. We shall see who comes home with the better prize."

"Colton, did you wait here simply to taunt me?" Dropping the other man's rank and Bloodname was a precisely calculated insult, paying Fetladral back for doubting Torrent's bidding. He turned toward the access gantry hatch, five meters down the curving corridor, a large well-lighted opening in the hull of the *Star Hunter*.

"No," Fetladral admitted, nodding an apology as he glided along next to the younger warrior. "I came to wish you victory and honor, Torrent, toward the success of the Steel Wolves."

Torrent paused at the gantry hatch, looked down at Fetladral's outstretched hand. He took it in a firm grip, stronger than a friendly clasp but not quite a test of strength. "Accepted. And appreciated."

"Just do not forget to hold to plan," Fetladral said amicably enough, "or I will see you dead in a circle of equals."

For the second time since the jump, Torrent laughed one of his loud, raucous laughs. "I would have it no other way between us. Do not worry. Star Captain Laren Mehta is a loyal executive officer. My forward forces will not break cover for at least another twenty hours."

"Your Trojan Horse gambit does not concern me. I only wanted to reinforce the need to hold Achernar's attention—and anyone else listening in—until the arrival of Sir Kyle Powers."

An impediment to Kal Radick's plans had been the arrival of Kyle Powers, a Knight of the Sphere, on Ronel. It was expected—demanded—that Torrent draw out the fighting in such a manner as to pull Powers's stabilizing presence from Ronel to Achernar.

Torrent nodded curtly. "I know Kal Radick's plan, and will hold to it."

"Then your victory will ensure my victory. So again, I will wish you success." Fetladral clapped Torrent on both shoulders, nodded, and then drifted back down the corridor and toward one of his own two DropShips.

Torrent watched the other officer's unhurried retreat, then ducked through the gantry hatch and moved into the *Overlord*-class DropShip *Lupus*. Eventually he would command over the DropShip's atmospheric approach from the bridge, but after his run-in with Fetladral, Torrent found himself turning his feet toward the ship's main cargo bay. Two decks down he slid along a transship corridor and then drifted through large doublewide doors that led into his primary 'Mech bay. Ten of the walking war avatars waited in their berths—five state-of-the-art designs, including his seventy-five-ton *Tundra Wolf,* and five industrial machines converted to military use. The empty BattleMech berths had been given over to a full star of his Elementals as a place for the genetically engineered super infantry to store and maintain their powered armor.

And in Bay Two, five more converted industrial 'Mechs and two stars of armored vehicles. Bay Three held all vehicles: fifteen well-maintained tanks ready for battle.

And in the *Wulfstag,* his second DropShip, Torrent brought along another two trinaries of vehicles and a second star of assorted armored infantry.

Torrent glanced over the smudged stains Fetladral had

left on each of his shoulders and smiled a predator's grin. No word of praise would ever be won from Colton Fetladral without a black look or whispered threat behind it. And as Torrent had said earlier, he would have it no other way between them. Friend and enemy—one came with the other as both men rose in power. The day Colton Fetladral ignored Torrent would either be the day Torrent no longer mattered among the Steel Wolves, or the day he would kill Fetladral.

With the forces under Torrent's command for this mission, that day would not be today. He had bid well, earning his place at the forefront of the Steel Wolves' plans, and even without his forward-deployed screen he believed he had enough strength behind him. Enough to assault, occupy, and finally wrest away control of Achernar from the Republic.

Tomorrow the Steel Wolves would take their first step toward conquering Prefecture IV.

3

Timing

Erik Sandoval-Groell stood at the bronze-tinted window of his fifth floor office, listening with perhaps half an ear to Michael Eus's daily report. A steaming mug of brandy-laced coffee warmed Erik's hands, his afternoon vice. The spicy aroma filled his nostrils as he breathed deep over the mug, and the brandy taste trailed a comfortable glow down into his gut.

From Taibek Mining's Corporate Headquarters Erik looked out over the sleepy mining town of Hahnsak. Below, the streets filled up as the 1600 shift change bled over into what passed locally for close-of-business rush hour. A car might have to wait through two traffic lights. Lifting his gaze past town, past the river and Taibek Mining's sludge-dumping processing plant, past the rail line which fed down out of the mines themselves, his hard gaze bore into the Taibek foothills which separated Hahnsak, himself, and his growing military force from River's End.

"And finally, Phillip Mendosa—he's your mine manager," Michael reminded him. "Mendosa forwarded another warning concerning the fall-off in production. With the conversion of so many of our IndustrialMechs, it is impossible to make quota."

Erik took a calm sip of his coffee. Brandy knocked off its bitter edge perfectly. "You pulled three more MiningMech's?" he asked. "One from each shift?"

"And reassigned their best drivers to field training," Michael confirmed. "Accounting bumped their pay, as ordered. I should mention that the profit-and-loss reports from almost every mining facility are grossly unbalanced with so many workers on paid—"

"The new conversions will be done on schedule?" Erik interrupted Eus's worry about the P and Ls. He was far more interested in the three lasers he'd finally worked out of Customs, and their installment on the IndustrialMechs.

"I understand there is some trouble, adapting the lasers to a conventional power source." Michael paged through screens on his noteputer, seeking information. "The engineers are attempting to install the necessary power amplifiers." He looked up. "Currently they are limited to a reduced rate of fire."

Eric had expected that. "Will they be ready on schedule?" he asked again.

Michael Eus was Taibek Mining's operations officer. He was not a military man, but he knew how to take orders and when to be politic. "Yes," he said.

Erik knew that somehow the corporate officer would get the job done. That was all that mattered. "Then the mines' failure to make quota doesn't matter."

"Local titanium buyers will begin to ask questions," Michael reminded him. "Our export schedule will fall off as well."

"Fill local orders first. All off-world shipping goes through Tikonov, yes?" He barely waited for Eus's nod, caught it in the man's ghostly reflection in the window. "Start filling those shipping containers with raw ore, tailings, old equipment—whatever it takes."

"Duke Sandoval will not be pleased."

Erik's gaze slid away from the Taibek Hills, rolling

back into town along the network of rust-streaked rails and rough roadways. He turned away from the window and spitted his corporate officer with a hard glare and a dry smile. "My uncle is well aware of the need to cut back on regular operations, Michael. Keep to schedule. That will please him."

Still, Erik could not help his nervous glance at the data crystal that waited for him on the corner of his large, kidney-shaped desk. The hardcopy communication had arrived on the latest DropShip. Michael had brought it in, delivering it before his report. From Lord Governor and Duke Aaron Sandoval. A reprieve from exile? Orders for a new operation, or modifications for Achernar? So few messages from Aaron Sandoval had held good news since Erik's failure on Mara that he wondered, and worried.

"Is that everything, Michael?" His tone came off more curt than he'd intended.

Michael Eus slid his noteputer into the pocket of his charcoal-brushed suit coat. Youthful, steel gray eyes seemed at odds with his salt-and-pepper hair. They also showed the intense will of a man determined to rise in the Sandoval empire. "I intercepted another call from Legate Stempres. He's still concerned that he failed to separate that new *Ryoken* from Customs."

"He's concerned about losing my family's investment in his career." Erik laughed, short and dark. "That man has hedged every bet since being named Legate under the planetary governor's emergency powers. Can you tell he's insecure in his job?"

"What would you like me to do about him?"

Erik did not miss the way Michael Eus immediately promoted himself as overseer to Brion Stempres. He smiled, and then took another taste of his brandy-tipped coffee. He savored the momentary warmth, deciding how he wanted Stempres cared for. "Handle him, Michael. Keep him at arm's length for now."

It also was not inconceivable that Stempres might try to convert Michael Eus into an asset of his own. In the legate's place, that's what Erik would attempt to do. The young noble wasn't too worried—Michael seemed to realize that power was gravitating around Tikonov, and Erik's uncle. Still, Eus bore watching. Erik had learned on Mara that he couldn't trust family. He wasn't about to trust a corporate suit with an eye on advancement.

"Now get out of here, Michael." Erik waved the man away with an imperious gesture. "I have some things to think about, and I don't wish to be disturbed. Not unless it is something you cannot personally handle."

The confidence playing over the other man's face said that he doubted there was any such situation. Michael Eus bowed shortly from the waist, spun and padded softly from the plush office.

Preparing himself for the coming one-sided interview, Erik strolled around the large and mostly-empty office taking the most circuitous route back to his redwood desk. His feet sank into plush carpet. The entire room still had a new-office smell to it that spoke of a lack of permanence to Erik. He paused over a small, glass-encased model of the new Achernar Industries Mining-Mech—the same model he was now ripping apart and rebuilding into military conversions—and again at a wide bookcase that contained almost every handy reference book one might need with regards to mining on Achernar.

The leather-bound volumes across the top shelf had little to do with mining, though. Michael Eus had stocked the office with a complete history of the Sandoval dynasty (Robinson Press, 3130 edition): twelve volumes, six centuries of family activities and profiles. Erik knew that a few events were missing from that "complete" history. He'd checked. Those were the secrets and dirty laundry the family would never allow a public airing.

Still, running his hand along the leather spines, feeling the raised lettering under his fingertips and watching some of the gold gilt flake off to the shelf's dark walnut surface, gave Erik a sense of the history that pushed at both his uncle and himself.

Early volumes where the Sandoval dynasty came to power, and had briefly stood in line for the throne of the Federated Suns. Princes of the realm.

Middle volumes. The fall of the Star League and the Succession Wars which followed. Here the Sandoval dynasty secured themselves as undisputed rulers within the Suns' Draconis March. Those stories involved so many tales of battle and heroics against House Kurita's Draconis Combine that Erik could reread them *ad infinitum*. The leather itself felt charged with electricity, jumping small sparks to Erik's fingers.

Volumes eleven and twelve. The last eighty years. Cold to the touch.

These troublesome pages detailed years of civil war and the Word of Blake Jihad. They contained bright moments, such as Tancred Sandoval's marriage to Yvonne Steiner-Davion—and once again a Sandoval sat on the throne, even if as regent to the son who would follow. But so many dark times overweighed the good.

3081: when Devlin Stone annexed twenty-five worlds from the Draconis March into his precious—and precocious—Republic of the Sphere. Several members of the Sandoval dynasty stood in opposition to this, but already a popular wave of support for Stone's reforms had caused a shift toward the decentralization of power.

3095: the power struggle on Robinson that permanently divided the family, creating a branch of true believers in Stone's work and a line of loyal opposition.

3124—and an event not recorded correctly by the histories—brought the two lines into conflict on Schedar. The opposition had sponsored border pirates as a means to test Republic resolve, and true believers from outside The Republic had chased them down. Aaron Sandoval himself—then an officer in the Republic military—had become involved, and managed to cover up the family's involvement.

And then, in an event not covered at all by the current history books, Devlin Stone abdicated power and disappeared. Erik knew how much Stone's desertion had hurt his uncle. So much that when the HPG network crashed, and Aaron was free to pursue his personal agenda, he had sent Erik as his military ambassador to the world of Mara. A world in Prefecture III with strong Sandoval interests, the idea had been to secure it and then invite the Robinson-based dynasty back into both Prefectures III and IV at the same time. Erik had opted for a military solution, but failed to take under proper consideration a cousin of his who was on planet—and sided with the natives.

Christine sent Erik back to Tikonov in disgrace.

Aaron Sandoval sent him away to Achernar.

Erik shoved himself away from the bookcase and the painful memories. After one final sip of the strong coffee, he left his cooling mug on the silver salver resting on a tray next to his door. The brandy taste stayed with him on the short path to his kidney-shaped desk, faded into a pleasant afterthought as Erik rolled up his chair. He fit the data crystal into a reader slot at one edge of the redwood desk. Pressing his thumb up against the nearby indentation provided his DNA sample that was compared to the digital key embedded within the crystal. A green light blinked its authorization. Motors hummed to life as the desk's glass inlay levered up into a vertical screen, and the strong countenance of Aaron Sandoval, Lord Governor of Prefecture IV and Duke to the Swordsworn, winked into existence.

Even reduced to a twelve-inch display, his uncle seemed to fill the room. With a proud chin and piercing blue eyes, Aaron Sandoval was no easy man to forget. He wore his blond hair shaved up into a topknot similar to Erik's, although he wore it combed back rather than braided. He preferred to dress in robes of state rather than military uniform, but he wore them with such precision, perfectly tailored and pressed, that the air he gave off was still one of military command.

"Erik," he began with no preamble whatsoever, "I have reviewed the reports on your progress. It is more than satisfactory. In fact, your sponsorship of Brion Stempres to replace Legate Rudy Maks was an inspired idea. I have similarly replaced the Legates on two other worlds where the Swordsworn hold dominance."

Imitation was the highest form of flattery. What his uncle didn't say spoke large in Erik's mind and helped stiffen up his spine.

"Regardless of your progress, nephew, I still feel that I must warn you not to exceed my directions. Achernar is a valuable world with its working HPG station. I should not have to tell you that. *How* valuable has been made apparent to me, however, in the latest communiqués delivered to Tikonov by JumpShip. We know of Achernar and Ronel, of course. In all the rest of Prefecture IV, I have rumor of only one other working station—one of Kal Radick's JumpShip hyperpulse relays. Three, perhaps, out of a possible thirty. My agents on Ronel tell me that they have made contact with Markab and Al Nair, and your report that Achernar has had sporadic contact with Genoa is also good intelligence. But, Erik, that is *all*."

Duke Sandoval paused, letting Erik consider that numbing fact. The young noble listened to the sound of footsteps running down the outside hall as he counted up the worlds. With a fifty light year range to any HPG, Achernar and Ronel could conceivably reach through all of Prefecture IV, most of III and V, and into pieces of Prefecture II and border worlds of the Federated Suns. A chill shook Erik's spine. He heard a shout outside his door—ignored it. Sixty . . . seventy worlds. And of all those, only five or six of them could talk to each other.

A recipe for worried populations.

Aaron Sandoval nodded, as if agreeing with Erik's thoughts. "Panic and civil unrest are highest on those worlds lost to the Blackout. News and rumors of fighting are not helping, either. Besides your ill-fated attempt to bring over Mara," always one to jab past failures back at Erik, the better to keep him mindful of orders, "I have confirmed major escalations on Dieron, Addicks, Liao and Ankaa. The Republic might be under attack. It might be eating itself up from within.''

However it was happening, Erik understood his uncle's unspoken context. The Republic was dying. On any given world there might be factions who recalled their old allegiances to House Kurita, Davion, Liao . . . to Clan Wolf or the Sea Foxes . . . to the Word of Blake. Ignorance and fear brought out the mob mentality. Devlin Stone's reforms—his efforts to encourage relocation, to spread the Republic's different cultures over many worlds— were now working against the Republic.

Who was it—a general for House Steiner—who had originally coined the term *Information is ammunition*?

From twenty-odd light years and several weeks away, Duke Sandoval sensed his nephew's conclusions. "The single greatest asset anyone can possess right now is a working HPG station," he said. "Achernar must remain accessible. It must eventually be brought under the control of the Swordsworn. *Eventually,* Erik. Do not rush my plans. Take no action unless provoked, and only if a diplomatic solution does not present itself.

"Our best, nephew. From the family." The message terminated with one sharp, decisive nod—

—and gave way to the sound of arguing voices and shuffling feet in the hall outside Erik's office. He thought he heard Michael Eus's voice, raised up on the far side of the argument. The loud voices faded, but Erik could still hear nearby offices emptying and people moving quickly down the hall.

"What in the blazes is going on out there?"

Erik pocketed his uncle's message, planning to destroy the data crystal as soon as feasible. He kicked up from his chair and crossed to the large set of double doors. A knock rapped through before he reached them, stopping him fast in his tracks. That would be Michael, no doubt. The warning bought Erik a brief moment to compose himself. Folding his arms across his chest, frowning his displeasure at the interruption, he barked out a single "Come!"

Michael Eus opened the door. Behind him, top executives for Taibek Mining argued and gestured to each other as they streamed down the hall. Michael did not bother to step through the doorway, which meant he had come to call Erik away for something. Something that had the entire building in an uproar if management was any clue.

Michael shook his head, as if angry with himself for disobeying Erik's earlier command, or at whatever problem had arisen to force him into such a position. He looked straight at his employer, and Erik actually read a touch of fear behind his impassive gray eyes.

"Lord Sandoval. We have a situation."

Achernar Customs Security
River's End, Achernar

A ceiling fan spun lazily overhead, pushing around the tepid air. Closeted away in his office at the Achernar Customs Security building, Raul Ortega hunched forward, dividing his time between a stack of paperwork, his noteputer, and the computer network station built into the top of his desk. A half-eaten maple bar lay forgotten on the desk's pull-out sideboard; its frosting melted slowly down onto the paper plate, sweetening the air with syrup and sugar. Warm milk remained untouched in a waxed paper cup.

Never enough hours in the day. Raul pulled up an on-screen memo from the joint directive of Legate Stempres and Planetary Governor Susan Haider. As of two days before, all hardcopy news delivered by DropShip would be duplicated, cataloged and routed—by Customs—to Achernar's chief executive and ranking military office.

Add *intelligence gathering* to the growing list of new duties for a Customs Security Officer.

And another hour cut out of any given workday.

Footsteps in the hall outside his office. Raul knew how most shoes sounded against the vinyl, stick-on tiles. The angry stomp of military, steel-toed boots. Nervous scuffing of patent leather when shipping agents wanted a favor, and purposeful patent leather when Carl Rossiter, his boss, wanted an explanation. Comfortable civilian shoes, uneven strides, lots of pauses—usually lost or misdirected to Customs Security when they really wanted the downstairs regulatory office.

These footsteps fell into one last class. Professional work shoes. Comfortable but not too relaxed. Customs officers preferred this kind of shoe: a match for the uniform and good for staying on your feet all day. Raul heard their dedicated stride make a line direct for the door at his back, step inside his office, and wait.

"Can't do it, wouldn't want it, got no time for it if I did," Raul said without glancing back. The usual line of excuses. "What can I do for you?" he relented on automatic pilot.

"Dinner would be nice," a warm voice offered with a touch of amusement.

Raul spun his chair around, a smile spreading over his face as if half the day's workload had been lifted from him. Jessica Searcy stood just inside his door, leaning back against the frame. Tall and well figured, she wore her strawberry-blonde hair pulled back severely from her face, accenting her dangling earrings and pronounced cheekbones. Eyes of brilliant, inviting blue teased him with their mischievous gleam. Her dress-suit was comfortable, but not too casual, and his fiancée wore the professional shoes also common to doctors who spend a great deal of time on their feet.

"But if you really don't have time for me anymore," she said easily, "I can take mother's advice and find a good-looking lawyer who only works sixty-hour weeks." She turned as if to go.

Raul vaulted from his chair as if it came equipped with a BattleMech ejection system, caught her up in a strong embrace and swung her back into his office while Jessica laughed. He almost sat her against the maple bar, caught her again at the last moment, and then lowered her into his own chair. "Remember our bargain, Jess." He shook a finger at her. "I don't take off-world assignment, and you stay away from the lawyers." A mostly empty threat anyway. Jessica's mother lived on Rio now, at one of the best retirement communities in Prefecture IV, and she adored Raul.

Jessica dropped her long hair loose from the severe clips, shaking it down around both shoulders. It fell in strands and curls, like a little girl's hair after a wild day on the playground. One strand settled between her eyes, resting down onto the bridge of her nose in a manner Raul found extremely cute. She shook off her smile and sat stiffly upright, as if consulting with a patient, tilted her head to one side and considered his offer. "I'm sorry," she finally said, "do I know you?"

"All right," Raul surrendered. He reached out to gently push the stray hair aside, tucking it behind Jessica's ear for her, and planted a tender kiss on her brow before dropping back into the stiff-backed chair he kept on-hand for most visitors. "Guilty as charged. I've been absent, lately, I know." He ran fingers back through his tightly curled, wet black hair. "But you wouldn't believe the workload being dumped on the agency."

She softened a bit, relaxing into the chair but never too comfortable in an office that wasn't her own, Raul knew. "I believe it, Raul. I simply don't know why you put up with it. I thought the spaceport was crowded with unions to prevent this kind of thing."

"That's for the longshoremen and technicians. People who actually *do* something for a living." Like doctors. Raul smiled at their shared joke, but thinly. He leaned back into the chair, feeling his fatigue now that the boost from her arrival had passed.

"You look awful," Jessica said, a touch of worry crowding into her voice.

"Thanks for noticing."

She shook her head. "No, I mean it. Have you been hunched in this room all afternoon?" A glance around. She prodded at the decomposing maple bar. "Let me guess . . . your idea of lunch?" She dabbed the back of her hand against her own forehead. "Don't you have climate control in here?"

Raul nodded at his office's narrow window, which looked out over the San Marino spaceport. From his angle, he could just see the rounded curve of the merchant-*Union* sitting on Pad Seven. "That window is it until we get the heat pump fixed, but I never open it. The dead heat that hangs over the 'port simply drifts in and makes the office hot and sticky."

"Well fine, then let me take you out of here. Dinner? Las Palamas?" She saw his hesitant glance toward the pile of work on his desk. "Margaritas and mariachi bands? I'll let you get me drunk."

A weary smile fought its way back over his face. "Now that's an offer hard to pass up." He waggled his eyebrows suggestively and tried to get some enthusiasm into his dark eyes for her to see, a leer which died with the return of professional sense. "Can you give me one hour?" he asked, saw Jessica's building anger. "An hour! I promise. Customs is on to a new smuggling operation, we're overseeing a snit between the legate's office and a private owner, we have an inbound DropShip that's been stuck in orbit for *five days*," he ran out of steam, his enthusiasm waning, "and we've just been designated Achernar's news police. Let me get a few of the big-ticket items off my desk and make them someone else's problem for a while."

Jessica stood, shaking her head. Her dangling earrings flashed and sparkled even in the room's dim light. "I don't know why I put up with you," she said wistfully, then bent forward and pecked him on the cheek.

Raul reached up, trapped her in his strong arms, and hugged her. He had pushed his sleeves up to his elbows while working, and his swarthy arms looked exceptionally dark against the pale cream skin of Jess's neck. "Because you have wisdom beyond your years," he offered, pulling out another old joke.

"And you've had another job offer from Bannson Universal," she reminded him matter-of-factly, standing back up again. "We'd have to move over to Agnetenar," Achernar's smallest continent, "but I can shift my practice."

"Not tonight, Jess." He exhaled a long vent of frustration. "Anyway, there's too much going on to entertain their offer." Raul wanted to kick himself for continuing. Hadn't he just said, 'not tonight?'

But he had opened the door. "There's always too much going on, Raul." Jessica sat forward, chin up and eyes boring into his, giving him her debate-team attitude. "You wanted to stay with the Reserves. Fine. You earned your citizenship. Congratulations. Now why continue to beat yourself up? Just for the sake of those holovids and histories you like so much?"

Here it came. Resident honor. The argument people gravitated toward when they have clearly made up their mind that chasing after Republic citizenship wasn't for them. That so long as you contributed your best work to The Republic—through its work force, professional service, or art—you had just as much right to claim the honors of the Republic if not the benefits of being an actual citizen.

It was how the two of them had met, actually, over that argument. Raul had come in to the hospital to visit a friend in his reserves unit who had been hurt in a VTOL transport crash. A freak accident, really. Jessica had been the attending physician, a few years older than him but only a year out of her internship. She'd made a comment—he couldn't remember it exactly anymore—something about the military providing her with more work even in peacetime. He had responded by telling her that Jonathan was simply trying to earn his citizenship. And it had begun. A nurse finally shooed them out of the patient's room, and they continued the debate in the hall, and then over lunch in the hospital cafeteria.

They were still at it after three dates, when Raul conceded that 'official' citizenship was certainly not required to be a good citizen. He'd said it mainly to forge a truce, thinking that he might be falling hard for the good doctor. He'd even gone so far as to admit that most privileges of citizenship were beyond the enjoyment of most who earned them. Jessica had told him that, at last, he was showing a hint of wisdom beyond his years.

He had never let her live down that slightly pompous remark.

She was right, of course. Raul was never likely to own significant land grants, and the idea of a noble title was so far above his station as to make him laugh. He would never own his own BattleMech. But he could vote. It was a right he had earned with his college years in MRTC, two years in the Militia Reserves, and in two years with Customs. But he also understood Jessica's position. After her drive to qualify for med school, her internship and residency, she had never had a chance to look at five years' service for citizenship. In her mind, she had done enough for herself and more than many others.

His continued stand—that citizenship was always best earned by taking that one additional step *beyond* your own goals—never failed to annoy Jessica. But he just didn't have the strength for it today.

Or so he thought.

"Will you at least consider the Bannson proposal?" she asked.

The buzz of an alarm in the outside hall interrupted his initial reply, jolting Raul with a quick burst of energy. As the distant wail of the spaceport's seldom-needed siren joined in, a real adrenaline rush flooded him with warmth and jangling nerves. He leaned past Jessica and snagged his wireless comms from the top of his desk. With practiced efficiency he dialed the building's switchboard with one hand while tucking the clip over his ear with the other.

He settled the microphone wire just next to the corner of his mouth, waiting for the circuit to connect. "Jess, I like what I do. It's important." He glanced through his door as a few other Customs officers scrambled by, heading for their own offices. "Bannson Universal wants a glorified rent-a-badge."

If he wasn't going to set the discussion aside, Jessica certainly wasn't either. His fiancée shuffle-stepped to one side, getting out of Raul's way should he need his desktop system. "Maybe Bannson is looking at a bigger picture. They claimed to be impressed with your BattleMech training."

"Every potential security position will claim that. How many of them will actually put that training to use? Yes, hello?" Raul held up a hand to Jessica as his call went through. Rather than fight his way through to Rossiter or the spaceport's command center, Raul went for Customs' switchboard operators. "Can you tell me what's happening?" The technicians down there always knew the good info first.

He gave the on-call tech only ten seconds, and then disconnected with a sharp stab at his comm unit. He dialed another number. "This is CSO 5589." He swallowed against the dry taste of adrenaline. "I need to register off-duty and out of contact."

Jessica frowned a question at him, and Raul raised his hand to cover the mic. "Bannson isn't the only one who needs a MechWarrior right now," he said, dark eyes wide with excitement. "The Steel Wolves have jumped in-system. They've deployed fighters, and are refusing all orders to stand down.

"We have twenty-two hours."

4

Change of Fortunes

Achernar Militia Command
Achernar
16 February 3133

Officially, the Achernar Militia's command post butted up against the spaceport's northeast border. In truth, Raul knew, that fenced-off portion of the garrison command was little more than a trio of old, rarely used landing pads. The militia manned it with a skeleton crew, usually reservists serving their two weeks out of a year, except for the days when a military DropShip was due. A small security team stood by, mostly to police that crew from taking too many unscheduled breaks. The base proper actually began twelve kilometers out with a large collection of bunker-style warehouses. From there, the militia's Reserve Training Command spread out to the east, like a common meeting ground between the military base and River's End. The standing barracks, maintenance bays, garages and administrative buildings belonging to the Republic Guard clustered in their own little protected world north of the RTC grounds.

The day before—the day of the alert—Raul had never known a longer drive than his trip back into River's End for uniform and gear and then back out to the base.

Jessica rode with him for the first leg, giving up on questions to which Raul had no answers and finally lapsing into a worried fret. She kissed him goodbye at his apartment, and then he had an hour of city traffic and highway klicks to imagine what the base would be like under a real military alert.

Except for a kind of frantic energy that crackled in the air like static electricity, Raul saw no difference. Routine had already taken over by the time of his arrival. A corporal signed him in and assigned Raul to shared quarters rather than the barracks, the perquisites of being a MechWarrior, even as a reservist. He was handed official orders activating him to full duty and asked to sign his name to them, and then was put on a five-and-dimes rotation working as an aide-de-camp inside the command center itself. Five hours on duty, ten hours off, with his first five-on taking the midnight shift where there was nothing really to do but monitor preparations and discuss the inbound DropShips.

Raul's second five-on made up for the uneventful night. Feeling a little lethargic after catching a fitful daynap, he walked into the command center wholly unprepared for the raised voices of argument and the blizzard of papers that struck him in the face.

Hot coffee sloshed over the edge of Raul's Styrofoam cup, scalding his hand. He quickly passed the beverage to his other hand, shaking his injured fingers dry and searching for his attacker. He recognized several of the voices, but knew which one in particular was behind the paper shotgun.

"You can cite Stumpy's directives and Republic emergency authority all you want, Colonel. You can't just take my 'Mech."

Tassa Kay.

Tassa stood toe-to-toe with Colonel Blaire, white-hot fury burning on her face. She had pulled her dark red hair back into a loose ponytail, and wore only shorts, boots, and a 'Mech cooling vest which left very little of her curvaceous figure to the imagination. A necessity in the often-sweltering confines of a cockpit. The unofficial 'uniform' of a MechWarrior wasn't designed for modesty. The crystal charm Raul had seen on Tassa before still hung around her neck, but now nestled very snuggly down into the swell of her breasts.

"Stempres," Isaac Blaire corrected her, his powerful voice carrying though the room. He held his ground before the fiery MechWarrior, only slightly favoring his prosthetic leg. "Lay-gate Brion *Stempres*." His face, normally a ruddy pink, had flushed a deeper, warning red. "And you know very well Ah can do it."

The militia commander's Zaurak accent showed through. Considered Achernar's outback, Zaurak natives always had a bit of a twang in their voices. Raul hadn't heard it in Blaire's talk since the officer—then a major—headed Achernar's Reserve Training Command. This argument had either been going on for some time or Tassa Kay had gotten under Blaire's skin exceptionally fast.

"Your transit papers on every world in The Republic included a binding agreement which allows me to press into service any military equipment—privately owned or not—Ah see fit to need."

That quieted the argument for a moment. Bending down, Raul scooped up a handful of the papers. He carried them and his half-full coffee over to one of the small metal desks shoved up against a wall. The entire room was listening in on the argument, talk held down to a minimum and eyes dancing in between workstation screens and the pair of verbal combatants. A nearby communications tech nodded Raul a nervous greeting.

"How long will it take you to prove that I was presented with that information?" Tassa asked.

Raul looked up sharply. He knew that she had. He'd handed it to Tassa Kay himself as a part of the Customs process, *and* obtained her signature over the document. But he kept quiet, unwilling to barge into the commander's argument and waiting to see, first, how he would handle her. Tassa Kay was formidable, he knew. Besides the fact that Raul had dealt with her once before, that she had managed to bull her way into the militia's command center—during an alert—spoke a great deal about her.

Colonel Blaire recoiled as if struck. His surprise was genuine, or well feigned. "On your honor as a MechWarrior," he asked simply, "you never received that information?"

Raul sipped at his highly sweetened coffee, glancing in between the rescued papers and Tassa Kay. He saw that Blaire's comment had struck right to her personal pride, and had maybe touched on something else even deeper. Tassa's tongue drew a slow line over her top lip as she thought about it, relented. "All right, I received it. But I still have the command codes, which means you cannot get more than a quarter power out of the reactor and the weapons remain locked out. So there is a bargain to strike here. My offer was good enough for your Exarch. It should be good enough for you."

"It would be. It is. However, that is not my call. The decision rests with Lay-gate Stempres. He has already ordered up Erik Sandoval's people, who are on a forced march over the Taibek Hills. Now he demands the codes to your *Ryoken*."

So that was Tassa's ace. Her command codes. No doubt Blaire's need to get them had facilitated her entry into the base. She had already pulled out the verifax from Exarch Redburn and placed that on the table as well.

Setting his still-hot beverage aside, Raul shuffled the papers back together. As Tassa had mentioned earlier, they were copies of the Republic's Emergency Powers Act and Legate Stempres' own decision to press civilian assets into military service. To wit: Tassa's *Ryoken II*. He didn't need to read the legal text, he knew it by heart. . . . *such as the needs of the Republic dictate, civilian assets may be confiscated and pressed into service with adequate compensation to be decided* . . .

To be decided and agreed upon by both parties unless the Republic will guarantee full replacement value on said civilian assets.

"Excuse me." Raul spoke up just as Tassa was warming to the next round of her refusal to cooperate. He strode forward. "Colonel Blaire. May I interrupt a moment?"

Blaire glowered at the uniform, at first seeing only Raul's honorary rank of lieutenant. Then, recognizing the reservist, he relented somewhat. "Lieutenant . . . Ortega. Ah saw your name on the lay-gate's report, didn't Ah?" He swallowed back his accent then, as if noticing it for the first time. His weathered face was filled with shadowed valleys, but a pair of unclouded blue eyes still stared out hard and bright. "Yes. I'd like your input."

"So would I," Tassa said, eyeing Raul with interest, obviously remembering him.

"I don't know how much you'll like it, sir." Raul remained properly deferential to his commanding officer. "The way I read the EPA statute," he handed the paper over to Blaire, "if MechWarrior Kay doesn't agree to your order, the only way you can trump her is by personally guaranteeing, up front, full replacement value on the *Ryoken*."

Blaire's face darkened again. "You want me to sign a marker for twenty million stones?" he asked, using the slang name for Republic money.

Smiling, her good humor replacing fury in the blink of an eye, Tassa said "Twenty-four. It is a custom design you would have to bring in from the Lyran Commonwealth." She awarded Raul a brilliant smile. "That's two I owe you."

Raul would have liked to say that he was only doing his duty, presenting useful information to the discussion, but the warm glow in the pit of his stomach put the lie to that idea. He had jumped in on Tassa Kay's side. Again. "Worth the story of Dieron?" he asked.

"Worth something," she promised.

Blaire was less amused. "Wipe that kay-det grin off your face and snap to, Lieutenant. Are you telling me that Customs' stand on this would demand Lay-gate Stempres sign a voucher for her estimate of twenty-four million stones?"

Careful. Raul swallowed, tasting the bitter traces of his earlier coffee. He shook his head. "That's my own read on the text, Colonel, though I'm fairly certain that Judicial would back me up on it."

"And if Ah allow her to pilot her own machine?"

"It's vague, sir. My opinion . . . it falls under the heading of an agreement between the civilian owner and the military."

Tassa shrugged. "Same offer as before. Guarantee me the closest you have for replacement parts, and maintenance time and workers, and you will have my BattleMech."

Which by Raul's way of thinking was either incredibly generous of Tassa Kay, or incredibly naïve. Under those terms, her *Ryoken* would suffer some degradation, and there was no offer of recompense for her services either. Colonel Blaire obviously worried at the offer as well, frowning, trying to see what it was he was missing in the deal.

"Colonel Blaire!"

"Now what?" Blaire rounded on the communications tech, more than a little frustrated at yet another interruption. "You have something to add to this, Corporal?"

"Yes sir. I mean, no sir." The tech looked confused, but only for a second. The excitement in his eyes was too bright not to quickly overshadow any worry of reproach. "Sir, we are getting a space-to-ground transmission from the Steel Wolves. A Star Colonel Torrent, of the Kerensky Bloodname, is requesting you specifically."

At the mention of the Steel Wolf officer, Blaire rocked back in thought while Raul swore he saw Tassa Kay suddenly lean forward in predatory interest. Could the Steel Wolves have been involved in her "trouble" on

Dieron? That seemed a bit far outside of Prefecture IV—through Prefecture III and into II—for Kal Radick to be involved.

"Ah, blazes! Time to DropShip touchdown?" Blaire asked.

A junior officer, this one overseeing several tactical workstations, straightened up. "At their present burn, not for four hours at least. We have some new craft fouling our clear-skies order . . . falling fast through the atmosphere . . . have to be civilian shuttles making ballistic hops from one of the other two continents. Looks like they may be landing out near Hahnsak."

"Sandoval," Blaire growled as if the name was a curse. "Thinks he can do whatever-the-hell he pleases. Clear them out of my no-fly zone," he ordered the junior officer. "Where will the Clan DropShips land?"

"Trajectory still puts them coming in at Eridanus, west-central, but I can't narrow it any more than that at this time."

Blaire nodded perfunctorily. "They could be dropping right on top of us." He eyed Raul and Tassa, backed them away with a gesture. "Maybe we can resolve this and negate any need for your *Ryoken*. All right, is there visual feed?" The corporal at communications nodded. "Give it to me on the main screen, and return full audio and visual."

A six-foot screen snowed to life on the forward wall, quickly filled by Star Colonel Torrent's visage. A large man, Raul thought, made more impressive as he loomed over the entire command center, with serious brown eyes and a no-nonsense expression masking any true emotion. Standing in front of his own video pickup at a modified parade-rest, he looked like a man totally in control.

"Colonel Isaac Blaire. I am Star Colonel Torrent, of the Kerensky Bloodname. Prefect Kal Radick has decided to move Achernar under his direct protection. I have won the right to carry out his will."

Blaire was no fool. "*Direct protection?* Is that his latest euphemism for armed rebellion, Star Colonel, or is it yours?"

Raul's memory tripped over Torrent's comment of having won the right to battle. Old Clan protocol, he remembered from his RTC days. Officers bid down to the smallest force needed to take an objective. The lowest bid won the privilege of combat. Kal Radick had kept alive more Clan traditions than anyone had apparently thought.

"Achernar has been reclassified as vital military infrastructure. The uncertain nature of your militia, and the presence of Lord Governor Sandoval's personal army, warrants Prefect Raddick's concern. My orders are to take control of the local situation."

"If you are under the orders of Prefect Radick, then you follow illegal orders and you damn well know it. Lay-gate Stempres has jurisdiction. If he doesn't like that, Prefect Radick can call for a vote of no-confidence." Blaire dialed for his command voice. "Stand down, Star Colonel. Return to your JumpShip."

"My JumpShip has departed," Torrent said evenly. "I will not require it. We will set down in your Highlake Basin and claim that as our staging area. I accept any offer of uncontested landing."

Next to him, Raul heard Tassa Kay whisper, "Safcon. He is asking for safe conduct."

All Raul could think of was the devastated territory of Highlake Basin, a good half-day's travel or better northwest of River's End and the military base. He'd never forgotten his last simulated battle, and could see why Torrent might choose that as his base of operations. Good open ground for landing fields, and there would be no covert marches against him.

"You want me to guarantee you uncontested access to Achernar?" Blaire asked, incredulous. "What possible reason would Ah have to grant that?"

Torrent grinned arrogantly. "To limit damage to your own forces. Are you truly prepared to resist me?" He glanced to one side. Raul couldn't say why, but it felt as if Torrent had just given an order to someone off video.

"Resist? Ah'll give you hell with a hand grenade, and welcome to it!"

"That is too bad. I hoped for a sensible attitude. I planned for stubbornness. Colonel Blair. With what forces will you defend Achernar?"

Tassa Kay visibly winced and Raul trembled with a cold thrill of adrenaline. This is not happening, he wanted to shout. This only thinks that it's happening. For all his protestations about serving the Republic and doing an important job, Raul never thought he would see real war. And certainly not between factions of the Republic! Civil war? Staged here on Achernar?

"What forces?" Blaire growled out, completely non-plussed. He calmed himself with visible effort. "I will defend Achernar with everything I can order, scrape together, and call in from outside."

"All you have set against all I have?" Torrent paused, shrugged. "Bargained well and done." His video fee cut out with a flash of static, and then light snow once again filled the forward screen.

The finality in Star Colonel Torrent's words left a new chill washing up Raul's spine. There had been a dark promise in them. And laughter. Torrent had been far from surprised, as if his plans had already factored in Colonel Blaire's response.

They had, and Raul learned how not a moment later.

Tension welled up in a surging wave that lifted several voices at once. "Target deviation . . . IFF transponders are lighting up . . . we have multiple incoming . . . Stone's Blood!"

The wave crested over and struck the command center a heavy blow, shaking the floor and dancing coffee mugs on desks. The large, forward view screen cracked as the entire wall buckled and threatened to cave inward. Lights flickered and several workstations tripped off under surge protection—one blew apart in a cascade of sparks and dancing electricity, peppering the hands and face of a young sergeant with shards of green glass.

Raul caromed off the corner of the comms station, then snatched up an auxiliary headset to keep plugged in as Blaire's aide-de-camp. Damage control reports flooded the system, but these Raul held off for any hard intelligence that came his way.

The communications tech was ahead of Raul and faster even than Blaire's tactical officer. "Aerospace fighters!" he warned, fast-switching in between two different frequencies and somehow making sense of both. "Second wave hitting in three . . . two . . ."

The floor jumped again, but not so severe this time. Raul dialed in on the corps engineers, found them debating the damage amongst themselves in an almost luncheon-calm discussion. "That was our monorail," Raul announced for Blaire's benefit. "We just lost the fast-track system."

Blaire glared his question at Tactical, who seemed to feel the heat spearing into his back. "We have three confirmed two-craft elements of aerospace fighters making high-speed passes. That's a full squadron. Third wave in thirty seconds. We have a DropShip . . . *Okinawa-CC* . . . making planetfall right behind the fighter's flight path."

An *Okinawa-CC*? That was a civilian-converted vessel, or supposedly so. Dread chill walked icy fingers up Raul's spine and he ran to Tactical. It was also the same designation as the DropShip that had been "stuck" in orbit for nearly a week. He reached past one of the technicians, selected the civilian band aerospace traffic control and fed it to his screen. The *Okinawa*-merchant was gone.

"Sir, Colonel. We've been had." Raul yanked off his headset, turned to Blaire and laid out his findings. "They put forces in orbit five days ago."

"*Okinawa*'s can't carry 'Mechs," Tactical said. "Fighters only."

Raul shook his head. "They don't carry them normally. Any DropShip can ferry BattleMechs, though, if you are willing to stack them in like freight. Or infantry or armor. We don't know what we're dealing with."

"Agreed." Blaire rounded on Tassa Kay. "You can have your *Ryoken* hot and walking in five minutes if you're willing to risk a VTOL. Ah'll release a Yellow Jacket to get you over to the spaceport. If Lay-gate Stempres agrees to full value in the next five minutes, you will turn the 'Mech over to one of my pilots." The floor shook again as the next wave strafed some other part of the base. "Otherwise, you are free to engage at your own discretion."

"Done," Tassa agreed. "Get me a jeep at the north entrance." She bolted for the door.

"Ortega, make it happen."

Raul pulled his headset back on, calling for a ready vehicle from the motor pool and keeping tabs on the Yellow Jacket Gunship that Blaire had asked for. He paced a short path in between the commander and his desk. The room smelled of spilled coffee and fear now, but slowly the trained routine of military preparedness was taking hold in the room.

Then a new strafing run slammed into the building.

Plaster fell out of the ceiling, raining down thick dust and adding premature gray to Raul's dark hair. He shifted to an active, tactical channel. Heard the report of a wounded enemy fightercraft as base assets finally responded to the attack. "Two VTOLs just crippled an enemy fighter," he reported. "It's trailing smoke but still airborne. One VTOL destroyed, one crippled." He relayed more estimates of damage and enemy strength as they came in.

"Colonel, we have a MechWarrior down!" the comms tech shouted.

Blaire was beyond surprise or even anger. "Ah don't even have a MechWarrior in the field yet," he complained.

"She was on the monorail when it took the hit. They medvaced her to the hospital."

"You're just full of good news," Blaire told the comms tech. "Who is it?"

"MechWarrior DePriest."

Charal. Not just a random name but someone Raul knew—had known well—was already a victim of the violence. This was getting very real *very* fast. Raul yanked the headset mic back from his mouth. "Is she all right?"

"Unknown," the tech told him, then stuttered a quick apology to Colonel Blaire. "No news on her status," he told the CO.

"Who's my ready-alert standby this watch and where's his post?"

Caught up in the moment, trying to juggle three incoming calls and follow the room's conversation and layout of the building battle all at once, Raul was caught unawares. Blaire's tactical officer consulted a duty roster on his noteputer, then glanced up sharply. "Sir, it's Lieutenant Ortega."

Raul snapped his head around so fast, he tweaked a muscle in his neck. That was right, though. Every second shift he stood in as a back-up MechWarrior or field officer.

Blaire caught him staring. "Ah got to spell it out for you, Lieutenant? Grab some togs, grab a jeep, and grab your ass out to the hangar. Move it!"

Except for nearly slipping in the puddle of spilled coffee next to his desk, Raul couldn't remember touching the floor as he fled the control center for the long hall outside. His footsteps echoed hollowly in the near-empty corridor, reminding him of distant artillery fire. Tunnel vision focused him on the door at the end of the hall, and it wasn't until he cracked that and saw daylight that he even remembered the headset he was still wearing. He yanked it off and clipped it to his belt, blinking the bright day out of his eyes and looking around for a vehicle to flag down.

Blaire's comms tech already had a jeep pulling up and a corporal waving at him, yelling that he should move it or lose it.

On his sprint to the jeep, Raul saw three enemy aerospace fighters flash by to the south on high-speed runs. He clambered into the vehicle, which started with a desperate lunge to get where it was going before a passing pilot decided it made a nice stationary target.

They raced east, toward the BattleMech hangars. Ahead of him, just taking to the air, Raul saw the Yellow Jacket that Blaire had called for Tassa Kay. She would be on the field as well. He might never hear about Dieron, he suddenly realized. And as a strafing fighter tore up the road in front of them with its nose-mounted autocannon, Raul quickly came to realize something more important about live combat.

He might never hear about anything again. Ever.

5

Face of the Enemy

Jagatai Aerospace Fighter
Over Achernar
Prefecture IV, The Republic
16 February 3133

Star Captain Laren Mehta thumbed the firing stud on his joystick. The twelve-centimeter assault cannon mounted into the nose of his *Jagatai* OmniFighter spat out a long tongue of flame and several hundred rounds of angry metal, laying down a storm of fire that tore through yet another line of monorail tracks. Earth and stone and splinters of metal struts exploded into the air. Then, with a thunderclap of displaced air and the roar of his Zeon 280 engines, Mehta's *Jagatai* flashed overhead like some vengeful spirit in search of a new sacrifice.

Already he had claimed a Demon armored vehicle and a very foolish Cyrano pilot who thought the VTOL's pitiful armor and single large laser could match up against his seventy-ton OmniFighter with its full array of heavy weaponry. Earlier he'd almost caught a Yellow Jacket gunship, until it ditched him by flying low between buildings. One close-in encounter with a JES missile car-

rier had already convinced him of the danger in chasing
VTOLs into ambushes.

Rolling his *Jagatai* off of its original line of attack and
then pulling straight back on the stick, he rocketed up
for a bird's eye view of the base. Behind him, Mehta's
wingman checked his maneuver. Leaving off their nape-
of-the-earth runs, they thundered out over the northern
stretch, leveled off, and cruised back in for an overview.

When Star Colonel Torrent had approached Mehta
with this mission, launching this surprise first strike
against Achernar, the Star Captain had resisted. Even
when his rank and part in the plans guaranteed him the
position of second-in-command, Laren Mehta only saw
that he would be second to an un-Bloodnamed warrior;
one who wanted to deploy the fightercraft on a ground-
strafing assault meant to buy conventional forces a free
ride to the planet's surface.

Kal Radick convinced Mehta of the merits concerning
both sore spots. Torrent's position was easier for the
pilot to accommodate, as the MechWarrior officer had
twice turned down opportunities to compete for a Bloodname. Such was not unknown among the Clans as young
ristars waited for a Bloodname with a long and valiant
heritage. Mehta's own Bloodname had been owned by
less than two dozen warriors. Twenty-one, to be exact,
dating back to the formation of the Clans some three
hundred years before.

With that kind of pedigree, Laren Mehta was destined
for leadership.

Which was Prefect Radick's second argument. As the
forward officer, claiming first blood from the enemy,
Mehta demonstrated his independence from Torrent. No
one was ordering him or his pilots to bomb civilian targets or strafe aerospace craft on the ground. Strategic
damage against the base was a necessity, of course. But
other than knocking the monorail out of commission and
inflicting some basic structural damage, Mehta and his
fighters were free to engage targets of opportunity as
they presented themselves.

No one would remember the need for their Trojan Horse gambit. Radick promised that Laren Mehta's codex would reflect only his command independence. For Clan warriors a codex—containing an accounting of their career victories and failures—meant everything.

"*Stealthy Paw* to Star Captain Mehta. Touchdown complete." Their DropShip, setting down in the hills northeast of the base. "Ground forces are breaking through. We have sightings on enemy forces both south and several klicks north."

So Colonel Blaire had finally rallied a response to the Steel Wolf assault. North . . . could that be the Swordsworn? If Erik Sandoval had force-marched his people over the Taibek Hills, it very well could be.

Mehta squeezed at his throat mic. "Ripper Flight, pull back and cover our brethren around the *Stealthy Paw*. Blood Flight, link up with Star Commander Orvits and guide them north. Form a shield at our backs, intercept the Swordsworn if they break two klicks."

No need to respond, Mehta's flight leaders signified their acceptance of his orders with double-clicks that briefly broke the channel's background static. Mehta pushed his own craft over and dove for the northeast, his own flight, Fang, making a straight-arrow approach over the River's Run Flatlands toward the twenty-story plume of smoke and steam that he knew hid the *Okinawa*-class DropShip. Then he saw the enemy ground forces, led by a dark-painted *Legionnaire,* and curved down on a soft spiral to come at it from an oblique angle.

"Incoming, incoming. Angel's three. Republic Guard has scrambled four—four!—fighters and a squadron of attack VTOLs."

Leveling off at three hundred meters, Mehta had just picked up a distance-lock on the *Legionnaire* when Star Commander Xera of Ripper Flight called in the spot on Blaire's fightercraft. Mehta's wingman moved up to safeguard his port side, buying the Star Captain time to take one stab with lasers at the lumbering *Legionnaire* below. One of the ruby lances scored an angry cut into the BattleMech's leg and then Mehta yanked back on the stick, once again clawing for air.

Two elements of aerospace fighters dove down on the Clan warriors with the fury of angered hornets. A mixed flight of F90 and F92 *Stingrays* paired off, leaving an element of heavy *Rapiers* anchoring their line. The Clan OmniFighters rose to meet them, weapons reaching out ahead to peel back paint and armor from the local defenders. One *Stingray* took a gauss slug directly into the cockpit, gutting the control section and leaving the pilot as little more than a smear over the back fuselage. The fighter rolled over out of control, falling for the budding battle between ground forces.

Laren Mehta wished he could take credit for such a handsome shot, but gave credit where it was due. "High marks, Pilot Sascha."

A rattle of autocannon fire skipped tracers off the forward spar of his port wing. Mehta rolled, but not before a half dozen holes popped through his armor like exploding blisters. He rolled out again, just for good measure. Then he was through the line of descending fighters, locking his sights on the lead *Rapier* that he knew would be the enemy wing officer's stick.

Sometimes the locals made it all too easy.

Agave Dales
Achernar

At the controls of his *Hatchetman,* Erik Sandoval-Groell swiped the BattleMech's large, titanium blade at a passing Shandra. Missed. His targeting computer more than compensated for the scout vehicle's high speed, however, and in the next instant he had tracked a stream of autocannon fire in toward its ridged tires. The slugs chopped into steel-threaded rubber and armored supports, cutting free the middle tire and sending it bouncing over the smooth rolls of Agave Dales. The Shandra slid sideways, recovered, and then quickly dodged behind a small hill to escape the 'Mech which probed after it with extended-range medium lasers.

Heat washed through his cockpit as the laser's energy draw spiked demand from the BattleMech's fusion reactor. Circulation fans pulled it away quickly, though, as the power level settled back into the green band. It hardly broke a sweat over Erik's forehead. Still, he was not about to let the daring crew off so easily.

"Sergeant Bosley, there is a Shandra coming up fast on your flank." If he was correct in placing his Gnome battle armor, in fact, the Shandra would be driving right into their waiting arms. "Weak right side. Finish it."

"Got him," the battlesuit infantry leader responded. "Missing one wheel. Now two. It's in our hands, Commander."

Quite literally. Erik paused at the top of a smooth rise, saw the Shandra being disassembled by his squad of Gnomes. He could almost hear the tearing-metal shrieks of wheels being ripped free from axles and armor shredded under mechanical claws.

"Commander, Able-Victor Six." Erik's lance of Mark II Scimitars. "We are still pushing back the Steel Wolf Elementals. Some trouble from strafing runs—got a couple of aggressive *Visigoths* over here—but they seem to be happy enough to hold us north of their line. Do we press forward?"

Having force-marched a mixed company of troops over the Taibek Hills, Erik still hadn't decided on how much aid he would give the local defenders. The Steel Wolves seemed content to poke and prod at his lines, but so long as he held back near the foothills that eventually became the Taibeks (and further north, the Tanagers), they were content to hold him off the main battle.

Able-Victor Six was the more expendable lance, as Erik preferred not to risk his valuable 'Mechs or any of his Swordsworn-converted battlesuits. Not beyond reason, anyway.

"Push them, Able-Victor. Don't threaten that DropShip, but drive for the Flatlands." Dropping from

the Dales and into the River's Run Flatlands would allow
his Swordsworn to link up and coordinate efforts with
the militia. "See if they will let you approach the Republic forces." Erik bet they wouldn't.

Of course, it wasn't his life he wagered with.

In his pause, Erik's own lance had caught up with him.
Three converted MiningMechs stormed up behind him,
their tank treads cutting at Achernar's ground. Diamond-
bit cutters slashed the air. One launched a brace of missiles from its shoulder-mounted launcher, the projectiles
falling far short of the nearest Steel Wolf target, blasting
small craters into a hillside.

"*Short*-range missiles," Erik berated his driver. "Short!
That Condor was half a klick distant. Watch your
range-finder."

"Yes, Lord. That is, I don't have a range-finder, Lord."

"Eyeball it, then," Erik snarled. "Better yet, don't fire
expendables unless you see another 'Mech fire them off
first."

Erik switched off the frequency for his own lance, not
wanting to hear any more sycophantic whining. The mining drivers were masters in their own right, but they
weren't soldiers and he shouldn't expect them to be. That
would come with experience.

He switched his frequency open again. "Forward at
your best rate," Erik ordered them. "Concentrate fire on
targets. Garibaldi, you call them out." He levered his
own *Hatchetman* into an easy walk, coming in behind the
MiningMechs, keeping an eye on his HUD and always
watching through the forward ferroglass for any sign of
a shift in battle.

Garibaldi put the trio of converted machines on a hoverbike squad, chasing after the fast-moving craft. One of
the mine drivers actually managed to cripple one hoverbike with a (probably) lucky missile barrage. Seeing
that speed meant a great deal on the battlefield, as op-
posed to the static course they had trained on, Garibaldi
started to angle after slower targets. Working together,

they managed to threaten a D1 Schmitt into breaking off its attack run.

"*That* stirred them up. Pull back, pull back!"

On Erik's HUD, one of his armored vehicles flared bright sapphire and then winked out of existence. "Able-Victor Six, report!"

From his height, swaying three stories above the battlefield, Erik saw his remaining Scimitars race back from a boiling fury of VV1 Rangers and Elementals. He balled up one fist, smashed it down on the armrest of his command couch.

"We opened a hole in their line," the lead Scimitar reported. "By accident more than intention," he admitted, "but for a second we had an open shot to rendezvous with the Republic Guard. Those *Visigoths* and a *Jaga*-something pounced on us and strafed us full of holes. Then the Rangers and Elementals hit with a vengeance. They don't want us getting through there, Commander."

Message received, Erik silently told the Steel Wolf commander. If the Swordsworn wanted to push through, these Clan wannabes would make them pay for it. Erik smiled grimly as his MiningMech converts cheered their own little victory, having pushed forward just far enough to hammer a squad of Steel Wolf Cavalier infantry with multiple missile barrages. They may have put two or three Steel Wolves permanently out of commission.

"AV-6, pull back north nor'west. Let them think they can split us. Do not make further attempts to press forward."

"Copy *that*."

Erik reigned in the cowboy warriors in the converted 'Mechs as well as his various infantry squads. With a bit of stage direction, he planned to pull them all back and westward, ostensibly to link back up with his lance of wayward Scimitars. It pulled his company out of the main battle, but allowed them to skirmish with whatever dregs the Steel Wolves wanted to throw their way.

It was how Erik would build warriors. He'd let the two larger factions battle each other, saving his troops for later.

"I've learned the hazards of jumping in too soon," Erik whispered to his cockpit, hearing his words echo in the tight confines of his neurohelmet. As his uncle admonished, this time Erik would exercise greater patience. He'd wait, and plan, and train his drivers into true soldiers. And then, he'd strike.

With any luck, the other factions would bloody themselves up so badly that when the smoke cleared, Erik would remain the uncontested commander on Achernar. Without a shot fired.

He laughed. It was a pleasant fiction, and whiled away the time as Erik pulled his forces further from the main battle.

6

Enemy Down

Raul Ortega used the dry riverbed as a natural bypass, able to move from one side of the Republic's strung-out battle line to another. Opening skirmishes and strafing runs by the overhead Steel Wolf OmniFighters had already cost him a damaged knee actuator. Throttling the *Legionnaire* up to a fast walk, favoring the right leg, Raul curled around tall stands of Ponderosa Pine and thorny monkey trees that weren't much better than very large cacti. A pair of hoverbikes abandoned the dead riverbank, following his lead, flying off the drop and kicking up a large cloud of dirt and debris in their wake.

"Ortega on the way," he said in an encouraging voice, willing the recovery team to hold out.

"Whatever you can do, do it fast," came a clipped, no-nonsense response.

Raul nodded to the empty cockpit, swallowed painfully, mouth parched from breathing the dry cockpit air. He tasted flatland dust and wondered just for a moment how wise it had been to rechannel the river away from Highlake Basin on a shorter path to River's End. Only five kilometers north of the military base, once-grassy plains had become a virtual dustbowl in the last thirty years. Except for summer storms, the River's Run Flats wouldn't see much moisture until late autumn. With temperatures outside peaking at forty Celsius, that made for a miserable battlefield.

Pivoting into the final river bend, the *Legionnaire's* feet nearly skidding out from beneath Raul on old hardpan and river rock, he judged the timing about right and turned into the steep bank. Flange-formed feet dug at the side of the river. Raul bent forward at the waist, throwing the 'Mech's center of gravity forward as his neurohelmet transferred his own sense of equilibrium down into the stressed gyroscopic stabilizers. The *Legionnaire* actually fell uphill, arms out to catch the upper lip of the riverbank.

Raul pulled himself out of the riverbed just as the hoverbikes chose a likely looking slope of their own and jumped the bank to either side of him. Working his footpedals and control sticks, he stumbled back up into a flat-out run and toward the beleaguered recovery team.

He couldn't fault the fix-it team for trying to salvage the Behemoth II after it took crippling damage to its drive train—an assault tank was no easy piece of technology to abandon on the field. He could have asked for a more defendable position, however. The isolated crew sat out in the open with their JI 100 recovery vehicle cowering behind the stranded Behemoth. Steel Wolf forces pressed in from two sides, sniping from long range at the fix-it team, kept off them only by Tassa Kay's *Ryoken* and the frantic racing of twin Condors which worked hard to guard both flanks at once.

Erik Sandoval was supposed to have closed in on this side of the battlefield by now. Obviously he was running late.

"Ortega has the right side," Raul offered, his *Legionnaire* limping forward at a still-respectable ninety kph.

"Tassa has the left." The *Ryoken* turned in a graceful, predatory leap even as she warned him, jetting up and over the Behemoth on fiery streams of plasma. The Condors gravitated to her as if drawn by a titan's lodestone.

Raul kept the hoverbikes. "You corral them, I rope them." The fast hovercraft sprinted out ahead of him, already worrying a lumbering JES Strategic Missile Carrier with their twin laser system.

If the JES crew thought they had time to deal with the hoverbikes and escape, they misjudged the speed of a *Legionnaire*. Raul stabbed his targeting crosshairs directly over the back hatch, exhaled an extra-long second waiting for his targeting computer, then remembered that Charal had either ripped it out or had it removed intentionally. Instead he carried a trio of medium lasers to supplement his rotary autocannon.

He pulled into his main trigger, holding it down as the overhead rotary chewed through several hundred rounds of high-explosive ammunition. Charge-loaded slugs blasted into the back of the JES Carrier, cratering large holes through its armor and feeding even more damage into the vulnerable crew quarters. The entire vehicle shuddered, swung around at an awkward angle, and then ground to a halt, dead on the plains.

It didn't hit Raul for another dozen steps that he had just executed a Republic-born military crew. He throttled off, slowing to a walk as he stared at the gutted carrier.

"Head's up," Tassa warned him. "Here they come again."

Twin lines of autocannon fire chewed up the flatlands ahead of him as two bone-white *Jagatai* skimmed the flatlands, strafing arrows at Raul's *Legionnaire*. He sidestepped out of the obvious damage path, but one of the pilots reacted on instincts and lightning-fast reflexes. The tail end of one *Jagatai* slewed around, correcting its aim. The craft thundered by overhead, and for a second Raul believed he was safe. Then the pilot flared wing flaps and pulled the OmniFighter's nose toward the heavens, angling his tail down at the *Legionnaire's* back and spraying a mix of laserfire from his aft-mounted weapons.

The blood-red lance burned the ground off to one side,

but bright emerald darts from a pulse laser stung all up and down Raul's backside. Armor ran down his BattleMech's legs and splashed into the dirt, smoking small craters into the flats.

Raul felt heat radiating up through the cockpit deck even before he checked his wireframe damage schematic and saw that he'd lost a good chunk of physical shielding around his fusion reactor. Temperature levels had jumped up to yellow-band equivalent, and now just about anything Raul did with the 'Mech, including an easy walk, would begin to bake him alive.

He suddenly felt a touch less sympathy for the Steel Wolf crew in the *Big Jess,* seeing how close he had come to a fiery death of his own.

"Unless you're in full shutdown, how about an assist?"

Tassa Kay's sarcasm cut through Raul's brief seconds of reflection, snapping him back to the here and now. He checked his HUD, deciphering the code of icons and IFF tags, saw that Tassa's *Ryoken* was herding a pair of Demon medium tanks around the far side of the stranded Behemoth. Both vehicles slid around into full view, saw the waiting *Legionnaire,* and then cut sharply out toward the middle of the flats and the safety of their own lines.

Raul reached out for one of them with a few long-range bursts from his RAC. Both missed, chewing up the ground just behind the lead vehicle. Tassa was not going to be denied so easily. Twisting her 'Mech's torso further to the left, she bracketed in the rear vehicle with her twin PPCs. The particle cannons spent incredible power into two hellish streams of blue-white energy.

One cut across the front of the rear Demon, a literal shot across the bow.

The second PPC smacked into the tank broadside.

The physical force of impact rocked the Demon onto its right-side wheels, shoving the vehicle over several meters, while the focused energy in the beam cut and tunneled its way through armor. The vehicle poured on speed, racing out from under Tassa's weapons. She tried to chase after it with her torso-mounted lasers, but the scarlet shafts cut down into the ground just short of their intended target.

The Demons slid in behind a screen of JES Tactical carriers and Elementals.

"Damn and blast!" Tassa yelled, then followed it up with curses in Deutch and a language Raul did not recognize. He checked his comms, saw that she was at least confining her transmissions to the MechWarrior's-only circuit.

"What happened to the Condors?" Raul asked, gasping for breath in the oven-temperature cockpit. According to his HUD, they had abandoned Tassa to chase after some Hauberk infantry and a Joust. That didn't sound like Republic Guard tactics, splitting your offensive force.

"I ordered them off," Tassa admitted. "Those were our kills, and we missed both." More curses.

"Lieutenant Ortega, this is Recovery Team Three. Thanks for the timely arrival."

Raul muted Tassa's input to prevent her anger from bleeding over into the support frequencies. "Welcome," he swallowed new life back into his throat. The taste of sweat burned on his lips. "Now get out of here ASAP."

"We need five more minutes and we can have the Behemoth operational again. Can you buy us that amount of time?"

"That's hardly been the problem." Tassa was back, her anger mostly spent. "The Steel Wolf ground forces are not pushing too hard unless they catch us off guard. We can hold a line here."

Raul had noticed much the same thing. "Probing attacks," he said, catching his breath as the *Legionnaire*'s heat levels settled back into a bearable range. "This entire assault was designed to throw us off guard while the main force lands. They're taking the opportunity to test our strength."

Already the enemy was shifting forces to the west, back into the area from which Raul had originally come. "Maybe we should take this chance to test theirs," Tassa said. Without waiting to see if he would follow, Tassa's *Ryoken* hit a long stride, stalking out toward the Steel Wolf lines.

Not to be left behind, Raul throttled up into a loping run. She was right. It didn't matter that this was not the main Steel Wolf push. The enemy was down on-planet, and it was a MechWarrior's duty to face the enemy.

Even when they had been part of the same army.

Jagatai Aerospace Fighter
Achernar

Add one *Rapier* to Star Captain Laren Mehta's list of kills. The wingman.

It had taken him longer than estimated to break apart the two-fighter element chosen as his targets. He accepted help from no one, determined to bring down the enemy flight leader on his own skill. But then he had latched onto the tail of the wrong craft!

He knew it within seconds—the uninspired way in which the pilot tried to shake him, twitching and rolling through the air as if Mehta was a raw cadet, to be fooled by such basic feints. Almost he pulled off, to go hunting better game. Almost. When you had the killing position, riding high in their six, you didn't throw it away out of ego. You splashed the enemy first, and then you moved on.

The *Rapier* had no aft-mounted weapons, and so it could only try to run. Laren Mehta played for the pilot's fear and inexperience, often letting his victim extend out just enough that he could bracket the other fighter with lasers and long-range missiles. As soon as he tightened up again, switch to the assault-class autocannon and scrape away more armor with flechette submunitions.

Finally the *Rapier* pilot dove for the ground, playing chicken with the star captain. Mehta hung in right behind, having played the game with braver men than some free born sparrowheart still hovering in the flight leader's shadow. Five thousand meters. At four thousand his own wingman peeled away, maintaining a high watch. Three thousand. Two.

The *Rapier* pulled up, right into Mehta's crosshairs.

The *Jagatai*'s autocannon started at the nose of the enemy craft and chewed large holes all the way back along the fuselage. High-velocity metal shattered the cockpit canopy, filling the tight space with flesh-cutting shrapnel, and then finally trailed off into the aft thrusters. The *Rapier* rolled belly-up and fell toward the ground even as Mehta rocketed by under a full power dive.

Laren Mehta yanked back hard on his stick and pulled for full flaps, digging into the air for every ounce of lift he could find. His altimeter read four hundred meters by the time it started to crawl back upward again. Seconds to spare.

A victorious howl died stillborn in his throat as Ripper Flight's Star Commander Xera claimed the *Rapier* lead.

"Verify!" he snarled, clutching at his throat mic.

"Aff," came an immediate response. "*Rapier* lead is burning, *Rapier* lead . . . has crashed." She paused, as if uncertain how much info her Star Captain was asking for. "Ripper Flight lead is operating solo. Wingman is down."

Still, an impressive victory for her codex. Not his. He glanced down at the octagonal data crystal, strapped to his wrist right over the pressure point. Mehta was one of the few pilots he knew who did not wear gloves, preferring to feel the full response of the OmniFighter.

Star Commander Drake had also reported in with one fighter withdrawn. That was one OmniFighter crippled and one destroyed for three confirmed enemy kills. Seven, if VTOLs and ground vehicles were counted. Not a terrible day's work. And according to his HUD, the enemy fightercraft had ceded control over the battlefield to Mehta's force. With the arrival of a second pair of *Stingrays,* the militia had three fighters and half a dozen VTOLs circling around the battlefield edges like jackals waiting to pounce on a weakened stray. Mehta would not give them that chance.

"Keep clear skies over the battle, but do not chase down

enemy *Stingrays*. Star Commander Xera, fly high alert and take command as you see fit to throw back any advance."

"Aff, sir!" She saw her elevation as a promotion. And it was, of sorts. Drake was the senior Star Commander, but Drake didn't have a squadron leader under his belt today. "Where will you be?"

Laren Mehta checked to make certain his wingman was back, holding position off his left wing. He dipped his nose down, and started a long, gliding dive down toward the ground battle.

"Hunting," he told her.

There was other game to be tracked, and just as big as an enemy squadron lead.

River's Run Flatlands
Achernar

Sweat beaded on Raul's bare arms and legs, trickled in tiny rivulets down his face, and stung at the corners of his eyes. His breath came in short, burning gasps as his lungs fought to pull oxygen out of the baking air. His reactor levels hovered almost constantly at the border between the yellow caution band and warning red. Only his MechWarrior's vest, circulating coolant through fifty meters of sewn-in tubing, kept his body core temperature down and prevented heat-induced blackout.

No time to rest or allow the *Legionnaire*'s heat levels to relax, Raul ran his 'Mech forward to keep pace with Tassa Kay's *Ryoken*. The two of them had pressed further forward than any other Republic unit, in sight of the Agave Dales although there was still no contact with Sandoval's Swordsworn. Not that they needed him anymore. The Steel Wolves seemed committed to their hit-and-fade strategy, which surrendered any advantage to the two MechWarriors' blitzkrieg offensive. All they had to do was keep their eyes open for OmniFighters and targets of opportunity.

Like this one. They raced up on either side of a re-treating Joust, the tracked tank straining along with obvious engine difficulty. Black, oily smoke trailed out of several gaping rents in the tank's armor. Battlesuit damage.

From earlier trade-offs with Tassa, Raul knew she would leave him to finish off the wounded vehicle. Her lasers spat out scarlet spikes which worried the ground to one side of the Joust, herding it closer to Raul's *Legionnaire*. The Joust's turret swung over as the tank tried to bully its way past the militia BattleMech, lancing out with its large lasers but missing. The ruby beam scorched a line of black glass into the ground at Raul's feet.

Cautious of his ammunition reserves, Raul spent two short bursts into the damaged side of the Joust. A tongue of fire licked out from the blackened rent—an orange flame spitting more fuel-tinged smoke into the air. The tank trailed to a stop, and Raul lifted his crosshairs away in search of a new target.

"You're getting soft," Tassa accused him. "If they get that fire under control and then put a laser into your back, you will wish you had finished them."

Raul's vision blurred, and he blinked some moisture back into his eyes. "You haven't noticed that we attracted a small retinue behind us?" he asked. Of course, Tassa's head's up display might not be fully conversant with Republic Identify Friend-Foe transponders, but her sensors should have picked up the two VVI Rangers and the double-squad of Cavalier battlesuit infantry following in their wake of dust.

"Honestly, no. If they are not hostiles, I tend to over-look lesser forces. And I do not trust my back to anyone but a MechWarrior. Sometimes, not even to them."

There it was again; a veiled—not contempt, but a lack of consideration—for conventional forces. Somewhere, Tassa must have been burned badly. "Learn that on Dieron?" he asked.

"You don't give up, do you?"

"Not easily, no. I've been told by . . . on good authority that I have a determined stubborn streak." By his fiancée. A guilty start shook Raul. Why hadn't he simply admitted that it was Jessica who often told him that?

Tassa took a moment out to pop her lasers off at some Hauberk infantry. The battlesuit troopers had tried to come at her from over a small rise. Her lasers burnt one into a desiccated shell, drove the rest back. "Stubborn does not work with me. When the answer is no, it stays no."

Was she just talking about her adventures on Dieron? "The answer hasn't been 'no' yet, now has it?" Was he?

"No. Not yet. Though if you do not get around to asking the right—Raul!"

Too late, her warning came. Sensors screamed at him as an enemy targeting system locked on, their high-pitched wail piercing his ears like the autocannon rounds which made short work of his right-side armor. Raul wrestled with his control sticks, fighting to keep his balance as the *Jagatai* OmniFighter screamed overhead at less than one hundred meters off the ground. A cyclone of dirt and debris blasted up behind its wake, pelting Raul's cockpit.

A second OmniFighter, higher and slower than the first, spent two ruby beams toward Tassa. She throttled into a reverse walk, pulling out of its line of fire, and managed to clip its tail assembly with one of her PPCs before it thundered by after its lead.

Kicking his left leg out into a wide-bodied stance, Raul barely managed to hold the fifty tons of metal and myomer upright. The *Legionnaire* bent far over toward its right, holding a precarious balance. Slowly, Raul straightened back up.

"You all right?"

His ears rang with the echoes of sensors alarms and the hammering reports of one hundred twenty millimeter ammo chewing into his armor. He tasted blood, and then realized from a throbbing ache that he'd bitten the inside of his cheek. Which was the least he deserved from flirting during a firefight. Idiot.

"Yeah. I'll live." He checked the wireframe, and tested out what he saw there by trying to flex the *Legionnaire*'s right knee. "That's it for my right knee joint, though. It's fused." Which would cost him about ten klicks on his top speed. "I'm going nowhere fast."

"Well how about you get turned around to the north," Tassa said casually, "because those fighters are looping back around."

It was true. The fighters had left the range factor on his HUD, but were still caught on an auxiliary sensor display circling at five klicks. Tassa moved to place herself in line, with Raul between her and the fighters' return path.

"Tassa, what are you doing? You don't put yourself in the path of a strafing run. You attack from the oblique so it's harder for the pilot to target you."

"It's harder for you to target them, too," she said with a curt tone. "If you really don't think I know what I'm doing, step aside."

Raul considered it. Everything in his training and the prickly hairs standing up on the back of his neck told him to avoid the fighter's pass. His targeting system would allow him to get one shot off at the *Jagatai* as it flashed by overhead, but his rotary autocannon couldn't match the OmniFighter's firepower. Not unless he held into the trigger and emptied his ammunition bins in one long burst.

"I think I'm good to go," he said, sounding braver than he felt.

No time for better than that, though. The *Jagatai* were already back.

The lead craft came in low again, hugging Achernar like an old friend. The tail of dirt sucked up into its backwash stood out several klicks away, which gave Raul all of three seconds to magnify for aerial targets and set his crosshairs into the OmniFighter's approximate path. At the last possible second, he shuffle-stepped to one side and squeezed into his trigger, held it.

Behind him, framed on his rear monitor, Tassa Kay's *Ryoken* rocketed up and forward into the air on its jump jets.

It was a maneuver—two maneuvers, really—caught on various gun-cam videos that Raul would end up watching over and over again once back at the base. Everyone had a piece of the exchange, but only the long-sniper squad of Cavaliers—rushing up from the backfield after dealing with the Joust's crew—caught the entire thing.

Raul stepping aside of the main strafing path just as the ground opened up in a new, hideous rent of damage that drew a line right between his old footprints.

Tassa Kay hovering her *Ryoken* in the air almost right over Raul's *Legionnaire*.

His *Legionnaire* cutting apart the air with hot, lethal metal, hammering several hundred fifty-millimeter slugs into the nose of the *Jagatai* and peeling away several layers of its thick armor plating.

Her *Ryoken,* stabbing out with lasers and particle cannon. The lasers actually burned in along the fuselage underbody, doing little more than scorching pristine armor. Her PPCs, however, struck into the *Jagatai*'s already-bloodied nose. Both beams fused into one hard-hitting punch, washing blue-white crackling energy over the forward third of the OmniFighter.

The combined damage might have been enough to penetrate to something vital. Raul wasn't so certain. Sensors blinded by the particle discharge and canopy no doubt awash in a white sheet of energy, it looked to Raul as if the Steel Wolf pilot attempted to quickly turn out of the firestorm, banking away hard to port.

At one hundred meters over the hard, unyielding earth, a pilot did nothing quick or hard. Not without consequences.

Air bled away beneath the wings and the *Jagatai*'s nose dipped just enough. The OmniFighter jinked away on a tight, horizontal loop, drifted down, and then clipped its wing on the same small rise behind which the Hauberk infantry had hidden. In slow replay, Raul would see the OmniFighter turn three complete somersaults in the air, shedding pieces and parts in a storm of falling metal.

At the battle site, he blinked, and it was all over.

The lead *Jagatai* was shredded wreckage spread over several acres of burning earth. The flames burned white for a few seconds, hot enough to consume metal, and then settled back into normal, yellow-orange flames. Raul felt the wave of heat slam into him as his own reactor spiked dangerously high. Shutdown alarms wailed for attention and he slapped the override, preferring to cook himself before being stuck on a battlefield in a dead 'Mech. He did reach back and punch his emergency escape release, as if vacating the cockpit through the manual hatch. The small door blew outward on explosive charges. Forty Celsius air fouled with smoke rushed into the cramped cockpit. Raul had never tasted anything so refreshing.

Tassa Kay stalked her *Ryoken* up to his *Legionnaire*. Her ferroglass canopy had three starred bullet holes in it. Fortunately, they were well wide of her actual command couch. "Now *that*," she said calmly, "I did learn on Dieron."

Raul coughed against the acrid taste of smoke, found his voice. "Now she starts with the stories."

He checked his HUD and all sensors. Nothing. The second *Jagatai* had broken off its attack run and bugged out. The remaining ground forces had disappeared as if someone had thrown the master switch on an elaborate simulation. Except that there was nothing simulated about this day's work, and he would never be able to erase it from memory. Not a computer's. Not his own.

7

Circle of Equals

Highlake Basin
Achernar
19 February 3133

Star Colonel Torrent had dimmed his shipboard office lights, relaxing his eyes after a morning spent sweating under Achernar's harsh sun. The air remained sluggish and warm, however, with a hint of old mud. The *Lupus*'s interior climate controls were set to minimum, scrubbing the air it pulled from outside the DropShip but adding only the slightest drop in temperature as Torrent forced his warriors to acclimate.

Sitting forward in his chair, arms resting on legs and hands clasped in between his knees, Torrent watched with intense concentration as the battlerom played out in three dimensions and vivid color on his holovid desk screen. Pulled from the OmniFighter belonging to Laren Mehta's wingman, the Star Captain's *Jagatai* hovered at the lower edge of the tableau during its furious, and final, nape-of-the-earth run.

The ground was little more than a beige blur except for where his technicians had cleaned up the image, showing the slow-motion approach of the two BattleMechs. One took to the air on jumpjets while the other sidestepped, both cutting weapons fire across Mehta's flight path. Torrent stared unblinking as tracers and bright metal shards skipped off the *Jagatai*'s nose, soon to be engulfed by the converging beams of twin particle cannon. He could almost smell the crackling ozone of PPC discharge as Laren Mehta banked and his craft curled out of the picture.

To slam into the ground a split-second later.

Torrent reached forward, hit the video-still and capture controls. The *Ryoken* hung in the air as if trapped in amber. He reopened his audio report to Steel Wolf Commander and Prefect Kal Radick. "I officially classify Laren Mehta's death as heroism under fire," Torrent said, his deep voice adding commentary to the video. "Two BattleMechs pushed our lines back. Star Captain Mehta attacked, and earned a warrior's end. His codex will reflect this." And new Steel Wolf sibkos would be born of his DNA. If Torrent owed anything to Laren Mehta, that was enough.

"I promoted Star Captain Nikola Demos as my second in command," he informed Radick. "She is senior to any officer on the *Stealthy Paw*. Also, Mehta's death created a disciplinary crisis between two pilots, both of whom are positioning themselves to replace the Star Captain. I expect that to be settled within the next few days." Another commander might have settled the issue by now, but Torrent would wait and see which one had the greater warrior's heart.

And of greater concern to the star colonel this moment were the two machines caught in frozen display. "The *Legionnaire* clearly displays the insignia of Achernar's Republic Guard. The *Ryoken* bears no crest. It is more advanced than anything we estimated facing." He frowned, noting how the *Ryoken* pilot worked almost seamlessly alongside the militia warriors. "I do not believe this MechWarrior is Swordsworn."

A theory Torrent had tested, nonetheless. His two probing attacks toward Hahnsak on the following days had turned up no sign of the *Ryoken,* nor anything more advanced than Erik Sandoval's *Hatchetman* and some converted MiningMechs. Torrent queued up battlerom footage from those probes, set it to spooling into the recorded report.

"My force can roll over the Swordsworn at any time." Torrent looked forward to that, given Duke Aaron Sandoval's position as Kal Radick's primary competition for control of Prefecture IV. "I am holding off on any major offensive, awaiting the arrival of Knight-Errant Kyle Powers. In the meantime, I will keep a wedge driven between Swordsworn and Republic, and stay open to contact from our lost wolves. Star Colonel Torrent, reporting."

He let the final battle footage play out, then cut off the video spool and batched the report into the files set for transmission. In two days a Steel Wolf JumpShip would pass through Achernar's system, staying just long enough for Torrent to upload reports. Even without the local HPG station, Kal Radick was slowly building his intelligence infrastructure.

Torrent switched off his desk's recording equipment and reopened his connection to the DropShip's communications board. Only a military emergency could interrupt him during a private session. Three low-priority messages queued up on his system, but were shoved aside as an open line from the *Lupus*'s bridge pushed through.

"Star Colonel." The on-duty bridge officer blinked into existence on Torrent's holographic screen. "Sir, you've an urgent request for your presence at the *Stealthy Paw*."

"From whom?" Torrent asked, irritated over having to ask for such basic information. Ship officers: lazy minds, most of them, as evidenced in the officer's use of contractions.

"The request came with Ship's Captain's authority. Rachel Grimheald. I'm not certain with whom it originated. I can find out, Star Colonel."

Torrent rocked to his feet and leaned over the desk

as if ready to pounce through the monitor. "Never mind. I already know. Spend your time learning how to deliver a proper report."

He switched off the call with a violent stab at the disconnect. Grabbing up his field jacket and the service cap perched on the edge of his desk, Torrent carried them into the DropShip's corridor and down to the lower cargo bay in search of transportation. The trip from his *Lupus* to the DropShip *Stealthy Paw* was less than four minutes by hovercraft. Torrent did not wait for a driver, coding in his personal override and firing up the lift fans on a Fox armored car, coasting it across the cargo bay, down the extended ramp, and then opening full throttle for the short dash across Highlake Basin's mud flats.

Achernar's sun was just hitting its late afternoon stride, the bright, blue-white star washing out the sky to a pale, pale blue. Nearby, the Tanager Mountains looked more forbidding by the harsh light of day than during the soft twilight by which the DropShips had landed three days ago. Torrent wasn't used to the bright days yet, especially when being called out of his office. He reached into a utility pack on his belt, pulled out dark-tinted goggles and pulled them over his shaven pate one-handed. Settling the dark glass over his eyes, he returned his attention to driving.

The three Steel Wolf DropShips formed a triangle around their primary staging area with two kilometers to a side. He reviewed that arrangement every day as he jogged the perimeter for a morning workout. Acceptable, he decided again. The *Lupus* had followed down their *Triumph*-class aerodyne, the *Wulfstag,* waiting until the massive troop carrier ground to a halt using Highlake Basin as a modified landing field. The *Stealthy Paw*'s arrival completed their defensive perimeter. Plows leveled a very rudimentary runway, and as his OmniFighters returned they coasted into the protective field at the center.

Four Omnifighters, returning without Star Captain Mehta. That was today's problem.

He had brought down two more *Jagatai* with the *Lupus,*

bringing his on-planet total to six craft. Three of the fighter craft remained under camouflage tarps. Torrent drove by close enough to make certain, passing between them and his first rank of VTOL craft. The artificial wind generated by his high-speed tugged at the tarp edges and stirred up yet another layer of dust. He knew that two *Visigoths* sat out on the runway as his ready-alert interceptors. Which meant there was still one fighter unaccounted for, being worked on inside the *Stealthy Paw*'s maintenance bay. Something told him he had a fifty-percent chance of guessing who that one belonged to, and his instincts sniffed at Star Commander Xera.

It was his own fault, leaving his decision open for as long as he had. But with the battles on Achernar to be decided by ground forces, the star colonel indulged himself in testing the pilots.

Torrent grabbed up a headset lying on the floor next to his seat, and held it next to his ear. Idle conversation—two tank drivers arguing about the merits of the Scimitar Mark II. Torrent ordered them to clear the channel and then used the frequency to contact the *Wulfstag*. His report, and seeing the aerodyne carrier, reminded him of more unfinished business. So long as he was out and about . . .

"*Wulfstag,*" an on-duty communications officer acknowledged.

"*Wulfstag.* This is Star Colonel Torrent." He gave the other man a moment to sharpen his wits. "Connect me with Star Captain Demos. Wherever she is."

"It will take me a minute to locate her, Star Colonel," the man said, trying to buy himself time.

"Bargained well." Torrent grinned to himself at the thought of the other man's sudden realization. "You have one minute."

Just to see, Torrent began a slow count of the seconds. He did not set impossible tasks for his crew, but he expected them to perform to high standards where he was concerned. He would give the communications officer sixty seconds, and then he would give him an extra shift.

The man came back within forty. "I have Star Captain Demos, sir. She is on maneuvers near the Taibek Hills."

Torrent placed her on his mental map of the area. Twenty kilometers away, where the Tanager Mountains bent north to go around Hahnsak and the B'her farming valley. "Commendable." His praise was short, but effective. "Patch her through."

"Star Colonel Torrent." Nikola Demos's voice sounded shaky, as if her Mobile HQ was bouncing her over some rough terrain. "How may I serve you?"

"Are you overly busy?"

"No, Star Colonel. Taking an aerial view of our forward posts."

She was in a VTOL. That explained the chopping noise cutting apart her voice—the blades of the aircraft. Torrent nodded. He guided the Fox in a gentle swerve that pointed him directly toward the *Okinawa*-class carrier. "Nikola. Meet me at the *Stealthy Paw*. We have matters to discuss." He threw the headset back down onto the floor.

Grounding the Fox hovercraft at the foot of the *Okinawa*'s narrow ramp, Torrent secured the vehicle and cracked his door. The full heat of Achernar's high desert plateau slammed into him with physical force. It felt as if the heat were sucking the moisture right out of his body. He shucked his jacket, stripping back down to field pants and a black tank top, and left the jacket and his service cap in the vehicle.

He paused halfway up the ramp, gazing over the dry lake, and inhaled deeply as if testing the air for the scent of predators, or prey. Achernar smelled dry and abandoned. From his staging area, it was difficult to believe that such an out-of-the-way world had suddenly become so important to Kal Radick and the Steel Wolves. Torrent wiped a large hand over the back of his head, brushing away sweat and dirt. Looks were often deceiving. Reviewing battleroms from the recent assaults had reinforced that old maxim.

The *Okinawa's* main bay—its largest space with most of the ship's OmniFighters and conventional aircraft grounded outside on the lake bed—had been converted into a primary maintenance area. From the wide-open bay doors Torrent noticed one thing immediately.

No one was working.

His disposition took a dark turn as he walked past torn-open vehicles and infantry battlesuits downchecked for preventative maintenance. He saw an abandoned welder, and only barely picked up the acrid, fading stench of hot metalwork. Grease and paint were much stronger, but then with so many barrels cracked open and bleeding fumes into the air, they would be. Whatever had happened here had stopped work better than thirty minutes before, and there had obviously been no resolution.

His workforce gathered around a *Jagatai*, the Omni-Fighter shining bright silver from fresh armor but only partly repainted. He bulldozed through the ring of spectators, shouldering aside those who were in his way without breaking his stride, and walked right up to the side of the craft where the pilot's name was painted.

Star Commander Xera. Just as he'd thought. And instead of listing her command as Ripper Flight, under her name was the new callsign Broken Fang.

No, it wasn't. Torrent yanked the dark glasses off his head, tucked them into his belt. Actually it read Broken Fan with the "g" still missing. Paint and stencils sat on a nearby work platform. That would be Xera provoking the situation by trying to co-opt Star Captain Mehta's flight callsign, slowly assuming his position. Drops of bright red blood darkened toward drier brown on the nonskid deck at his feet. A fight.

He swung about, and the look in his eyes sent most people back to work. The ones who hadn't slipped away after his obvious arrival, that is. The slow-learners. Those who stayed behind shifted about on nervous feet, the techs waiting to finish work on the aerospace Omni-Fighter.

Except for two.

Star Commander Drake stood closest to him. Torrent studied him head to foot, noting the dark smear of blood under his split lip and the righteous fire burning behind his pale green eyes. The man had fallen into Xera's trap, pulling her away from the *Jagatai* and earning a fist or foot for his effort. Not even the five minutes it must have taken Torrent to arrive had slackened his fury. Or it had been incredibly strong.

Xera stood a more relaxed post off to one side. A master tech and two apprentices separated the two pilots. Not keeping them apart—lower-castes did not interfere in a fight between warriors—but showing support in the way they stood closer to Xera than Drake. Torrent noted that, too.

"You two should have taken care of this three days ago." He kept his deep voice under careful control, simply pointing out the facts. "A hot stick is not enough. If either of you had an ounce of Laren Mehta's leadership potential, you would have challenged sooner."

Neither Star Commander said a word, which was to their credit. He glanced at Xera. "You struck Drake outside a circle of equals?"

She nodded. "He laid hands on me without permission. That is an attack."

As Torrent had already surmised. "Do either of you have an official challenge?"

Xera preempted Drake by being faster off the mark. "I have restored my own honor. And, as I was the one Star Captain Mehta last placed in command, I assume his authority."

"Then I challenge," Drake argued at once. "The position is mine."

Torrent nodded. "I forbid augmented combat while we are on a military footing." By custom, choice of hand-to-hand or live-fire combat belonged to the 'hunter,' the one who challenged. "Drake. For that, I offer you choice of venue."

"Here. Now." The pilot couldn't wait to think if he enjoyed an advantage someplace else.

Torrent glanced to the remaining technicians. "Give them five meters." Starting near their star colonel, the six remaining men and women formed a loose circle around the pilots, leaving them approximately five meters for their circle of equals. "First one forced out of the circle," Torrent said, a time-honored condition of victory. Then he set himself in a wide, comfortable stance, and waited.

The two combatants circled each other warily, watching for any telltale sign of weakness. Xera's sharp, hazel eyes missed nothing. A warm anger radiated out of Drake, who was beyond patience. He rushed in, coming low and fast to maintain his center of gravity and not get simply *toreadored* out of the makeshift circle.

Xera accepted the full brunt of his attack, protecting herself by balling up and rolling away, losing skin from her hand against the nonskid deck and coming dangerously close to the circle's edge. By intention, as it happened. Greedily, Drake pursued, thinking to kick her the rest of the way out of the Trial. Xera rolled back toward him, speared out one leg in a low sidekick and connected solidly with his knee.

He stumbled forward and Xera could have won the Trial right then if she had helped him to fall over and past her. Instead, the female pilot struck out again, bringing her foot up fast and cruel, spearing Drake in the groin and stopping his fall cold.

Torrent couldn't help his wince of sympathy.

Drake backed off, doubled over and trying to catch his breath. Jumping back to her feet, Xera gave him no time to recover. She danced in graceful as a striking snake, throwing a roundhouse kick into Drake's stomach, folding him in half and then bringing her elbow down on the back of his neck. Then she waited for him to rise again.

The star colonel had Xera's measure now. Rather than take the victory when she could, she was winning this challenge and any future challenges of her new position. She waited for Drake to concede. Torrent respected that, even if it might cost him a pilot for the better part of a week. Such a commanding tactic was one of many reasons why women were considered the most dangerous competitors for a Trial of Bloodname or any other rough contest. They simply did not try to win. They tried to destroy.

Drake didn't know enough to thrust his hand out of the circle and slap the ground. Instead, Torrent watched him crawl painfully back to his feet. Dogged persistence was an admirable trait in any warrior stock, the star colonel granted Drake that.

Xera moved in again. This time Drake threw every ounce of his remaining energy into one vicious punch. His uppercut caught the female pilot a glancing blow as Xera rolled her head in the same direction. She sagged forward as if falling, grabbed two handfuls of Drake's coveralls, and then rolled backward dragging him with her. Planting her foot into his gut, she used their combined momentum to throw Drake up and over, slamming him down on his back against the cargo bay deck. The air rushed from Drake's lungs in a forced exhale.

Still on the ground, Xera pivoted on her shoulder blades and threw a backfist that connected with Drake's nose. Torrent heard cartilage and bone crunch. A gout of blood splashed down over Drake's mouth and the man lay still.

Xera climbed back to her feet.

Drake lay prostrate near the circle's edge, but still no part of his body had broken the perimeter. Torrent stepped forward, violating the circle. Xera would now be within her rights to attack him as well, taking his interference as a slight to her own honor. It depended on how much respect she held for her commander. Torrent did not even glance at her as he stepped past, giving her his back with full confidence. He paused near Drake and used his foot to shove the pilot's hand so that it fell outside the circle. Then he stepped over the unconscious man and left the circle behind.

Star Captain Demos jogged over from the bay door,

her sharp gaze flying past Torrent to seize upon the ended Trial. "You did not wait?" she asked, obviously upset. "I would like to have seen that."

"And gamble on it, no doubt." Torrent shook his head. "As I recall, you still owe . . . Yulri . . . on a previous wager."

"I have not forgotten. I took a bondsman yesterday, after the skirmish near Taibek Mines. But he is an infantryman and is proving . . . intractable."

Taking defeated enemy warriors as *isorla,* making them bondsmen to the Steel Wolves, was a Clan practice Kal Radick encouraged among his forces. Torrent was less sanguine about the idea, looking only for those who truly supported the Steel Wolves. They were out there on Achernar, and they would come over to him at the right time.

He merely needed to provide it for them.

"You had something you wished to discuss?" Demos asked him after several paces in silence.

"I do." Torrent mentally thumbed through the Achernar briefings he had memorized. There were two local reservists who had once petitioned for active duty under Kal Radick's command, citing their blood ties to Clan Wolf expatriates. Freeborn, but still of warrior stock. It was a guess, where he'd find them, but the briefing mentioned their dissatisfaction driving LoaderMechs and short-haulers.

"I would like you to take a run over to the San Marino spaceport," Torrent told his second, "and pick up two packages for me."

8

Rendezvous

San Marino Spaceport
Achernar
23 February 3133

Strapped into the ConstructionMech's cracked vinyl seat by an ordinary lap belt, the militia's newest MechWarrrior wrestled with unfamiliar postures and controls as he tried to pick up the tangled section of chain link fence. His left-hand vise grabbed at the wire mesh, pulling it to one side so that his bucket hand on the WorkMech's right arm could dig out the buried pole. For the third time he misjudged, bringing the bucket down on the fencing and tearing it out of his own grip. Biting down on his frustration he pulled back on the controls, preparing to start again. The going was slow, but there was little hurry.

"Not like we'll be using these landing pads anytime soon," he whispered.

He had certainly seen this section of the San Marino spaceport in better shape.

The military's "secure landing" zone was neither after the Steel Wolf raid two days before. Bunker-thick walls lay in untidy piles, protecting nothing better than a fire-gutted hangar and two collapsed warehouses. The trio of landing pads were scorched and scarred by errant lasers and artillery-made craters. A section of tunnel—one of two that connected the once-secure site to the underground service area on the larger, civilian side of the spaceport—had caved in, forming a long, deep depression into which a Republic militia Marksman had fallen. The second tunnel would need an incredible amount of shoring before safe access could be guaranteed.

Work teams, mostly civilian volunteers, had spread out over the ruined area in an attempt to clear the debris and recover whatever useful material remained to be salvaged. Like ants toiling to rebuild their shattered colony, people carried and fetched, formed a brigade line for moving dirt and rock out from around the second tunnel entrance, drove dozers and cranes and one of the ever-rarer IndustrialMechs. One team worked with body-sniffing dogs, searching for any of three missing reservists who might be buried under a pile of rubble. *That* was a duty Raul had no stomach for. Fortunately, there were other options.

Volunteering some of his off-time, today Raul substituted for the ConstructionMech's usual operator who was now being trained to drive a combat-converted Work-Mech. Soon, he knew, this vehicle would be pulled in to the base. A rocket launcher would be mounted over the top of the engine housing, and one of its arms might even be modified to carry some kind of light autocannon or small, one-shot missile system. In the last week Erik Sandoval had proven that converted IndustrialMechs could hold their own against ground vehicles, and The Republic militia was not too proud to learn from the ambitious noble.

"The enemy of my enemy is my friend," Raul said to himself, and sounded half-convinced.

Well, this was the right planet for making such conversions, he knew, with Achernar IndustrialMechs one of the planet's largest companies. Loaders, Forestries, Miners, ConstructionMechs . . . and that brought him back to his volunteer job.

He gazed through the scratched ferroglass canopy, studying the violently-disassembled fencing. This was his last task for the day, before having to report back to base. With a sharp exhale, he grabbed for the mesh again and tried to dig out the connecting pole.

Missed.

Raul levered up the 'Mech's throttles until its combustion engine roared with new life. The chassis shook and dark exhaust smoke belched into the air. Raul opened the vise wide, gathering as much of the fencing mesh as possible in one giant handful, then tightened down on the grips as he shuffle-walked backward. The ConstructionMech ripped the fencing out into a long carpet of tangled metal, quickly winning a brief tug-of-war match against the buried post. That accomplished, he balled up the chain and posts into one ungainly mess, grabbed it in an awkward hug, and lifted it high overhead ready to carry it to the waiting dump truck.

Jessica Searcy stood on the far side of the ruined ground, hardhat perched awkwardly on her head and a portable cooler in hand.

From twenty meters away she likely missed Raul's guilty start. He quickly waved her over toward the truck, using exaggerated gestures she was sure to catch. Raul shuffled the WorkMech into a wide turn, careful of his load, and marched over to the waiting vehicle where he 'Mechhandled the ungainly mess of fencing into the back. Stepping back, gritting his teeth at the obnoxious bleating alarm that sounded to warn others of the backpedaling machine, Raul found a clear area to park the Worker.

Grounding both long arms for stability he shut down the engine, feeling as if the entire world had come to rest without that laboring rattle at his back. Shucking his earplugs and tossing them to the littered floor, he kicked open the stuck door and jumped down to the ground, ignoring a short ladder.

Jessica didn't look ready to work. Her casual blouse would never stand up to the abuse and she had chosen slacks instead of jeans. But she was here, and that alone left Raul feeling better. He had called her this morning, asking her to join him on the work party. This time their old argument had turned on a sharper edge, and she had eventually slammed the phone down on him.

"I thought you had *real work* to do?" he asked. Not mean, but not completely forgiving either.

Jessica shrugged, and had the good manners to look a bit ashamed at her earlier, heated words. "I thought someone told me this was real work." She sounded apologetic. Leaning forward, she kissed Raul's sweaty cheek. "I made up my mind too late to be of much help, so I made a large lunch and brought it out. There's plenty." She glanced around, counting the number of volunteers. "Maybe not, actually."

Raul took the cooler and set it aside. "It's appreciated." He was glad she'd come, talking through the vidphones wasn't enough to ease the ache of missing her, but her timing left a great deal to be desired. Pulling a rag out of his pocket, Raul wiped down his face. "I wish you had come out earlier." He nodded toward a waiting shuttle bus. "I'm about to be relieved."

"Early day?" Jessica frowned. "Have you at least eaten something?"

Raul glanced guiltily at the container of food. "I'm taking a meeting this afternoon where there will be food provided. I'll eat. Honest." He even sounded guilty, and there was no reason to.

She nodded, skeptical. Likely remembering the last time she had come after him with an offer of dinner and found a half-eaten doughnut. "Are you being careful?" she asked suddenly.

Now that was a loaded question. "As careful as I can be, Jess."

He couldn't think of anything else to say, especially after their argument on the phone. Raul knew that his fiancée worried for him. This was not the kind of life Jessica had in mind to lead. He saw his replacement walking over, took Jessica's arm and pulled her aside.

"Look, I know this is hard. I trained for this, once, and it's hard on me too." Raul had tried to tell her about his misgivings on the battlefield, that first day, but it was like they spoke different languages. "Help is on the way, Jess. There's a Knight-Errant coming over from Ronel to survey the situation and call up additional support as needed. That's the advantage of having a working HPG station."

Jessica nodded perfunctorily. "A Knight. That's great." She certainly didn't sound very enthused, although she made an effort to smile. "So maybe this will all be over soon and you'll be home."

"I hope so," Raul said, shifting from one foot to the other. The shuttle bus honked, warning him that it was about to leave. Raul waved his replacement aside for a moment, then embraced his fiancée. "Look, I have—"

"To run," she finished for him. "Duty calls." She glanced around. "If you take another off-day to come out here, or anywhere, let me know. I'll be there." She exhaled a long sigh. "Or I'll come out to the base to see you. If they'll allow that."

"They will," he promised, greatly relieved. "Just call first and make certain I'm there. Love you."

"I love you too." Jessica shook her head. "Damned if I know why sometimes."

Raul grinned at her sudden start, Jessica realizing the opening she had given him again. "Because you have wisdom beyond your years," he teased. The base shuttle blared its horn again. "That's for me!" He dodged over to the replacement driver, gave him a sketchy outline of the work he had managed to get done, and then sprinted for the shuttle. He was seated, belted and in the middle of catching his breath before he remembered that he had never looked back, or waved once, to Jessica.

Jessica Searcy watched her man dodge up the shuttle bus steps. For all his energy there at the end, she had seen the deep-rooted exhaustion beginning to pile up behind Raul's dark brown eyes.

The medical doctor in her couldn't help looking for symptoms and trying to diagnose people. Raul suffered from wounded beliefs. He seemed lost to her—trapped between what he had thought he wanted out of Republic citizenship and what he was getting. If he wasn't careful, she worried that the Republic would chew Raul up and spit him aside. Always assuming, she shuddered, that the Steel Wolves didn't first do the job in a physical sense.

"Over here," someone shouted, dispelling the dark gloom blanketing her thoughts. "Hey, we have a live one!"

The call wasn't for Jessica, but she responded to it out of a habit born from several years of medical internship and residency. She saw a large crane lifting an armored tank from a collapsed underground area—a basement or tunnel? Someone rode on top of the vehicle, waving frantically for attention. Jessica was one of several people who ran over, arriving just as the tank settled to the ground. Workers forced open a large hatch at the rear of the large metal juggernaut.

The waving man jumped down. "He crawled back into the ammunition storage locker trying to find a way out. Poor bastard's been half-buried for two days."

Half buried and half dead by the looks of him. Jessica shouldered her way in. "I'm a doctor," she said, backing off several larger men with an air of authority. Pulse was thready but there. Aside from multiple contusions and an obviously broken clavicle, the only thing he had to worry about was internal bleeding. "Get a blanket on this man and call in for an emergency pick-up. He needs a chopper right away."

"You'll have one in ten minutes," a man promised. He was one of the men she'd shouldered aside, and had a rough but competent look to him. "I'll call it in myself."

Jessica spitted him with an exasperated glare. "Call it in to the spaceport and we can have it in five," she said, nodding at the distant terminal on the far side of the tarmac. "They'll have a helicopter somewhere over there."

The foreman nodded and made it happen. Water and blankets were brought, and a VTOL emergency transport thundered across the landing field to set down only a few minutes later. Jessica helped two corpsmen get the patient aboard, gave them her evaluation, and then ducked clear as the fast-copter leapt back into the sky and made a beeline for River's End.

As was common after any emergency situation, the fading adrenaline rush left Jessica empty and lost for a moment. She wandered back toward where Raul had left her. The foreman caught up with her there.

"Hey. I wanted to thank you for your help." He sounded frustrated, having to make that admission, but manners won out over pride. "No one thought to have paramedics out here two days later." He took in Jessica's civilian clothes with a quick glance, measured her, and then made a guess. "You need a ride back to River's End?"

"I have a car," she said haltingly. Then, "But I'm here, and already filthy. What can I do?" It wasn't in her to simply turn her back on work, even physical work, now that she was here. Not to mention her recent emotional investment.

"I don't know," the foreman said. He had tangled blond hair and a scar at the edge of his left eye. His voice was respectful, especially after her earlier help, but held no time for games. "What *can* you do?" he asked.

"Besides be on hand for injuries?" Jessica smiled thinly. "I can drive simple vehicles, organize shift schedules, and apply bandages as necessary to bruised egos." She remembered her cooler, found it where Raul had set it down. "I have a cooler full of sandwiches and apples, and I know where I can get more."

The foreman laughed, then nodded. "You're hired. Pull anything you need from the spaceport and I'll sign my name to it. And thanks again for coming out." He glanced with a readable amount of disdain toward the distant capital of River's End. "Most people don't want to get involved."

Including her. Jessica did not tell him that, though. As

she'd said, she was here and there was work to be done, and it wasn't in her to turn her back on people who needed help.

Not so different from Raul after all, she decided.

Perhaps.

Officer's Club, Achernar Militia Command Achernar

The militia's base facilities were limited but had all the basics, including an officer's club.

After checking back in with the duty officer, Raul barely had time for a shower before he met Tassa Kay coming off a work shift. His dark curly hair was still damp, and he had grabbed nothing more casual than the utility fatigues all militia members preferred for everyday routine. His one concession to comfort, and maybe to Tassa's presence as well, was to roll his sleeves up to the elbow. Raul had strong arms, and his tawny coloring shone with a burnished hue under Achernar's bright sun.

The two placed an order at the bar for food and drinks, then chose an outside table. A late afternoon breeze worked its way over the low wall that protected the club, stirring the edges of the tablecloths. Raul nodded toward a table with an umbrella awning well away from other dining groups. Most others sat alone, or in subdued pairs talking about the hard press being dealt out by the Steel Wolves, and Raul did not need their dark moods coloring his talk with Tassa.

Taking his seat, Raul spread his hands on the table, suddenly nervous and still feeling a little guilty that he'd left Jessica at the spaceport. He hadn't lied to her. Not exactly. Relieved by the new driver, his standing orders required him to report back to the base. And this wasn't a dinner date. It was dinner, and the chance to finally learn something more about Tassa Kay.

Okay, so Tassa was attractive. Raul didn't see any reason why that should make him feel guilty. Except that it did.

"You look bothered by something," Tassa noticed. She pulled the sweatband off her head and used it to tangle her hair back in a makeshift ponytail. Tassa wore dark leathers and looked perfectly at ease, an attitude Raul wished he could adopt as easily. "I hope it's me," she said with a sly grin.

Digging some money out of a pocket, Raul threw it on the tray as a server brought their drinks. "I had to rush away from the spaceport to make it here. I may have left . . . a bit of a mess behind me."

"I have noticed that about you, Ortega."

Raul tasted his drink, grimaced. The iodine taste burned all the way down his throat. The bar whiskey was not Glengarry Reserve. "Then why are we here?"

Tassa stirred her drink by sloshing the ice around in a quick circle. "I didn't say that was a bad thing." She took a healthy sip. "I came along to see who you were going to upset today."

"No one. Unless you don't like questions."

"Still trying to get something out of me?" she asked, giving him a dark smile.

He coughed into his glass. The alcohol burned up into his sinuses. "Maybe," he said, trying to recover. "You did say that you owed me. Twice."

Tassa Kay regarded him long and cold over the rim of her glass. Her green eyes narrowed to razor slits. "I think I paid one of those debts out on the flatlands. Gimped *Legionnaire*. Persistent *Jagatai*. Any of that ring a bell?"

"Fair enough," Raul agreed.

In fact, without Tassa in the field, the Republic militia would have been hurt badly that first day. Since then she had gone out twice more to push back Steel Wolf probes, but never again with Raul who always seemed to draw alternate duty as the ready-alert. He missed her, truth be told. Tassa lived the life he'd dreamt of for so long, and never once seemed bothered by the same moral qualms that pricked at Raul's conscience. When he was with her, he could set aside some of those problems. Unfortunately, Tassa did not always share his sense of camaraderie.

Though she relented, slightly, when Raul didn't press. "All right. I still owe you and that is why I am here," she admitted. "You backed me up twice off the field, and I appreciate your timely arrival that first day." She downed a slug of whiskey. The alcohol fed a warm blush to her cheeks.

"You're welcome," Raul told her, guessing that it was as close to a thank-you as she was likely to offer. Tassa glanced over sharply, as if suspecting sarcasm, but then relaxed. The woman seemed to have a gift for switching between states of readiness in the blink of an eye. The security officer in Raul wondered where she had needed to develop such a hair-trigger defense mechanism. One more mystery concerning Tassa Kay.

"And you want to know about Dieron?" she asked.

Feigning casual interest, Raul shrugged. "That's your choice, Tassa. You'll give it up, or you won't." Throwing innuendos back at her for a change felt good.

Tassa Kay gave him an appraising stare, so long that he began to feel warm and uncomfortable. Finally she set her glass down and said, "All right, then, here it is. I have no idea what really happened on Dieron. How it started, or how it ended. I arrived in the middle of a firestorm. The DropShip was blindsided by fighters from two factions, but we made a safe landing in the middle of a swamp. I slogged out of there and discovered that everyone seemed to be shooting at everyone else. Dracs, Fists, Foxes, pro-Republic and anarchists—I spent the first week fighting for my life and the lives of a patched-together mercenary company."

The names blurred through Raul's mind. Even after the chaos here on Achernar, he had trouble picturing the kind of confused warfare Tassa described. Combine supporters and Commonwealth troops? The Sea Fox merchants?

"By luck more than anything I hooked up with your Exarch. He never told me why he was there, though I am sure it was an attempt at damage control at first. He made me an offer, asked me to help him regain possession of the local spaceport, and I accepted. Then I left."

Raul shook his head, as if trying to clear away a thought he couldn't understand. "You left?" He'd been sitting on the edge of his chair, waiting for some kind of glorious finale. Their food arrived, but Raul suddenly wasn't hungry. "You abandoned the Exarch?"

"He is not *my* Exarch. Anyway, he seemed competent." High praise indeed. "By the time I shipped through Northwind, I heard that he had made it safely back to Terra." She looked at him askance. "What? Dieron wasn't my fight, what reason did I have to stay?"

Rocking back into his chair, Raul tried to reason it out. Failed. "And Achernar?" he asked. "Is this your fight?"

"It's closer," Tassa admitted, her brow creasing in a light scowl.

"Closer to what?"

"To what I am looking for."

Raul leaned forward again, the security agent in him defaulting into interrogation mode. She was holding something back, something big, and he wanted it. "And what are you looking for?"

Tassa Kay settled back calmly, cradling her drink in one hand. She offered him half a shrug. "Whatever that is," she said, "I think it left this table. You and I are done talking for a while, Lieutenant." She rose to leave.

Raul couldn't help asking, "Are you going to walk away from Achernar too, Tassa?"

Staring down at him, something closer to a predator's grin than any true smile crept over her mouth. "Lieutenant. Don't you trust me anymore?"

"I don't know you." He had never really known her, which was part of the damnable attraction he felt, and what she was capitalizing on.

Tassa bent forward at the waist, leaning down until

her face was only inches from his. For a moment, Raul thought she meant to kiss him. "You know me," she said. With a slight smirk, she straightened and then brushed by him. Back over her shoulder she said, "I'm just like you."

9

Desperate Alliances

Taibek Mining
Achernar
24 February 3133

The Taibek Hills stared up at Erik Sandoval-Groell with vacant eye sockets as his personal VTOL thundered low over the eastern mines. Ore carts trundled out of dark tunnels, pushed or pulled by small, overworked tractors now that the MiningMechs from this site were all down-checked for military conversion. His labor force milled about the three active tunnels or worked the loading area where ore was transferred from carts to open-box rail cars. To a man they avoided the northwest quarry where rifle-toting infantry guarded Erik's local staging ground and his primary maintenance facility.

Gray wisps of rock dust bled from the mine entrances and hung over the loading platform in a large cloud. As Erik's military-class Warrior H-9 banked across the complex, the downdraft of its rotors swept the air clean. For the moment. The thirty-ton craft extended landing gear and settled to the ground next to a smaller Ferret light scout copter. Erik jumped out as soon as the skids touched earth and met the elder man waiting for him with an outstretched hand.

"Legate Stempres," Erik smiled a mostly-sincere greeting. "Always a pleasure to see you."

"Truly? That is why you are nearly an hour late for our meeting?"

At forty-eight and wearing a conservative gray suit, Brion Stempres still looked the part of a warrior. He kept his silver hair cut short in a flattop and his face had a younger man's blue steel shadow where his thick beard kept trying to grow in. He had served a distinguished career with the Standing Republic Guard on Caselton, coming to the attention of Duke Aaron's father and then later to Aaron Sandoval himself. His transfer to Achernar and into semiretirement had come four years before after the death of his wife. Blind fortune for Erik that the man was available when it came time to shop for a new military leader of Achernar.

Erik did not take the man's gruff nature personally. "I received a report that the Steel Wolves had launched a major strike toward River's End. I had my pilot swing out over the Agave Dales to check it out."

A slender eyebrow rose over one of Stempres' muddy-brown eyes. "You take chances, Lord Sandoval."

"To endeavor without risk is to win without victory," Eric quoted, calling on his studies in martial history. "General Gregory Cox." Not that Erik worried. Star Colonel Torrent had held off his OmniFighters for the better part of a week, now, relying on conventional aircraft. Erik's VTOL had likely been in little danger.

"And what did you see?"

"Another probing attack," Erik told the old general. "Perhaps a bit stronger than recent assaults, but hardly a threat to River's End. The Republic Guard called out reinforcements, just to be safe." He shook his head. "Someone needs to convince that sheep in wolf's skin to make a real push one of these days."

Legate Stempres assumed an air of innocence. "Someone does, eh? Well, until that happens, might be you should think about this." He pulled a digital verifax from his jacket pocket, thumbed his own DNA imprint over the security device, and then passed it over to Erik.

The young noble paged through the document quickly, skipping over most of the introduction. It notified Stempres that Knight-Errant Kyle Powers would arrive in a few days, a fact Erik already knew through his network of supporters and spies among the regular militia, and the list of briefings he requested. Then Erik hit the meat of the verifax, skipped back to the top and read through it all again. Carefully.

"This is a serious offer?" he asked Stempres, looking up from the reader when finished.

"It is. Sir Powers has asked me to feel you out on a formal alliance for the defense of Achernar. His proposal establishes you as 'a legitimate foreign-auxiliary commander.' That's the designation used when competing branches of military service—or foreign militaries—work together on a joint mission."

It wasn't formal recognition by Exarch Redburn, Erik noted, but damn close. It elevated his Swordsworn to a politically supported entity at the very least, and the fact that Powers even proposed such an alliance meant only one thing. "The Republic is in bad shape," he whispered aloud. A political push here, some military action there—how much could the Sphere government stand up under? His uncle had been right all along. Best to salvage what they could. Drawing a reference from the Unfinished Book—or was it the original New Testament?—it was time to *render therefore unto Caesar the things which were Caesar's*.

Or, more to the point, they would take back unto Sandoval those worlds which were Sandoval.

"Legate Stempres," Erik finally said. "Have a message ready to send Powers as soon as his JumpShip arrives in system. You discussed the matter with me but have been unable to secure my official cooperation. Yet. Please attend to that right away."

"You sound as if you're in a hurry to be off, Lord Sandoval."

"I am." Erik nodded toward his northwest quarry. Visible over a rocky outcropping of pale stone, one could catch the profile of his *Hatchetman's* elongated head. "If I push, I can be over the Taibeks with a small force and coming to the aid of the Republic before their own reinforcements arrive." Engaging lightly, ready to draw back as needed, Erik could seem to be the rescuer and still put very little of his own assets at risk. "It will do well for Powers to see me contributing even without his official sanction. Then, when he sends you to try again, I can—*reluctantly*—agree."

"What possible reason can that serve? Why not *reluctantly* agree now and save yourself the damaged resources?"

But Erik only smiled at the old officer's lack of political shrewdness, stepped back onto the Warrior's skid and grabbed a handstrap on the side. He rapped against the ferroglass window for the pilot's attention. Made a circling motion with his finger. Cut his hand over toward the quarry. The pilot flashed him a thumbs up and throttled the VTOL to life, leaving Stempres behind as they lifted off for the short hop to Erik's local military compound.

And it wasn't until they were airborne, far from Stempres' ears, that Erik answered the legate, his words lost in the beating thunder of the H-9's rotor blades. "When you are playing Caesar's game," he said, "it is always best to cement your alliances.

"Before you take advantage of them."

Taibek Foothills
Achernar

Raul Ortega had his back to the wall in the moments before Erik Sandoval's arrival. Or, more to the point, the Steel Wolves had forced his *Legionnaire* back to the Taibek's lower foothills.

The battle had started in the Agave Dales, with the Steel Wolves caught trying to loop around River's End to hit the industrial sector or perhaps moving further afield toward the lower dams near Vera-Stiago. Tassa Kay had chased off after a pair of Demons, stretching their line thin. Raul might have held strong if not for a pair of raiding *Visigoths* and a new push by conventional forces.

Culled out from the main body of his task force by a solid line of Condors backed by Hauberk battlesuit infantry, Raul managed to keep a Schmitt and a pair of Rangers with him as the Steel Wolves threw into the gap a trio of 'Mechs led by a laser-bearing *Blackhawk*. The *Blackhawk* chased after him, pulling a squad of Condors and two SM1 Tank Destroyers with it. Faced with running a deadly gauntlet at the side of the slow-moving Schmitt or trading ground for time, Raul allowed himself to be slowly driven back, waiting for Tassa Kay to fight her way free of two *Pack Hunters* or for the reinforcements he'd summoned from River's End to arrive.

That was almost an hour ago.

An hour of standing up under several missile bombardments and being pushed around the Agave Dales by powerful hovercraft. An hour of hit-and-fade tactics that was finally taking its toll. His armor profile didn't look healthy, and his ammunition supply was red-lit—down into the last half-ton of fifty-millimeter rounds. In the northern Dales Raul had traded one of his Rangers for an SM1 Destroyer—both vehicles shredded into scrap metal and left leaking fuel and the blood of their crews onto the thirsty ground. But even keeping up such tactical victories, in the end the Steel Wolf MechWarrior had more than enough force under his command to outlast Raul.

He watched the Destroyer and half of the Condors power away to the northeast, on another flanking attempt he guessed wrongly. Then an electronic crackle in his ear warned Raul of an incoming transmission. "Republic force, this is Sword-One. Can you use assistance?"

Surprised by the designation, it took Raul several long seconds to recognize Erik Sandoval's voice. His HUD was dialed in for short-range maneuvers, searching for hidden infantry or stealthy armor, but Raul found the neutral-blue blip of Erik's force on his long-range sensors.

"All I can get, Sword-One." Raul's voice cracked, whether from a lack of moisture or the galling taste of being rescued by Sandoval, he wasn't certain. He swallowed painfully. "I have more units pulled off to the south, but can't reach them."

"I've inherited part of your problem," Sandoval said, his voice growing more serious. "Thanks for the Destroyer! I just lost a convert." A pause. "Look, get moving. I can hold here and pull back into the Taibeks if it gets too difficult. Go find your people."

It was still *his* people and Erik's, Raul noted, but wasn't about to question the offer. If Sandoval wanted to play with the *Blackhawk,* he was welcome to it.

Raul ducked his *Legionnaire* under the sweeping path of a Condor's autocannon, centered the vehicle under his crosshairs and spent a precious burst of his limited ammo into its side armor. The Steel Wolf *Blackhawk* wasn't about to let Raul get into him for another tank, though, and stalked forward to threaten again with torso lasers and the Streak-equipped missile launchers mounted on either arm. The arcing warheads fell all around and over him, shaking the ground and knocking his *Legionnaire* with fiery punches.

"Are you trying to draw him after you?" Sandoval yelled. "I can shift his attention toward me if you get moving."

Raul ordered the VV1 Ranger to lead the way with the Schmitt to follow, but hesitated himself. "Are you sure?"

"You are the hardest people to help," Sandoval complained. "Go now!"

Not even the Condor hovercraft could keep up with Raul with his *Legionnaire* at a full run. He turned and throttled up, moving out of the *Blackhawk*'s reach and trailing after the Schmitt. Reaching its side, he slowed back to a walk and paced the tracked vehicle south.

"This is Ortega. Tassa, where away? We've picked up some help, finally."

"I heard." Her response came back wreathed in static likely caused by the discharge of her own PPCs. "Middle Dales. No sign of reinforcements and—damn!—I can't shake these two loose." She faded from the air for a moment. "They broke us into three pieces. I held out as far north as I could, hoping you would rejoin. But if you're still up by the foothills, you are a good twenty minutes away."

Raul measured the distance in his mind. "Ten," he promised her. Then he ordered the VV1 to blaze a trail for the Schmitt, both of the vehicles taking a roundabout path back toward the base. He throttled up. "I'm at a run and heading your way."

"I have a bottle if you have glasses," Tassa said, then cursed again and turned her attention back to the fight.

A lot could happen in ten minutes. In ten seconds, even, on a live battlefield. Raul stomped his way over the rolling Dales, his cockpit swaying dangerously far to each side as he pushed the *Legionnaire* harder than he should for the uneven terrain. Tassa checked on his progress every few minutes, helped guide him in. Raul smelled fuel and saw smoke before he ever found the battlefield, running up on a militia Scimitar overturned and burning. From there Tassa knew exactly where he was, and bent her battle toward him to help link up faster.

Tassa Kay had one of her two Condors, a Behemoth and pair of tactical *Jessies* left at her side when Raul found them. She would push at the Steel Wolf force, and then the pair of *Pack Hunters* pushed back. The thirty-ton BattleMechs each wielded a PPC and eight General Systems micro lasers. With a top speed of one hundred twenty kilometers per hour and the full energy array, *Pack Hunters* were designed to harry and pursue and eventually wear down the opposition. With Shandra scout vehicles and Hauberk infantry chasing around in their specially modified Maxim carriers, it was no wonder Tassa couldn't shake her pursuers.

Raul's arrival gave them something else to think about.

Suddenly the weight seemed to shift into the Republic's favor.

"Are you feeling sick or something?" Tassa asked him, pulling her *Ryoken* even with the *Legionnaire*. "Lay into one of them."

Easier said than done. Even outmatched, getting a *Pack Hunter* to hold still long enough for a solid lock wasn't easy. Also, "I only have about a dozen pulls left in my rotary," Raul admitted.

"They don't know that. And you still have lasers. Threaten them if you can't hurt them! Chase down the left-most *Hunter*. I have the other."

Although not in the chain of command, Raul defaulted this time to Tassa's authority. She had the strongest 'Mech on the field and she had been involved in a cat-and-mouse game with these two Steel Wolves for the better part of the day. He spent more of his precious ammunition at the *Pack Hunter* she'd assigned him, tried to split it away from its partner.

The other 'Mech reminded him that it had teeth as it sliced a particle cannon across Raul's left arm, blasting away armor and cutting into the myomer and mechanical joint. The Behemoth saved him further damage by putting a gauss slug just over the *Pack Hunter*'s shoulder, making the pilot think twice about getting too close.

Able to go one on one with the other enemy BattleMech, Tassa used her jump jets to grab a side-deflection shot. At the height of her arc, she laid into the *Hunter* with both PPCs. One carved a glassy trail into the ground behind it. Her second shot burned into the *Hunter*'s leg, spilling a ton of molten armor over the Dales.

Tassa dropped down in between two of the Maxims, staggered back toward Raul's position with infantry missiles chasing after her, pockmarking her armor with ragged holes.

"Rotten, waddling *lilliputaner-nadels*!" It sounded German to Raul, and hardly complimentary. Her next few curses he couldn't begin to place.

"If those were Elementals," Raul admonished her, "you'd be ripped into shreds right now."

"If those had been Elementals, I would have taken out the infantry carriers much—blazes!"

Tassa's *Ryoken* disappeared from view as fiery explosions blossomed over her head and shoulders and the ground around her exploded in a series of unnatural geysers. Raul knew from recent experience what had caused that, and found the *Blackhawk* cresting a hill on their near left flank, launching missile spreads from short range.

"Damn Sandoval, you were supposed to hold him up." He watched as Tassa limped out from underneath the cloud of smoke and debris, her *Ryoken* stripped down to a walking skeleton. "*Jessies* on the Hauberk battlesuits. Condor . . . Six," he pulled its operations tag out of his HUD code, "distract the Shandras."

Raul left the Behemoth to its own choice and threw his *Legionnaire* forward at the *Pack Hunters,* leaving the *Blackhawk* in Tassa's hands. He'd had no time to check Tassa's status or form any plan more complex than engage and overcome. All he knew was that allowing the *Pack Hunters* to link up side-by-side with the *Blackhawk* spelled a complete rout for the militia forces. Tassa's *Ryoken* had the only weapons capable of putting the missile-capable 'Mech down quickly. She was either fit to take it, or they were both as good as dead.

Doubting that Tassa wasn't good enough to cover his back was never an option.

Whatever the two *Pack Hunters* had expected with the arrival of their larger brethren, it certainly had not been a full-push offensive. Raul's *Legionnaire* was just as fast as they were, and given a few second's lead he covered ground in long strides to set himself between the *Hunters* and the *'Hawk*. His lasers spat ruby arrows at the smaller machines. His rotary autocannon chewed down through his reserve bins as he peppered first one 'Mech with armor-piercing slugs, then the other.

The Behemoth added some misery of its own as it

spread missiles from its twin Holly racks over the shoulders of one *Hunter*.

Tassa had stumbled up into a loping run, shaking off the assault with characteristic speed. Her PPCs stabbed out angrily once, and again. On the second salvo, her beams fused into a single, hard-hitting strike that rocked the *Blackhawk* back on its heels.

Raul's *Legionnaire* shuddered as a PPC cut down through his left leg, slicing through myomer but missing any critical mechanisms. He emptied his rotary's drum with one last, long pull. Then committed himself to a slow walk forward with lasers still flaring bright, bejeweled energy. He kept one eye on his rear-facing monitor the entire time.

Wading through the *Blackhawk*'s return fire, shrugging aside more missiles and hard-stabbing lasers, Tassa blasted two, red-tinged wounds across the *'Hawk*'s chest and then hit it with the two Streak six-packs she'd held in reserve. A dozen of the wide-bodied missiles burst from their box launchers, drawing gray lines of corkscrewing smoke from her *Ryoken* to the Steel Wolf BattleMech.

Only two missiles missed, scraping by to either side of the *Blackhawk*'s head. Half of the rest burst into large fireballs against the 'Mech's chest, some burning new damage deeper into the engine and gyro housing. A pair of missiles slammed into the bulbous cockpit, cracking ferroglass and no doubt shaking the warrior hard against his restraints.

Raul gave credit for the *Blackhawk*'s fall to one of the torso-striking missiles, though. The way the entire BattleMech shuddered and drunk-staggered to one side, he knew that it had cracked through the gyro housing to upset the high-speed gyroscopic stabilizers inside. The *Blackhawk* toppled to one side, burying half of its raptor-like profile in the earth. Tassa stood over it, weapons ready to cook the MechWarrior alive should he try to rise again.

That was enough for the *Pack Hunters*. The fall of

the larger 'Mech, and watching Raul's slow, purposeful advance, sent them in full flight north. Monitoring them on his HUD, they did not begin to slow down for a good half kilometer. The remaining Steel Wolf armor and infantry followed at only a slightly slower pace.

"You have anything left?" Tassa asked.

"A pair of lasers and maybe an ounce or two of armor." Raul checked his wire frame, saw that he wasn't far off the truth. "And if I'm reading my sensors right, our friends just picked up the *Blackhawk*'s support team." He counted three Condors and an SM1 Destroyer deploying at the far reach of his sensors, giving the *Pack Hunters* a secure flank. They must have forced Erik Sandoval back into the Taibeks. Raul supposed he should thank the noble for delaying them as long as he had.

"They aren't going to stand by and let us drag our trophy back to River's End, then." Tassa held her vigil, though, waiting as the Condor glided up and sent two armed guards out to take the fallen MechWarrior prisoner. "Pity," she said, once the man was secure.

Then she raised up one large, metal-taloned foot and crushed the cockpit into ruin.

Raul had never thought to see someone treat a BattleMech with such disregard for its worth. "Tassa! What are you doing?"

"Sending a message," she shot back. "If the Steel Wolves are going to keep playing in Achernar's backyard, they are going to lose toys. Star Colonel Torrent needs to know that it is time to get serious or go home."

"How do I know you're hoping he 'gets serious'?" Raul asked in a resigned voice. Still, he couldn't help his sharp thrill of excitement at the other MechWarrior's resolve.

The way her *Ryoken* swiveled around toward him, it was easy for Raul to imagine Tassa staring at him through the ferroglass shield, her head bent quizzically to one side. "If you actually believe that Torrent will just pick up and leave, you are going to be sadly disappointed. Trust me. If he is a Kerensky, then he is not the type to leave empty-handed." Then she turned to follow after the Condor, slowing only to keep pace with the sluggish Behemoth.

They were still in radio contact, but Raul could tell she meant it as one of her infamous parting shots. "She does that a lot," he whispered, careful of the voice-activated mic. Then he throttled up for the long walk back to base.

10

Kyle Powers

Achernar Militia Command
Achernar
26 February 3133

"Ortega!"

The corridors at Achernar's command post bustled with activity as aides and junior officers swept in and out of offices, running errands and putting on their best show of martial diligence for the visiting Knight Errant. Raul was still trying to wake up after a short night of restless sleep, debating between coffee versus the pair of caff-tabs in his pocket, when his former roommate called to him.

Raul Ortega waited outside the briefing room door for Captain Jeffrey McDaniels to catch up. The newly promoted armor officer had opted for dress uniform, making Raul's utility greens look shabby by comparison. The other man *tsked* at Raul's casual dress, brushed some imaginary lint off his own shoulder. Raul smiled and gave his friend a familiar wave—having been recently promoted himself.

"They don't enforce much discipline among you 'Mech-jocks, do they?" McDaniels had an easy smile and a sharp tongue, two traits that complemented his thick shock of red hair. His pale blue eyes were shot through with red, evidence of another hard night out with the guys. When the going got tough, the Irish went drinking. "Colonel's pet."

The wintergreen scent of several breath mints barely covered the whiskey-tinge on McDaniel's breath. Raul smiled thinly, and then nodded at the other man's captain's bars. "Is that what Colonel Blaire told you at the O-club last night? You're only one step out from major, gotta start showing time with the old man, right?"

McDaniels nodded, but slowly. "Yeah. We're making new officers pretty fast out there."

The thought sobered both men; each had moved up— Raul from the reserves, in fact—due to battlefield attrition. The MechWarrior ushered his friend into the briefing room ahead of him, trailing after with an additional concern on his mind this morning. If rumors were to be believed Raul might actually be on his way back down, and he wasn't exactly sure how to feel about that. If they were true.

They were.

Or, at least, partly true. Halfway to the bank of coffee urns, the silver-armored sentinels standing guard over trays of morning pastries, Raul saw that Charal DePriest had indeed returned to active duty. She sat at the round table on Colonel Blaire's left, shuffling some papers into order. Her once long brown hair had been cut back during her sickbed time, and a shorn patch behind her left temple still did not hide the suture scars. Charal had the same gray hospital pallor Raul had seen on her during a visit while she was still unconscious. Her sapphire eyes looked a bit unfocused, but she nodded with confidence when Colonel Blaire turned to her for a question.

"Ouch," McDaniels offered in sympathy as he grabbed a glazed doughnut. "Hope they left a chair for you." He slipped away to find his spot next to Major Chautec, Achernar's ranking officer for conventional forces.

Raul had already begun a survey of the room. After Charal DePriest, and the possible demotion waiting for him, Sir Kyle Powers drew his gaze next. He sat next to

Colonel Blaire. A bona fide Knight of the Sphere, Powers was tall, pushing one hundred eighty centimeters but slender with wiry strength. There was a kind of intensity about him, too, about how he wore a Knight's white uniform with religious attention to sharp military creases and the set of his cape of rank, the crisp edges to his platinum flattop, and the way he focused himself forward as if alert for the slightest detail which might escape him.

Powers sat in serious conversation with Legate Brion Stempres on his right and Erik Sandoval-Groell one seat further down. Stempres had pushed his own chair back so the three men could talk evenly. Following the table around Raul found Captain Norgales, Major Chautec and Jeffrey McDaniels, what looked like two empty seats and then MechWarriors Clark Diago and Charal De-Priest and finally Colonel Blaire on Powers' left.

Raul peeled a caff-tab out of its protective shell, then swallowed it down with a jolt of bitter coffee. Carrying a refilled mug to the table, he slipped in next to Captain Diago, leaving a single open seat in between himself and McDaniels.

He had wanted to be unobtrusive—an errant student slipping in late for his lessons—but as he took his seat Raul saw two pairs of eyes glance his direction. The first was Erik Sandoval, his amber gaze registering Raul's arrival with a touch of recognition and confusion. The other glance belonged to Kyle Powers, whose piercing, flinty gray eyes stared out from beneath sharp, platinum brows. They held Raul for a long second, measuring him. The Knight-Errant allowed him a single nod of greeting, as if Raul had passed some kind of test, and slipped back into his conversation with Stempres and Sandoval as though nothing had ever distracted him.

Raul had time for half his coffee and a few whispered words with Clark Diago before the room's clock finally ticked its way up to seven a.m. and Kyle Powers' immediate transformation from private conversation to command of the morning briefing. It was nothing more than laying his hands flat on the table and slowly pushing

himself into an easy stance. Other talk died away and a
corporal who had slipped into the room to refill the urns
finished with haste and shut the door behind him as he
left. The room suddenly felt a great deal closer to Raul,
who realized that it was Sir Powers who simply took up
more of the space now.

"Thank you all for being here. We're short one person,
though. Does anyone know when we can expect Mech-
Warrior Tassa Kay?"

Raul hadn't even known that she'd been invited. Talking to the civilian MechWarrior had apparently fallen to
Diago, who nodded. "No offense, Sir Powers, but Tassa
Kay claimed to have better things to do this morning
than rehash old news. If we want to find her later, she
said that she'd be seeing after repairs to her *Ryoken II*
or interrogating her prisoner."

Her prisoner. That would be the *Blackhawk* pilot recovered from the wreckage of his BattleMech.

Kyle Powers took Diago's news with a raised eyebrow
and a tight smile. Raul thought that he read more than
professional courtesy there. Amusement? Powers had
been on-planet less than four hours, and already he
seemed to know something more of Tassa Kay than
Raul himself.

"Well. I'm certain that we'll bump into her sooner or
later." Powers' voice was dry, but in no way suggested
insult. He retook his seat with the same, slow grace in
which he had stood. "In the meantime, let's get started.

"First, let me say that my presence in no way reflects
poorly on your performance. You have all done an incredible job, given the situation you were handed. Working together, True Republic and Swordsworn, in the face
of the Steel Wolf assault shows a remarkable depth of
duty in all of you. If the sporadic fighting on Ronel
hadn't looked to be tapering off, and if Lady Lakewood
had not been inbound, I would still be there, in fact,
counseling you via the HPG. And we all know how reli-
able that is now considered."

Powers left the opening, and Brion Stempres stepped

in with the question. "Has there been any confirmation yet about the Blackout? How far it reaches, and to what extent we've lost the hyperpulse web?"

"ComStar is researching the problem." A venerable agency, with its founding at the fall of the original Star League, ComStar was responsible for the majority of HPG operations within The Republic, although they quite often relied on private subcontractors. "The latest reports I've seen show better than eighty-five percent blackout. Not just within The Republic, but reaching into every Inner Sphere nation around us. Some cases look like sabotage. Others like hard-wired viruses that didn't get purged after the Jihad. And then there are stations which appear to be working fine, but simply cannot bridge space as they once did."

Over eighty-five percent failure. In Prefecture IV, that meant Ronel and Achernar might have the only two working HPG stations. Was it any wonder the Steel Wolves were here? And if so, what about—

"Regardless," Knight-Errant Powers interrupted Raul's train of thought, "what we have to deal with is right in front of us. The Steel Wolves are making aggressive moves, cloaked under Kal Radick's questionable authority as Prefect, and we have to deal with that accordingly. Lord Erik Sandoval is here at my request, representing Republic forces who have swung their nominal allegiance over to his uncle, the Lord-Governor." He raised a hand. "*That* is not under debate at the moment. We all have a vested interest in keeping Achernar under local authority.

"We must all hang together, or assuredly we shall all hang separately," Powers said.

"Benjamin Franklin." Erik Sandoval was quick to identify Powers' quote. "At the signing of a Declaration on ancient Terra." He smiled. "All in all, a fitting maxim."

Raul bit down on his tongue until it throbbed, staying his own opinion on making any deal with Erik Sandoval and the Swordsworn. He trusted that Kyle Powers knew what he was doing. The Knight-Errant's not so subtle warning in the ancient quotation, and the terms of the alliance which he put forward to the entire group over the next two hours, proved that he did. He placed Erik in the chain of command, on par with Colonel Blaire and under the jurisdiction of Legate Stempres. Kyle Powers himself retained the Exarch's authority on all matters military, placing himself as a watchdog over the entire operation.

"My Swordsworn will carry our end," Erik Sandoval promised. "And I can offer more than a dozen tanks and my own *Hatchetman*. We have converted several of our IndustrialMechs over for military use—six of them, to be exact." That number more than doubled what anyone else in the room had thought, and Raul noticed the way a few eyebrows raised at the claim. "We lost one of those recently, coming to the aid of a Republic patrol, but even so an extra lance of converted MiningMechs thrown into a battle can do a lot of good."

Hanging out there, unfinished, Erik seemed to be saying, *Trust me, I know.*

Sandoval kept far too many secrets for Raul to completely trust him. Still, Powers seemed to have the young noble's measure and Raul doubted the Knight-Errant would get caught unawares.

"Excellent," Powers agreed. "And on the militia's side, I understand we are welcoming back a MechWarrior?"

Isaac Blaire nodded. "Captain Charal DePriest is returning to active duty as my adjutant and will oversee BattleMech logistics. Raul Ortega will continue to pilot the *Legionnaire,* however. Charal has been assigned our one converted ForestryMech to pilot as necessary."

Raul saw the wince of memory on Erik Sandoval's face, wondered where the noble had run into a converted ForestryMech before. A flush warmed his own neck, of pride and embarrassment both. Charal should have moved back to her position above him, taking the *Legionnaire*. Part of him had hoped that she would, he realized, saving him from the burdens that seemed to add to the pile with each day of conflict. A stronger part did not want to give up the BattleMech. Everything he had ever dreamt of . . . thought that he had wanted . . . it was still there for the taking.

Wasn't it?

Morning marched steadily toward noon as Powers turned the meeting to recent battles fought with the Steel Wolves. Raul spoke up to direct questions, but otherwise felt content to sit back, observe and learn. The room smelled heavily of stale coffee and melting doughnuts by the time Colonel Blaire queued up gun-cam footage from the most recent battle, where Raul and Tassa had taken down the *Blackhawk*. Raul swallowed back the bitter aftertaste of his coffee and narrated his own footage, trying to give the Sphere Knight an idea of the larger battle not shown on the video.

"This Steel Wolf MechWarrior," Powers asked after the footage had run through again showing Tassa Kay stomping the *Blackhawk's* cockpit into ruin, "what was his name?"

"Yulri," Charal DePriest answered, consulting a file on her noteputer, "of the Carns *redname*. I've been rereviewing his secret."

Legate Stempres leaned in. "His what?"

"Codex." It was Powers who answered. "Clan-descended warriors still follow the tradition of carrying some kind of data crystal on their person—a complete record of their personal victories and awarded honors."

Charal pulled up a new screen. "Yulri's secret proves that he is from a promising red-redname, and has risen slowly but certainly through the Steel Wolf ranks. Most of his greatest trophies have come on the coattails of Star Colonel Torrent, though. He's a follower." She frowned. "Although that doesn't debate his offers to stab his former commander."

"What's that?" Powers asked.

"It seems that Star Commander Yulri is making repeated offers to bolt sides and d-dance for The Republic." Charal huffed out an exasperated sigh. "Is very insistent on it, in fact."

Powers frowned, his eyes glossing over as if looking inward through mental files for some explanation of the Steel Wolf's behavior. "Maybe it's time I met with this prisoner," he finally said. "Colonel Blaire, if you would accompany me?" To everyone else he said, "We'll meet again after lunch, and discuss plans for a stronger defense of Achernar. Thank you."

Raul rose with the others, waited for the Knight-Errant to pass behind him before stepping away from the table intent on Charal DePriest. He had just laid a hand on her arm when Kyle Powers called from the doorway, "Mr. Ortega? I'd like you to accompany us as well." Powers was out the door before Raul responded.

He nodded at the Knight's back, but did not follow immediately. He met Charal's unsteady gaze with concern. "Are you okay with this?" he asked.

"Okay with what, Raul?" Charal blinked hard, as if clearing her vision. Her sapphire eyes did have a glossy look to them.

"You should have the *Legionnaire* back. It was your 'Mech before you got hurt. I"—he swallowed hard—"I don't want to give it up," he admitted, "but it's not right to keep you sidelined."

Charal smiled sadly. "I appreciate that. I nod." She screwed up her elfin face into a frustrated scowl, then slowly eased it back toward a disciplined, false calm. "The hopscotch diagnosed me with . . . with Nonfluent Aphasia. It's a brain dysfunction that interferes with my speech patterns. I substitute worms without meaning to."

Hopscotch? It took Raul a few seconds to understand what Charal meant. "The hospital?" The other Mech-Warrior nodded. "Is it serious?"

"It's a brain dysfunction, Raul. My neural connections are a bit spilled up." She glanced away from him. "I'll never pilot a real BattleMech again."

Not when a finely tuned neurohelmet might read her crossed brainwaves and trip up one of the near-priceless

BattleMechs. But a converted IndustrialMech, with its much more basic neurocontrol system, that she might be allowed to pilot. *If* the situation was desperate enough to allow her on the field. Raul winced. "I'm sorry, Charal."

"You're a fine pilot, Raul. I'm glad it's you." She nodded after the absent command officers. "You do . . . gold . . . by Achernar."

Not sure what else he could say to her, Raul simply nodded and left. Her words chased him from the briefing room. Do good by Achernar. That was what she had meant to say. And he was trying, dammit.

He was trying.

11

Calm Before the Storm

The arrival of Knight-Errant Powers acted as a shot of adrenaline for the entire militia. Leaning back in his chair at the on-base officer's club, listening as Jeffrey McDaniels regaled the table with yesterday's scuffle between Fourth Armor and the Steel Wolves, Raul Ortega took its measure from the spirited conversations warming up the lounge. He couldn't hear more than snatches of two or three at a time, not over the general background buzz of conversation and the upbeat guitar solo someone had coined into the music system. By the sweeping gestures and excited flush lighting each face, he could tell that, like McDaniels's, most were telling of recent battles—but now the stories had an air of pride-in-service rather than the anxiety that had colored the tales of holding actions of only three days before.

At the next table over, a pair of fighter pilots shouted down a VTOL squad as to which had made a larger impact on that first, desperate day of the Steel Wolf assault. They held up wildly bent straws and folded napkins to represent airborne craft, dogfighting each other and strafing an array of salt and pepper shakers set out over their table. Some armor jocks had claimed most of the dance floor, pushing chairs around in tank formations, and a trio of bulked-up infantry lieutenants hovered at the nearby bar, adding the sweet aroma of their cigars to the already-thick air while discussing battlesuit tactics.

Recital night at the O-club.

McDaniels dropped heavily back into his chair. Thirsty from all his talk, he picked up a tall glass of iced juice and drank heavily. He'd hit his four-drink limit early with highballs of Glengarry Reserve, making up in quality what he couldn't get in quantity. Raul continued to nurse his second margarita, enjoying the sweet ice and tangy bite of bar-stock tequila.

"You're sure?" he asked his friend. "Morgan and Brightfoot?" The two men who were still missing in action from the spaceport mess Raul had been helping clean up . . . was it only six days ago?

Major Eligh Chautec nodded, backing up McDaniels. "Gun-cam footage doesn't lie. I know their faces. By the Unfinished Book I should, they were such thorns in my heel a few years back." Chautec had commanded Achernar's armor corps when Colonel—then Major—Blaire was still overseeing the RTC. Chautec's steel gray hair had streaks of black in it still, though they were hard to find with his hair cut into a tight flattop. "Always bothering after a transfer to active duty. They weren't good enough then, and they weren't good enough yesterday."

Not if McDaniels's story was to be believed, and the 'captured' reservists had been put back into the field under Star Colonel Torrent's command. Driving Shandra scout buggies wasn't a huge vote of confidence in their abilities. Especially when they try to tangle with McDaniels's crew in an M1 Marksman.

"Jeff had no choice," Chautec said. One man dead—Corporal Morgan—and Brightfoot retreating with severe damage.

Clark Diago and Tassa Kay rounded out the small table of officers. Tassa sat with her chair partially pulled back, as if trying to disassociate herself from the men. Diago stared at his wedding band, the gold all but glowing against his caramel-colored skin. "Better to know what happened to them, I guess."

McDaniels didn't seem so certain. "Say that when it's one of your MechWarriors turning coat." He realized belatedly that all three Achernar BattleMech pilots were, in fact, represented at this table. "I meant one of the conversion pilots."

Raul dipped a finger into his drink and flicked a drop toward his friend. "Right." He smiled as he said it.

"We'll set it all to rights soon enough," Chautec promised. Weathered hands gripped a hammered-metal beer stein—made out of the armor of his first tank, if the unlikely tale were to be believed. "We knew—we know—that we have Swordsworn and Steel Wolf sympathizers mixed in with the Standing Guard. But most of them continue to follow orders and do their jobs. Likewise, Torrent must have Republic-loyal troops under his command who are torn between what they know is right, and orders coming direct from Prefect Kal Radick. If we can hit Torrent hard enough near *his* base for a change, and isolate some of those men and women—"

"You will have your head handed to you," Tassa interjected.

Raul downed the last draught of his margarita and waved the empty, bowl-shaped glass at a passing waitress. "Here she goes again," he whispered, never loud enough for anyone else to hear. Tassa glanced at him from the other side of the table—a coincidence, although Raul still felt a sizzle of heat pass between them.

The back of his neck itched in a guilty flush, remembering his last rendezvous with the MechWarrior, and how he had learned the next day that Jessica had stayed out at the work site pitching in to help. Since then, his fiancée had gotten more involved in civilian efforts to support the military.

If Tassa sensed Raul's discomfort, she didn't let on. Instead, she glanced over at Chautec. "No offense." She paused, then reconsidered, "Well, offense or not, Major Chautec, it is still a bad idea."

"And why do you think so?" the major asked calmly, too seasoned a veteran to bite back in anger.

Tassa thought a moment, obviously deciding how—or *if*—she would answer him. With sudden commitment she rocked forward in her chair, her necklace charm swinging from her neck, leaned elbows onto the table and stabbed a finger down into the middle of a knot in the table's wood grain. "Highlake Basin. Star Colonel Torrent has concentrated his forces here for their proximity to River's End and the Swordsworn stronghold near Hahnsak. His advantage is that he can strike in either direction at a multitude of targets, carefully allocating his strength.

"But if *you* go after him where he is strongest, he will commit everything. All or nothing, Major. There will be no middle ground. Are you ready to strip River's End bare of every last militiaman? Because you will have to. Is Blaire or Powers ready to do that?" she asked, cat's-green eyes intent on Chautec.

So intent that she missed Kyle Powers' approach from one side. "No," the Knight-Errant said, obviously catching the last of her question. "I doubt that we are."

All five men stood out of respect for the Sphere Knight, who had traded his bright, spotless dress uniform in for more practical gray utilities. His platinum hair looked ivory in the club's subdued lighting. His only concession to rank was a collar pin that had been shaped like a forked banner, red with a gold clasp around the middle, on which erupted a platinum starburst: the heraldic of the Knights Errant.

Tassa Kay reclined back into her chair again, making a point of not rising. Powers noted this with an amused smile that reached into his eyes. He waved everyone else back to their seats, then turned to pull a chair from the nearby table filled with Aerospace and VTOL pilots. Raul did not miss the way the pilots' gazes followed the Knight Errant, filled with hope and maybe some hero worship as well. A touch of awe that Powers quickly set aside by ordering them a round and making a point to ask each one something personal. A name. Unit. Hometown. In thirty seconds he had them laughing and joking again, relaxing while they could.

Raul caught himself smiling, warmed by the Knight Errant's care for men with whom he had never served.

"I'm afraid I have to agree with MechWarrior Kay," Powers said, returning with his chair, seating himself between Major Chautec and Clark Diago. "Star Colonel Torrent is a trueborn. He's also of the Kerensky Bloodname. That makes him a most dangerous adversary."

Raul accepted his new drink from the waitress, tipping her heavily. He turned back to the conversation with renewed interest. Tassa Kay had said something remarkably similar to him after their last tangle with the Steel Wolves, and in a few short days Powers had proven himself of sharp mind and instincts as well. His battlefield analyses were always spot-on. "I'd like to know why you say that, Sir Powers."

"So would I," Tassa agreed slowly, drawn back to the table and to Powers as if against her will.

The Knight-Errant had carried over his own tall glass. He sipped at what looked like pale, iced coffee, and Raul could only guess what it really was. Setting his drink back to the table, Powers traced the smooth line of his chin with one finger. "I don't know as much as I'd like about the inner workings of the Steel Wolves. Kal Radick is much more a student of history than I am, and he seems to be truly invested in returning the faction toward true Clan Wolf traditions and ambitions. But I remember some of the history behind our expatriate Clan population, and I've been forced to learn a great deal more since the Blackout.

"In the Clans," Powers continued slowly, as if dredging up each memory from deep inside, "a warrior is judged mainly on their own accomplishments, but they can also carry a heavy burden of shame or great expectations from previous generations. Star Colonel Torrent is more than a rising star among the Steel Wolves. He comes from Bloodname stock that is most revered among every Clan. Kerensky. General Aleksandr Kerensky led seventy . . . eighty percent of the Star League army into exile back in 2784. He was the Great Father to his son, Nicholas, the Founder of the Clans. Nicholas organized them into a warrior society unlike anything Humanity had ever seen.

"A later descendant, Ulric Kerensky, led all the Clans at one point as their ilKhan—supreme war chief. His efforts on behalf of the Inner Sphere fractured Clan Wolf, although Katya Kerensky reconciled many of the outcasts when she joined Devlin Stone's reformation. And of course, the greatest outcast of them all was Natasha Kerensky—they called her the Black Widow and she was one of the greatest MechWarriors and mercenary officers ever known to the Inner Sphere. She eventually returned to the Clans and was even elected saKhan of Clan Wolf for a time. To a martial people who believe that at thirty years of age you are looking past your prime, her sixty-year career is the stuff of legend."

"You're saying that Torrent has a lot to live up to," Diago summed up in his usual sparse style. "Beyond the usual need to prove himself."

Powers shrugged. "I'm saying that you should try to imagine yourself descended from Anastasias Focht or Victor Steiner-Davion. The son of Genghis Khan, Erwin Rommel, Michael Cameron, or Takashi Kurita. You start so close to the top, but it's also a very long fall if you miss."

Major Chautec shook his head. "So we wait around for him to grow into his role as Dictator-General of the Inner Sphere? Or to prop up Kal Radick into that title? Maybe we should hit him with everything we have, now, and be done with him or us. What are we waiting for?"

"Maybe we're waiting for the return of Devlin Stone," Raul said quietly to himself. Not quiet enough, though, as half the heads at the table swung around toward him. He hadn't realized until voicing the idea how strongly he

believed in Stone's return. "Well, wasn't that the promise?" he asked the Knight. "When we need him, he
will return?"

"Ye-es," Powers agreed hesitantly. "But do we truly
need him—or want him—to save us from our own weakness?" The Knight Errant gazed over Raul's head. "We
need our father because we are afraid of the dark? I
think Devlin Stone would be sorely disappointed."

Raul had not considered such an argument, and found
it compelling. But how much of that was the words, and
how much the man behind them? And did it matter?
Powers knew how to command, and he knew how to
create alliances as well as friendships. Raul could see
himself putting his trust in this man.

Others were not so charitable. Major Chautec set his
stein down hard on the table, wiped froth from his upper
lip. "So we sit back and wait for Torrent to gnaw our
bones clean and maybe choke on a splinter. Wonderful.
Well, if he's going to scavenge among our forces, I say
we should seriously think about returning the favor."

"We do not need to," Tassa said. "Not in the same
way, at least. Torrent's warriors are more than content
to join our side, according to Star Commander Yulri."

Raul's new drink sat untouched on the table. Yulri
was the prisoner Tassa claimed out of the fallen *Blackhawk*. Raul remembered Powers' first meeting with the
man, watching as Yulri all but swore his allegiance to
the warrior who had bested him in combat.

Powers had looked at a loss at the time, though now
he showed no regret for having denied the man's petition
without prejudice. "True. The taking of bondsmen is another tradition Kal Radick seems to have revived." Powers picked up his drink, but simply cradled it in his hands.
"Eventually, such prisoners expect to earn their way
back to warrior status. And there is no loss of honor.
Yulri seems to believe that he belongs to you," he
winked at Tassa. "But I'm not comfortable with the practice." He hesitated, just for a second. Then he continued,

his voice strong, "In truth, I'm not entirely comfortable with giving the man over to you."

Tassa responded to his blunt statement with an honest shrug. "Why not? I already have two Condor tank crews who are routinely assigned to me at their request. Are you concerned that I will start my own army and take Achernar with a bare lance of men?"

"No. But such . . ." he trailed off, looking for the right word, "such *recruits* could do a great deal of damage if they decide to break against us at the wrong moment."

Tassa scoffed. "I can keep them in line."

"Yes, but will you put your *Ryoken* up as a bond on their loyalty?" The Knight Errant sat forward, suddenly very intent on the other MechWarrior. His gray eyes were sharp as splintered slate, and stared unblinking into Tassa's pause. From comrade to commander just that fast, Raul noted.

"I will put myself up as a guarantee," Tassa finally said, rolling with the change. "The *Ryoken* goes where I go."

"You're asking me to put a lot of faith in your word of honor, Tassa Kay. Do you have anyone who can vouchsafe *your* loyalty?"

To her credit, Tassa never once looked in Raul's direction. Not a glance or even a partial shift in the line of her shoulders. But he felt the question that hung between them. Raul knew she waited for his decision, and his alone. "I will," he said, speaking up before he could think better of it or argue himself out of the gut-sense call.

Powers raised an eyebrow. "You know Tassa Kay well enough for that, Captain Ortega?" The tone of his voice—a timbre of expectancy—made Raul think that Powers had been waiting for the junior MechWarrior to speak as well.

"I don't know her at all, Sir Powers, except that she's about the best damned partner you could ask for in a battle. And if I can trust her with my back on the field,

I can give her my support here." He shrugged, feeling the burden of Powers' judgment weighing on his shoulders. "And like she said, what can she really do with one lance?"

Kyle Powers seemed less interested in Tassa Kay and more in Raul, as if he could measure the other man's depth of devotion and empathy in a single glance. "All right, Tassa Kay." The judgment came down slowly, and with almost ceremonial reverence. "You can have your man. But he does not get anything better than medium armor."

"He will be a technician on my 'Mech for at least a week," she said, dismissing any concerns. She tugged at the dark forelock hanging down from her widow's peak. "Then maybe I will find him an infantry battlesuit."

Raul shuddered, trying to imagine giving up his *Legionnaire* for one of the tinman suits enjoyed by ground soldiers. Now *that* was desperation.

Clark Diago thought so as well, though along another train of thought. "You're pretty trusting, giving the enemy access to your *Ryoken*."

"I can use someone else with knowledge of cutting-edge technology to oversee repairs. Besides," she shrugged, rising, "I think we are all pretty trusting to give Sandoval access to our plans and stockpiles." She threw down the last of her drink, then set the glass on the table and used it to hold down her bar payment of crumpled bills. Without another word she left, gracefully weaving among tables and scattered chairs on a path toward the O-club door.

Most of the men watched her departure. More used to Tassa's cryptic personality, Raul shrugged it aside. Moreover, the same uneasy feeling had plagued him as well, ever since the staff briefing on Powers' arrival. How could the militia embrace one wayward faction even while fighting off another? "She's right," he said, then asked the question out loud for the opinions of the others.

"The Swordsworn aren't acting nearly as predatory as

the Steel Wolves," Chautec said. Then, hedging, he added, "Yet."

"Enemy of our enemy," Jeffrey McDaniels said with a casual shrug. "It's not like we're going to suddenly side with Aaron Sandoval when this is all over."

Powers offered nothing at all, staring at the table but obviously alert to the conversation. Raul pressed forward. "But we are choosing sides," he pointed out. "With all due respect, Sir Powers, we've given the Swordsworn legitimacy, and I'm not so certain that's a good thing."

The Knight-Errant glanced up. A shadow of doubt flickered in his gray eyes just for a second, enough for Raul to be sure it had been there, and then was suppressed. The MechWarrior felt certain he had been meant to see it.

"I'm not so certain either, Raul." Powers voice betrayed nothing of his own doubts, though. He had made his decision, and was standing by it. "It's a terrible answer to a worse question, though. And the Swordsworn have helped keep Achernar free, haven't they?"

Raul stood, abandoned his melting margarita. "No sir," he said with a sad shake of his head. "I think they were just here first."

He gave the Knight and then Major Chautec a respectful nod, and clapped Jeffrey on the shoulder as he stepped away and followed Tassa's path to the door. He paused there to look back. Powers already had the table turned back toward an upbeat mood, encouraging Jeffrey McDaniels to recount another tale. The Knight Errant glanced his way, once, and saluted him with a noncommittal nod. Raul pushed his way outside.

Tassa waited, standing in a large patch of evening shade, letting the dry, evening breeze tug at her dark red hair. Somehow Raul had been certain he'd catch up with her, though she looked surprised to see him. "Not staying for the party?"

"You know," he said, answering her in a roundabout way, "you have a knack for throwing water on other people's fire."

Tassa shrugged, not agreeing or not caring. Likely the latter. "I need to get Yulri out of dock. Can you give me a hand?"

"It's going to take Sir Powers's authority, likely countersigned by Colonel Blaire, to do that." Raul shook his head. "No way he'll get to it before morning, so relax, Tassa."

Hands on her hips and a jaunty tilt to her head, Tassa swung around to regard Raul with a poisoned stare. "You do not like the idea of freeing the prisoner either, do you?" She quickly doused her flare of temper, though. "Still don't trust me?"

Raul shrugged. "I don't know you," he said. "But I'm trying."

"Yes. Sometimes you are very trying."

If that wasn't the *Atlas* calling the *Jupiter* overpowered . . . Raul shrugged, stared up into the pale blue sky. Achernar's evenings were often mild and beautiful. Only a touch of the day's heat remained. He suddenly doubted his decision to walk out on the O-club, but wasn't about to go back inside. "You know," he said with hesitant strength, gaining momentum as he talked, "it's still early, and I left my third drink sitting on the table."

"What of it?" Tassa Kay asked warily.

Another brief itch of guilt, which Raul ignored, having pushed this far already. "So, I have a bottle of whiskey stashed in my room," he told her. "It's not reserve label, but it's true Glengarry stock."

Tassa considered it for all of ten seconds. "One condition. None of this ridiculous four drink limit."

He doubted that Tassa missed him wince at the headache he'd have in the morning, but nodded anyway. "Deal," he agreed.

And Raul would deal with whatever the Fates had in mind for him tomorrow, he promised. Just so long as they didn't call a military alert this evening.

12

Bait and Switch

Sirens' Pass
Achernar
1 March 3133

The last high peaks of the Tanager Mountains, the ones that anchored the short march down toward the Taibek Hills, had swallowed Achernar's sun not quite an hour before. A pale sky hung over valleys and narrow clefts now being drowned in shadow. Sirens' Pass, the last—or the first—major break in the Tanagers, which faded down into the B'her farming valley, swam in an artificial twilight.

The perfect place for an ambush.

Erik Sandoval-Groell waited with his forces inside the lower pass, hands sweat-slick on his *Hatchetman's* dead control sticks. Reaching into the storage under his seat, he fished out a pair of neoleather gloves and pulled them on with determined tugs. Better. He wouldn't let anything betray him here. Not damp hands, and certainly not second thoughts. Five days before he had set himself to watching for a chance to ratchet up tensions between the Steel Wolves and the Republic forces on Achernar. Now was that time. There was no turning back.

Outside, a violent wind cut through the pass, howling

and wailing as it brushed past the dark shafts that were an old Taibek Mining venture. The mine openings were such an obvious ambush site that Erik had ordered them left clear. Five MiningMech conversions and his own BattleMech crouched against cold rock, concealed on precarious ledges or half buried in ancient tailings. They would hit first.

And soon.

Through his sweating ferroglass shield, Erik watched as Steel Wolf infantry concluded their sweep of the first few shaft entrances, calling them clear and scrambling to the next set of dark openings even as the main patrol worked their way down out of the knife-edged Tanager Mountains. A converted ForestryMech led the way, flanked by two JES strategic missile carriers. A line of supply and support vehicles trailed behind them in column formation, ready to rape the B'her valley agrocombines of foodstock and machinery, and at sound military positions several infantry carriers and light armor paced the column. The JES's slowed a bit, no doubt on alert with magres imaging throwing back so many metal-lode returns. Ore, abandoned dump carts, an old drilling rig— there was too much clutter for them to read solid outlines and Erik's forces had been in place long enough for thermal shadows to cool on everything except his *Hatchetman*'s fusion engine. *That* took them several critical seconds.

He saw the carriers finally react to his presence, accelerating forward and swiveling their turrets against his position. Trembling with pent-up adrenaline, Erik banked the BattleMech's fusion fires to life, checked that he was selected to force-wide comms and ordered, "Now, hit them now!"

Priorities had been assigned earlier. His quartet of missile-equipped conversions rained fire and destruction down on the lead ForestryMech, Erik not wanting to take any chances against the design. His ultra-class autocannon hammered out eighty-mil slugs at double any normal rate of fire, chewing through armor with good-sized bites as the ForestryMech raced for the cover of a large pile of tailings.

Erik's final IndustrialMech conversion ended the Steel Wolf Mech's flight, spending its banked capacitor charge through a power amplifier to light off a large laser. A ruby beam stuttered a half-powered lance into the ForestryMech's left arm, severing the autocannon at its elbow joint. The modified IndustrialMech toppled awkwardly, crashed to the valley floor, and skid out of sight behind the tailings.

Standing the *Hatchetman* up from its crouch, Erik called for his infantry and armor as blossoms of fire erupted all around him. The JES carriers peppered his location with long-ranged missiles, throwing enough ordnance up-slope to trigger a possible rockslide. Erik rode out the jostling, trusting the regenerative feedback loop created between his neurohelmet and the *Hatchetman*'s massive gyroscopic stabilizer to keep him upright, then throttled forward into a careful down-slope walk. His autocannon barked out more hot metal, and the torso-mounted extended-range laser stabbed several mega-joules of scarlet energy into the lead *Big Jess* carrier. Not enough to do any real damage. Didn't have to be.

While dismissing the mine shaft entrances from his earlier plans, what Erik had counted on was that the infantry would miss the blind draw—a narrow cleft in the pass's south wall which opened up into a fair-sized canyon, and inside which he had hidden a heavy complement of armored vehicles.

A pair of SM1 Destroyers barreled out of the blind canyon, leading Erik's flanking charge as they struck into the forward head of the column. Long licks of fire and smoke burst from their assault-class autocannons, ripping into a Joust tracked vehicle that lay directly in their path. The Joust's engine erupted, bursting the side armor and blowing the turret skyward on a column of greasy fire. The scrapped mass of metal fell hard on the side of one SM1, grounding its skirt in a long, dragging scrape. It rebounded, and both Destroyers wheeled over to race for the rear of the column, spending thousands of rounds into lightly armored support vehicles on their way.

Behind them came a squad of Demons, a Behemoth, Erik's elite hoverbike unit, and two Maxim heavy troop transport vehicles carrying Hauberk and Purifier infantry. Most began spitting laserfire and missiles before even clearing the draw. More convoy trucks erupted into flaming debris.

Momentarily thrown back on their haunches, the Wolves rallied faster than Erik would have thought. The JES carriers charged forward, missile systems belching out flight after flight of armor-pounding warheads. One of the Swordsworn's MiningMech conversions got in their way and was left scattered in pieces over a blasted stretch of smoking ground. Another two Miners were pressed back into a nearby shaft and then sealed in by carpet-fire missile barrages.

Elementals vaulted from the backs of several convoy trucks. A point of five battlesuit soldiers seized onto the sides of a Maxim, ripping through plate armor and breaching the troop pen. They spent several of their back-pack missiles into the interior before the Hauberks inside managed to stagger out and engage them point-blank.

Erik's men struggled and died at the hands of the genetically bred infantry.

Off the pass wall and throttling up into a run, Erik dodged his *Hatchetman* around one particularly large pile of tailings and met one of the JES carriers coming around from the other side. With its LRM racks severely hampered at close range, the carrier pivoted on diamond-track treads and raced for open ground.

The *Hatchetman* was faster, cutting it off in only five long strides. Erik's autocannon opened up several gaping rents in the carrier's armor. Then he raised the right arm, which carried the massive titanium hatchet from which his BattleMech took its name. The hatchet fell once, twice, each time crushing large wedge-shaped bites into armor.

His third strike split open one of the launchers, and

live munitions rolled and tumbled out to litter the floor of Siren's Pass.

Erik's laser touched off spilled fuel. One warhead burst open still in its launch tube, then another. Erik spun the *Hatchetman* away, racing for distance. The horrific explosion of the JES carrier and its payload of missiles shoved the *Hatchetman* with a brutal fist to the back. The BattleMech sprawled forward in a facedown slide, shaking Erik against his restraining harness like a rag doll caught in the teeth of a mastiff.

A growling mastiff.

Tearing . . . trembling . . . buzzsaw teeth . . .

His tongue throbbed in pain and he tasted a hint of blood in his mouth, but it was the sound of tearing metal that shocked Erik back to life. Shaking off his dizziness, he blinked away the dark threat of unconsciousness as he recognized the shriek of a diamond-edged powersaw against armor. His armor. It was a sound he was unlikely to forget, having been under the blade of a ForestryMech one other time before. That time of his earlier disgrace.

The ForestryMech. Felled during the opening moment of battle, its pilot had apparently collected himself well enough to dive back into the fray. Missing its autocannon-arm, the gray machine still had use of the massive, tree-killing blades by which it primarily practiced its trade. With one foot stepping down on the broad ax-head of Erik's hatchet, the WorkMech used the powersaw to sever the haft and take from Erik his most potent close-in weapon.

Most potent, perhaps, but not his only weapon.

Thumbing an activation stud on his right-hand control stick, Erik released his BattleMech's grip on the ruined hatchet. Shoving that hand against the ground, he propped himself up enough to lean in with his torso-mounted autocannon, thrusting the barrel into the ForestryMech's armored crotch. He pulled his trigger, holding it down, spending thousands of eighty millimeter, high velocity rounds. Lethal metal tore into the ForestryMech's gyro housing, boring through the stabilizers and then hammering away at the engine shielding above that. Fuel oil mixed with hydraulic fluids spilled down in a black gush of 'Mech blood, staining the lower legs of the ForestryMech which staggered and then toppled back.

Climbing slowly back to his feet, Erik surveyed the wreckage his forces had made of Star Colonel Torrent's foraging column. Some of the Steel Wolves' faster vehicles had broken past his one remaining Destroyer, fleeing back the way they'd come. A few of the supply trucks had escaped as well, mainly because of their large initial numbers, and were hardly worth chasing down with valuable military assets.

The rest lay in ruins, smashed, broken and burning from one side of Siren's Pass to the other. Sharp winds fanned any flame into crackling infernos and lifted the oily smoke higher up the mountainside. Even through the cockpit's sound suppression, Erik could still hear the wind's whistling echoes. He counted two down MiningMechs, two others lost behind a cave-in but easily rescued, a lost Maxim and several dead Hauberk infantry, and a destroyed SM1. According to the reports which now bled in over one another, his Purifiers had captured one JES carrier and some supply vehicles.

"Now we'll see where things fall," he whispered out loud, just quiet enough not to be picked up by the neurohelmet's voice-activated mic.

The price had run slightly higher than Erik had wanted to pay, but the loss to Star Colonel Torrent would be galling. It would bait him to some kind of action. And whether the Steel Wolf commander came for Erik in Hahnsak, forcing him to call in his new allies for protection, placing them in between himself and danger, or went straight for Kyle Powers himself, the Swordsworn position on Achernar would only improve. But by how much? That was the question.

Erik's answer was just as easy. By however much he could squeeze from the situation. His uncle, his family, his people, expected no less of him.

Erik expected no less of himself.

=== 13 ===

The Challenge

Steel Wolf DropShip **Lupus**
Achernar
2 May 3133

"I will allow the death of Star Captain Laren Mehta to be recorded as a fitting warrior's end, though my review of the battle-rom footage is not nearly so generous, Star Colonel. Mehta should have held cover over your insertion. That is the last bit of charity I expect you to need from me."

The voice floated in from Torrent's office, calm and steady yet still possessing a rough-edged threat that promised that this was a man used to giving orders. Every word had been chosen with care and the smallest pause followed after each as the speaker overenunciated, making certain that he would always be clearly understood. It was a voice for the Senate floor, command-level staff meetings, and battlefield frequencies all three.

Leaning over the washbasin of his office's small, attached lavatory Torrent glared at himself from beneath angry brows. He had no need to watch the holographic message again, having spent enough time in Prefect Radick's company to know that his commander's face betrayed no personal thoughts. He left it playing so that

Kal Radick's orders would set themselves firmly in his mind, and as a reminder that Achernar was only one stepping stone toward the Steel Wolves' ultimate goal. On the far bank waited Tikonov, Duke Aaron Sandoval, and control of Prefecture IV.

Torrent's lip twitched up into the beginning of a snarl, which he quickly suppressed. Palming a handful of oily gel, he smeared it back over his head. Thick, black stubble scraped against his hand. The unscented gel smelled caustic, almost rancid.

Picking up the curved blade at the side of his washbasin, Torrent raised it to his scalp and set the laser-sharpened edge against his skin starting at his widow's peak. With a long, slow pull he shaved it back—careful, calm—over the crown of his pate. Softened to wire brush stiffness, the stubble rasped against the knife's edge. He took another stripe to the left of the first, then used the side of the basin to scrape the knife clean of gel and shavings.

"Now. You should remember enough from our planning sessions to know how much I value Achernar *and* Ronel. Colton Fetladral's report, which I have attached, proves that we underestimated the dedication of Katana Tormark's forces and the resolve of CEO Bannson to resist our offers of alliance." A longer pause, for effect Torrent felt certain. "That man has a private agenda, I swear."

Torrent contemplated the edge of his blade. It glinted a cruel, steel blue in the lavatory's dim light, and reminded him of his previously delicate position on Achernar balanced between the Swordsworn and Republic. A position that had changed overnight. Jacob Bannson was not the only one with a hidden agenda, he knew. Sandoval. The name crept back into his thoughts. Erik Sandoval. Returning to his morning ablutions he shaved another rasping strip from the side of his head, careful of his own ear as the blade whispered against it. The personal maintenance forced Torrent to calm, focus.

"Still, Bannson remains of secondary importance so

long as Katana Tormark continues to devil our worlds.
The Dragon Lady professes complete ignorance, of
course, but I know that it is she. One of her suicide
samurai buried a *Visigoth* into the bridge of Fetladral's
Bloody Hunt during his insertion run." A chime sounded
in the office as someone rang through from the corridor.
"It never recovered."

Torrent leaned back through the door, called,
"Come." He cleaned his blade again, and then went to
work on his right side.

He knew it would be Nikola Demos, and he knew
the holographic image that the armor-driving star captain
walked in on. It was the kind of image that haunted
every ground-force commander. Even him. A once-
graceful *Gazelle*-class DropShip, though you could never
tell from the strewn, fire-blackened wreckage that was
left of it. In one terrifying moment following the
Miraborg-death of an aerospace fighterpilot, Colton Fetladral lost a star of converted WorkMechs, an armor bi-
nary, and any chance of taking Ronel.

Without help.

"It comes down to this," Kal Radick promised.
"Choosing between taking a harder line with the enemy
I know, Aaron Sandoval, and the enemy I do not know
as well, Katana Tormark. In this, I must choose Tormark.
She is an accomplished military leader with an aggressive
force backing her. It is of long-term importance that we
convince her to stay on her own side of the Prefecture
border. In fact, opposing her in this manner will cement
our position on Achernar as well. In the end, we prove
that what we are doing is both prudent and sound in
directly occupying important worlds."

Cleaning his blade one last time against the basin's
edge, Torrent returned the wicked little knife to its scab-
bard at the small of his back. Grabbing a damp towel
hanging nearby, the star colonel draped it over his scalp
and rubbed away the remaining gel as he stepped back
into his office. Nikola Demos stood defiantly near his
desk, arms akimbo, staring at the diminutive projection

of Galaxy Commander Kal Radick. She had pulled her gleaming black hair severely back from her face, giving her a hard, hawkish profile. Her dark blue eyes held no warmth for the orders she sensed—even from just a short lead in by the Steel Wolf leader—were coming.

"This change in priorities comes at an awkward time and through no fault of your own. Star Colonel Fetladral concedes that his victory shall be your victory. Your victory, Star Colonel Torrent, is mine. Anything you might accomplish on Achernar will only add to our honor. You have my greatest confidence."

Nikola Demos turned as the holographic message winked out, recycled, and then began again with the Steel Wolf icon floating ominously over Torrent's working desk. "His greatest confidence? Great Father! What about the occupation force?"

"Shifted to support Colton Fetladral," Torrent acknowledged as he thumbed off the holovid player. He moved with a slow economy of motion, deliberate and controlled. "We are abandoned."

"Can we still win?" Nikola jumped right for the neck, seizing hold of the problem and dragging it to the ground. "Can we take Achernar?" She pressed her mouth into a thin, hard line.

Torrent felt his lip curling again. "Before or after Erik Sandoval's Swordsworn gutted your foraging unit?" He felt the white fury building up within him again. Overriding the impulse to lash out, knowing that Nikola Demos had, in fact, set a sound escort for the B'her Valley raid, Torrent moved behind his chair and exercised his muscles against the back rest.

"We might," he said slowly, evenly. Although they could never hold onto Achernar if Aaron Sandoval pushed out against them from Tikonov. The Steel Wolves would have opened up the world for the Swordsworn to take. "Perhaps. If we can split the alliance between Swordsworn and Republic."

"How will you do that?"

Torrent relaxed his grip on the chair back, turning his

mind away from Erik Sandoval and the Swordsworn's ambush even as he turned away from Nikola to grab his uniform jacket off a hook. "By destroying the man who forged it," he said. Sandoval would be dealt with, in time. Before that, Torrent would deal with Knight-Errant Kyle Powers.

Achernar Militia Command
Achernar

The world shook and Raul Ortega bolted upright in his bed. Achernar's furious, late-morning sun slammed into the window of Raul's base-assigned quarters, slashing by the cheap, vinyl blinds to stab blinding pokers into the forefront of his brain. Light birdsong and the rolling crush of heavy trucks—those were his first coherent impressions of the morning. His tongue felt thick and gritty. His mouth tasted like the birds had nested in it. There was no good reason to wake up feeling so awful, but about a dozen poor reasons.

Each one had come served in a shot glass.

The door rattled in its poorly hung frame as someone outside pounded again, gave up, and simply barged into his room in the company of more painful sunlight. "Dogs and togs, MechWarrior. Going to be a busy day." Tassa Kay.

Raul groaned, fell back to his pillow in a flop that, he felt, conveyed his sense of enthusiasm for Tassa's early company. He pulled the top sheet over his head, which lasted all of five seconds before his visitor stripped his bed in one brutal yank. Raul scrambled to cover himself, then realized that he had gone to bed in slacks and socks and a white undershirt.

"I do not have the time or patience to play, Ortega. Get up or get left behind."

More awake this time around, Raul blinked some moisture into his eyes, noticed that Tassa also looked a little less polished than normal. She had pulled her hair back into a severe tail, secured by a leather tie. She wore camouflage pants and a black tank wrestled over firm breasts. Her eyes were well shielded by a pair of leather-wrapped, reflective aviator's glasses, the kind that rested right up against the brow and let in very little light.

Memories from the previous night came staggering back as he stumbled from his bed in the studio-style apartment to the kitchenette sink. Cold water slapped against his face and on the back of his neck helped put them back in order. He had matched Tassa Kay shot for shot, trading tips, technical facts and history in between rounds of Glengarry amber. Even half-drunk, Tassa had said very little about herself. Raul remembered something about her meeting Evan Kell of the famous—or infamous—Kell Hounds. More about her fighting along-side Exarch Redburn. She had seemed curious—pleasantly so, even—when Raul told her about Jessica Searcy and their differing opinions on duty to the Republic, and . . .

And why was she here so damned early?

"What happened?" he asked, knowing that Tassa had not volunteered for wake-up duty. "The Wolves?"

"Round-about," she said. "More like your Sword-sworn. Erik Sandoval stirred up a hornet's nest last night. Sir Powers is taking a formal call from Star Colonel Torrent in about fifteen, and he wants us there."

"They're not *my* Swordsworn," Raul reminded her, gathering up a fresh uniform and slipping into the small closet of a bathroom to change. He listened through the cracked-open door as Tassa filled him in on Erik's ambush, the destructive tactics Sandoval had favored against support units, and Torrent's likely violent response.

"All right," he finally said, emerging from the bathroom with a toothbrush clenched in one hand. "So Erik caught the star colonel's forces in an ambush, using over-matched firepower. Sounds like sound military doctrine to me. Why would the Steel Wolves be insulted?" He scrubbed the first layer of paste from his teeth and tongue.

"Clan warriors limit damage to civilian and support forces whenever possible. It is considered the epitome of skill to take their target with the fewest possible forces, concentrating on opposing leadership and important front-line units. Sandoval's assault borders on treacherous—even cowardly—tactics. In Torrent's eyes," she added as an afterthought.

"What do you think he'll do?"

Leaning back against the standing locker, Tassa massaged her temples. "What would you do?" she asked. "You have suffered a large military set-back. Additionally, you feel that your personal honor has been smeared in the process. How do you regain your equilibrium?"

Although part of Achernar's older Latino population, Raul had never subscribed to the same level of machismo honor as so many of his counterparts. Still, he felt he could place himself into Torrent's shadow enough to draw a few conclusions. "I would challenge Erik Sandoval to a duel. *Hombre-en-hombre.*" Except that that was thinking too much with emotion, and not a head for strategy as well. "No," he decided. A chill shook him. *Leadership and important front-line units.* "I would challenge Sir Powers."

"Count on it," Tassa agreed. "And we have about ten minutes to be there when it happens, if we want a chance to get in on it."

Raul spit into the kitchenette sink, rinsed his brush out with tap water. "You think that Powers will accept?"

"Jousting is back in style, or have you not noticed?"

He had. Raul used a handful of cold tap water to slick his dark curls back. Icy trickles bled down his neck, but he trusted to Achernar's bright sun to dry him off before the two of them made the command center. Grabbing some dark glasses for himself, he nodded toward the door. "I still think it's a risky proposition, even for a Sphere Knight." He half blocked the doorway with his shoulder. "Unless there's something more?"

"There is always something more, Raul." She shrugged. "Today, though, is about a challenge."

"And what will tomorrow be about?" he asked, pushing at her for more information.

Tassa paused, exhaled her frustration, then elbowed her way past him, ducking into the bright, warm morning. "The Steel Wolves have landed assault forces on Ronel."

That was something more, all right.

Tassa had picked up a military jeep somewhere, and left it idling in a parking space out front. Grinding the transmission into gear, she jumped it back out of the stall and then forward on a wild pace across the small military base. Speed limits meant little to her and stop signs even less, it seemed to Raul, and she finally slammed the vehicle into a spot near the central command building that was marked as officer's parking only. From there it was two minutes and a short, painful jog down the last hallway before the two of them slipped in through a knot of junior officers and senior enlisted men to grab a patch of wall in Blaire's command post.

The large wallscreen was back in working order, and Torrent's large visage already filled it in a portrait of barely-checked rage. Everyone stared at the face of their enemy. But where were Powers and Blaire? The station reserved for senior officers was abandoned and dark.

"Our practices and traditions will be honored," Star Colonel Torrent demanded, looking down from his position. "If they are not, I can only name you among the *stravag* treachers who raid out of the Confederation, and I should just as easily believe the Republic capable of hiring assassins and stabbing in the dark with a poisoned blade. This is unacceptable!"

Raul had no idea what the term *stravag* meant, but it did not sound complimentary. He was still searching for Powers, to watch him give his reply, when Tassa elbowed him in the side and nodded toward a small auxiliary station not four meters past them along the same wall. Sir Kyle Powers stood, looking down into a camera pickup and a diminutive screen filled with Star Colonel Torrent. He wore his full military dress, no doubt anticipating the formal occasion. "Perhaps," he offered, "you should direct your attention to Lord and Captain Erik Sandoval-Groell. I believe it was his force that threw you out of the Tanager pass."

"As I have seen no honor among your subordinates, Kyle Powers, I demand satisfaction at your expense instead."

The Knight Errant considered that for a moment, long enough for Raul to see his purpose behind using the auxiliary station. Facing away from the main wall, Kyle Powers could not be intimidated by Torrent's looming presence. Instead, the Knight Errant kept his opponent carefully scaled down to manageable size. It might not mean much against the Steel Wolves' grand scheme for Achernar, but not even a small detail escaped Powers' attention.

"What if I should refuse you?" Powers finally asked.

"Do you seek total war? An assault on civilian transportation lines and the local industrial base? Aerial bombardment of the HPG station? I can bring that to Achernar if it is your wish." The thought sent cold chills walking up Raul's spine. "The Steel Wolves will not be denied."

"But they would, Star Colonel. You would see to it with such tactics. A population may be held only by popular support or overwhelming force. Such terrorist tactics would ensure that you could never earn the first, and I believe that the Steel Wolves do not have enough manpower for the second. Not"— he held up a hand—"without abandoning all other military considerations."

Torrent calmed, but in a glance at the wallscreen Raul could tell it was by sheer force of will over emotion. The Star Colonel's brown eyes looked deadened and flat as he asked, "You are willing to gamble on that?" Raul thought that the entire room might be holding its breath.

"Of course I am not." Powers spoke in a sad, formal voice. "My first charge is the safety of Republic citizens and residents on Achernar, as it should be with you, Star Colonel. I had not realized that you had so completely foresworn your own oath of service."

Tassa actually leaned back, as if expecting Torrent to leap through the airwaves with hands ready to grab for Powers' neck. "And you stain my honor again! I will have justice. A Trial of Grievance, Sir Powers. I will require you to accept personal responsibility for all Swordsworn actions."

Which Raul believed was only proper, no matter Sandoval's directions. The Swordsworn were Republic troops. Kyle Powers, however, had the larger picture still in mind.

"I accept your challenge," the Sphere Knight said with formal grace and a half bow. "In return, I call on you to answer for the Steel Wolves, and swear on your personal honor that there will be no escalation of manpower on Achernar."

Powers would pull the teeth from any Steel Wolf threat to bring larger forces to bear against the world, limiting the fighting to forces at hand. Of course, if the Steel Wolves were also hitting Ronel, they likely did not have the strength to bring a secondary assault against Achernar anyway.

Still, Torrent balked. "What you are asking is beyond the scope of a personal Trial, Sir Powers."

"Then we shall expand on our Trial. A small, combined arms force each. A test of your command against my own." He nodded to one side, and Blaire fed a crystal into a data slot. "I am already transmitting my force composition. I expect you to match them with equal strength."

Caught out by the Knight Errant's preparations, Star Colonel Torrent paused for only a brief second. Then, "Bargained well and done! I will meet you on the River's Run Flatlands in two days time."

And then his transmission cut out to a field of gray static.

The attending soldiers cheered as Powers also stepped back from the comms station, secure in their belief for the Sphere Knight. Already a daring oddsmaker was calling out wagers, but of course there were no takers in this room. Even at long odds, no one would put money on the Steel Wolves. Except perhaps for Tassa, Raul amended, but even she was apparently politic enough not to answer the wag's challenge.

Or perhaps it wasn't politics, he noticed, following her gaze to the data crystal that Colonel Blaire retrieved from the station and then handed back to Kyle Powers. Her pointed gaze betrayed her hunger to be involved in this challenge. Raul figured she had as good a chance as any. Powers might go with heavier armor assets and battlesuit infantry alone, of course, but the junior MechWarrior was willing to guess that Powers had rounded out his combined-arms force with a second BattleMech. Would the Knight Errant publish the list beforehand? Or summon a briefing among command-level officers first?

Then Powers turned, and saw Raul through a gap in the crowd. "Captain Ortega," he called, interrupting Raul's thoughts. He gestured Raul forward, then turned for a word with Blaire as Raul and Tassa elbowed their way up through the charged crowd of soldiers.

"Sir," Raul answered, presenting himself to the Sphere Knight.

Powers handed him the data crystal, pressing it securely into the MechWarrior's hands. "Pull the duty records for every man on that list. Bring them to Colonel Blaire's office in one hour. We'll go over them together."

"You want my input?" Raul asked, feeling a small swell of pride for at least being invited in on the review session.

Powers looked a great deal graver, though. "I think I should have it," he told Raul. "Your name is on the list, after all."

His warm surge of pride gave way quickly to a sharp, two-edged thrill as hands slapped him on the back and a new cheer went up for the 'defender of Achernar.' *He* had been chosen. Not Tassa and not Clarke Diago despite Diago's seniority. Then the immensity of the task before them reared up and washed over him like the final deluge sweeping over a drowning man. "S-sir! Captain Diago—"

"Is a fine officer and MechWarrior," Powers agreed. "And he helped me create the list to begin with, so let's concentrate on more important details."

Raul's head swam with important details, not the least of which was his quick rise in importance among the Achernar militia. If only his father had lived to see this. If only Jessica understood. He shook his head lightly, trying to clear the wayward thoughts. "Such as?" he asked, looking for guidance.

"Such as preparing ourselves against the best Star Colonel Torrent can throw at us." Powers leaned in closer, dropping his voice for Raul alone. "Make no mistake, Raul, this is one battle that Torrent is going to take very personally." He pulled back, and gave Raul a heartening smile. "Now how about those files?"

"Yes, sir," he said, forcing some cheer into his voice for the sake of those soldiers around him. Raul knew that he didn't fool Powers for a moment. The Knight's sharp eyes cut through any cloak of pretense. What was more disconcerting, however, was the fact that Powers was obviously quite busy maintaining his own pretenses with Raul.

And *that* was a sobering thought for Raul to take with him as he fought his way free of the room.

14

The Show

Sonora Plateau
Achernar
4 March 3133

Achernar's sun hid behind a thick gray shroud. Sharp, westerly gusts pushed around a few heavier, lower thunderheads, swirled dust up off the Sonora Plateau, and tugged at Raul's dark curls as the MechWarrior jogged a short distance from the mobile command vehicle to The Republic's ad-hoc staging grounds.

Kyle Powers stood in conference with Tassa Kay and Colonel Blaire at the foot of his *Jupiter*. He wore the same stripped-down uniform as Raul—combat boots and shorts, a cooling vest worn over a light T-shirt—ready for the heat of a BattleMech cockpit. As in the briefing rooms and command centers, the Sphere Knight drew the eye, focusing himself at the center of all around him. It was the confident set of his shoulders, and his encouraging gaze. It was the way he seemed simply to exude a stronger physical presence.

Powers glanced over, as if feeling Raul's gaze on him, then nodded once, decisively, and continued his conversation.

Swinging a wide berth around the assembled news reporters, Raul also veered away from the other officers, looking for a moment alone. He couldn't help being pulled toward the impressive *Jupiter,* though. Thirteen meters tall and weighing one hundred tons, the titan easily overshadowed his nearby *Legionnaire.* Raul saw the 'Mech's origins as a Clan design in the narrow, turret-style waist and the modular-looking weapon ports. Heavy LRM racks at each shoulder, two PPCs riding low on either side of the slender cockpit canopy and a quad of fifty millimeter autocannons mounted in pairs on the lower arm, the *Jupiter* could deliver 'Mech-shredding damage at long or short ranges. For some reason, Kyle Powers had not painted the BattleMech in standard camouflage, instead opting for bands of tans, yellows and faded reds with one great red spot swirling in a storm over the *Jupiter*'s left chest. Unconventional, but not wholly inappropriate for the plateau's high-desert terrain.

It possessed a commanding presence, much like its master.

"So what do you think of *Jove*?" Powers asked, stepping over to Raul's side.

"Magnificent," was all that Raul could think to say at first. "I'm surprised that Star Colonel Torrent didn't balk at facing you in his *Tundra Wolf.*" He gazed across the plateau, toward the Steel Wolves who readied themselves for the challenge. At four kilometers, only the bulky outline of Torrent's *Tundra Wolf* was clearly distinguished. The other silhouettes belonged to a pair of converted IndustrialMechs, Raul knew, and a low-profile Marksman.

Powers followed Raul's gaze across the plateau. "That's one of several reasons why we are fighting in combined-arms lance strength. The star colonel made up the difference in armor and infantry. Make no mistake, Raul, Torrent is out for blood. This battle is everything he wants."

"If he wants it, then why should we give it to him?"

"First and foremost, it's something the people of Achernar can *see*." Powers nodded toward a line of journalists and camera-toting news hounds, held back behind a rope barricade and by several sentries in Purifier battle armor. During the actual challenge, a select few would be allowed to board noncombatant VTOLs for shooting live footage.

"Until now, Legate Stempres has allowed them to get by on rumor and second-hand reports. Now we're getting news from Ronel, and the Steel Wolf forces landing there. They need to know that we are doing all that we can. They need hope, and we can provide it."

"Unless we lose," Raul said, only half in jest. It fell very flat.

Fortunately, Tassa was there to pick it up and dust it back off. "You won't," she said, joining the pair. "You can't. This is what it is all about, Raul." She surveyed the open plateau, a hint of excitement shining in emerald eyes. "A call to arms. Trial by combat."

"That's the Steel Wolf position. Now we need to convince them that they didn't bring enough to do the job right." Kyle Powers nodded to both of them and traded grips with Raul, each of them clasping the other's wrist. "Strength and honor," he offered a Knight's salute. Turning for his *Jupiter,* Powers eschewed a nearby hoist and used the roll-down chain link ladder to ascend to his cockpit.

"You know," Raul said, watching the Knight climb and then salute the cameras before ducking through an access hatch, "you really don't appreciate the weight behind the term 'civic obligation' until it comes rolling over you like a Behemoth."

"Why let it worry you? Today is about battle and victory. What else matters to a MechWarrior?"

A very good question, and one Raul had been attempting to answer for himself for two days. At first, being chosen over Captain Diago and Tassa to fight alongside Kyle Powers in the challenge, what Star Colonel Torrent called a Trial of Grievance, had felt like an award of validation to Raul. He had arrived. Then the young MechWarrior had recognized the false sense of superiority for exactly what it was—no different than being chosen first for dodge ball in the third grade or making varsity on the swim team in college. His ego out of the way, Raul was left shouldering only the obligation for holding up his end of the coming battle. What else mattered?

"Responsibility?" he finally offered. "Why else do we fight, except for the hope of not fighting in the future?"

Tassa shrugged. "Some people might say that the glory of battle is its own reason for being."

He stared at her, shook his head. "Torrent might. And maybe you would, Tassa. But that's not me." He laughed, at himself more than her. "Sometimes I wonder if we have anything in common."

Tassa grinned, reached out to grab Raul under his chin. "And again I ask, why let it worry you?" Then she pulled him in, planting a firm and lasting kiss on Raul's mouth.

Despite the attraction and the flashes of heat that had passed between them, Raul was caught completely off his guard. So much so that it took a moment for his brain to catch up, only to realize that he had wrapped a hand around the back of Tassa's head, pulling her in stronger, tasting her. The MechWarrior did not melt away before him, holding her own, challenging. He broke away first, though reluctantly. A sharp intake of breath nearly drowned him in her lavender scent.

"Luck," she said in a husky whisper.

"Funny." Raul shook his head lightly. "I wouldn't have thought that you believe in luck."

"A little good luck never hurt anyone. Neither did a morale boost." She made a show of looking coy. "So, are you boosted?"

Tassa's grin was infectious, spreading from her mouth to his. "The Wolves aren't going to know what hit them," he said, then turned away for his nearby *Legionnaire,* securing the last word for once.

He felt the hot caress of Tassa's gaze follow him as he walked around to the side of his BattleMech's foot and took hold of the chain link ladder. Remembering Kyle

Powers' ascension Raul swarmed up the ladder to his access hatch, and then threw a jaunty salute back toward the waiting cameras and a second one to Tassa. Fifty meters away, a pair of JES tactical carriers fired up their lift fans, blowing out twin halos of dust and debris. A Saxon personnel carrier also fired up as a squad of Purifiers finished loading, the APC and infantry filling out the Republic's augmented "lance."

A warm raindrop splashed Raul's ear and he glanced up into the heavy skies just in time to catch another pregnant drop against his face. Licking the gritty taste of desert rainfall from his upper lip, he ducked inside his cockpit before the skies truly opened up. Local storms, like Achernar's usual heat, were often severe.

Settling into his command couch, Raul fastened himself into the five-point harness and then reached up to a shelf to draw down his neurohelmet. He pulled it over his head, shifted it about to make certain the sensors made decent contact with his scalp. A coil of metal braided hose and another cord of flexible nylon sat between his feet. Raul threaded the metal-braided hose into a restraining ring on the hem of his coolant vest, then snapped the lock-tite fastener into the vest plug. The initial coolant charge jolted him, standing gooseflesh out on his bared arms and legs. He shivered, then set about fastening the nylon cord with its socket plug into some velcro straps on the vest front, finally threading it up to connect into the chin of his helmet.

The neural connection complete, Raul released the dampening field on his *Legionnaire's* fusion engine and fired the massive furnace to life. Up through the cockpit deckplates came the massive thrum of barely-controlled power, massaging his lower legs with radiated warmth and subsonic vibrations. The *Legionnaire's* computer brain ran through several systems checks on an auxiliary screen, returning all-green indicators and a final prompt for MechWarrior identification.

"Raul Ortega," he identified himself. "Captain, Republic Standing Guard."

"Identity confirmed." The computer's synthesized voice was only slightly more feminine than masculine, devoid of any real inflection or feeling. Just enough, Raul guessed, to make a MechWarrior feel comfortable with the disembodied voice without paying it too much attention. "Proceed to secondary security protocol."

Because voiceprints could be faked, and there was a very real threat in having a BattleMech captured and put back into service against you, security systems used a second line of defense that stopped all but the best-trained code breakers from making the attempt. A simple quotation, created by and known only to the Mech-Warrior, which would be checked for accuracy using voiceprint and neural wave patterns. A personal key.

Raul looked out through his cockpit's ferroglass, past the streaks of broken rain that trickled down the transparent shield to the now-animated *Jupiter* which moved to take its place at the head of the Republic formation. "To be all that we are," he dredged up his quotation from an ancient Terran author, "to become all that we are capable of becoming, is the only end of life."

"Lockouts released," the computer responded. "*Legionnaire* is now weapons-able."

And with a live BattleMech at his command, and the memory of Tassa's lips still warm on his mouth, Raul was finally ready for battle.

He hoped.

15

Trials and Grievances

Sonora Plateau
Achernar
10 May 3133

A hard deluge hammered down as if weapons fire had opened mortal wounds in the skies over Achernar's Sonora Plateau. Fat water drops carrying desert grit splashed against the *Tundra Wolf*'s ferroglass shield, pushed into horizontal bands by sharp, gusting winds, smearing the landscape into a gray watercolor. Sight was hardly an issue, though, as target-lock warnings screamed for Torrent's attention, giving the star colonel a scant three seconds' warning before a new rain of warheads fell over and around him. Blossoms of fire tore into the armor mantle protecting his right shoulder and gouged new craters over the 'Mech's left leg. Geysers of smoke and earth erupted down a line right in front of the seventy-five-ton *Tundra Wolf*, throwing up blackened, smoking dirt that pattered down against his cockpit's ferroglass, mixed with streaks of actual rain and clotted against the shield.

Torrent sidestepped his *Tundra Wolf* several meters to the left, anticipating the follow-up. A single, coruscating particle beam blasted through the gray downpour but passed wide to the BattleMech's right. One PPC less than the *Jupiter* could have—should have—used.

Light damage and a defensive enemy posture. That was Torrent's immediate assessment.

Still, he throttled back, wary of the *Jupiter*'s long reach and not quite ready to commit to a full press. His extended-range laser stabbed blood-red energy into the assault 'Mech's side, carving a deep, angry wound into its armor. The whistling screams of hard-burning propellant slashed by his left ear as the *Tundra Wolf*'s shoulder-mounted launcher spread a score of missiles into the air. His computer counted better than half of the missiles peppering the *Jupiter*'s lower legs.

It wasn't enough to goad Kyle Powers into a premature advance, though. Trusting to his assault machine's impressive armor, the Sphere Knight ignored Torrent's assault to turn his weapons against a second Steel Wolf, inviting return fire from both warriors.

Torrent grinned at the implied insult—that he was not worth the Knight-Errant's full attention. Grinned, and continued to orchestrate an envelopment.

His *Tundra Wolf* held the center of the Steel Wolf line. Of course. Early on in the shaping battle, just after his Elemental infantry lost their Maxim heavy transport vehicle to the *Jupiter*'s PPCs, Torrent had swung two AgroMech conversions, each modified with medium-grade autocannons, wide to the left and right. Now they were almost on the direct flanks of the *Jupiter* and *Legionnaire,* waiting for his orders. He had kept the M1 Marksman tank and his surviving Elementals in close, putting them on his *Tundra Wolf* in vanguard positions. Once his AgroMechs tore into the Republic flanks, his abbreviated unit would be the jaws snapping for their neck.

Kyle Powers seemed to invite the encircling maneuver. He kept the much-faster *Legionnaire* pacing alongside his *Jupiter,* and never too far away. The two Republic 'Mechs protected a Saxon hover transport, which waited in their immediate backfield, while both JES hovercraft carriers ran a picket line out front, daring any Steel Wolf to close on against their short-ranged missile barrage.

Torrent would dare, but he would do it on his own terms.

One of the *Jessies* limped along on damaged lift fans, the result of an earlier run-in with an AgroMech conversion. It was the key to Torrent's plan. He opened up a channel to his Marksman, identified the JES carrier as its primary target, and then traded another salvo with Powers' *Jupiter*.

Again the Knight-Errant divided his fire, spending new flights of LRMs and a single PPC on Torrent while he used his second PPC and half of his ultra-ACs to back off the advancing left-flank AgroMech. The Steel Wolf pilot did not return fire, under strict orders to leave the Knight to Torrent. Instead, the AgroMech's autocannon hammered fifty-mil slugs into one of the tactical carriers, chasing after as the hovercraft spun and dodged back for the right side of the field.

With calm deliberation, Torrent opened an all-hands channel. "Begin," was his only command.

Like hunting dogs cut loose from their leash, the Agro-Mechs vaulted forward on huge strides, coming in with autocannons belting out long swatches of destructive power. Catching the SRM-toting JES carriers in a blistering crossfire the wounded hovercraft stuttered and paused, losing armor and precious time.

It was all the Marksman needed.

Packing a Lord's Thunder gauss rifle, the M1 turned its rail gun against the damaged JES. A one hundred kilogram nickel-ferrous mass slammed through the air with enough kinetic force to shatter rain into bands of spreading steam. The gauss slug smashed into the hovercraft's turret. Impact peeled back the turret like an opened can, ruining one of the launchers and exposing the crew quarters.

A second salvo accelerated a new mass into the lift skirt, punching through to shatter vanes and drive gears. The front edge of the carrier caught the sloppy ground and flipped the vehicle up into a spread of medium-range missiles. Several warheads speared through the damaged turret, erupting deep within the carrier. Raw destructive force bulged the sides of the vehicle outward, erupting through seams, ports and panels to eviscerate the hovercraft. It twisted and rolled across the ground, digging up large globs of mud and earth and flinging them like dark blood spurting from an opened artery.

Star Colonel Torrent slammed forward his throttle, pushing his *Tundra Wolf* past its usual best running speed of sixty-five kilometers per hour. Geared with myomer accelerated signal circuitry, the MASC-equipped machine was capable of short sprints nearer to eight-five. The storm-ruined plateau made such speeds dangerous, but Torrent never doubted his own ability to control the BattleMech as he pushed past his Elementals and the M1 for a head-to-head match with Kyle Powers.

The Knight certainly didn't miss Torrent's charge, though standing true to form Powers again divided his attention between Torrent and the charging AgroMech. Torrent doubted that it would have mattered even if Powers had known—or guessed—that the AgroMech pilots were under strict orders to leave the *Jupiter* alone. The *Jupiter*'s dark silhouette moved to put itself in between the AgroMech and the surviving JES carrier, ready to bear the brunt of the offensive and protect the lives of men under Powers' command.

What Torrent had predicted, and counted on.

The *Tundra Wolf* was an impressive design, especially at seventy-five tons. But Torrent had known from the start that it would all come down to closing with the *Jupiter* at point-blank range if he were to have a real chance of bringing down the Sphere Knight.

A PPC blasted away armor from over his BattleMech's chest, splattering molten composite to the wet desert floor where the bright embers quickly congealed into black-crusted, steaming puddles. Warheads threw a risky stutter into his pace, and a single missile clipped the side of his cockpit shield, scarring a long, deep fracture into the ferroglass.

Torrent kept his attention divided between his HUD and the gray-scale picture resolving itself on the other side of his mud-streaked shield. The *Legionnaire* and remaining JES carrier had stopped one of his AgroMech's cold, holding it off with blistering counterfire. The Republic's Saxon APC burst forward as well, thrown into the fray on the side of the smaller of the two BattleMechs. Torrent ordered his M1 in to assist the besieged AgroMech. It looked more and more like Kyle Powers was ready to accept the duel of single combat. Warrior to warrior, the way it was meant to be.

Except that Kyle Powers turned away.

He actually turned his *Jupiter* aside, ignoring Torrent's charge and putting up a blistering wall of particle beams and missile barrages against the AgroMech.

A warm flush of anger heated Torrent's brow as he pulled into a full barrage of every weapon at his disposal. Lasers flashed with ruby brightness in the gray rains, a few sparks scattering off into brilliant prisms. The LRM rack dumped out another score of warheads even as he dialed his right-arm advanced tactical missile system down to short range and let go with it and his four-pack of SRMs as well. The salvo chewed and blasted into the *Jupiter*'s armor, demanding Kyle Powers' attention.

For a moment, Torrent thought that he had gained it. The *Jupiter* half turned in his direction, and cut loose with a bright PPC beam that flashed past him on the left-hand side. He considered it a hasty shot and braced for the follow-up. Then he counted one less Elemental on his HUD. The report of the PPC's effective blast was radioed in to him over his channel to the armored infantry even as Powers turned back to the AgroMech, pummeling it to a broken standstill.

Torrent might be victorious or he might be defeated—it was all part and parcel to a MechWarrior's life—but he would not be ignored! The AgroMech stumbled, falling to its knees and digging its threshing blades into the ground for support. The star colonel charged forward, closing rapidly with the *Jupiter* and running his heat quickly into the red band as he fired again, and again.

Now Kyle Powers turned. And he blasted Torrent with everything the *Jupiter* had left. Two particle cannon arced brilliant scourges between the two machines, flaying away armor and rocking the *Tundra Wolf* back on its heels. Four ultra-class autocannons spat out long tongues of fire and longer streams of depleted-uranium slugs. Armor flew off in shards and splinters. And behind all this damage, missiles corkscrewed in to blossom two-dozen destructive fireballs that lifted the *Tundra Wolf* up and set it back several meters.

Hunching forward, throwing every bit of his equilibrium into fighting gravity, Torrent kept the *Tundra Wolf* on its feet by sheer force of will. Waves of heat slammed into him with almost physical force, and his vision swam with heat stress and the blurred ferroglass shield.

His wireframe schematic showed better than sixty percent armor loss, and the telltales on two medium lasers and one of his missile racks lit up to signify that they had been destroyed. He didn't need to see a readout on his engine—he could tell from the rising temperature levels that Powers had cracked the reactor's physical shielding.

Damning his heat curve, Torrent wrestled his 'Mech to a full-front profile, biting and clawing with every weapon left to him. There was no planning now, no grand strategy. His simple counterattack was brutal and effective. Lasers cut deeply into the *Jupiter*'s leg. His Streak Missile Rack misfired, holding back the four short-range warheads, but his ATMS locked on and managed to spend more crippling damage into an already-ruined knee joint.

The *Jupiter*'s right knee actuator crushed in on itself, staggering the mighty titan. It fell to one knee as if bending down in supplication. But rather than shove back, Powers threw his arms out wide and divided his weapons again. In what Torrent might have considered a spectacular display of targeting any other time—any other time when the tactic wasn't insulting *him*—the Knight-Errant scoured away more of the *Tundra Wolf*'s armor with PPCs, gutted the engine on the rising AgroMech with his left arm autocannon, and even managed to score double-wounds against the advancing M1 Marksman with his right arm ACs.

The martyr son-of-a-Blakist was still taking on all-comers.

Grinding his teeth together, Torrent rocked his throttles forward and advanced. Drawing his targeting cross-hairs in a line across the *Jupiter's* shoulders, he counted his thundering heartbeats until the reticle burned the flashed a golden tone of targeting lock and then waited a second more until he could steady the shot with a confident touch on the controls.

He would show the Knight-Errant's foolishness in disregarding Torrent as a worthy adversary. Steel Wolf or Republic Knight. One of them would die trying.

Raul Ortega caught on to the Knight-Errant's plan from the start. By keeping Raul's *Legionnaire* in close, and always dividing his fire, he acted as a lodestone, drawing Torrent in and making certain the Steel Wolf remained focused exclusively on the *Jupiter* even while Powers was free to whittle away at the enemy defenses.

Long-range jousting caught the enemy Maxim APC in a series of devastating scourges, left it dead or dying far in the Steel Wolf backfield. The AC-toting AgroMechs were a threat, flanking the tight Republic force, but Powers let them come, always adding a brace of missiles here, or a scouring pull from his autocannons there. Waiting. Waiting for Torrent to make his move.

And then he unleashed hell.

Too late. Raul knew it, and was certain that Powers had known it even beforehand. Powers had warned Raul, after all, that Torrent was out for blood. If the fire-gutted *Jessie* wasn't proof of that, the star colonel's pincer-charge confirmed it.

Raul bit back any further warnings, inhaled deeply against the steel-band grip around his chest, and worked his rotary autocannon in a series of long and short pulls to hammer one of the AgroMechs into submission. The surviving hovercraft missile carrier had slid around behind the Torrent's Marksman, threatening its slightly weaker rear armor and trying to pull it away while their Saxon APC dropped Purifier infantry in a skirmish line around the AgroMech.

He was looking away when Kyle Powers' *Jupiter* stumbled to one knee.

He turned back in time to watch Sir Kyle Powers die.

Not two hundred meters distant through the gray downpour, Star Colonel Torrent's *Tundra Wolf* towered over the kneeling outline of Kyle Powers' *Jupiter*. Raul watched as the Knight Errant divided his fire in three directions, a stunning display of BattleMech command but dangerous—so dangerous—point blank with the *Tundra Wolf*. Raul pulled back around his own weapons, coming to Powers's aid despite the Knight's earlier orders. His *Legionnaire* swiveled at the waist. His right-arm laser had barely acquired targeting lock when Torrent proved just how deadly he could be. Even at a distance and through the curtains of rain, Raul saw the glowing wound of a laser-cut slicing from the *Jupiter*'s chest up into—and through—the ferroglass canopy . . . which was all that stood between a MechWarrior and a closed-casket service.

Raul knew a moment of hope—a moment of denial—when the *Jupiter* shifted as if adjusting its weight to stand back up. A trick of the rain. The great machine twisted around on its knee, showing him the horrible, red-wealed scar that now ruined the cockpit. Then it pitched forward and slammed facedown into the desert mud. He knew that Powers was dead. Knew it in the same way he felt the Sphere Knight enter a room—

down in his gut. This time it was a hollow feeling, the loss of something Raul had come to rely on in recent days. The sinking sensation as he realized that the entire battle—the expectations of a watching planet—had just settled on his own shoulders.

"Down! *Jove* is down!" A frantic call from the JES carrier's crew shook Raul from his stunned lethargy. "Captain . . . Captain Ortega, we've lost Sir Powers."

They had. But Raul would not let them lose Achernar in the same battle.

Before he had even considered a proper tactical response, the MechWarrior pulled into his primary triggers. Medium lasers stabbed ruby knives into the *Tundra Wolf*'s side while his overhead rotary spent a long, lethal stream of fifty-mil slugs hammering into the *Tundra Wolf*. The autocannon roared out hundreds of rounds. Two hundred. Three. Four, five, six . . .

And jammed. Pressed too hard too fast, the spinning barrels locked up with a grinding screech of metal against metal.

Stupid, stupid, stupid. Raul cursed himself silently as the *Tundra Wolf* shook off his desperate attack and swiveled around to come at him over the ruined *Jupiter*. The BattleMech stalked forward like a predator in search of prey, slow and with malicious intent. Its large laser sliced in at Raul's *Legionnaire*, splashing armor off of his right arm. An earth-shaking spread of fifteen separate missiles pummeled Raul's 'Mech and the surrounding desert floor. Two individual warheads slammed in on either side of his cockpit, like a one-two punch, shaking Raul against his harness and leaving behind the taste of blood from a bitten lip.

To add injury to Raul's insult, the AgroMech opened up behind him to drill through his back armor. He stumbled forward, recovering just in time to save himself from a three-story drop to the desert floor.

Reactor alarms spoke their general discontent into the cacophony of sirens and audio alerts as the stream of hot metal chipped away at the engine's physical shielding.

Failsafes threatened to dump a dampening field over the fusion chamber, but Raul slapped at the override to keep his 'Mech up and fighting. He turned to present fresh armor against the converted AgroMech, and worked to clear his jammed weapon.

"Purifiers, get control of that Agro. *Jessie-one,* worry the *Wolf.*"

Throwing a hovercraft against the *Tundra Wolf* would not have been Raul's first choice, but he had to buy himself a few critical seconds. He worked the ammunition dump on the autocannon, clearing the jammed breach. Status lights blinked from red back to green as he stood up under another withering assault, again from both sides as the remaining AgroMech and the *Tundra Wolf* worked him over with autocannon and missiles.

Then the AgroMech went down with half a dozen Purifier battlesuits clinging to its back, ripping through armor and engine, and the tactical carrier launched a full spread of short-range missiles into the *Tundra Wolf*'s face.

They bought Raul the extra few seconds he needed to set his feet firmly beneath him, pulling his targeting crosshairs over the *Tundra Wolf*'s blocky outline.

Short pull. Long pull. This time Raul varied the way he ate into his ammunition reserves, careful of the weapon's needs. When he needed to rest the rotary, he chopped at the tall BattleMech with his trio of lasers. Between the damaged shielding and his nonstop fire, temperatures in the cockpit climbed slowly but steadily through the yellow band and into the red. And all the while Star Colonel Torrent worked him over with more missiles, and more. A pair of medium lasers. Missiles . . .

Torrent had lost his large laser!

The realization slapped Raul back into a semblance of coherent thought. He had not been weighing his chances, or worrying about what the best strategic opportunity might be. In those first moments after the fall of Sir Powers, all Raul could think of were Tassa's earlier words. They wouldn't fail. They couldn't. He understood her better now. Kyle Powers had drawn a line in the sand—right here. And right here was where Raul had unconsciously decided to hold that line until he broke under Torrent's guns.

But now he glanced more frequently between his targeting and a readout on the star colonel's 'Mech. One of his autocannon salvoes had crippled the laser, and both shoulder launchers looked to be off-line as well. Also, Kyle Powers had done a number on the *Tundra Wolf*'s armor before falling to its weapons. Raul counted three deep rents in the upper chest, one of them glowing with the golden hue of the BattleMech's internal fires.

The *Legionnaire* stood up under all the abuse Torrent could give it. Another glancing blow to the cockpit. Left arm chewed down to a twisted, skeletal stump, right leg fused into little better than a BattleMech peg leg. Sweat poured down his face, stinging at the corners of his eyes, his lips. Every gasp for breath pulled hot coals down into his lungs. He outlasted the *Jessie* as it finally grounded out after a series of hammering gauss slugs from the M1 Marksman. He ordered his own Purifiers after the tank, intent on capturing it for the Standing Guard, but never once took his eyes off the rock-steady *Wolf*. The desert shook with natural thunder, and the rain beat down hard enough to drum a deafening roll over his head and shoulders. The *Legionnaire*'s ruined right leg trembled beneath Raul, threatening to give out at any second, but he held his BattleMech up, squinted through the pouring rainfall, spat out another set of ruby darts and then lashed out again with an extra-long pull from his autocannon. If Torrent wanted him, he'd have to be willing to trade 'Mechs. Maybe trade lives. It was a decision Raul was ready to make.

Star Colonel Torrent, apparently, was not.

The *Tundra Wolf* took an actual step backward, then another. Then, with a violent lurch that seemed able to convey the star colonel's anger as well as his frustration, the seventy-five-ton BattleMech showed Raul its back, high-stepping over the *Jupiter*'s stilled legs and then kicking in with its MASC equipment to put immediate distance between the two MechWarriors.

His finger already crimped around the trigger, pulling it back into the control stick grip, Raul hammered another several hundred rounds into the back of the *Tundra Wolf,* but against fresh armor there was no real chance to harm it. The M1 Marksman drove in between the two, guarding the star colonel's flank. Raul called off the infantry, ready to save lives now that Torrent had bowed out of the challenge.

Now that Kyle Powers and at least one armor crew had already paid the highest price for the Republic's pyrrhic victory.

"Raul? Hey, Ortega!" Tassa's voice, filled with a healthy amount of respect and enthusiasm. "You did it. Do not ask me how, but you actually backed off Star Colonel Torrent."

Breathing shallow, trying to pull oxygen out of the cockpit's reactor-baked air, Raul slumped back into his chair and let the automatic safeguards shut down his reactor. Panel lights died, leaving him one red-tinted backup and the rain-dampened gray which filtered through his ferroglass shield. Drenched in sweat, utterly spent, his arm felt like dead weight as he tied his comms system into the battery reserves.

"Torrent got what he wanted," he said, voice cracking. Raul swallowed dryly, tasting blood from his bitten lip. "I just denied him the trophy." And ran the cost up on the Steel Wolf commander as well, with one converted WorkMech destroyed and another captured.

"Take the victories you can get, Raul. There is not much more to a MechWarrior's life."

Raul nodded to the darkened cockpit, his neurohelmet pressing down with insufferable weight against his shoulders. Kyle Powers had put a similarly low price on his own life with the way he had fought the battle, and Raul couldn't help but believe that the Republic had lost more than it gained this day.

"But there should be, Tassa." He stared out into the rain. "There should be."

16

Spectators

Rain continued to pound the River's Run Flatlands just as it had hammered through the Taibek foothills and Agave Dales. Sand-choked rivulets streaked the ferro-glass shield of Erik's *Hatchetman*. Desert wash flooded the old river course that raged along as if the river had never been diverted to better serve the city of River's End.

"Something coming through, Lord Sandoval." Michael Eus had commandeered a spot inside the heavily armored mobile HQ vehicle. His voice cracked on Erik's title. It might have been the static of transmission. "Erik . . . sir! Knight-Errant Powers has fallen. Patching through the trans—"

One of the HQ techs cut Eus off, splicing the intercepted transmission onto Erik's command frequency. A Republic soldier reported back to base, informing Colonel Blaire that Kyle Powers had been gravely injured—possibly killed—in battle. A tingling chill walked up Erik's spine. Listening to those reports of the challenge battle's final moments, he pulled his *Hatchetman* out of

A CALL TO ARMS 181

the column line and stomped it up to the crest of a small, mud-slick rise. A deep roll of thunder cheered the Republic. Rain applauded against the elongated head of Erik's BattleMech for the assembled Swordsworn force.

A half dozen converted MiningMechs continued their dedicated march alongside the old riverbed, rolling along on tank-tread feet. A Behemoth, two Condors and a squad of four Jousts followed, leading a double-wide column of command and support vehicles. Nearer to the column's rear the mobile HQ pulled out of line as well, leaving its place next to a MIT 23 M.A.S.H. unit, grinding to a halt in between Erik and his tail-end military force. Ranger scout vehicles mixed in among infantry carriers. A squad of veteran Demons rolled along, unconcerned, while JES carriers wove in and around the back of the column as if eager to move up when called.

Everything he could muster in a timely fashion when Michael Eus brought his uncle's orders to him.

Enough to hold River's End. He hoped.

"More time," Erik whispered to himself. Another week of attrition among Republic forces would have helped. Two would have been better.

"Excuse me, sir?"

"Nothing, Michael." Erik scolded himself for forgetting the voice-activated mic. "I was worried about the time. The river is forcing us into a long detour." Not exactly true. Even without the flashflooded watercourse, Erik had planned to swing far around the militia-controlled base to come at River's End from the east.

"Estimated time of arrival is still holding at fifteen hundred hours. I can pass along an order to increase our pace."

Erik bristled, feeling his anger rising in the warm flush that spread along the nape of his neck. "I can give my own orders when I am ready to, Michael. Continue to monitor the Republic military bands."

"Yes, Lord Sandoval." Michael was properly respectful, even though he paused before answering.

Well, what should Erik expect from a man who had

stepped forward as his uncle's soldier, bought and paid for? Michael Eus had brought the Duke's orders to Erik personally, a coded verifax commanding that all Swordsworn forces move against the Steel Wolves at once or otherwise confound Star Colonel Torrent's plans so that Kal Radick's faction could not send more support to Ronel.

"Keep them tied down on Achernar."

That had been Aaron Sandoval's order. Standing in full regalia, no doubt about to attend a highly visible—as highly visible as one could get without HPG service—function as Lord Governor, the Swordsworn's leader nodded imperiously. No questions clouded those bright, cerulean eyes. This man was the master of all he surveyed.

"Do not allow Torrent to withdraw for Ronel, Erik. Do not allow him to seize control of the local HPG station. Kal Radick *does* have a working, JumpShip-based hyperpulse generator. If we allow him to establish the spine of a communications network, our Swordsworn will be hard pressed to resist him. Listen to Michael Eus. He has been my eyes and ears—and occasionally my hands—on Achernar since before your arrival there. He will have suggestions."

And Erik had been cautious of Eus being suborned by Legate Brion Stempres.

"Have you been in touch with our friends inside River's End?" Erik asked over his private channel to Eus. Reports from the Sonora Plateau had trailed off, confirming that Kyle Powers had indeed been killed in combat. Martyring himself, by all indications. "Our reception is readied?"

Michael's voice bled confidence through the transmission. "News agencies friendly to your uncle's—to *your* agenda are on hand to put a positive spin on our arrival. Industrial areas owned by Taibek Mining, Steyger Railways, and the Fronc Granaries are cleared. Together they form a defendable staging area and can house all equipment inside warehouses. Logistical support in food and ground services has been put into place."

Which, when all added together, would give Erik a fair base of operations on the outskirts of River's End, in between the city proper and the militia's outlying command post. It might even buy him a measure of goodwill among the populace. Good PR never hurt.

But he would still have preferred another week.

Throttling his *Hatchetman* into a forward walk again, pacing the column at fifty meters, Erik shoved the thought aside and tried not to let his uncle's interference worry him. Even such surprises as Michael Eus's perfidy were to be expected in the long-reaching game the Sandovals played, though it was hard not to feel slighted, in at least some sense. Duke Aaron Sandoval was not here, not in person, and Erik was. That counted for something more than a title. Erik should not—and would not—be made to feel the part of a spectator. No. He remained on the board and in play.

A knight. At worst, a pawn. That idea appealed to him at some remote level, and Erik felt an upward tug at the corner of his mouth. A pawn in Caesar's game.

And pawns that survived to the final rank became powerful pieces indeed.

River's End
Achernar

Jessica Searcy bit down on her lower lip. Not hard enough to draw blood. Just enough for the pain to reign in her emotions.

Heavy, golden curtains drawn across her living room windows filtered Achernar's already gray day down to gloomy twilight. She sat on the couch, feet pulled up beneath her, trivid remote balanced on one leg. Her left thumb rested down against the memory timer. A mug of forgotten coffee cooled on the end table as she pressed

in, backing up the once-live holo footage, eased back for
a moment, then brushed the feathertouch sensor once
more so that the entire scene played out again, and again,
as she watched with dry, aching eyes.

Watched Raul Ortega kiss another woman.

Jessica had it memorized. She wasn't even certain anymore what she looked for in the trivid's memory buffer.
She caught Raul's slight recoil over something said or
gestured. Then the red-haired woman grabbed the front
of his MechWarrior togs and pulled him in to plant a
hard kiss on his mouth. That was hard enough on her.
But it was Raul's hand coming up, cupping the back of
her head with desperate need, that stabbed a shard of
ice into her heart every time.

He broke it off, finally, but with no obvious look of
regret or shame. Words passed between the two, tram-
pled by a news anchor's voice that Jessica had long since
muted. She didn't need anyone else's imagination filling
in the blanks. She didn't need to see again Raul's half-
amused smile, the determination behind his dark, dark
eyes. Didn't need it. Not at all.

Biting down harder, Jessica backed the footage up
again.

17

New Deal

Night's chill grasp clutched at the morning, unwilling to let go even as the northeastern skies brightened to a pale rose. Raul Ortega glanced around at the few dozen ranks of soldiers and civilian contractors—reserves mixed in among standing guard, logistics among infantry and tank crewmen. Only the MechWarriors and Brion Stempres stood separate, ten paces out from the nearest row, filed by rank from Legate Stempres and Colonel Blaire through to supernumerary Tassa Kay. Raul's place was in the middle, between Captains Diago and Charal DePriest.

They stood in silent reverence as lottery-chosen technicians extinguished the fusion-flame funeral pyre and removed the ashes of Knight-Errant Kyle Powers.

Raul turned back to the service and shook his head, slowly, carefully, keeping his opinions to himself. There were hardly enough warm bodies to fill one side of the parade grounds. Yet he knew that except for a skeleton watch crew in the command post, all on-base personnel had turned out for Sir Powers' funeral. Blaire had even gone so far as to secure Star Colonel Torrent's assurance that the Steel Wolves would also observe thirty minutes of respectful silence in honor of the fallen Sphere Knight. There would be no military maneuvers. No alerts.

And there still were not enough bodies to turn out a decent honor guard.

Twelve hundred and thirty-odd beating hearts. Gooseflesh prickled up Raul's arms. This was the Republic's strength on Achernar, and lucky to have it, he knew. There were worlds of The Republic that no longer knew the necessity of fielding a BattleMech, even for show. Some which no longer supported a garrison of any type, having lived for so many years under Devlin Stone's umbrella of peace and prosperity. As rents tore through the fabric, spilling drops of blood onto their soil, would those worlds be better off, or worse?

How many citizens would prefer to bow their heads to an occupying force rather than suffer as Achernar was suffering? How many residents simply did not care?

Twelve hundred and thirty-odd.

Raul wouldn't even wager money on the ultimate loyalties of everyone present. There were more Steel Wolf sympathizers, he felt certain. Two infantry squads had all but attached themselves to Tassa Kay's mixed-arms lance for no other reason than out of respect for her bondsman, Yulri. Some Swordsworn armor jocks stole an SM1 Destroyer on hearing of Erik Sandoval's occupation of River's End, running to his side as if the young noble's treachery—and Brion Stempres's legitimizing it—wasn't bad enough.

The techs finished cleaning out Kyle Powers' cremation chamber, created by two of the Knight's own technicians who had pulled the fusion engine from the crippled *Jupiter* and jury-rigged the device. They deposited his ashes in the warhead of a specially prepared missile. Colonel Blaire looked back over one shoulder. "Atten-*shun*." Uniformed soldiers clicked heels together and stood ramrod straight. Civilian contractors clasped hands in front of them in respectful homage.

Satisfied, Blaire glanced down the line of MechWarriors. "Post."

Stepping out on their right feet, the entire line of MechWarriors marched out toward a waiting *Stingray* aerospace fighter. The craft had been painted a stark, bone white for the occasion. Blaire took a position nearest the fighter, and the rest of the MechWarriors strung out in a line between the *Stingray* and the fusion incinerator. The ashes were passed to Tassa Kay with reverent slowness, who then handed them on to Charal DePriest. It passed through Raul's hands and those of Clark Diago to Colonel Blaire. The Colonel ducked beneath the *Stingray* and loaded the missile through a groundside access port.

Raul swallowed dryly, followed the Colonel as they retreated back to their original line. The fightercraft fired up its engines with a throaty roar, taxied to one end of the parade grounds and then screamed down its length. Timed perfectly, the *Stingray* leapt into the air and banked immediately into the just-rising sun, flying straight on until it was finally lost in the glare. The pilot would turn off his heading moments later, cruising south and finally firing the missile over the Sonora Plateau, scattering the ashes of Sir Kyle Powers over the battlefield on which he had died.

Colonel Blaire allowed another moment of silence. Then, without any preamble, barked out, "Dismissed!"

Raul completely agreed. What more was there to say?

Until later that evening.

The briefing room felt empty with only the four of them: Raul and Colonel Blaire on one side of the table, Brion Stempres and a man introduced as Michael Eus on the other. A pitcher of iced water sat untouched and sweating on a sideboard. The low hum of air conditioning seemed to grow in volume as the awkward silence stretched out behind Michael Eus's demands.

"You expect—" Blaire began.

"Lord Erik Sandoval-Groell expects," Eus was quick to interrupt. "I am simply here as his adjutant, Colonel."

Raul wasn't so certain. Dressed in a civilian suit and slightly stoop-shouldered, Michael Eus cultivated the look of a civilian administrator, not the kind of man who would be worth much as a military advisor, or as a hostage against Erik Sandoval's ambition. Still, he had a strength behind his gray eyes that promised something more about him than his previous position as the operations officer of Taibek Mining.

"And as Sandoval's *adjutant,*" Blaire sounded as if he wanted to substitute a less flattering title for Eus, "you will be sitting in on all command-level planning sessions and advising us on the need for support for Swordsworn operations? This sounds more like an ultimatum, Mr. Eus."

Raul agreed. And it wasn't helping that Tassa had warned him of the Swordsworn not too many days ago. The Sandoval faction hadn't been interested in the mutual protection of Achernar. They had simply been here first, before the Steel Wolves. "We are supposed to trust Erik Sandoval now? After what he has done?"

"Lord Sandoval considered it in Achernar's best interest to abandon his own financial concerns and move to protect River's End."

Colonel Blaire scoffed. "It seems that Lord Sandoval—or is it Duke Aaron Sandoval?—has something in common with Kal Radick after all. Both of them seem ready to tell us what is in Achernar's best interest, as they move to occupy our world."

"Our new position forms a second line of defense for River's End, protecting the population of the capital as well as the HPG station. It goes without saying that the station is of extreme value to The Republic. Lord Erik has shown a commitment that I should think you would admire, Colonel. He has even placed two converted MiningMechs outside the facility on a twenty-four hour guard."

"Besides which," Brion Stempres stepped into the conversation, "Erik Sandoval was named a legitimate foreign-auxiliary commander by Knight-Errant Powers. He is, in all respects and matters military, your *equal*, Colonel. The Republic recognized him as such. And," he added, "Erik is not occupying River's End in the military definition. I invited his assistance, do not forget."

"I haven't forgotten that, *Lay*-gate Stempres. Governor Haider also called me this morning, to express her confidence in your decision."

With two 'Mech conversions leveling weapons at the HPG station, Achernar's tenuous link to the outside universe, Raul bet that Governor Susan Haider had little choice but to back up her military counterpart.

Therein lay the entire problem. Erik Sandoval-Groell was holding the HPG—and River's End itself—hostage against the garrison's behavior. Stempres had chosen to side against the Republic, and he had enough clout to drag Achernar's top political leader along under duress. Everything was falling apart as the Republic continued to fracture into disparate factions.

It left a cold void hollowing out Raul's stomach to think about it. He couldn't sit any longer. Shoving his chair back, the MechWarrior paced the long way around the table to get some water. He poured for the Colonel first, ice clunking into the bottom of the glass, and delivered it, pointedly ignoring their *guests*. A second glass for himself, which he sipped leaning back against the sideboard. The crisp, clean water could not wash away the sour taste in his mouth.

"Colonel." Michael Eus seemed determined to keep his ambassadorial voice calm and confident. "Colonel Blaire, we simply must reach an agreement that Achernar is better protected, at the moment, with Lord Sandoval's assistance. Now, can we count on you to work with us? Or not?"

With Legate Stempres no doubt on hand to relieve Blaire in the face of any negative response, the colonel nodded reluctantly. "Achernar must come first," he agreed.

The bargain struck, Raul assumed his duties as advisor—hardly needed in the face of such overwhelming pressure—were no longer needed. "With the Colonel's permission?" he asked, abandoning his water glass and taking long strides toward the door. For the first time since his drunk with Tassa Kay, he felt the acute need for something a touch stronger than water. And were he to stay any longer, he might say something that he'd have plenty of time to regret after Stempres bounced him off active duty.

Which might not be a bad way out of this mess.

Which would only go to prove that citizens had no stronger investment in the Republic than residents.

Oh, yes. He needed something very much stronger than water.

His walk from the base command post to his BOQ room left Raul miserable as well as upset. The day's humidity had spiked over forty percent thanks to the previous days' rainstorms, and then the temperature had hit a new high of forty-two centigrade. His uniform clung to him like flypaper, bunching up around his waist and sticking to his back. Sweat beaded on his forehead and left a salty rime on his upper lip. He stomped up his front steps and unlocked the door to his dark apartment, paused near his vidphone, but then gave it up for the bottle still sitting out on his kitchenette counter. Two fingers poured into a water glass. The amber liquid swirled around in the bottom like liquid smoke.

"So did you think about calling me just a moment ago, or her?"

Raul nearly fumbled the glass, ended up grabbing it with both hands as he turned to find Jessica Searcy waiting in a dark corner, sitting on a folding chair rather than at the table or on the utilitarian couch.

"Jess! Where have you been?" Raul set his glass next to the sink. "I tried to reach you all yesterday."

Rocking up to her feet, standing almost motionless, she folded her arms and nodded. "I know. I screened your calls." She must have seen his confusion in the evening light spilling through the still-open door. "I was home, Raul. Watching the trivid. They've been running the fall of Kyle Powers on every station. Truthfully, I've been drawn more toward the preparations. You know. Choosing the support forces. Gearing up your machines. The speeches and the private words. How long have you been wanting to kiss that woman?"

Raul found the lights, switched them on even as Jessica's question reached a cold hand into his gut and twisted him up. She looked awful, hair pulled back into a simple band and eyes dark from lack of sleep. Not the polished resident from River's End General. In the aftermath of battle, Kyle Powers' death, and Erik Sandoval's move against the capital, Raul had forgotten about the video teams on hand for the challenge.

Jessica, it seemed, had been thinking of little else.

"Jess, I can't even begin to tell you how surprised I was at Tassa's move. I honestly didn't see it coming." He moved toward her, but she held up a hand to freeze him in place.

"You kissed her back."

Raul nodded. "I did." There was no denying it. He'd wanted to, and so he had.

"I thought . . ." he began, then shook his head. "It doesn't matter what I thought. And to answer your first question, I don't know. I guess I felt an attraction toward Tassa the day she arrived on Achernar, three . . . four days before the Steel Wolf assault." Raul remembered that late afternoon meeting—had it only been three weeks ago? Tassa had promised to be on Achernar *"As long as it takes."* And then the Steel Wolves followed—

Jessica took three quick steps forward and slapped him. She looked awkward doing it, unsure of herself the way she frowned at every move. Medical school and residency had never prepared her for this. She reacted woodenly, as if this was something she had simply been instructed to do from the Guide to Feminine Behavior.

Raul saw it coming, began to flinch away but then forced himself to stand there and take it. Jessica had put more force behind the blow than he expected, watching her hesitant motions. The side of his face stung warmly, and his right ear rang.

Something tickled his chin and Raul swiped at it, the back of his hand coming away with a smear of blood. He winced and a stab of pain cut at one side of his mouth. Jessica's engagement ring had cut the corner of his lower lip. He nodded, and a surreal side of his mind almost prompted him to ask her, *"So, we good?"*

He didn't.

"You embarrassed me in front of the entire planet, Raul. How do you expect me to react?"

All their arguments and fights over the last few years, and this was the first one that rang with any sense of permanence. The slap notwithstanding, Raul saw it in Jessica's haunted eyes. "However you feel you have to."

There were likely a dozen other comments he could have made that would have gone over better. He just couldn't think of them right then. Raul had a feeling that he had missed a great many such opportunities in the last few minutes—in the last few days, or even weeks. Important opportunities to make things right. To change the events which had unfolded in the wrong direction. But he couldn't go back.

Jessica proved that to him as she stripped the ring off her finger, picked up his hand and placed it in his palm, and then calmly folded his fingers over the circlet.

"Good-bye, Raul."

He stood there, watched her cross the floor and exit through the open door. The perfect end to a terrible day. Raul fought down an urge to run after her, knowing it would do no good, and instead turned back to the kitchenette and his depleted liter of Glengarry's Best. He picked up the glass and dashed its contents into the sink, wasting every drop. Before he could think better of it, he also upended the bottle and allowed it to drain. He didn't need the drink anymore. Raul had been looking for a bit of numbness.

He'd found it without the bottle.

18

Escalations

Achernar's blue-white sun tore a brilliant hole through the pale afternoon sky, flooding Highlake Basin with heat and bleaching light. Temperatures ebbed higher, past the usual tidemark of forty-two Celsius and lapping up toward forty-three. With no moisture left to the cracked-mud plains the air remained dry and baking, and puffs of dust swept up from each pounding stride Star Colonel Torrent took as he turned away from the *Stealthy Paw* and eased into the last leg of his run back to the DropShip *Lupus*.

Torrent's khaki shorts and dust-smeared tank top were damp with fresh sweat but hardly soaked through. The thirsty desert air drank in the moisture quickly. Still, his shaven scalp and his arms glistened as if painted with a diamond glaze. His lower legs were streaked with mud—desert dust mixed with sweat, drying to gray streaks along both well-muscled calves.

Unsnapping a plastic water flask from his hip, Torrent swigged its last draught without breaking his stride. It tasted stale, tinged with the sweat on his lips and the plastic taste of the flask, and completely failed to wash away the sour taste of yesterday's performance. He hooked the strap back into his belt, fastened it, and forgot it as his concentration turned back to the run and what might have been.

Kyle Powers was dead.

He knew it before any announcement was made. Torrent had watched his laser cut up over the *Jupiter*'s chest and into the thin strip of ferroglass that protected the cockpit, the ruby-bright beam punching through into flesh behind. The star colonel had to keep reminding himself of that or else lose himself in the anger of having been forced to flee. Torrent had defeated the Sphere Knight, had certainly driven a hard wedge in between the Swordsworn and Republic forces, and that had been his goal, after all. The Steel Wolves had required drastic measures and he took them. And he won. He always won.

But not one hundred percent, this time.

Not a flawless victory.

That single *Legionnaire* had held the line, battering back no matter how much Torrent's *Tundra Wolf* threw at it. Raul Ortega—according to the staffing reports, a recently promoted *reservist,* not a regular line officer at all. He should have broken with the loss of Kyle Powers. He should have quailed beneath the *Tundra Wolf*'s heavier weapons. He should have.

Instead, Ortega's threatening rotary autocannon had carved into Torrent, worrying his armor and chewing new damage into critical systems like his engine shielding and weapons. The star colonel's anger—and his pride—had encouraged him to hang in, to push forward and live gloriously or die honorably by the next few minutes. His instincts, his many years of experience, his loyalty to Kal Radick—those all told him to take his limited victory over Powers and withdraw to fight again another day, perhaps to claim Achernar despite Fetladral's misfortune and Kal Radick's shift in priorities. This time he listened to the saner voices, but it had been a close call. Muscles tight with frustration, he had levered the *Tundra Wolf* away. One step. Then another.

Torrent continued his run—one stride, then another—picking up speed as he pushed himself for the DropShip.

A stinging tear of sweat leaked past the seal of Torrent's dark goggles, burning at the corner of his eye. His vision blurred for a moment, but Torrent blinked it clear. Not that there was much to see in any case. A flat, dry basin pounded by the harsh glare of a strong sun. His dark lenses filtered out much of the painful brightness but did little to help the stark, colorless landscape. The desert looked more gray—maybe a dry dun—than the yellow he had expected. His *Lupus* commanded the horizon, but painted the stark, stellar white so common among space navy. Even the sky of this world looked washed out and lifeless to him.

But the world was not lifeless. It was an important world now, with its functioning hyperpulse generator station. So long as he had a means to pursue it, Torrent would not abandon Achernar. He would take what victories he could, build on them, and rise to greater honors than ever before.

That was what it was time to do. Build.

Pounding up the DropShip ramp and charging into the BattleMech bay, Torrent quickly dropped down into a brisk walk as he forced himself through several cooldown laps of the shaded work area. He stripped his goggles away, tucked them into his belt as well. His breathing strong but even, muscles burning with the pleasant ache of an honest workout, Torrent lapped the bay in slower circles, considering, planning. Seeing who was on hand.

"Star Captain Xera!"

The aerospace pilot stood within a small cluster of pilots and tank crewmen, looking over a grounded Scimitar and pointing out its weak spots. With her hands she had been showing attack angles, and the best way to strafe ground targets for maximum destruction. Now she snapped to attention, found Torrent, and jogged over to her commander.

"Yes, Star Colonel."

The woman had bound her blue-black hair into a ponytail, secured by a steel-spring clip. Her bright, hazel eyes missed nothing as she scanned her commander's face for any sign of displeasure.

"Your pilots. They are ready for a new mission, quiaff?"

"Aff, Star Colonel."

He would have been surprised at any other answer. But, "Even Star Commander Drake?"

"Drake has adapted, sir. He was quiet for a few days after our Circle of Equals. Then a pilot in his star questioned my orders in front of him and other witnesses. Drake took it as a challenge to his own authority, and . . . he put the pilot in the infirmary for two days." She saw the slight crease to Torrent's brow. "I chose not to bring it to your attention as it was a pilots' matter. I fully support Drake's resort to personal discipline. Sir."

Torrent hid his smile. Good. Xera would make a fine aerospace commander. "I want all aerospace forces ready in two days. They will provide escort to our DropShips."

"We are not leaving?" The thought seemed to worry Xera, as if giving up Achernar would be a blotch on her personal honor. "Have we been recalled?"

"Neg, Star Captain. The time has come to heighten our profile on Achernar. We will be moving our staging area to a more appropriate venue." Such plans had been discussed before, when the Steel Wolves first planned their assault on Achernar and, since, after every difficulty noted in staging raids over distance on this planet.

Xera remembered their secondary plans as well. "Are you thinking, perhaps, of the River's Run flatlands?"

"I was thinking River's End," Torrent said, a choice that had not been among their original plans. He noted the predator's gleam that immediately brightened up behind Xera's eyes. "Or something very, very close to it." He turned for the bay exit and a shower, leaving her behind to stew of excitement.

"Bring Star Captain Nikola Demos to my office in thirty minutes," he said, "and we will plan."

River's End
Achernar

Erik Sandoval-Groell walked around the lavish apartment that had been recently given over to him by the president of Steyger Railways, readying a few last-minute details. Music was selected, placed into the playback unit, and piped through at low volume to the dozen speakers hidden throughout the suite of rooms. He opened the wine to let it breathe. Its dry, oakwood scent perfumed the air.

The door chimes rang for attention, and at Erik's nod Michael Eus left the room to answer it and invite in Erik's guest. The nobleman heard Eus' welcome, and knew that the door shutting would be Eus on his way out, leaving the two of them alone. Such rendezvous were best handled in private.

Especially if it worked out completely to Erik's liking.

"Come in," he called, moving to the table and pouring two glasses of merlot. He heard footsteps move into the room, but did not look up until both glasses were poured full. "I hope you enjoy red," he said, placing the bottle back in its cradle and lifting a glass to his guest.

Tassa Kay accepted it with raised eyebrows and a shrugged nod.

The female MechWarrior was doubly attractive to Erik—and likely to most men, he assumed—being both a warrior and a beautiful one at that. While she tasted the wine he drank in her curled-back red hair and the arched slant to her eyebrows, green, inquisitive eyes, and her full, hard-bodied figure. Yes, this could go very well indeed.

"Not bad," Tassa said, cradling her wine glass expertly in a cupped hand. "When your man asked for a meeting between us, he did not mention that it would be a social occasion." Her smile did not quite touch her eyes. "I would have dressed more appropriately."

Erik shrugged. "I see no problem with the way you are dressed." Tassa's everyday uniform usually consisted of a leather jacket with steel buckles, worn open, jeans, and a shirt of breathable cotton. This evening she wore dark gray jodhpurs and a black, collared blouse with red buttons up the front—like the bright warning markings on a poisonous snake or spider. Her earrings dangled a few inches below her lobes, flashing red-enameled spiders. They played up wonderfully the red highlights in her dark hair. Erik shrugged out of his uniform jacket and threw it over the back of a nearby chair. Lifting his own glass, he said, "To casual comfort."

They both drank. The wine was a dry variety, tasting of blackberry and currant with the barest proper hint of charcoal. Erik breathed deep the heady fumes.

"Let's sit, shall we?" He led her over to the open-plan living room, holding out one hand to seat her at the couch but properly taking his seat across from her in a deep-plush chair.

"You are an incredible warrior," he told her. "Honestly, I doubt I've seen your like before, and I think it's safe to say that without your help, the Republic militia would not still be functioning."

"Well *that* is a lot to lay on a girl on your first date." Tassa Kay sounded amused, though she did not exactly deny Erik's compliment.

"You know it's true. That's how you managed to hold out against Colonel Blaire on that first day, knowing that he needed you and your *Ryoken*." He sipped his wine. "It is a handsome design."

Tassa's smile turned down a few watts. "Which is why you wanted to confiscate it before the arrival of the Steel Wolves?" she asked.

Careful. Erik busied himself with a long taste from the glass, feeling the light smile curling at the edges of his mouth. "I believe it was Legate Stempres who originally tried to secure your machine, and obviously with good reason. If you had been working hand-in-glove with the Steel Wolves, I doubt we'd be sharing this wonderful wine right now." A wary tightness around Tassa Kay's eyes gave her away, as if she steadied herself from revealing anything. Erik grasped for what it might be, failed, and pursued his original proposal. "In fact, given your value to the local militia, I'm surprised that you have not renegotiated your original deal with Blaire."

Tassa shrugged. "I gave my word on the matter. As, I believe, have you."

"I can appreciate that." Appreciate it, but never agree with it. "Still, if my reading of the regulations are correct, I concur with Raul Ortega's original assessment in that you could demand a bond of somewhere in between twenty-one and twenty-four million Republic bills for the continued availability of your BattleMech and your skill."

"You are very well informed about what went on inside the militia command post," Tassa said, eyes narrowed.

"I am very well informed about everything—and everyone—on this world." Erik could not sit still. He rose in a fluid motion and began to pace around his side of the room. "Everything, that is," he said then, "except you. Who are you? Where do you come from? What are you doing here?"

She shrugged. "I thought men liked a touch of mystery in their lives."

Erik laughed into his glass. "Sandovals prefer to keep the secrets, not have secrets kept from them." He sipped carefully. "Although in this case, I might be willing to live with the mystery. Especially," he said with a frank stare of interest, "if it were on my side of the line."

Stretching back into the sofa's comfortable embrace,

Tassa kicked her feet up onto the glass-topped coffee table and lounged in a more relaxed posture. "I'm listening."

Erik leaned over the back of his vacated chair, amber eyes staring unblinkingly at his guest. "Twenty-four million," he said bluntly. "In Republic Stones or in a Federated Suns account. I'll give you the deal that Colonel Blaire wouldn't—a fully bonded contract for your services on Achernar, to be used for repair or replacement as necessary. And when you leave, you can keep ten . . . twenty percent of the balance for services rendered."

Tassa considered it and Erik watched as her eyes blurred for a moment as she seemed to be looking back at something. She gazed down into the red pool swirling about in her glass. "You are very generous," she finally said, and softly, barely more than a whisper.

Erik began to pace again, circling the room now in long, slow strides. "When it's something I want, I don't haggle over the price. I think you're worth it, and I'm willing to pay."

Tassa continued to stare into her wine. "Quite the compliment. You know. For a woman like me."

"I never believed there *were* women like you, Tassa Kay." Erik stopped behind her, reached down with one hand to trace the back of one finger along the warm curve of her ear, and across her flawless cheek. He heard her sharp intake of breath, felt the slight hitching tensions. Was she choking back sobs? Erik leaned down behind her. "We could be very good for each other, you and I," he whispered.

That was when she finally started to laugh.

Not a nervous titter or an appreciative chuckle. No. Tassa threw her head back in a full-bodied, riotous laugh warm with her amusement and complete rejection. "Oh. My. You know, Erik, I thought I could hold a straight face through all of this. I really did. But it was too much."

She rocked forward, slipping out from under his touch and coming to her feet with the grace of a hunting animal. "You are completely without any sense of honor or shame, except possibly where it impacts your public-relations campaign, and you're a poor judge of character. You think you can buy me as one of your 'Yes-my-lord' people, both on and *off* the field? You are impetuous, self-centered, and, perhaps worst of all, impatient.

"Good for each other?" she scoffed, coming around the end of the couch at him. "I doubt I could trust you not to dampen your uniform the first time I whispered in your ear."

Erik had known refusal, even defeat, in the past. But never—ever—had anyone torn into him in such a manner. His ears burned with an embarrassed flush, and his fingers felt numb with a kind of distant cold.

"That was a mistake," he promised her, voice flat and dark.

Tassa looked ready to dash the rest of her wine into his face, then reconsidered, but not because she feared him. Her sorrowful glance made it clear that she wouldn't waste good wine on him. She drained off the merlot, then tossed the fragile glass over one shoulder.

"I've made others in the past," she said to the musical accompaniment of shattering crystal, "and I'll make more in the future, I'm sure. But I'd rather make mistakes than have no idea what I am doing. You don't, Erik, on or off the field." She turned for the apartment's foyer, dismissing him as easily as Erik might a servant in his uncle's home.

"Quite frankly," she said, "I have had better offers." Tassa cast a single, appraising glance back at him. "In all respects."

Achernar Militia Command Post
Achernar

The hard pounding on his BOQ door roused Raul from his silent contemplation. He had never turned on the lights after Jessica's departure, feeling more comfortable sitting alone in the dark. His room still smelled of the wasted liquor, smoky and sharp, and his face remembered the stinging slap of his ex-fiancée's hand.

Another round of knocking. It sounded like someone might be kicking the door on the other side.

He considered not answering it, considered sitting quietly in the dark until the person simply went away, but then a third, more commanding, series of poundings drew him reluctantly off the kitchen chair and around to the door. Whoever it was, they could be made to go away. Just then Raul didn't care if the Steel Wolves were at the edge of the base, ready to overrun the capital. He wasn't going out to answer an alert—he'd be of no use to anybody right now if he tried, and McDaniels wasn't going to haul him over to the O-club either. He wasn't going out, period.

He yanked open the door, and Tassa Kay stepped up to plant a long kiss over his mouth.

Like their moment on the Sonora Plateau, he didn't expect it. Unlike then, he didn't respond, and that threw a momentary hitch into her approach. Tassa stepped back, sized him up and down, and then said, "So you going to invite a girl in?"

Raul almost told her no. Then he inhaled the taste of her off his lips, and felt a spread of warmth along the back of his neck. Did he really want to sit in the dark for the rest of the night? Tassa's mercurial moods might never bring her back to his door again if he turned away now. And he wasn't up to forcing another woman to walk away on him. One had been enough.

He didn't answer her directly. Didn't need to. Raul simply shoved the door open wide and then backed to one side, allowing Tassa to slip past and into his room.

Then he kicked the door shut behind them both.

19

The Day After

Achernar Militia Command
Achernar
7 March 3133

Memories of the previous night invaded Raul's morning thoughts, teasing him awake with whispers of flesh and the promise of long, passionate kisses.

He remembered deep green pools of life swimming under his own gaze, acres of tanned skin and a few thin scars he did not remember on Jessica's body. Not blond hair hanging down into his face. Coltish red hair, long and damp. The scent of lavender soap and honest sweat, and the cool, sharp touch of a steel-bound crystal pressed against his chest.

As long as it takes . . .

Hearing the husky whisper in his mind and placing it with a face, a body, Raul opened his eyes. He stared at the ceiling of his quarters, still dim in the early morning light. An arm, draped casually across his chest, pressed down with unfamiliar weight. He turned his head far enough to find Tassa Kay, sleeping on her front, head turned toward him. Her eyes remained closed and her breathing deep and even, yet somehow Raul knew that she was awake as well. He suddenly *knew* a lot more than that.

"You're Clan," he said softly, though not quite whispering.

Tassa's eyelids rolled back like gunports opening. Bright, intelligent eyes stared back at Raul without a trace of guilt. "I did not know you could tell . . . this way."

Hearing her confirm it, Raul blinked rapidly as he cleared sleep from his eyes and the haze of time from his memories. "No. I mean, it's been a lot of little things. Adding up over the days. But you're Clan. Trueborn?" he asked.

"Yes."

Raul wasn't certain why that should make a difference, that Tassa had been born from iron womb technology. Maybe she seemed a touch more alien because of it. He stared back up at the ceiling, trying to sort through his thoughts.

"You don't speak like a Clanner." Then, "Not always," he amended. "You use contractions. And you don't follow strict bidding practices in combat."

"A wise warrior once commented that slavish adherence to tradition is the sign of a weak mind. I'd like to think that I'm a bit like her."

" 'As long as it takes,' " he quoted her. "You came here to wait for the Steel Wolves." He remembered another of her evasive answers. "What did you come here looking for, Tassa Kay?" His vidphone chirped for attention, but he ignored it. "Is that even your name?"

"It is name enough," she said with formal cadence, letting her eyes drift back to half-mast. "And I came here looking for battle, which is its own reason for existing. I wanted to test the Steel Wolves, and test myself against them, and that is all the answer you are going to get, Raul Ortega. It should be enough."

It should be. As much as anything else was an answer for him these days, living from day to day with little else on his mind except where the next attack would come from and how soon would it take to get his BattleMech fixed up afterward. The vidphone chirped again. Raul glanced toward it, then shrugged. Tassa might have refused to answer questions, but she had never outright lied to him.

He just needed to ask better questions.

Throwing the covers aside, Raul padded over to the wall-mounted conference phone and turned the camera off. Then he stabbed at the connection. The screen scrambled to life, showing a middle-aged man in a business suit and a silver goatee. In the lower left-hand corner the antenna-and-globe sigil for Stryker Productions Limited, the local ComStar affiliate, revolved on a vertical axis. Not the early-morning call Raul would expect. Right then, he wasn't certain what to expect anymore.

"Yes?"

"Mr. Raul Ortega?" the man asked. Raul nodded, then remembered he had turned off the camera. He repeated his earlier question. "Mr. Ortega, my name is Hanson Doles. This is a courtesy call to let you know that you have a message addressed to general delivery at our HPG station."

Raul was at once intrigued and cautious. With the failure of the HPG network, any message was golden. A personal message? It bordered on the unbelievable. Raul's security-trained mind didn't trust it. "Is it verifaxed?" he asked.

"It is not."

"Then why not send it by conventional transmission? I'll pay for the charge."

Hanson Doles rubbed one hand over his goatee. "I can only repeat, sir, that you have a message waiting here at the station. Conventional transmissions are . . . I guess you might call them suspect at the moment."

Raul stiffened. Erik Sandoval had troops stationed near—or inside—the HPG station. But if that was the problem, and Doles was trying to circumvent any monitoring, then he was taking a risk merely contacting Raul. "Who is it from?" he asked, still not willing to let it go. It wouldn't be the last time he asked one question too many.

Doles frowned, his wide face taking on extra years. He shifted in his seat, but his duty to deliver outweighed any discomfort. "Lady Janella Lakewood, Knight of the Sphere." And then, obviously having said enough in his own opinion, Hanson Doles cut the transmission from his end.

Tassa was sitting up in his bed, sheet draped over one shoulder and her necklace charm dangling down over her exposed breast. "You are becoming more popular by the day, it seems."

Jessica was gone. River's End lost to Sandoval. Star Colonel Torrent might attack again at any time, and Raul had a Clan warrior lounging in his bed. He felt pulled in five different directions. No. Pushed. Pushed from five different directions, each one of them trying to force him in a direction he wasn't certain he wanted to go. Tassa was here, she was waiting and he definitely had to have a talk with her, but Raul suddenly felt a need to step away and think. *Me time,* as Jessica would have said.

"I have to go out," he told her. It was the start of something, whether an apology or a promise he wasn't certain.

Tassa cut him off with a simple shrug. "I am not surprised."

ComStar HPG Station: Stryker-A7
Achernar

Two MiningMech conversions dominated the courtyard of the River's End ComStar compound, their weapons covering the broad avenue. Dark patches the color of wet concrete augmented their usual utility gray paint, putting together a rudimentary cityscape camouflage. Short-range missile packs sat double-stacked over the MiningMechs' left shoulder. A pair of anti-infantry machine guns replaced the grinder heads normally found on

the left hand. Both converted IndustrialMechs stood in
frozen profile as Raul rounded the corner. Arriving in a
military jeep, though, he quickly drew their attention.

And their aim.

From the corner to the compound's main lobby Raul
was stopped three times, asked for identification twice,
searched once, and generally made aware that Erik
Sandoval-Groell had invested more security around the
HPG station than the militia base used to cover their
main gates. A Demon medium tank guarded the front
door, parked in the shadow of the large parabolic dish
that rose over the bunker-style compound, angled cross-
wise across the sidewalk. Hauberk armored infantry
walked posts around the station perimeter and Raul spotted another squad on the roof.

Just inside the door a uniformed squad bearing assault
rifles inquired to the business of every customer, adding
further intimidation to any traffic not daunted by the
outside show of force. No customer was about to forget
that the station was under Sandoval "protection." Raul
submitted to a second check of his identification and
stated his business very simply as a personal—not military—pick-up. A corporal checked to see that Raul Ortega did have a post waiting care of general delivery.
With a glare the duty sergeant let him pass.

Hanson Doles met Raul at one of the two dozen service desks, taking over for a customer service agent who
wore the white mantle so commonly known on Achernar
as the duty uniform of Stryker Productions. There was
no way to tell if Doles was a ComStar corporate officer
or part of the local affiliate in charge of caring for the
massive station—as before, Doles wore a simple suit, although Raul noticed up close that the showing tail of his
breast-pocket handkerchief was monogrammed with the
globe-and-antennae logo of SPL. They sat on opposite
sides of a glass-topped surface, a small monitor sitting
between them on a swivel-base.

"Good afternoon, Mr. Ortega. May I see some identification, please?" His voice was cultivated for calm assur-

ance, but the man did not even try to disguise the suspicion that clouded his hazel eyes. "And for a requested secondary verification, can you provide the verbal key? 'The Swordsworn are not necessarily here to help . . . ?' " he began, trailing off into the question.

After so many security and I.D. checks, Raul began to question whether he was really himself. Then he remembered one afternoon at the Officer's Club. "They were just here first," he finished, wondering how Janella Lakewood had known of his conversation with Kyle Powers. He must have passed it along to her. Which meant that Powers had been looking ahead toward his own injury or death days before Torrent challenged him.

"They are *still* here, Mr. Ortega." The way Hanson Doles pitched it, Raul felt certain the man was simply voicing his own negative opinion of the situation. "Thank you for your patience. You may use this terminal to view your message. I have a dedicated earpiece for you," he passed over the plug-shaped device, standing, "and if you would sit in my seat, no one else should be able to view the screen. When the message has played through, a computer glitch will erase it automatically."

Raul stood, shifted his weight from one foot to the other, and then moved slowly around to the working side of the desk. "Do you perform this kind of service often?" he asked.

"Twice since Kyle Powers' arrival on Achernar. Before that, the records show our last reception of a heraldic code to be more than five years ago." Doles moved off with casual aplomb, stationing himself several meters to one side.

Heraldic! Of and for the Knights of the Sphere. Raul slipped into the vacated seat, hands itching to reach for the video controls but stayed by a touch of nerves. Lady Lakewood wanted something from him. He wondered if he had anything left to give after this last chaotic week. Exhaling sharply, Raul reached forward and tapped the playback controls.

He expected trumpets and regalia, Heraldic crests, the public trappings that usually followed around a Knight of the Sphere. Instead, Janella Lakewood winked into existence without flourish or fanfare, the picture flat and dark. The transmission had not even come in as a holographic message.

It was difficult to tell, with so little detail besides her face and shoulders captured by the camera, but Raul thought it very likely that Lady Janella had used a BattleMech cockpit vidcam to record her message. Her thick, black hair looked matted, as if she had only recently removed her neurohelmet. Her green eyes were bloodshot with dark circles beneath from lack of sleep. Even so, she radiated *something*, even through a transmission that had originated forty light years away. Competency, perhaps. Trust.

"Raul Ortega." She nodded at the screen. Even through a poor recording, she showed an animation that had Raul believing she stared back at him, knowing him on sight. "I have, only a few short hours ago, learned of Sir Kyle Powers' unfortunate and tragic death. I will confess to you that I did not immediately see the necessity for Sir Kyle to sacrifice himself in the manner he chose. Not for Achernar alone. Not in these dark times which will demand so much of every Knight, citizen and resident. So let me begin by assuring you that if his death has led to any amount of personal guilt or shame, it should not. Kyle looked beyond the battle. Beyond, even, the challenge for Achernar. What he did, and the way in which he did it, fostered a continuing rivalry between two Steel Wolf commanders. This has aided Ronel—and myself—directly, as well as assisting any future efforts against Kal Radick's growing faction."

It was a lot to take in over a very short count of words. Raul *had* felt some guilt over the loss of Kyle Powers. Lady Lakewood's efforts to assuage that guilt helped, but also showed how little Raul himself actually knew about the enemy, the situation on other Republic worlds, and even about the Sphere Knights. Wanting to think over her words, he reached forward and tapped the view-screen's PAUSE key.

It flashed twice, but Janella Lakewood simply shook her head.

"Do not worry if you don't understand everything I tell you at once, Mr. Ortega. We do not have a lot of time, and I have several directives with which I hope you can assist. First and foremost, do *not* trust Legate Brion Stempres. If he has not shown his true colors by now, he will do so at the most inopportune time. Stempres is a Sandoval man, bred and bought."

Raul nodded, mainly to himself. His eyes roamed back toward the main lobby, where a distrustful sergeant continued to glance over with dark suspicions. "That has become more than apparent," he said aloud.

"Which is as we feared, but could do nothing about." Janella Lakewood could just as easily have been answering Raul's comment. "If he is actively working against Republic interests, you may be forced to collaborate, for the sake of remaining involved. Do not let this discourage you, Raul. I have already forwarded by JumpShip a report to the Exarch on such possible tactics. You will be absolved."

With the last few days on his mind, and this morning in particular, Raul shook his head. "I may be past absolution."

"We are never past the need for absolution, Raul. When everything else is lost, forgiveness is often the first step toward vindication."

Shocked by her direct response to his outburst, Raul gazed long and hard at the screen where Janella Lakewood waited for him to work it through in his mind— and believe it. "Yes," she finally admitted. "This is not a recording. But do not say anything unless critically necessary. It is better if no one suspects that I am personally tasking you with orders."

A warm thrill ran down Raul's spine, firing out through nerve endings and quivering his muscles with new tension. He tried to picture in his mind the convoluted programming necessary to hold a real-time conversation between planets. Janella Lakewood sitting in her BattleMech, transmitting on a coded channel with the Ronel HPG station. The fragile connection as two HPG antennae synched up perfectly for transmission and reception both. And the expense! Stryker Productions on this end (ComStar, or a second affiliate on hers) could not batch and send messages so long as the two of them tied up a dedicated channel. They had to know.

Raul glanced sidelong toward Hanson Doles. *He,* at least, had to know.

Deciding to risk some amount of privacy, Raul scratched at his upper lip—as if deep in thought—and talked behind his hand. "Stempres has handed Erik Sandoval the keys to River's End. He controls the capital and HPG."

Janella nodded, understanding. "Still, better him than Star Colonel Torrent. I hate to give up access to one of our few working stations, but with Ronel falling to the Steel Wolves in ten to fifteen days, we cannot allow Kal Radick easy access to so much potential intelligence."

Ten to fifteen . . . Raul swallowed past a tight throat. Janella Lakewood was admitting that the Steel Wolves would take Ronel. She said it matter-of-factly. "But to simply hand it over to the Swordsworn . . ."

"Damned if we do," Lady Janella agreed, "but, believe me, damned faster if we don't. Can you trust me enough to believe this? I need eyes and ears and willing hands on Achernar, Raul. Kyle Powers thought you able. More, he was highly impressed by your instinctive sense of honor and duty. His report promised that you felt your way through things as much as reasoned through them. That is why you were selected to fight alongside him. That is why I am contacting you now. Do what you have to do to keep the Steel Wolves from completing their own, private HPG circuit. If you can keep it out of Swordsworn hands, so much the better." Raul lifted his hand again, but she shook her head. "No, don't tell me your ideas or plans. I am not in any position to advise you at this time.

"Serve the Republic, Raul. Serve the people of Achernar. When necessary, and you will know when that is, serve yourself. I wish I could invest in you some additional authority, to help you carry out my orders, but I cannot. That would be premature at this time. Use what talents you have and what authority is appointed to you, and work toward the better end.

"That is all any of us can do right now."

Raul faked a cough. "But if I need to contact you . . ."

"I think you know who can help you. Be confident, Raul, be calm. But above all else be *cautious*." She nodded one last time, both encouraging and accepting.

"Strength and honor," she saluted him in farewell.

Static bled through and erased her image as the real-time network fell apart before his eyes. Raul took the earplug out, set it on the desk. Hanson Doles was beside him as he stood up.

"Was your service satisfactory today, sir?"

Raul shook his head. "Not particularly. There was a great deal of static and I couldn't hear much of it. I believe it may have fallen apart there at the end."

"I understand. We will try to recover the data for you." Raul received the impression that this would be the equivalent of Hanson Doles trying to recover dropped eggs using a hammer. The only thing ever recovered would be bits and fragments. "Will we be seeing you again soon?"

Raul glanced around at the mostly-empty offices, and back at the bottleneck being squeezed ever tighter by the inside post of Swordsworn infantry. The entire draconian routine smacked of population control as practiced by House Liao, not the supposedly free nation of House Davion's Federated Suns. Were the Sandovals willing to give up their supposedly long-cherished ties in the very pursuit of them? Perhaps. Which was one more reason why Raul should fight to keep Achernar out of their hands as well.

"You never know, Mr. Doles." He shrugged uneasily. "You just might."

20

The San Marino

San Marino Spaceport
Achernar
11 March 3133

The San Marino Spaceport's siren wailed a deep, mournful bawl, chasing low notes and then a higher, louder tone with its synthesized Doppler effect. It rolled over sun swept tarmac, echoed off the flat hull of a grounded *Kuan Ti*-class DropShip, and was turned into a flat background drone by the Praetorian's thick armor. Erik Sandoval-Groell barely heard it anymore. There were too many other things on his mind, each one of them having to do with defending the spaceport from a Steel Wolf assault.

"I want an update on the waterworks raid," Erik demanded, his command chair sliding across the vehicle's interior on an articulated arm. He knuckled the back edge of a sergeant's helmet. "And get me some kind of trajectory on those DropShips. They aren't up there for the view!"

"We're getting on top of it now, Lord Sandoval."

A mobile HQ, even one of the vaunted Praetorians, was no place for a MechWarrior Erik belatedly realized. Six meters tall and nearly as wide, the massive, sixty-ton half-track maneuvered in the backfield behind the Swordsworn's full protection and still Erik felt exposed, vulnerable. A dozen staffers worked the vehicle's command deck, manning consoles and talking over one another, sweating through their uniforms; a more claustrophobic environment than a BattleMech cockpit could ever be. Erik's hands itched for control sticks and the touch of weapon triggers under his fingers. He wanted targeting data and crosshairs.

He wanted—he suddenly decided—out of the mobile chair.

Slapping the quick-release on his harness, Erik all but launched himself from the seat as he made for the Praetorian's front. The drivers' station took up most of the forward ferroglass shield, but there was an observation seat and gunner's console to one side, domed in at the mobile HQ's forward corner, which allowed Erik an eyes-on appraisal of the battle.

Why the open view should give him a sense of relief, Erik didn't know. Except for two JES strategic carriers that flanked the Praetorian for protection, most of what he could see involved distant ground shadows and flashes of laserfire while speed-blurred darts tangled in the skies above. Without a head's up display there was hardly any telling his own forces from those of the Steel Wolves or the Republic militia. He knew that the Swordsworn held a rough line across the spaceport's sun-blasted landing field, committing half of its available defenders from River's End including four of his six remaining WorkMech conversions. The balance, including his own *Hatchetman,* waited inside the city's industrial sector or continued their watch over the local HPG station, giving him a strong fallback position and all the leverage he needed to keep the militia in line.

In fact, quite literally in line. Layered in between the enemy and his own people, and also wrapping around one flank of the Steel Wolf formation, was Achernar's Standing Guard. Although minus a large contingent drawn away by a morning raid against the Brightwater river control facility, the militia still outnumbered his Swordsworn by almost two to one. It had taken some work, drawing them into the gap between his people and the Steel Wolves, which Erik had accomplished by surging ever backward onto spaceport grounds. Eventually, one of their *Legionnaires* had slipped into the break with a double-squad of vehicles, forcing a stand rather than allowing the Steel Wolves a stronger approach to the spaceport. Erik had quickly spread his forces thinner, slipping several squads onto the Republic rear lines, tying the formations together but, more importantly, cementing the militia in place. But would it be enough?

So long as the militia soaked up the balance of any casualties, it hardly mattered to the Swordsworn or to Erik.

"Sir!" A call for him, drifting forward from the command deck. "Lord Sandoval, we have those updates."

Rather than abandon the observation deck, Erik slipped into the vacant gunner's seat and tucked the comms headset up into his right ear. "Gunner's channel seven," he yelled back, dialing himself over to the correct frequency. "Report."

"DropShips." The aerospace monitor was first in queue. "They've completed a turn at apogee. Without a secondary course correction, they will drop right on top of the spaceport in less than ten minutes."

A metallic dryness crept into Erik's mouth. So the big push *was* for the spaceport. Or at least, that was what the Steel Wolves wanted them to believe. "Do we have intel on the Brightwater raid?" he asked, wanting confirmation.

The Brightwater river control facility stood halfway between River's End and the Tanager Mountains. The Steel Wolves had targeted it once already, and been rebuffed. This morning's raid had looked to be a stronger push, led by Star Colonel Torrent himself. Despite the facility's importance—able to force a drought on River's End or, during high rains, possibly flooding the city by opening sluice gates—Erik had let the militia handle it.

Cautious of his position, the smaller on-planet force but in control of the capital itself, he had to allow attrition to work in his favor.

Another staff sergeant waited with the news. "All indications are that the raid was diversionary. MechWarrior Kay is down. May be dead. Before she fell, she reported back that several of the APCs were empty, and what they first pinged as armored tanks were actually convoy trucks."

Erik had followed Tassa Kay's efforts on Achernar's behalf with something akin to jealousy. Piloting an impressive 'Mech, successfully inserting herself into the Republic's order of battle, she was the wild card of which he could never be certain. If she was indeed down and out, then he was well rid of her.

But what mattered now was *this* battle, and how to handle the incoming DropShips. The vessels represented a significant amount of firepower, and even with the militia's help and his own reserves he doubted they could be stopped. "I need a run-down on all available forces. Give me units and numbers." He wanted his own terminal, and was half-tempted to walk back to the command deck and appropriate one.

Then he realized he had one, right in front of him.

Listening to the follow-up reports with only half an ear, Erik strapped himself into the gunner's place, firing up all sensor bands and targeting consoles. A laser-painted HUD leapt up onto the ferroglass shield, drawing icons in gold, neural blue, and enemy red. What he saw gave him no more information than an aide could have fed him on the command deck, but it felt better. He read the battle with a practiced eye, gauging strength, calculating odds off the cuff and coming up far short.

Shaking his head, Erik once again gave way to caution and the certainty of his current position within River's End. "Operations. Begin to stagger back some of our stronger units. I want one of our converted Miners limping off the battlefield in minutes. Make a good show of it. Have a unit press forward on the attack, and then fall

back the second they draw any hard resistance. Prepare
for full evacuation on my command."

If Star Colonel Torrent wanted the HPG, he would
come for it in a fight on Erik's terms, not his own.

Raul Ortega shifted around in his seat, throwing his
own sense of balance behind the *Legionnaire*'s fifty tons.
The BattleMech twisted at the waist, bent forward, and
rocked back off the left-side edges of its square-shod
feet.

"Can we expect relief from these strafing runs anytime
soon?" The militia had only a pair of *Stingrays* over the
spaceport field, and they were being shoved around like
schoolyard children at recess. The one-two punch of
ground-fire and aerospace fighters had thrown him off
balance twice since Erik Sandoval pulled back his
antiaircraft-capable vehicles.

Clark Diago, anchoring the militia's attempt to encircle
the Steel Wolf flank, was more direct. "Base, Diago. Get
us some support out here!"

Promises and regrets were forwarded by Colonel
Blaire himself. Aerospace was still tied up in attempts to
divert the Steel Wolf DropShips. "You're about to get
all the cover we have," he said in clipped tones. "But it
won't be enough."

Biting back his response, Raul throttled into a backward walk and put some distance between himself and a
pair of M1 Marksmen. The assault tanks rolled past the
dismantled corpse of the final Swordsworn WorkMech,
working it over with short-range weaponry, just for good
measure, before turning their attention forward. Their
gauss rifles were too big a threat for Raul to ignore.
Switching over to his company's tactical frequency, he
called a missile barrage down on their location.

Gray tendrils of smoke fell down from the sky, marking the four-score warheads that blasted into armor and
ripped through the polished tarmac landing field. Before
the smoke cleared, a squad of DI Schmitts pounced, their
rotary autocannon blazing with long, sustained rates of

fifty-mil fire support. Raul shifted back for a forward run, cutting along behind the Schmitts, adding his own hard-pounding rotary to the assault.

The Steel Wolf crew rallied quickly—too quickly. With artificial thunderclaps splitting the air, both Marksmen punched rail-accelerated gauss slugs into the lead Schmitt. One carried away a turret missile launcher, ripping it clean off the tank. The second gauss slug impacted over a wheel, smashing it back into the drivetrain and fouling the right-side independent drive mechanism.

The Schmitt turned in a sharp circle, crippled, unable to withdraw.

"At them! Hit them now." Raul drove forward, feeling each of the *Legionnaire*'s pounding steps at the base of his spine.

Centering his crosshairs over the Marksman with greater armor fatigue, he burned into it with a hammering cascade of fifty-millimeter slugs tipped with depleted uranium. More missiles rained down on the Steel Wolf position—and more than one flight was returned against Raul's BattleMech—as the three remaining Schmitts followed their MechWarrior's lead and drilled deep into the gauss-toting tank.

Protected by deep armor reserves, the Marksman and its comrade vehicle managed one more volley, completely smashing through the side of the crippled Schmitt, and left it a gutted shell. Then a blistering scourge of laserfire chewed into the wounded Marksman. A burst of flame scattered out of several gaping holes as fuel caught fire, and dark, greasy smoke swirled out to commingle into a dark funeral shroud.

The remaining Marksman rolled backward into the protection of the Steel Wolf lines, quickly flanked by two advancing *Pack Hunters*.

And that was when hell opened up, throwing a long line of fire and destruction into the midst of the exposed Schmitt trio.

"DropShips! Angels-twelve. Straight up but drifting back."

Like Raul needed the warning. His alarm systems had
failed to register the DropShip arrival, sensors cluttered
up with too many ground targets to worry about overhead threats, but there was no mistaking the fire pattern
laid down from above. "Break and run," he ordered the
Schmitts. "Strike Squad Two, evade and escape."

Two of the three Schmitts crawled out of the blasted
landscape. One of them had plunged into a cratered strip
that could only be a collapsed service tunnel. It might
have survived, but even so it was out of the battle.

Craning to one side, looking up past the thick, rotary-
linked barrels of his overhead autocannon, Raul found
the bright drive flare of a hovering *Okinawa*-class
DropShip as it passed overhead by half a kilometer. The
DropShip crew had put a rotating spin on the vessel, and
now long beams of gem-brilliant energy lanced down
from three weapon ports at a time as lasers and particle
cannons mixed into terrifying salvoes. As one port fell
out of line-of-sight, another came around to walk new
destruction down among the militia line. LRMs fell out
at regular intervals, spreading more impersonal death
over the ground-bound vehicles.

And it continued drifting north, toward the militia
rear!

"Support forces, scatter and evade," Raul ordered,
knowing the confusion he was about to unleash in his
own backfield. He selected an all-hands channel, one that
the Swordsworn would also be monitoring. "DropShips
are not—repeat, *not*—grounding in support of Steel Wolf
advance. 'Ware behind!"

Then a pair of *Jagatai* aerospace fighters tore over the
landing field, cutting down with a mix of autocannon and
lasers, and Raul had all he could do to angle out of their
strafing line before they yanked the rug out from under
his feet again. The *Pack Hunters* prowled forward, waiting for a single misstep. Their PPCs spat out twin forks
of manmade lightning, but they grounded out short of
Raul's *Legionnaire*.

As more reports of air-based strikes filtered through

the command levels, Raul understood that a low-passing *Overlord* had ravaged Clark Diago's position before moving down the militia's back line and into the hesitant Swordsworn. Sweat burned at the corners of Raul's eyes. He blinked them clear and twisted his *Legionnaire* about, watching as the two leviathan vessels lowered themselves on massive drive flares, one to either end of the grounded *Kuan Ti*. The trapped DropShip made the mistake of firing on the *Overlord*, one final act of defiance, and suddenly the aerial assault dealt over the militia line looked like a casual wave by comparison.

The *Overlord* pounded down at the nose of the civilian-conversion with gauss rifles and enough laser energy to light up the city of River's End. Although limited in firepower after its military decommissioning, the *Kuan Ti* still mustered its assault-class autocannons and a heavy missile barrage. Then the *Okinawa* bit in from behind, trading lasers and PPCs against the civilian vessel's aft pulse lasers and missiles.

It was an uneven fight from the beginning, and lasted until the *Overlord* pounded silent every one of the *Kuan Ti*'s forward weapon bays.

About sixty seconds.

Wary of being caught between the DropShips' anvil and the hammer of the Steel Wolf advancing force, Raul herded his two remaining Schmitts and a scattered flock of mixed battlesuit infantry back toward their ravaged rearward lines. M.A.S.H. units and a JI 100 recovery vehicle had rolled up from the southwest, making pickup on broken units and fallen comrades. He stomped past a fire-gutted Joust and the twisted wreckage of two broken hoverbikes. One still had hands clamped onto the steering bar, but was missing the rest of the driver. A technician emergency response team fell hard at work over a captured Demon, getting it battle-worthy again and detailing a new crew out of their auxiliary ranks. Raul gave the working ERT a wide berth, swung around to one side of them, and then slammed his throttles down to a full stop. Being hauled up into the embrace of the JI recovery vehicle was Charal DePriest's converted LoaderMech.

With Tassa leading a small force in defense of the Brightwater facility, Charal had been called up to help defend the spaceport. Raul had thought to keep her safe, relegated as she was to a support role, even when she followed him into the wedge between the Swordsworn and Steel Wolves. 'Safe' was a relative term in a live firefight, though, especially when two DropShips began redefining the battle. Still, there were any number of injuries that even a converted WorkMech could take and the MechWarrior could walk away from. Crippled gyros. Destroyed legs. Ruined engines.

Charal's WorkMech was missing its cockpit. All that remained was a melted stump of support structure.

Standing there, his *Legionnaire* grounded to a dangerous halt while Steel Wolf forces continued to stalk up from the south, Raul became a lodestone to stragglers. Scattered reserves and retreating forward units gathered in around his position, inadvertently creating a strongpoint that worried the advancing Wolves. Sensing a possible counter-thrust, they also slowed, drew together in concentrated ranks. A converted ConstructionMech joined the *Pack Hunters,* forming the spearpoint on a thrust that would not be long in coming.

The Swordsworn pressed forward now as well, goaded back into the fight as enemy DropShips landed behind their position. On one of the auxiliary channels, Erik Sandoval recommended—ordered—a full retaliatory strike against the advancing Steel Wolf line. "Bloody them now, and they'll pull back. DropShips and all."

His mobile command vehicle lumbered up from the far rear, protected by a pair of JES carriers. A pair of *Jagatai* fightercraft turned in his direction, laying down a long line of fire that swept up and over the Praetorian. Both *Jessies* belched out thick clouds of proximity-fused missiles, filling the air with heavy flak. The lead *Jagatai*

pulled up so sharply Raul could almost believe the pilot
had defied all laws of momentum.

The second craft was not so skilled, or lucky. It drove
through the thickest part of the antiaircraft barrage, bull-
dozing through the far side with streamers of fire and
smoke, a stunted right-side wing, and a lethal roll that
pitched him up, over, and into the tarmac.

"Where was that support five minutes ago?" Raul
asked aloud, not caring who heard him over the comm
channels. But he knew, he knew.

Like those Swordsworn "reserve forces" held back
within the capital, the JES carriers were being denied to
the militia so that the standing guard bore the brunt of
the fighting. The perfect Sandoval partnership. So long
as Erik's people held the HPG station and could force
fighting in the streets before being removed from River's
End, the militia operated with its hands tied. The only
choice was to cooperate—collaborate . . .

Or give Erik Sandoval exactly what he was asking for:
complete responsibility for Achernar.

A trio of missiles slammed into the side of the *Legionnaire,* cracking into more armor, while the azure
lightning-whip of a particle projector cannon snaked past
Raul's left knee and cut into a stalled Fox. The armored
car swung around on lift fans and scurried back, like its
scampering namesake.

Swinging around, Raul pegged one of the encroaching
Pack Hunters dead center with his crosshairs. A pounding stream of autocannon slugs chipped away at the
Hunter's gyroscope housing, shoving the BattleMech
back by several meters and threatening to topple it. It
fell back among the building Steel Wolf forces.

Raul turned back to the waiting militia units, and
Charal's decapitated WorkMech. *Do gold . . . good . . .
by Achernar.* From all their difficult conversations in the
last week—difficult only because of her speech impediment—those were the words he remembered. The same
ones echoed by Janella Lakewood. But what happened

when serving the Republic and serving Achernar conflicted? Was that what the Sphere Knight had meant, telling him to then serve himself?

Tie goes to the MechWarrior.

"Captain Ortega?" Diago. According to the HUD, he too had fallen back, stretching the militia line into something more of an abbreviated arc than any serious encirclement. The Steel Wolf forces were knotted up into a thick wedge, with the tip pointed straight at Raul's position. "Raul? You've got about ten seconds to get turned around and ready to meet a full charge."

Raul shook his head, feeling more than his neurohelmet weighing down on his shoulders. "Not happening," he said, voice pitched low. Then, with gathering strength, "No, Clark. Wrap 'em up and back to base. Carry or drag along our wounded equipment as we can. Ruin it rather than leave it for Torrent."

He passed the same order down through several channels, making certain that the support forces rallying around his position had a clear idea of the order of retreat. The M.A.S.H. trucks and salvage vehicles led, protected by hovercraft flankers. Raul's *Legionnaire* and their heaviest tanks would guard the militia rear. If the Steel Wolves wanted to force a longer battle today, he would make them pay a butcher's price.

"Disregard that order." The plans had finally worked their way over to Erik Sandoval. "Achernar militia, hold your line and prepare for a joint offensive."

Long past caring for Erik Sandoval's tactics, Raul keyed open a channel to answer for himself. "We've seen your brand of joint offensives, Sandoval. And it's the last time we walk into one without reading the fine print." He rocked forward on his foot throttles, stepping out into a crisp march to the west, out from under the Steel Wolf sword, exposing the Swordsworn line.

"Captain Ortega, what the hell do you think you're doing?"

"I'm ceding Star Colonel Torrent the San Marino spaceport. I would suggest you do the same." There would be hell to pay with Colonel Blaire. At least Clark Diago was willing to follow his lead, for now. The militia's western flank had drawn itself into a skirmish line to protect the retreating middle. "The militia is withdrawing," Raul said.

"And leaving you to the Wolves."

21

The Hardest Lessons

Brightwater River Control Facility
Achernar
12 March 3133

Strapped into one of many passenger seats inside the older Trooper-class VTOL, Raul Ortega labored to breathe shallow. The wide passenger compartment smelled its twenty years as an infantry carrier, tainted with rancid sweat and aviation fuel fumes. His seat had lost most of its thin padding years before, with only a few remaining strips held together with duct tape or stapled into the rigid plastic seat. Trying to ignore the knots pressing into his legs and lower back, Raul twisted around to stare out through a copper-tinted window as the infantry carrier thundered up the Rio Sangria.

The reddish, mud-colored waters still ran high as mountain rainfall continued to pour down into the lowlands, but was hardly in danger of flooding so long as the Brightwater River Control Facility remained in Republic hands. A system of locks and sluice gates, the Brightwater facility could, for brief periods, dam up the river completely or channel excess water into one of many old dry washes. From above the facility, he could see that water was indeed being diverted into two older arroyos.

The VTOL followed the larger of the two runoff channels, banking southwest and leaving the river course a moment later to run out over yesterday's battlefield.

From five hundred feet, the area did not look so bad. Some scorched desert grasses and a few charred husks that had once been vehicles or a military-modified IndustrialMech. As the 'copter settled, however, more of the personal cost became clear. He saw the pieces and parts of other machines, scattered leavings after salvage crews had worked the field over for whatever useful equipment they could find. Raul also counted better than two dozen armored battlesuits littering the area like the molted cicada husks, each one a potential fatality.

Three M.A.S.H. tents covered makeshift triage, surgery, and hospital care areas. Corpsmen loaded two stretchers onto a small chopper, which rushed them airborne even as the Trooper hit the ground and an infantryman rolled back two large doors so that Raul could jump down.

Jogging over to the hospital tent, Raul slowed only once as he passed the blackened and severed arm of a BattleMech. It was from Tassa's *Ryoken*. He had already seen the laser-blasted wreckage hauled back by a recovery crew, missing its arm and showing a tangle of twisted scrap where its gyroscope stabilizer had once been housed. He mentally tagged the severed limb to be recovered. With some hard work, it might be reconditioned and reattached.

There would certainly be no ordering a new one up from stores. Not for a *Ryoken*.

There would be no ordering up a new MechWarrior, either, which was why Colonel Blaire had dispatched Raul first thing this morning. With Charal DePriest dead, the closest thing that the militia had to another backup was Captain Norgales—Legate Stempres's man. Any others were barely capable of handling a *Legionnaire*. Raul might be able to handle the powerful *Ryoken II* design, leaving his 'Mech to a lesser pilot, but he didn't want it.

He wanted Tassa Kay back.

The hospital tent smelled of old canvas and the strong disinfectants used to keep wounds clean. Several dozen men and women still waited for evac back to River's End. Blood-soaked bandages and elevated casts gave Raul a close-up look at the cost of this ongoing struggle. He caught whiff of a septic wound—a latrine scent at which he wrinkled his nose—and stood aside as two bulky civilians who looked more like construction workers than corpsmen helped a nurse hustle one of their patients from this tent and likely back to field surgery.

Raul waited for the door to swing shut, then began walking the long rows again, studying faces—when he could—and reading names from charts clipped to the end of the cots. Near the end of the first row he glanced ahead, saw Tassa lying back on white sheets with an IV stuck into her arm and a compress taped to the side of her head. A physician bent over her. A civilian physician, checking vitals and then straightening up to stare down in question. Raul's breath hitched.

It was Jessica.

Raul had already been feeling at odds with what had happened the other night with Tassa Kay. His conversation with Janella Lakewood was forcing him to reevaluate many things, in fact. His liaison with Tassa had been all passion and need and proximity. Not solid emotion and certainly not love. In the holovids, the ones Raul had loved so much while dreaming of a post within Achernar's militia, romantic trysts were part of a MechWarrior's due. "Because tomorrow we may die," and other such trite excuses. But this was real life, and real people got hurt both on and off the battlefield. Any decision, or lack thereof, could cost lives, ruin equipment, and shatter relationships.

"I'm sorry," he whispered, not really meaning to speak out loud. He wasn't even certain to whom he was apologizing just then. Charal, for failing to protect her. Jessica, for how things had turned out. Or Tassa, who had fought and bled for a world that wasn't even hers to defend.

Jessica was the one to hear him. She glanced up with a guilty start, then quickly darkened to a brooding hostility when she saw who stood nearby. "Well," she said, and a lot of judgment weighted down her words. "We've been here before."

It was a lot like their first meeting—over the bed of a military patient. Raul could even feel the old arguments warming up in the mental bay where he stored those weapons. Raul swallowed dryly, fighting the tightness in his throat. "What are you doing here?" he asked.

"I'm being a doctor, Raul." She stood slowly, showing fatigue and stiff joints, then walked over to the foot of Tassa's bed where they could talk more quietly. "Between Brightwater and San Marino yesterday, apparently you swamped the militia's medical capability and they called in several civilian auxiliaries to help out here, where the fighting was over and danger was low."

Raul saw the dark circles under her eyes, and could only imagine how little sleep she had gotten since the previous day. Or the previous week. "I'm glad. These are good people, and they needed your help."

"What they need is transport back to River's End. We've ferried them out two at a time all night, and at this rate we won't have everyone back until late tomorrow."

"I came in a Trooper." Raul saw her frown of concentration, guessed at her question. "Infantry carrier. Seats twenty-eight. You could lay half a dozen out in stretchers and take any of the wounded who can ride in a sitting position."

"Only right, I guess, considering that the military put them here."

"I didn't come out here to fight with you, Jess."

"Why not? Fighting is what's caused all of this, isn't it? More battle and bloodshed. The natural order of things. Right?"

"That's not what I believe, and you know it." Raul

stepped up closer, lowering his voice into a harsh whisper only for Jessica. "Though maybe you'd rather we just hand over Achernar to the first tyrant to challenge our Exarch."

"No, I wouldn't," she said with a violent stomp of one foot.

She looked as if she wanted to slap him again. Or maybe deliver a good sharp kick to the shins. Raul had never seen Jessica looking so completely angry and yet at a loss for a target: her short, pounding breaths, the way she bit down hard enough into her lower lip that she'd leave marks, the little shake of her head. It had only started to occur to him that she was actually angry about the situation, and herself, before she admitted it openly.

"You don't know how difficult it is to accept that one of the core beliefs you've held for so long doesn't measure up when challenged, Raul. I watch the news footage, I go out to the sites on civilian volunteer parties. Then I hear the pundits spouting knee-jerk opinions and going on about how they'd run things if they were in charge—and you know what? I find myself arguing your side of the discussion."

He started to say something, thought to comfort her, but she held up a hand. "Let me finish." She glanced around at the wounded. At Tassa. "I believe that war is evil. I have to, Raul. But in the last few weeks, I have also forced myself to realize that you—and the Republic Guard—did not bring war to Achernar. The Steel Wolves did that. The Swordsworn did that. And we can't simply sit back and allow one military action after another to roll over our world unchecked. So we need soldiers. And we need citizens with a vested interest in The Republic, who can hopefully affect non-violent changes to prevent this from *ever* happening again."

Raul had never heard such capitulation in Jessica's voice. Raising the white flag. And right when he was about to tell her . . . "Ah, hell, Jess. You lay all that out, and here I was ready to concede the entire argument to you. I don't know that I ever wanted this for the right reasons. So maybe we were both wrong."

Her eyes held enough anguish for them both. Still, she offered bravely, "Or maybe we were both right. A little." Then she glanced between Raul and Tassa, her professional demeanor taking charge and erecting a shield over the breach she had allowed in her defenses. "She's going to be all right. Mild concussion and hairline collarbone fracture. I have her resting on a sedative just now." She swept her gaze over nearby patients. "Most of them are resting, with the really critical cases already flown down to River's End. Your helicopter will help move the rest out today."

Which was a decision Raul needed her help in making. "I'd like to talk to you about where you'll take them."

Jessica frowned. "If your militia hospital can't handle the load, I'll take them back to R.E.G." River's End General.

"I'm not certain that's such a safe place for them anymore. Erik Sandoval has men keeping tabs on the hospital now, and with the Steel Wolves in control of the San Marino, it's only a matter of time before they push for the city itself."

A touch of fire leapt back into Jessica's weary blue eyes at the thought of military intrusion at her hospital. She licked her lips, then asked Raul, "You have another idea?"

"That's what I want to ask you. The Trooper has a good range on it and it can refuel on the other side of the Taibeks if necessary. Where else can you take them? Take them, and hide them?"

"Hide them?"

He exhaled in a long breath. "I don't want Sandoval to get wind of how many soldiers we return to active duty in the next few days. And for those who need longer to heal, it would be best if they were far out of the way in case we lose Achernar and have to go underground. If you can, I'd like you to classify many of them as deceased or critically wounded."

"Underground. As in resistance?" She blinked away her surprise. "Are you really planning that far in advance?"

"We're planning for everything, except for whatever we haven't thought of. Jess, I wouldn't be here if it wasn't important, for Achernar *and* The Republic. We need to work together here. Please."

Jessica laughed, short and sad. "Sharing the glory, Raul?"

He shook his head, then gazed around at the wounded and the dying. "There is no glory, Jess. No romantic adventure. What I have—what we have—is duty. Resident honor, if you want. Whatever the cost, we have to try." He paused, then, "Charal DePriest is dead."

"I know. And I'm sorry, Raul. I know you got on with her. I also heard that Colonel Blaire reprimanded you for abandoning San Marino to the Steel Wolves. Is that true?"

"I know what I'm doing," he told her. He wanted to explain about Janella Lakewood, and his hopes that the Steel Wolves' proximity to River's End might force the Swordsworn to finally commit to a stronger position than before. In the end, though, he could only say, "You'll have to trust me."

Jessica actually looked as if she had expected the request, and surprisingly did not laugh in his face. "What about her?" she asked, nodding at Tassa's sleeping form.

Steeling himself for the reopening of a raw wound, Raul asked, "How soon until we can have her back?"

"Normally, I'd suggest twenty-four hours rest and another twenty-four under observation. She's lucky to be alive."

He knew that. By all reports and the limited footage he'd seen of the battle for Brightwater, the Steel Wolves had struck with a ferocious assault. Led by Star Colonel Torrent, the "diversionary raid" had involved more military forces and generated more casualties than any other action so far on Achernar save the San Marino battle and the Steel Wolves' initial assault against the planet.

Tassa had worked with a heavy armor contingent to hold them back, keeping her *Ryoken* up long after a lesser warrior might have succumbed to the beating she took.

Torrent had already withdrawn from the field, to take command at the San Marino, when Tassa ran into a trio of tactical *Jessies* and one of Torrent's converted Agro-Mechs. She accounted for two of their number before falling under a final missile barrage. Her squad had rescued her by driving off the last two JES carriers. It had been a heroic stand and was the very reason why any final defense of Achernar needed Tassa Kay on the line.

"We need her by tomorrow, Jess. I don't know when things are going to start happening, but we can't do without Tassa."

A touch of color blushed high on Jessica's cheeks. "You'll have her back, then," she said coldly. Raul started to speak, to tell her he didn't mean it that way, but she stopped him with a raised hand. "Look. Just tell me what you need and I'll do my part. Whatever else you're about, Raul, I know you've got Achernar foremost in your thoughts. Just don't try to work on *us* right now. All right?"

He nodded, a couple of short, shallow dips of the head. "All right. I've got to get outside and make similar arrangements with the local salvage crews, but I'll be back later to discuss plans. In the meantime, the Trooper crew knows that the local medical staff will be directing them, so get started on whomever you need to fly out first." He should have left it there, he knew, but he couldn't resist adding, "And Jess?" He waited for her to look up, and the sorrow weighing down her eyes almost made him stop. "It's good to have you with us."

"Yeah."

She gave him a shrug, leaning more toward a nod than a dismissal. But barely. Raul took that and left. It was a start. He hoped it left him something to build on later.

The hardest lessons, he was learning, were not those that came at high cost to himself. They were the lessons that others kept paying on his behalf.

22

Stage Directions

Achernar Militia Command
Achernar
16 March 3133

Erik Sandoval saw signs of the militia's strain in the little things. A lack of casual traffic on the base. Tired guards in bedraggled uniforms, both at the central post and standing a weary honor guard in front of Colonel Blaire's office. The corridor floor not buffed to a military shine. And Colonel Isaac Blaire, holding himself upright with elbows on the desk, eyes red-rimmed from drink or lack of sleep. The militia commander looked such a state, in fact, that Erik missed the office's second occupant for several heartbeats. Then—

"What is he doing here?" Erik demanded, staring with venomous fury at Raul Ortega.

Ortega had pushed his chair to the inside wall, as far back from the desk as he could conceivably get. He sat extremely still, with arms laid out carefully along both sides and hands gripping the end curve of the armrests. The MechWarrior said nothing in reply. He broke his stony repose only long enough to glance over at Erik, and then cautiously at his commanding officer.

Gesturing Erik to the chair across from his desk, Blaire did not bother to look over at his officer. "He is here because Ah ordered him to be here, should you have any questions."

The colonel's tone, Raul's silence; the two did not appear to be on the best terms. Erik might find a way to use that. "Questions? How about a request for his immediate dismissal?" The young noble turned his chair just enough to be able to watch Ortega out of the corner of one eye. "He abandoned the field, Colonel. Pusillanimous conduct in the face of the enemy."

Now Raul leaned forward. "Said the commander who parked himself a good kilometer behind the fighting."

"That is enough, Captain!" Blaire's bark still had some of its old power.

Erik measured the way Raul stiffened up again, as if turned to stone by the Colonel's basilisk stare. It gave him a moment to compose himself; Raul's contemptuous charge had struck a nerve. Since Tassa Kay's cutting remarks and his recent reversals on the battlefield, Erik found his temper fraying at the least provocation.

"My position that day had nothing to do with cowardice," Erik said softly, slowly, "and everything to do with setting a strong second line to protect River's End. When the DropShips arrived, my plans shifted and I ordered an immediate counter-thrust, which would have prevented the Steel Wolves from lodging a foothold so close to the capital. *You!*" he said, stabbing a finger toward Raul. "You gave it to them."

Raul folded his arms across his chest. "Now it's the Swordsworn facing the brunt of any Steel Wolf attack. And you need us—the militia. I like being on this side of the arrangement. No wonder you hid in Hahnsak for so long."

"Dammit, Ortega." Blaire's outburst cut off Erik's heated response. "You're acting like a peace-spoiled *kay*-det and you're not making this any easier." With a strained peace imposed between the other two men, the

236 Loren L. Coleman

colonel shifted focus and asked, "What about yesterday's raid? Did you suffer anything in the way of major casualties?"

"Two damaged JES carriers and a limping MinerMech Mod." Reminded of the short but brutal engagement forced on his people the day before, Erik felt a second flush of anger work up and outward from the nape of his neck. His voice remained civil, barely, as he outlined what had happened.

"The Steel Wolves weren't making a serious push at River's End. They struck in a pincer movement but with hardly enough forces to penetrate the industrial sector. It was a probe. We made it cost them a Demon, which we captured with no help from the militia I may remind you."

"Ah can try to provide you with anything you might need in the way of parts and supplies." Another hard glance at his captain. "We've had our own troubles since the spaceport battle."

"I've seen the casualty report," Erik admitted. "What concerns me more is the number of outright defections." Erik searched his memory, drawing up numbers provided to him by Michael Eus. "Eight infantrymen, six of them with battlesuits. Also a trio of hoverbikes, two APCs, and a pair of conventional VTOLs, all with crews. And a Destroyer, Colonel? How do you let an SM1 slip through your fingers?"

Blaire sat up straighter, as if his pride had been wounded. "How did you hear about those?"

"More to the point," Erik leaned forward, "where have they gone?"

Raul whipped at him with an exasperated laugh. "If they did not go over to you, and you have just basically told us they haven't, then they fled into hiding or went over to Star Colonel Torrent."

Erik's assumption as well, and one that had him sleeping less well every night. "If the Steel Wolves have grown so much in strength, then I expect them to attack soon. One final, all-out push for River's End." He wrapped himself tight in his noble demeanor, remembering that he now had the full weight of Brion Stempres *and* the planetary governor behind him. "I must now insist, Colonel, that you stand ready to answer my summons, instantly, once Star Colonel Torrent masses for that advance. I believe Legate Stempres has communicated this to you on more than one occasion in the last few days."

"Ah've talked to *Lay*-gate Stempres," Blaire admitted. He tried to sound unconcerned. Failed. "When we're needed, the militia will be there."

"Not good enough, Colonel. Instant response. I'll have your word on that now, if you don't mind."

The colonel struggled with it. Erik gave the man that much; he was still enough of a Republic man to not go easily into the Swordsworn embrace. But because of that, as well, he would honor his word. "If you call for us, we'll come," he finally granted Erik.

"And I want Raul Ortega dismissed from duty. Now."

That made the upstart MechWarrior sit up and pay attention, mouth gaping open like a landed fish. Dismissed. In effect, dispossessed. MechWarriors dreaded losing their BattleMechs. It was like telling a hawk that it could no longer fly and hunt. Erik knew first-hand, having lost a 'Mech before, how much it hurt. After the half-dozen slights, insults and setbacks he had faced at Raul Ortega's hands since first meeting him as a Customs Officer, Erik reveled in imposing the sentence, slapping the man back into place.

Blaire hedged. "Now that may be a bit hasty, Lord Sandoval. To remove one of our only MechWarriors from the order of battle—seems to me that we're handicapping ourselves." He searched for an argument. "Neither of us wants the Hyperpulse Generator to fall into Steel Wolf hands, after all."

"That no longer concerns me, Colonel Blaire. The Steel Wolves will never be allowed possession of the HPG. After consulting with Governor Haider, my forces have been hard at work rigging spoilsport charges on the antennae superstructure as well as throughout the compound. We've decided to blow the equipment before surrendering it to Torrent's marauders."

Or back to the militia, Erik did not have to say.

For once, Raul Ortega looked speechless. The MechWarrior glanced rapidly between Blaire and Erik, trying to guess which way the colonel would eventually lean. As if the man had any choice.

Blaire slumped in defeat. "Raul, you're sidelined." He saw the expected outburst coming, and headed it off with a stronger argument. "Ah should have done it days ago, and you know it. Tassa Kay can take over the *Legionnaire* until and unless her *Ryoken* is repaired to adequate function. After that, well, Ah'm certain that Lord Sandoval has ideas for a replacement."

"Captain Norgales," Erik said at once. "Legate Stempres' aide." He had wanted to claim the *Legionnaire* outright and invest Norgales in it, but had not figured on Tassa Kay's *Ryoken* being so badly damaged.

And since the woman did not have the good graces to die during the assault on the Brightwater facility, Erik would be happy to see her pushed in front of the blades once more.

"Colonel," Raul began, then hesitated. "Sir, I request assignment to an IndustrialMech conversion. I can still pilot."

"We have men who are better trained for those machines, Raul, and you know it. You'll have to wait for another BattleMech. I think you know what those chances are."

Another BattleMech arriving on Achernar, with or without a pilot? Erik counted the odds somewhere past the chances of the sun not rising tomorrow. He stood. "I'm so glad to see that we are at an accord, Colonel. With the militia's help, we'll keep Achernar free of Kal Radick's clutches yet." He nodded a dismissal to the militia commander. "Colonel Blaire."

To Raul he smiled thinly. "Agent Ortega," he said in leaving, reducing Raul in rank to his original position as a Customs Officer. Raul's surprised start told him the arrow had gone deep, as Erik had intended.

Everything, he decided, was going to go as he intended. Now, with the militia. Soon, with Star Colonel Torrent. And, eventually, with the position and honors his uncle would bestow on him. Erik was not about to let anything stand in his way.

Especially Raul Ortega.

23

Final Decisions

The tactical planning room of the DropShip *Lupus* was an outboard space, strangely shaped as it nestled up against the *Overlord*'s curved hull. Rather like a trapezoid, with a concave, sloping base. Utilities covered one of the inside bulkheads, caught between decks in a frozen cascade of pipes, electrical conduit and wave guides. The other held a large, darkened monitor and a computer terminal. The trapezoid's top had been punched through with one vent for warm, sterilized air, one for recirc, and the only door in or out.

Star Colonel Torrent was always the last to arrive. He stepped through the door at precisely eight a.m. local time, shut and locked the door behind him. Any officer who did not deign to be present found themselves not only shut out of the room, but would be fighting—literally—for their job before the afternoon was over.

A crescent-shaped metal table stood bolted into the center of the room with a curved bench around the outside and a single, swiveling seat positioned on the crescent's inside. A small holographic emitter rose up in the table's center, currently displaying a three-dimensional model of the local HPG station. Torrent took a roll call by eye, then stood over the empty seat with large hands resting on its high back.

"Today," he asked the trio of senior officers, "or tomorrow?"

No one jumped to give him the bad news, and so he knew long before Star Captain Demos spoke up. "Tomorrow," she said. She reached up to tug at a long curl of her shiny, black hair, what Nikola herself would have called a 'tell.' The armor commander was beginning to feel the pressure. "My technicians are still rebuilding the engines on two hovercraft, hoping to replace the Demon we lost the other day. Our Condor drivers could use the extra time on simulators, as well, and the Elementals are still too slow in dismantling so many charges."

A childish effort on Erik Sandoval's part, Torrent thought. Breaking the toys he cannot play with. The Star Colonel's people would strip away enough of the spoilsport demolitions that any damage would be easily repaired.

He glanced at the next officer in line, but MechWarrior Franzia also demurred. Two of his IndustrialMech pilots had light injuries that could use the extra day of rest.

"Xera?" Torrent turned back to his senior pilot.

The raven-haired warrior never hesitated. "My warriors will be ready to go when you command it, Star Colonel."

What few warriors she had left. The toll on aerospace was always highest on extended missions such as these. Taking the San Marino had cost the Steel Wolves two good pilots and two locally irreplaceable fightercraft. A double-flight of four *Jagatai* was all that remained.

Torrent gripped the chair back with frustration, wanting to tear it out of its floor-mounted socket. Then he relaxed, setting aside his bloodlust by sheer force of will. He spun the chair around, took his seat, and then swiveled back to face his advisors.

"Tomorrow," he said. "Dusk. I want the best possible

conditions for our air support. I will make a challenge to Erik Sandoval, and to the people of River's End, right after our meeting. No one will ever say that my Steel Wolves did not conduct themselves with due honor. Now," he ordered Franzia, "tell me about the militia."

The other MechWarrior was slight of build and had a tendency to stutter when extremely nervous. He was neither trueborn nor even of Clan Wolf origins, but one of the Republic freeborn who had come to Kal Radick and petitioned for acceptance. On the surface, he was a poor replacement to Star Commander Yulri as one of Torrent's planning staff. But the man was a gifted MechWarrior, no doubt about that. It was the one mitigating fact in his favor.

"I-I've . . . I *have* been going over the reports, Star Colonel. The militia has reported high casualties from the B-Brightwater diversionary assault and from our taking the San Marino. There are also rumors that they've—they *have*—suffered several d-d-desertions in the past week."

At least the man tried to correct his lazy grammar. Torrent tapped a thick finger against his jaw. "MechWarrior Franzia, you say 'reports and rumors' as if you do not believe them."

Franzia slid out from his place at the end of the bench, typed rapidly into the nearby computer terminal. The staccato fire of the keyboard reminded Torrent that the man had been a computer slave not so long ago. An accountant! And now he commanded a BattleMech.

"I do not, Star Colonel." Columns of numbers filled the wall monitor. "The casualty reports are extremely high compared to their survival rates in previous engagements, by a factor of seven-point-five to one. And these desertions? By all accounts, they have led to no *defections,* which I find interesting. A dozen men and women of shaky allegiance to the Republic, and not one has contacted us? Statistically speaking, that is highly unlikely."

Torrent noted the other man's confidence once he slipped into the realm of numbers. Franzia lost his stutter and all indications of doubt. And in Torrent's presence, too. That, more than anything, convinced the Star Colonel.

"What about the Swordsworn?" Nikola asked. "Perhaps the defectors went over to them."

Franzia nodded, paused as if confused, then shook his head. "Except that you yourself assured me, Star Captain, that no vehicles could move into River's End without our being aware of it. Where did the APCs go? Why haven't we seen Cavalier suits among the Swordsworn infantry posts?" He caught the contraction too late. "Excuse m-my base language. The militia may have suffered some losses, but I believe they are also using this to hide forces from the Swordsworn as well as us."

Torrent nodded. "Preparing for an underground resistance," he said, "*or* a surprise attack."

Demos dismissed that with a wave of her hand. "Give them exactly what they had when we took the spaceport, and I will still lay five-to-seven odds in our favor."

"And if the Swordsworn and militia actually join forces?" Torrent asked.

"If they work together seamlessly, under one authority? Five will get you eight." She smiled. "If Sandoval hangs back again, and does not engage? The morale hit alone will improve our odds."

The commander could not resist his indulgent smile. "Nikola, looking to recoup your earlier losses?"

"Aff, Star Colonel. I would. Except that I find Achernar's position to be a poor wager, and I have learned not to bet against you regardless."

Torrent rose, leaning over the table and fixing each of his advisors in turn with a hard stare. "Always a good lesson," he said. A predator's grin slowly crept up on his face, stretching the edges of his wide, wide mouth. "Now, let us go teach it to Achernar."

River's End General
Achernar

Every tri-vid on the floor—likely in the entire hospital—was turned on to the announcement. Jessica Searcy caught snatches of the beginning from every door as she made her rounds, then finally stopped in a room once she understood what was happening. A public address by Star Colonel Torrent of the Steel Wolves: another challenge.

"For the safety of all," Torrent was saying, "I ask that you remain indoors and away from the spaceport, the industrial sector, and any location where our opponents have gathered. That Prefect Kal Radick's orders have been ignored, rebuffed, forcing us to bring violence to your world, is a tragedy. Do not let it visit unnecessary hardship on you or your families. Do not come in between the Steel Wolves and their prey."

The hard glint in Torrent's dark eyes, his savage appearance with the shaved head and white, white teeth— Jessica shivered with a cold thrill. This man meant exactly what he said. And more. The warning was meant for the militia as well as any civilian. The Steel Wolves were coming for Sandoval and his Swordsworn forces.

Coming tomorrow.

"Dusk," Torrent promised. "Our forces may be met at the spaceport or at any venue between us and our goal. As the challenged party, that decision belongs to your defenders. It is the final decision they may make. All of mine against all of theirs. That was the bargain struck. That is the bargain they must now live up to.

"Bargained well," he said without warmth, "and done."

The video cut back to a long shot of the San Marino spaceport, and the Steel Wolf DropShips commanding the field. Then it switched back to a news anchor, and Jessica slipped from the room.

Questions paraded through Jessica's head and her legs shook with sapped strength. She leaned back against the wall in the deserted corridor. One way or another, it looked as if tomorrow was going to decide the fate of Achernar. Had Raul had enough time? Would the militia wait and form an underground resistance, or move to meet the threat now, while they could?

Did she truly believe anymore that her resident honor

saved her from taking a stand, if not for The Republic, then at least for Achernar? As Raul had said, there was no glory in war. But there was duty. Didn't she have the duty as well, citizen or no?

It was a very lonely question, and the empty hall at River's End General contained no remedies. If it was answers she wanted, she would have to look elsewhere. And she would need one other thing, she knew then.

Help.

From the person least likely to give it. And the one she should be least likely to ask.

24

Ascending Jove

Achernar Militia Command
Achernar
18 March 3133

Achernar's sun was barely a hint on the northeast horizon, a pale smudge hardly discernible against the black of night when Raul Ortega arrived in his jeep at the command post staging grounds. Warehouse and hangar doors had been rolled open, spilling yellow fluorescent light across the blacktop in deep, yellow pools. Headlamps and spotlights on two score of military fighting vehicles brightened up the staging grounds to an artificial dawn. Technicians and logistics corps ran everywhere, servicing equipment and turning out every last tank, battlesuit and VTOL.

Tassa Kay and Clark Diago met him near the pool of utility vehicles, coming up together as Raul shucked off his jacket and stripped from a jumpsuit to the cockpit-ready gear of fatigue shorts and a gray cooling vest. The pre-dawn chill bit at him, puckering his lean arms with gooseflesh. Clark clapped Raul on the shoulder, gave him a stiff shake.

"The old man wants a word."

Tossing his gear into the jeep, Raul slapped some

warmth into his arms and then nodded Diago ahead of him. "Your team ready to go?" he asked Tassa, falling into step with her.

She thrust her chin at the two nearest of eight military VTOLs. "Both of those are loaded—overloaded, in fact—with gear and good men. You are certain that this will work? This is not your newest attempt to deny me a separate command?"

"Deny you? Tassa, I'm counting—desperately counting—on you making rendezvous with . . ." Raul trailed off at her poorly hidden grin. Suckered. He licked his lips. "Just don't go haring off after Erik Sandoval before I give the word, all right? And remember, that's a fifty-tonner you're in today. Don't expect it to hold up like your *Ryoken,* and bring it back in as intact as you can."

"You still don't trust me."

He shrugged. "I don't know you."

"You know me," Tassa said. And this time her words carried on more than one frequency.

Raul smiled, but not with the same amount of interest he might have once.

The two of them had stepped lightly around their brief liaison since Tassa's recovery under Jessica's care. Raul knew that—while the passion was there between he and Tassa Kay—there wasn't the emotional bond he truly wanted. In between planning sessions and on-site reviews these last few days, Raul had tried to mention that to her. Talk to her. Tassa had shrugged off his attempts, working first at becoming healthy and then gearing herself up for today's battle.

Though he still wasn't certain whether to feel relieved or slighted that she had set him aside so readily.

Bright, hard white lamps drew them through the maze of vehicles and personnel to the militia's Tribune-model mobile HQ. Colonel Blaire waited for his three Mech-Warriors under a rollout canopy, studying a contour map of River's End and the surrounding area. The old officer carried himself in full field uniform today, with sidearm and sword. You couldn't tell, until he tried to walk, that he balanced on a prosthetic leg. Once the task forces moved off on their objectives, there wouldn't be a fighting man left to command inside the base perimeter. Blaire would follow Raul's larger force, offering them the direct benefit of thirty-six years of military experience.

Raul had readily accepted. He knew they'd need all the help they could get.

Blaire glanced up from the map, on which he had drawn force lines and time indexes for every stage of the day's maneuvers. "It's a very dangerous game we're playing today, Raul." He shrugged. "Ah hope you're certain."

A smirk twitched at the corner of his mouth. "You can court-martial me if it doesn't work. Sir."

"Give me one of your *kay*-det grins, Captain, and Ah'll wipe it off with low-wattage laser. You're the one sitting in the jaws of the trap. If it doesn't work, you'll be dead."

Raul smiled fully, though no humor touched his dark eyes. "There is that."

The colonel gave each one of them a once-over, then nodded his approval before pulling Raul aside. "You know what we're up against and what we have to do today. If you need to make any last-minute changes to the force allotments, now is the time."

He didn't think twice about it. He barely thought once. "I trust each member of the task force with their part today, Colonel."

"All right. Ah trust you, and that's good enough. Post," he ordered the younger man. To Raul's back, he said, "And you make Kyle Powers proud of you, Captain."

Raul nodded, but kept quiet. Jove waited.

Powers' *Jupiter* waited on the far side of the Tribune, standing on wide-spread feet next to the paired *Legionnaires*. While not at full capability, with two autocannons out of commission and still suffering some targeting glitches, the one-hundred-ton assault 'Mech nevertheless loomed over both nearby machines, in height and in raw, physical presence. It was painted in the same colored bands as before—a layering of tans, yellows, and faded reds. Raul's gaze was still drawn first to the great red spot that swirled in a storm over the right breast of the BattleMech.

Which may be how he missed Jessica Searcy at first glance, standing at the foot of the *Jupiter*.

"Jess?" Raul stopped flat in his footsteps.

Setting aside the way his heart pounded against his chest, he could not help but think there was no way his fiancée—ex-fiancée—should be here. Not with the base locked down on full military protocol. When Tassa walked on by, trading a nod of encouragement with Jessica, shock won out over decorum. "What the hell are you doing here?"

Her sharp, answering glare barely kept from cutting into his skin. "Tassa cleared me onto the base. Civilian contractor, temporary warrant officer commission." He hadn't noticed the small, golden caduceus shining on the collar of her paramilitary jumpsuit. He did now. "I'll be in charge of a M.A.S.H. truck. You soldiers have a way of keeping doctors busy."

M.A.S.H.? Jessica was on board for the maneuvers? "I really wish you weren't here." Also not the best way to reopen a conversation. "I can . . . appreciate what you are trying to do here—lord knows we'll need your skills before today is done, but I don't need to be worrying about you out there."

"Don't you mean, you don't need to be worrying about me, *too*?"

Raul held no illusions about whom Jess was referring. She wasn't going to make this easy on him. And it was no less than he deserved. But, "No. I don't mean that at all. Counting every crewman, infantryman, and specialist on the field today there will be over two hundred warm bodies, and I can't afford to worry about any of them. I can only trust them to be there, doing their jobs, because this is how we've all chosen to serve."

She nodded. "Then you can trust the same from me. Yes? Isn't this what a citizen does? Take that extra step?"

Hearing his own argument thrown back at him, and now of all times, left Raul speechless for several seconds. Was she doing this to impress him, or prove something to herself? Either way, it wasn't necessary. Tassa had proven to him over the last month that you did not have to be a registered citizen to carry yourself with honor. And if comparing his fiancée with a one-time *liaison* was not a way to tie himself into knots right before battle, Raul wasn't sure what else qualified.

"Jess, you've been a citizen your entire life in any possible way that it matters. You've always had the right side of that argument. Why are you doing this now?"

Biting down on that lower, pouting lip, Jessica gave in. "Because it was the only way to see you, and wish you luck." Flustered, she clasped one hand around the back of her neck and shot him a new, withering glare. "I'm not through being mad at you yet, and I don't want you to cheat me out of my due by getting killed out there today. And don't get wounded either, because then I'd have to think too long about whether or not to put you back together, and that wouldn't be fair to someone else who deserves help. What's more—"

Stepping forward, Raul held up one hand to cut off her building tirade, placed the tips of his fingers against her lips and readied himself to be slapped again for daring to touch her. She stood mute, the beginning of tears softening her glare, and he leaned in close with eyes never once wavering from hers.

"Thank you," he said simply, choosing only to acknowledge her first, better wishes. Backing his hand away from her mouth to his own, he kissed the backs of his fingers as if she might feel it through the brief, earlier touch. "Today we'll need all the luck we can get."

"I haven't forgiven you yet, you know."

"I know. But there is always the possibility, and that's enough to keep me safe." He stepped aside, reaching for the chain link ladder that hung down the inside of the *Jupiter*'s leg. "Not one wound, then. I promise."

"Maybe a little one," she said to his back. Raul thought he heard a trace of actual humor in her voice. "Couple of painful stitches, and a good scar."

It wasn't much, as far as good wishes went, but Raul would take what absolution he could get. Lady Janella Lakewood had been right about that, too. One was never past the need for forgiveness.

"I'll see what I can do," he said, and then scaled the ladder for his new cockpit, three stories up.

25

Early To Rise

River's End
Achernar
18 March 3133

Star Colonel Torrent habitually rose before dawn on Achernar, his diurnal rhythm set to the twenty-three-hour Tigress clock. Here, he always seemed to have more time than he needed. Most days Torrent wrote it off to an impatience instilled in him over the course of the protracted campaign. This morning, though, an urge drew him down to the *Lupus*'s 'Mech bay and his readied *Tundra Wolf*. One last round to search out any forgotten thoughts before the evening battle. Before victory.

The bay's cavernous interior was still on the half-lights order for nights, which Torrent immediately countermanded. Darkened overhead panels flickered and then shone brightly. A few night-duty technicians made a busier show of loading munitions through the back of a *Catapult*. Torrent ignored them for the open bay door, checking that two sentry vehicles—Scimitars, as it happened—properly blocked the access ramp.

That was where the alarm found him.

The metallic gong of a shipboard general quarters alarm sent the Star Colonel sprinting for his BattleMech, preferring to learn of any danger with seventy-five tons of myomer and armor wrapped about him and his fingers on the triggers of a Longbow missile XX-rack and Series 7 laser. This was what had drawn him down here so early, he knew, scaling the gantry and gaining quick access to his cockpit. With practiced efficiency he released dampening fields from the BattleMech's fusion reactor and cycled through a dozen prestart checks.

A comms headset held up to the side of his right ear connected him with the DropShip's bridge. "Torrent."

"Star Colonel. Remote listening posts have contact with a militia column, coming down out of the base heading east-southeast."

Achernar's militia thought to steal a march on the Steel Wolves? He cast aside the communications set and drew down his neurohelmet from its resting shelf. Plugging himself in, he asked, "Any response out of River's End?" he asked.

"Neg, Star Colonel. River's End is quiet."

MechWarriors Verin and Rheese made the 'Mech Bay within seconds of each other, scrambling for their pair of *Pack Hunters*. Torrent sped through his security procedures, answering with identification and his verbal key without being prompted. "To each, his own," he said, putting emphasis in a slightly different place than the ages-old saying.

His computer released full control about the time his ready-scouts checked in from the ground. A pair of Shandras had beat him out from another bay, but then Torrent had cleared a BattleMech in less than three minutes from alarm to his first, confident step. He would be the first officer on the scene, and if the militia thought to seriously challenge him here, now, he would be first to draw blood today.

By the Great Father, he swore it would be true.

And it would be, because even from the bottom edge of the ramp, calling the Scimitars to him on an auxiliary channel, his HUD lit up with a chaotic jumble of enemy icons. *Legionnaire*. Joust. A trio of JES tacticals. He read the IFF tag codes with a veteran's ease. DI Schmitts. Two Giggin APCs, no doubt brimming with armored infantry. *Jupiter.*

Torrent read it again. *JP3-a.* The same tag his computers had assigned to Kyle Powers during their Trial of Grievance. The Knight had returned from the dead—or at least his BattleMech had. Switching to thermal imaging, he centered his crosshairs over a distant red smear and then called up magnification on an auxiliary monitor.

There it was, standing at the edge of the spaceport tarmac where the razed military field bumped up against the larger civilian side. Torrent smiled. "And today I thought my best victory would be over a *Hatchetman.*" If the militia wanted to gift him with another kill on the *Jupiter,* Torrent would oblige.

His *Pack Hunters* had cleared the bay, and from all three of his DropShip's vehicles and infantry poured, along with a converted ConstructionMech and an Agro-Mech, Star Captain Demos in her personally modified SM1 Destroyer. All that Star Colonel Torrent had left to him on Achernar. Enough to deal with the militia and still take River's End away from Erik Sandoval.

"Form on me, line abreast," he ordered, strutting the *Tundra Wolf* forward toward the far end of the field. "No one fires until I have chosen my target." He wanted the *Jupiter,* of course. If the militia pilot would agree.

He dialed over to a common military band, one which all Republic forces scanned. "I am Star Colonel Torrent, of the Steel Wolves. Who challenges for the San Marino Spaceport?" Not that he expected a true call to Trial, but the forms had to be observed. So Kal Radick expected, and so Torrent of the Kerensky bloodline would do.

The militia had shaken itself out into an inverted wedge, inviting him in toward the center by placing a line of weaker tanks and infantry carriers there, surrounding a Tribune mobile HQ. It was on the closer flank, though, where the *Jupiter* stepped out.

"Captain Raul Ortega, Achernar Militia. We do not

challenge, Star Colonel. We are here to force you from Achernar, or whittle you down to size so that Lady Janella Lakewood will wonder where all your forces went."

The bluff was so transparent that Torrent was inclined to dismiss it for bravado. Still, with thirty seconds to close, he allowed himself the caution of turning over the threat in his mind. By his count, the militia mustered two BattleMechs and one converted ForestryMech, a trinary's worth of tanks—what the regular forces might call a strengthened company—and an estimation of twenty-five battlesuit squads. With the Swordsworn fighting alongside them, working fist-in-gauntlet, perhaps. But not like this. Not now.

"It will take more than a knight's BattleMech to back such a call to arms. Allow me to demonstrate." And from extreme range, Torrent let fly with every long-range missile at his disposal.

The XX-rack dumped a full score of warheads into the air. His Advanced Tactical Missile System automatically selected for extended range and chased the first flight with another nine missiles. Before these had arced over, Torrent was already in range for his laser and timed it so that the spear of bloodred energy carved into the *Jupiter* at the same time as his missiles pummeled the enemy 'Mech.

"Steel Wolves," he said calmly, waiting for his weapons to cycle, "engage at will."

River's End
Achernar

If Erik Sandoval had not demanded quarters befitting his new station, River's End might have been lost.

Ducking his *Hatchetman* into an alleyway, its shovel-blade feet kicking a dumpster along in front of him as Erik might a tin can, the young lord escaped the crossfire that had been set up at the nearby intersections. The *Demon's* lasers angled up and past him, slicing free only a small ridge of armor from his left shoulder before he made his full escape. Safe for the moment, Erik throttled back, planted one wide foot through the alley's thinner ferrocrete and then shoved himself back the way he had come, ax poised in the air overhead and sensing more by instinct than any sensor shadow that one of the Demons, at least, would chase him into the narrow side street.

One did. Saving his autocannon ammo, Erik smashed down his titanium hatchet once, twice. His first cut crushed both laser barrels into mangled ruin. His second caved in the tank's cockpit, bursting ferroglass shields into a rain of splinters and jagged shards that littered the street and sparkled dully in the yellow glow of a street-lamp. Erik kicked the end of the Demon around, letting him gaze down through his own shield at the telltale insignia.

Achernar militia.

Backstabbing sons-of-a-Liao.

Michael Eus had been able to tell him very little, rousing Erik from the president's apartments at Steyger Railways' city offices. Erik was not one to dwell on creature comforts, not usually, but the office complex also had the good fortune of being located only a dozen blocks over from the Achernar HPG station. From his new living room window he could see the massive dish suspended over the compound by geared towers. An impressive underground vault, left over from pre-Republic days, was large enough to house his BattleMech as well as two Condors.

Most of the Swordsworn had mobilized for the city's edge by the time Erik fired up his *Hatchetman* and set it on a similar course. He still could not say for certain why he had spread the Condors out in a flanking search except his inherent distrust—now—of Michael Eus. Erik's care had tumbled the militia's plans several minutes sooner than would have happened otherwise, as first a dark-running VTOL and then a hostile VV1 Ranger was sighted.

Erik's small unit claimed the Ranger, but then lost one Condor to a prowling *Legionnaire* and an AgroMech conversion. Since then, the nobleman had traded block by crucial block, summoning up both MiningMech conversions from the HPG station and calling in VTOL support and fast tanks from Eus.

The second Demon was missing, likely trying to head him off further down the avenue. Instead, Erik turned again for the station, intent on regrouping his forces as close to the HPG as possible. He chose the larger city streets—those which had been reinforced to allow 'Mech movement without collapsing. Then, rounding a corner, he stepped into the middle of an infantry firefight with Hauberks routing a rooftop emplacement of his Purifiers. A Saxon APC waited in nearby shadows while a converted AgroMech disappeared around the next corner.

Erik dealt with the APC first, again slamming down with his handheld ax. Better than against wheeled or tracked tanks, however, the impact was enough to ground out the hovercraft and hold it in place while its lift fans tore themselves to pieces against the concrete walk. A few Hauberks turned on him with their missile-firing backpacks. He easily shrugged aside these detonations while the Purifiers leapt down for hand-to-hand combat. Erik lent a hand—and a foot—as he could. One Hauberk moved too slowly, and ended up a smear of mangled metal and flesh.

"Back to the station," Erik ordered. "All free units, converge." He set off again, this time giving a ride to a few of the Purifiers while more ran and leapt along in his wake.

The militia plans became clear enough as pieces fell into place. A heavy push at the Steel Wolves, to draw everyone's attention, while a covert strike force penetrated River's End from another direction and tried to reclaim the HPG. Except that now he had the small raiding force nearly surrounded, cut off from the spaceport battle by the same soldiers he would have sent to aid against the Steel Wolves. Aid in a limited and self-supporting manner, perhaps, but the militia could have expected some relief.

Now, instead, he would hunt down the raiding force and deal with them personally, leaving the rest to Torrent. And when the Steel Wolves tried limping back to their DropShips, bloodied and weak, then Erik would be waiting.

But first, the *Legionnaire* and its supporting force.

Ortega. No matter that Eus claimed to have intercepted a transmission, placing the militia warrior at the spaceport. Erik bet family money on the *Legionnaire* being piloted by Raul Ortega, who had made a point to defy the noble at every turn since the two of them met. Even before the customs officer turned MechWarrior, he had shown a penchant for disregarding Erik's authority. Like a mosquito, biting and biting at him, always just out of reach and believing that he could not be smashed. Well, he would learn.

All of them would learn before this day was finished.

Some faster than others, he decided as his sensors painted a Warrior H9 attack helicopter cruising over a shopping mall and parking itself over the top of a bank. Its missile system reached for a lock on the *Hatchetman*. Erik pulled his crosshairs over the fragile craft, held the shot for a solid tone, and then pulled into the trigger with a gentle caress. Eighty-millimeter slugs roared out of his left-arm autocannon, tracking in over the VTOL's thermal silhouette.

The pilot tried to sideslip, banking his craft over the main avenue, but Erik corrected his aim faster and the armor-piercing metal chopped into and through the H8's light armor. Walking the stream of hot metal up into the rotor blades, he chopped away one, long vane and chipped up another. The unbalanced craft slewed through the air, losing altitude and finally dashing itself into the middle of the wide avenue where it erupted into a ball of orange fire and spreading pool of greasy flames.

Erik watched the fall, the fire. He rocked his throttles

forward, kicking up into a walk, before he saw the *Le-gionnaire* standing on the far side of the wreckage.

A gout of yellow flash-fire erupted from the *Legion-naire*'s overhead rotary, and fifty-mil slugs buried themselves in the *Hatchetman*'s chest and upper right leg. The hammering impacts shoved Erik back, but could not knock him completely off his feet. The young noble brought his left arm up again, drew a bead over the *Legionnaire* and chased it into a side street with a long pull from his Imperator Class-10 autocannon. He chipped more stone off the bank's facing than he did armor from the fifty-ton BattleMech. Before he could lower his aim, a pair of militia Jousts burst from the opposite side of the same street, crossed the main avenue, and chased off after the *Legionnaire*.

"*Legionnaire* spotted," Erik broadcast, walking in pursuit of the militia machines. "Madison and Ninth, heading south on Ninth. Disregard previous orders. Station guard, protect the HPG. All other units converge on my position."

A JES tactical and his Condor had already homed in on the light of the burning VTOL. Two other ground units radioed in confirmation while a pair of Swordsworn VTOLs raced up from the south to take spotter positions overhead.

Michael Eus called in with other contacts. "Lord Sandoval, we have heavy infantry contact across the southwest edge of the city and as many as half a dozen vehicles reported. They hit and run. Our forces are being pulled southeast and northwest at this time. My bearing on you, one hundred ninety relative, distance point-eight kilometers."

Erik felt his upper lip twitch toward a snarl, worked to keep his voice level and authoritative. "They are opening up a hole for the *Legionnaire* to escape through. Close it!" He pivoted into the corner, ordering his tanks forward and checking that the other two vehicles racing up behind were also his own.

The Purifiers leapt onto the bank roof, skipped over to the shopping mall . . . and disappeared inside a conflagration of missile impacts and converging lasers.

Forewarned, Erik was not about to walk into an ambush. "Five second delay," he ordered his armored lance, then slammed down on the jump jet controls with both feet. His *Hatchetman* leapt skyward on jets of superheated plasma, rocketing in a short arc up and over one corner of the deserted mall while Erik counted, "Five . . . four . . ." At three he began the sharp, short fall into the wide parking lot on the building's other side. Two found him raising back his five-ton hatchet, ready to decapitate the *Legionnaire*. One.

Landing on bent knees into a ready crouch, Erik stepped forward and delivered a shoulder-level swipe at the nearby *Legionnaire*. The blade bit in just below the BattleMech's armored mantle, crushing through protective plating and some myomer musculature but failing to sever anything critical.

His blow staggered the *Legionnaire,* shoving it forward into a tall lamppost, which could not bear the weight of a fifty-ton 'Mech. Sparks flew as the lamp heads shattered against the street. Erik's VTOLs dipped down long enough to spray some lasers into the *Legionnaire*'s face. He would have wanted his armored vehicles to take further bites out of the resilient design, except that as they raced around the corner they fell into a point-blank firefight with the Jousts and one of the Agro conversions.

From down the local boulevard, a hoverbike squad raced up to support Erik's assault. He left the smaller forces to them, concentrating on the *Legionnaire*. Thumbing the firing stud on his autocannon, he smashed several hundred rounds of hot metal into the BattleMech's back. Armor rained down over the parking lot and street in a fury of shards and splinters.

Then the *Legionnaire* regained its balance, spun back at him and bit into his side armor with lasers and a furious stream of autocannon fire. Erik felt his control slipping—his *Hatchetman* falling backward under the terrible onslaught. Fighting against gravity, he managed one stumbling step backward, then another. Enough to slam up against the shopping mall's three-story facing, protecting him from a bone-jarring fall.

Also enough to rob him of several crucial seconds. Erik rocked forward, putting his BattleMech back on stable footing. He traded one last burst of autocannon fire, and that much more armor, with the retreating *Legionnaire*. Then it squeezed in between a corner building and a burning Condor, and was gone again.

The fire-gutted Condor was Erik's, as was a crippled but safely landed VTOL. He counted a militia Demon and the smashed ruin which had once been a Joust also among the victims of the short, violent firefight.

Raul Ortega had stung at him again, but not without losing blood of his own. Erik would make it cost him again.

"*Legionnaire* and Agro—two Agros—heading east on Carrington." Erik's remaining VTOL pilot, back on observation. "Count three . . . four . . . *five* vehicles now. They're spreading out over two streets, on parallel tracks."

Giving up on their attempt and heading for the spaceport, Erik throttled up to his best walking speed, just over forty kilometers per hour, and struck a parallel course to the fleeing raiders. This street had not been reinforced, not even in the old days, before the Succession Wars, when Achernar IndustrialMechs was one of the region's largest producers. His feet punched down through brittle-thin ferrocrete, like a man walking over hard-crusted snow, and forced the *Hatchetman* to slog forward at less than optimum speed. It slowed him down too much. Not that he doubted it would matter.

Erik had only a basic idea of where all his units were, but he had to imagine that three 'Mechs working together would find a hole and crush whatever light resistance he might toss at their feet. City streets were too confining—too favorable for the smaller, mobile force. They had a slight advantage. Until he could pin them in the open, inside the industrial sector which lay in between the San Marino and River's End proper. That was where he would hit them with everything he could muster.

That was where he would kill them all.

26

The Gemini Gambit

River's End/San Marino Spaceport
Achernar
18 March 3133

Raul Ortega shook his head furiously as if trying to clear it of the noise. Comm channels bled over each other as reports, orders, and shouted warnings were passed up and down the militia line. Static crackled in between words and sometimes through an entire order. A moment of clear reception was rare, rare. And when it happened, too often it was the lull before a storm of new, concentrated fire savaged the militia and drowned out transmissions with thunderous explosions.

Fire and shrapnel raged constantly in the no-man's-land that separated the Steel Wolves and Achernar's determined militia. Bright lances of light speared back and forth, reflecting against ground haze built up from the smoky discharges of missile exhaust and burnt autocannon propellant. As the night gave way to sunrise, the only signs of battle falling off were the vehicles left broken and burning in the firefight's wake. Raul counted a militia Fox armored car and two hoverbikes among their early casualties, lost back on the southwest side of the spaceport landing field where the firefight had begun. At least four APCs had been crushed and mangled over the tarmac since then in trying to deploy screens of battlesuit infantry, marking each gruesome shift north and east.

Two of the APCs had managed to disgorge their cargo of armored soldiers. Two had not.

Despite the cost in lives and material, Raul knew that the militia so far had staved off heavy casualties. Their advantage, so far, was their combat VTOLs, the low-altitude craft giving the militia air superiority for the first time since the initial Steel Wolf assault against Achernar. A Yellow Jacket, in fact, a flying version of the Marksman or SM1 Destroyer, could worry even Star Colonel Torrent with its nose-mounted gauss rifle. The militia would not keep that advantage much longer now that daybreak was upon them, but it had been enough to help move their ragged line to the spaceport's northwest border, past the Steel Wolf DropShips and about even with the main tower and various administration buildings.

Nearly at the back of Tassa Kay's retreating picket force.

It took some effort, mentally untangling the cluttered HUD, but so far everything held more or less in accordance with the militia's rough planning. Raul's late positioning was the less. Tassa's early arrival, the more. Tassa had led most of her people from the capital just as dawn broke, turning back on the pursuing Swordsworn and holding them at the city's edge, making feints as if trying to regain the industrial sector.

"Sandoval is getting edgy, Raul. Make this happen soon." Tassa fell back a few more paces, limping on a ruined left knee actuator.

Using his twin PPCs and light autocannon to drive back the Steel Wolves' one remaining M1 Marksman, Raul bracketed it with lances of azure energy and then blasted deep, angry wounds into its armored flank. It pulled back and Raul let it go, wary of the next head-to-head push by Star Colonel Torrent and still fighting toward Tassa's position.

Torrent's attention had been diverted again as a Giggins APC successfully delivered a squad of Gnome battle armor into his line. As Steel Wolf Elementals worked to keep those Gnomes clear of the *Tundra Wolf*, Raul threw two *Jessies* down the enemy line, strafing the seventy-five-ton BattleMech and the wounded Marksman with flight upon flight of short-range missiles.

It bought him a handful of seconds. A moment, perhaps.

Raul pivoted the *Jupiter* toward the admin buildings, claiming another two hundred meters in long, five-meter strides. With white-knuckle grips on his control sticks, Raul shied away from one of the open DropShip landing pads, saving himself from a three-story fall to the underground service area. He still felt unsteady at the controls of such a large assault 'Mech, but the natural touch which had originally recommended him to the militia reserves held strong for him now.

Backed by two Schmitts and flanked by VV1 Rangers, Raul reanchored the militia line another dozen steps—two dozen . . . three . . .

Where he stepped into a barrage of missiles, drawing fire from a Steel Wolf Behemoth and paired JES strategic carriers.

Weathering the storm of hammer blows, shedding some of the *Jupiter*'s armor reserves, Raul wrestled with his control sticks and then turned in to back off the Behemoth. "Blocked again!" Two icons on his HUD flashed dangerously close to the militia line. "Shandra scout vehicles at nine-five relative. Pick them up!"

He wasted no time on the fast but lethal scout-runners, trusting the Rangers and some forward Cavalier infantry to handle them, and the Schmitts had already leapt forward to hammer long-range fifty-mils at a *Big Jess*.

Raul pulled his crosshairs over the Behemoth's large outline, pounding away double-flights of long-ranged missiles as soon as he struck good tone and chasing them with blue-white arcs of lightning from the *Jupiter*'s chest-mounted PPCs.

Unfortunately, the one-hundred-ton tank could stand up to that kind of abuse, though after forty minutes of sparring the tank crew had to be worried about their armor. The tank rolled back on its massive treads, ceding a few scant meters. As if they needed further encouragement, a Yellow Jacket VTOL slid over the north side of the field and skipped a gauss slug off the ferrocrete tarmac next to them.

Sensing opportunity, Raul shifted his own aim over to one of the forward JES carriers. Combining PPCs with his two light autocannon this time, he worried through the missile-boat's armor. The hovering VTOL spent several dangerous seconds following Raul's directed fire, punched a gauss slug through the carrier's weakened armor and then spun around to race back south and west.

Both Schmitts pounced, tearing into the carrier's interior even further, and did not shy away until an ammunition magazine ruptured under their hard-hitting rotaries. The *Jess*'s sides bulged outward and then burst. Flipping side-over-side, the disintegrating hulk rolled up against the retreating Behemoth and added impetus to their temporary retreat.

For just that moment, Raul found himself with no viable targets and a nearly open run between the militia line and spaceport tower.

"Best chance we'll ever get, Colonel." He shoved his throttle forward to its stop, lumbering the *Jupiter* forward at its best speed of fifty-four kph.

Blaire wasted no time doubting Raul's word. "All units, swing echelon left."

VTOLs pressed forward, and a laser-equipped Cyrano fell under the flak-assault from another JES carrier, while most skirmishers dropped back and pulled into their new position. Stealing a quick-march on the Steel Wolves, the militia line swung around in a ragged but effective arc, following Raul's lead and closing the spaceport off from River's End. Their line now held back-to-back with Tassa Kay's smaller force, giving her safe refuge.

Raul toggled his private channel to Tassa Kay, in case

she was not already falling back. "All right, Tassa. Lead them out." A waste of breath, as she first sent her damaged vehicles crawling for the safety of the militia lines and then followed in the borrowed *Legionnaire*. Raul turned back to the battle in time to count up the cost of their maneuver.

His Rangers had overtaken and overturned one of the Shandra scout-runners, but not without losing one of their own to a salvo of concentrated laserfire. Raul had also traded one of his tactical *Jessies* for a Steel Wolf Scimitar—hardly equitable—and enemy *Pack Hunters* had nearly cut Captain Diago out of the militia formation. He escaped back to the safety of their formation, but minus a great deal of armor and losing one of his *Legionnaire*'s arms—severed at the elbow by a *Hunter* PPC.

And worse, Star Colonel Torrent in his *Tundra Wolf* was left pressing forward right into the weak middle of the militia line. Frustrated with Raul's evasion of any straight-up match, now the star colonel took it out on a nearby APC. Breaking the Saxon in less than ten seconds, scattering its load of Purifier infantry with well-placed kicks, he then turned his heavy firepower on the militia's mobile HQ, and Colonel Blaire.

Blaire had organized the enticing weak middle in case Torrent went for it early on in the fight, allowing the militia to encircle and neutralize the Steel Wolf commander once and for all. Up to and including the arrival of Tassa's force at the city edge, that might have worked in their favor. Now it threatened to unravel their final maneuvers, should Torrent manage to split the militia line.

"Fill that gap," Raul ordered. "They break though, and we're done!" They had to hold. Hold and wait, as Tassa lured the Swordsworn out of the city's edge.

Their modified ForestryMech made an attempt, stalking in between Torrent and the Tribune. Autocannon chipping away some of the *Tundra Wolf*'s armor, the pilot managed to draw Torrent's attention long enough for the HQ to fall back a safe distance. Before Torrent could vent his full ire on the Forestry Mod, however, Raul stalked forward of the formation and lined up a long-range shot, carving one of his particle cannons into the *Tundra*'s flank.

It worked. Torrent shifted his BattleMech's weight and turned it for the *Jupiter*. "Raul Ortega. You have deviled me for the last time."

Raul swallowed dryly. "If you can't keep up, don't blame me. Hold on and I'll call off the dogs." Switching over to the militia's all-hands frequency, he ordered, "Lay off the *Tundra*. Let him come." Then a dozen missiles cratered his *Jupiter*'s lower legs, and Raul once again fought to remain standing. Recovering, he backpedaled, returning to his place in line and drawing the star colonel after.

His fury unleashed, Torrent made his earlier displeasure known by keeping up a sustained rate of heavy fire as he stalked down the militia line. Missiles, laser, missiles again. With the militia units leaving off the *Tundra Wolf* as a target, the star colonel ignored all but Raul. A distinction of sorts, and one the MechWarrior might have felt better about had not the *Tundra*'s place at the center of the militia line not been filled almost immediately by the PPC-toting *Pack Hunters*. The Steel Wolves fielded too many 'Mechs for the militia to keep them contained much longer.

In the meantime, Torrent advanced. And with him, drawn in his wake like filings to a lodestone, came the Steel Wolf line.

Fighting side by side with Tassa now, their BattleMechs facing different directions as each concentrated on a different enemy, Raul checked his head's up display and saw that the two of them formed the point of a new, thin wedge. Squeezed in between the Swordsworn and Steel Wolves, Tassa sniped at Erik Sandoval while Raul held up under Torrent's determined assault. Only a slender line of militia forces connected them back to the spaceport's northwest corner. It was time.

Such orders should be given with dramatic presentation. Some kind of timeless oration that would stand up to history. Or so Raul had once thought. Now it was with a strange mixture of relief and disappointment that he opened up a channel and simply said, "Tassa. Now."

Like a steeply pitched tent with its supporting prop yanked out from beneath it, the militia wedge folded back in on itself as Raul and Tassa herded scurrying infantry and wounded vehicles before them. Raul opened up his general channel. "Retrograde maneuver," he ordered. Colonel Blaire seconded the command, and began handing out the secondary assignments, which would pull the entire militia force back into a strong, secure fist.

The idea was to swing the Swordsworn *and* Steel Wolf line into close proximity. One errant missile, a laser stabbed in at their former enemies: it wouldn't take much. But first they had to maneuver into close range.

Tassa was the first one to notice. "Raul. It's not working."

Raul rocked back three hurried steps as Torrent sliced a small laser beam across the shield protecting the *Jupiter*'s cockpit. Molten ferroglass streaked down and recrystalized. Raul blinked to clear his vision of the ghost image temporarily burned into his retina. "Give it time."

As the militia continued to fall back, too often leaving a body or the fire-gutted shell of another vehicle behind, the Swordsworn and Steel Wolves were drawn forward, ever closer to each other. At the base of the collapsing formation, in fact, retreating soldiers reinforced each side, spreading the wings out in a north-south push that shoved the factions into three wedges of an asymmetrical pie.

The Steel Wolves were still the largest, but it was the militia who fought on two fronts. So far.

"Ortega . . ." Blaire's warning growled in Raul's ears.

Someone else not privy to the officer's worries noticed yet another problem. "The Wolves are getting up aerospace fighters."

That was true. With the militia finally pushed completely away from the taxiing strip, a squadron of four fightercraft rolled out from beneath the protective wings of the *Triumph*-class DropShip. Once in the air, with daylight to gauge their strafing runs, the Steel Wolves would heap more misery onto the militia's plate.

"VTOLs!" Raul knew he was sending good men and women to their deaths, but knew as well that Achernar wasn't quite done demanding its sacrifice. "Forward and harass the fighters. Buy us time." Two Yellow Jackets and the one remaining Cyrano thundered forward. The Cyrano never made it over the enemy formation, swatted down by a *Catapult*'s multiple missile barrages.

Still the Swordsworn and Steel Wolves pressed in, close to fighting side-by-side now and hardly acknowledging each other's presence. An SM1 nipped in and cut a leg from their ForestryMech, sending it crashing to the tarmac. Diago cut in on the senior officers channel. "Raul, maybe we should think about—"

"It'll work," Raul promised, cutting him off. "Give it time." He dropped crosshairs over the *Tundra Wolf*'s outline, lashing out with PPCs and running another ton of molten armor over the field ferrocrete. It had to work. Achernar was out of choices, and out of time.

River's End/San Marino Spaceport
Achernar

Erik Sandoval-Groell had nearly given up on the *Legionnaire*, counting it and the rest of the raiding party as lost once it cleared the capital's southeast industrial sector ahead of him.

On a private channel Erik railed at Michael Eus, who had set the entrapment the way *he* saw fit rather than as Erik had directed. The operations manager had many hidden talents, and even more hidden loyalties, but military planning did not rate highly among them. He had tried to close the net with slower-moving, tracked vehicles, thinking that their heavier armor would mitigate any losses. Even a first-year cadet understood that one used fast-response craft to pin an enemy in place, then rolled in the heavy guns to obliterate them.

Erik's rage was short-lived, however, the heat draining from his face when he gained the city's edge and found his forces holding off repeated attempts by the *Legionnaire* to regain the capital. Adding his own autocannon into the defensive enfilade, the young noble concentrated on the *Legionnaire* or one of the modified IndustrialMechs whenever possible. After he personally laid out the converted LoaderMech, his crosshairs found no other target than the *Legionnaire*.

As that BattleMech pulled back from the city, joining the rest of the militia force on the outskirts of the San Marino landing field, Erik cautiously followed rather than be denied his due after the treacherous attempt. Between his Swordsworn's carefully laid fire patterns and the brute-force cascade of firepower spreading out from the Steel Wolves, slowly they hammered the Republic's wedge flat and then caved it in. Likely they could have continued on until little was left of the Achernar militia but memories and a ready garrison post for Swordsworn forces to occupy.

Might have, in fact, except for a daring Shandra scout vehicle that shied too close onto Erik's flank in trying to avoid a passing Yellow Jacket gunship.

With casual need, Erik ordered up a pair of hoverbikes to birddog the Shandra, run it off. Light weapons fire stitched dark holes in its side armor, and was returned with interest as twin, ten-millimeter gatlings burned one driver from the hoverbike's seat.

Setting his jaw, teeth grinding together at the death of another Swordsworn warrior, Erik felt the warm flush return as he leveled his powerful Imperator autocannon at the Shandra and shattered its rear drive train with a long, deadly burst of hot metal.

And Erik might have let it go at that. He had not wanted to waste a precious amount of his dwindling ammunition supply on the Shandra, except that it had de-

manded some response from him as their leader and—
when necessary—avenger.

He tensed when the alarms wailed their warning blast
only seconds before the missiles hit all around his position. A half dozen smashed into the side of his *Hatchetman*'s elongated head, rocking it to one side like a
prizefighter caught by a series of left hooks. The cockpit
shook violently, body-checking Erik against his harness
straps until a seam ripped and Erik slid half out of his
command couch.

Neurofeedback works two ways: for the MechWarrior,
when he can use his own sense of balance to help a
stressed gyroscope; against him, when any personal dizziness or faulted equilibrium is translated into a signal that
is then used to alter the gyro's normal function.

Erik's vision swam and his gut clenched up as the
Hatchetman toppled over. He heard the shouts of alarm
on the comms system, could imagine his warriors turning
quickly to his aid, and opened his mouth to countermand
their likely actions.

Then the BattleMech struck against the ground, keel-
ing over on its side and jarring Erik most the rest of the
way out of his seat. Scraping along, it rattled the hapless
MechWarrior against his faulty harness. The world
dimmed to gray tones and blurred angles. Not long. Only
for a few seconds.

And by the time Erik had fought his way back to full
senses, it was already too late.

San Marino Spaceport
Achernar

Star Colonel Torrent heard the alarm, that the Swordsworn had also turned on his warriors. Heard it, noted
the expected treachery, and filed it away for future
consideration.

Chopping the *Jupiter* down to size filled his entire consciousness, and he pursued that goal almost to the exclu-

sion of all else. The militia tactics hardly mattered, and even the threat of two Yellow Jacket gunships thundering after his vulnerable aerospace fighters did not drag him away from his personal challenge.

Then his Behemoth crew reported that they had felled Sandoval's *Hatchetman,* and Torrent was forced to take notice if for no other reason than to confirm that one of the Steel Wolves' primary opponents on Achernar was finished.

Erik Sandoval was down, though far from finished. And Torrent himself became personally involved a few seconds later when two Swordsworn *Jessies* layered four score long-ranged missiles over his position. Blackened, smoking gravel pelted his 'Mech as warheads gouged the ferrocrete tarmac, and the *Tundra Wolf* shook with forced palsy as fire blossomed along his chest and shoulders.

Too many times today other units had forced their attention on Torrent, interfering with his second Trial against the *Jupiter* and against Raul Ortega, the only MechWarrior so far to walk away from him in combat. Anger twisted the star colonel's face into a snarl as he dropped crosshairs over one of the Swordsworn Mining Mods. A flight of missiles and two slices with his Series 7 laser—left, right—and the Mod lost the arm carrying its rock-cutting blade.

More Swordsworn had turned against the Steel Wolf position, drilling lasers and streams of autocannon fire into their ranks. Torrent divided a few seconds in between his head's up display and what he saw through his own ferroglass shield, then barked out his first of three orders.

"All 'Mechs, press the militia." He might lose a *Pack Hunter,* maybe one of his modified IndustrialMechs, but Ortega's people would know they had been struck. "Star Commander Orvits," he called up one of his remaining JES carries, "swat those Yellow Jackets and protect the aerospace fighters." He might need the air support after all.

"Star Captain Demos, destroy the Swordsworn and prepare to move on River's End at once!"

By the time this battle was over, there would be very little left in their way. He would make certain of that, starting—and finally finishing—with the *Jupiter*.

River's End/San Marino Spaceport
Achernar

"I think we've got them."

Pulling back in the face of Star Colonel Torrent's renewed assault, Raul targeted the advancing *Tundra Wolf* with PPC arcs while keeping an eye on his auxiliary monitor. He saw a few shots traded between Swordsworn and Steel Wolves, enough to put him on pins and needles until a Steel Wolf SM1 Destroyer led an entire star of heavy vehicles into Erik Sandoval's flank.

"That's it, Tassa. Now go!"

The *Legionnaire* surged forward on new legs, barely favoring its ruined left knee actuator. Tassa called to her side what was left of her squad—a Condor, Joust and Demon. No IndustrialMech conversions this time. And no APCs followed her. If everything had gone even half-according to plan earlier, the Trooper transports had dropped armored infantry squads near the HPG station and were already waiting in place.

This time there were far fewer defenders to stand in her way. The reconstituted lance drove back around the end of the Swordsworn line, caught their mobile HQ on the edge of River's End, and blasted their way past it in less time than it took Raul to lose Torrent's *Tundra Wolf* for what was likely his last opportunity.

Erik Sandoval's mobile HQ was not the only one in trouble. Torrent's *Pack Hunters* had finally slipped their leash, leaping forward on jump jets to savage the militia middle, relying on their excellent speed to dodge back when necessary, and then bounding forward yet again.

Colonel Blaire was in trouble, but had nowhere to call

for help. Diago had his hands full with a *Catapult* and an AgroMech Mod. Blaire's hoverbike escorts held back a lumbering ConstructionMech conversion, but likely not for much longer the way both vehicles slewed around, spilling critical air from damaged lift skirts.

Raul waded in with PPCs arcing out manmade lightning and his autocannons blazing with extra-long pulls, hammering lethal metal into a *Hunter* again, and again. Both *Pack Hunter* BattleMechs spun around, kicking themselves up over one hundred kilometers per hour in order to close rapidly on the assault machine. Or at least, for one of them to do so. Blaire ordered his Tribune turned into the path of the second, stalling it for several critical seconds.

A mobile HQ vehicle is slow and awkward, never meant for tactical maneuvers, but as a temporary wall it served. Raul faced down the single, thirty-ton machine with something less than trepidation. He rode lightly on his triggers, still running high heat from matching earlier salvoes with the *Tundra Wolf*, but even so a single PPC and paired autocannons could be devastating.

The *Pack Hunter* shed armor the way a true wolf might lose its winter coat. Its return fire cut a dangerous swath of armor from Raul's gyro housing to the left shoulder, but failed to penetrate into the *Jupiter*'s critical equipment.

Eight minilasers created more trouble for Raul, blistering paint and armor from half a dozen places and coring one weak beam directly into Jove's head. Raul could smell the ozone discharge, and something more, caustic yet sweet. As he flushed with warmth, suddenly conscious of the sweat standing out on his chest draining down his sides, he realized that the *Hunter* had crippled his life support system, somewhere rupturing a coolant line.

With no time for niceties and not about to take another biting return, Raul risked the heat and blasted the *Pack Hunter*. Lightning scoured armor away from the other 'Mech's chest and upper arms. If the Steel Wolf warrior thought that he'd get so lucky twice, though, Raul dissuaded him of that notion as autocannons ripped in and mangled the *Hunter*'s gyroscope into scrap. The *Pack Hunter* quivered, staggered awkwardly to the left, and then collapsed like an unstrung puppet.

Its companion 'Mech, having cut in jumpjets to sail over the Tribune, altered trajectory and landed between two APCs, one of which it overturned with a vicious point-blank PPC blast and the second with a well-placed kick.

The militia infantry was doing its part, providing a scattering of small, hard-to-hit targets. Raul saw two Hauberk squads sacrifice themselves in an assault against the Steel Wolves' ConstructionMech so that a Cavalier Specialist troop could seize and take control of the Mod.

"Two!" Colonel Blaire called out over the officers' channel. Two 'Mechs in as many minutes. And then in the next moment, the militia lost their final WorkMech Mod to the Swordsworn front. Still, "About even," he judged.

Raul nodded. "Now let's see if we can't finally tip things our way for once." He tied in a frequency routinely used by Customs Security. "Palos, is everything set?"

CSO Palos Montgomery jumped right in. "All set, Captain."

"Do it," Raul said.

A longer order wasn't needed. Alarms wailed for attention, and Raul managed only half a turn before Star Colonel Torrent finally caught up to him with full weapons blazing. A series of lasers, one large, blood red lance and four smaller, scarlet arrows, splashed away armor from all along Raul's right side. Missiles exploded in a series of thunderclap detonations, walking up the *Jupiter*'s tall form, blossoming fireballs at the knees, waist, chest, and then finally slamming two short-range missiles into the BattleMech's head.

Ferroglass squealed, fractured, and then burst inward as flaws and stresses finally gave way to the concussive warhead. Shards sprayed and struck Raul along the side of his neck and chest. One hand slipped from the *Jupiter*'s controls and the towering leviathan toppled off to its right side, surrendering itself to gravity and the tarmac's rough embrace.

Raul had a split second to remember his promise to Jessica that he'd come through the battle safe and whole.

Then he didn't even have that as the cockpit slammed forward and darkness swam over him.

27

Serving Achernar

River's End/San Marino Spaceport
Achernar
18 March 3133

The wire-frame damage schematic of Erik's *Hatchetman* showed critical armor loss down the entire left side. Back on his feet now, he blasted several hundred rounds of eighty-mil into a nearby Steel Wolf Condor and continued his backward retreat to the city's edge. He considered calling up the reserve force he had left guarding the HPG station, but then decided to hold them back as his final ace.

"Here they come again!" his remaining Mod pilot warned.

Running in pack formation, the five armored hovercraft bent around to continue their saber-dance tactics. Led by one of the deadly SM1 Destroyers, flanked by two Condors and another pair of JES tactical carriers, they would slice in at an angle, burn off a salvo of autocannon, lasers and missiles, and then turn out again to slip away before any concerted effort could be made against them.

Not this time.

"Grady, get in their way." Erik ordered the MinerMech forward. "Stall them."

Then he cut in his jumpjets, venting plasma down into the *Hatchetman*'s Luxor reaction chambers and burning skyward on glowing jets. The *Hatchetman* arced up in a short hop, falling just short of the SM1 while the gray and black Miner rolled forward on the far side to try and force a stand.

Just a little too late, Erik was forced to turn against one of the trailing Condors rather than taking a swing at the lead vehicle. His titanium hatchet cut down, smashing into the front of the hovercraft and forcing a stall.

With the glider's momentum arrested, Erik trained in an autocannon and ripped several long stripes of hot metal into the Condor's ruined front. He saw blood spatter over the interior cockpit ferroglass as his cannon tore holes through the forward shield and riddled the crewmen inside.

He would not be allowed to enjoy his brief victory, however.

The SM1, showing a veteran's touch on the controls, swung around the backside of Grady's MinerMech. Running forward on momentum alone, the Destroyer banked and cut its drive fan, rotating in a free-powered turn and using its assault-class weapon to show Erik exactly what an autocannon could do. A firestorm of flame and lethal metal burst from the twelve-centimeter bore, blasting into the Miner's lower back and erupting out the front in a gut-coring strike that left the Miner dead on its feet.

With a kind of slow grace, the six-meter tall machine drifted to one side, then toppled over to lay still.

Permanently.

A pair of JES carriers rained several score missiles over the retreating SM1, but it sailed out from under most of the damage and then powered after its three remaining lancemates.

"We can't compete," Erik spoke aloud, but mostly to

himself. Not spread out in a skirmish line, waiting to be picked off by the deadly Destroyer. "Fall back," he ordered. "Regroup, regroup!"

No sooner was the order given than a new crisis erupted over the communication net. "Station guard, station guard. We are under attack."

Erik stabbed at the comm panel, toggling for his reserve frequency. "Who is attacking?" he shouted. Who was left, not already involved at the spaceport battlefield?

"Sir . . . sir. Mix of infantry emplacements in the facing buildings. More on the roof. Armored tanks—militia vehicles, lord—have seized the intersection. *Legionnaire!* BattleMech on the grounds!"

Reading his HUD, Erik counted only one *Legionnaire,* and that one at the far side of the fighting from his position. "Where did it go? What happened to the *Legionnaire* we chased out of the city?" Caught up against the pressing Steel Wolves, he had made the dangerous assumption that it had finally fallen in battle.

His Behemoth driver—now the ranking second-officer on the field—answered. "Blasted the hell out of our Praetorian and escaped back into the city, Lord Sandoval. While you recovered."

Erik had seen the battle-damaged Praetorian still moving in the backfield, but there had been no transmissions and he had written that off to Eus not really knowing what to say in the midst of such a heavy-scale fight. Thirty seconds. Maybe sixty. That was as long as Erik had been distracted, picking himself up after the fall.

Fortunes changed that quickly in battle.

Ortega. It could only be Ortega.

He spent several more critical moments trying to disengage, moving back for the city's edge. A pair of Steel Wolf Destroyers cruised in, forcing him back, and then a lone Condor delayed him in a sacrificial run that eventually traded itself for one of the Swordsworn Marksmen.

Finally, turning for the city's edge and throttling up to

the *Hatchetman*'s full running speed, Erik gazed over some of the large industrial centers nearby at the top crescent of the HPG compound's titanic dish. If he moved quickly, sent his faster hovercraft ahead and left the Behemoth on guard at their backs . . .

A solid plan—it might have worked.

It all fell apart as the first eruption of fire and smoke rose up into the sky, climbing the HPG superstructure.

"Stone's blood!" someone swore. "Was that . . ."

. . . the spoilsport charges Erik's people had rigged to the HPG equipment.

Another series of explosions blossomed on the antenna's upper structure, and lazy swirls of dark gray smoke rose from all around the neighborhood. As easily as that, the entire Swordsworn position had been rendered moot. Erik throttled down to a slow walk, shaking his head at the militia's stupidity. They hadn't left things well enough alone, and now what had they wrought? He sat back hard against his command couch and read his future in the black, thickening air.

A future that would no longer include Achernar.

River's End/San Marino Spaceport
Achernar

Lost!

Star Colonel Torrent stared over the battle scene at the pall of angry smoke hanging over the southeast industrial sector of River's End. Through the haze a lick of tall flames could be seen, running up a red-orange flag of defeat next to the charred and scarred HPG dish. Everything the Steel Wolves had fought for, all that he personally had challenged to accomplish, ended in just a few short seconds of treachery.

No victory. No honor.

He rounded his *Tundra Wolf* against the rising *Jupiter,* white-knuckle hands gripping the control sticks. The *Ju-*

piter regained a shaky footing and teetered in place. "Your doing! Like a jackal vomiting over what it cannot eat, you would deny the prize to the victor."

"It was never about a prize," Ortega said, his voice shaky but growing in strength. "This was about Achernar. If you didn't see it that way, it's no fault of mine."

With each use of debased language, Torrent's rage doubled. He felt a flush of crimson warmth on his face, the tremble of anger in his muscles. "So you expect us to simply leave?"

"There's nothing for you here anymore, Star Colonel."

Torrent smiled, thin and cruel. If the militia MechWarrior had seen it, the star colonel felt certain he would have cowered away. Deactivating his targeting system to prevent any warning, Torrent pulled dark crosshairs across the *Jupiter,* aiming by dead reckoning.

"There is still you," he said, then toggled on full targeting and pulled into his triggers.

River's End/San Marino
Achernar

In between his shaky dialog with Star Colonel Torrent, Raul muted his voice-activated mic and coughed, clearing his lungs of acrid smoke. The taste of burnt plastic coated his mouth and his tongue felt thick and swollen from dehydration. A stabbing pain had lanced into his right shoulder with every movement until he managed to pull from it a long ferroglass shard, dagger-shaped and bloody. The wound bled slowly, trickling red paths down his bare arm.

Another minute, Raul asked silently. *Keep him talking.*

Four hundred meters off of the *Tundra Wolf*'s left side, one of the lowered DropShip landing pads flashed warning lights as massive machinery warmed to life and raised the platform. For the service-tunnel workers to choose that moment for a test, or to pop their heads outside for a look, would be too much of a coincidence for Torrent. It might warn him that something else was afoot.

Not to worry. The Star Colonel had eyes only for the *Jupiter*.

Raul couldn't say for certain what had warned him of the impending attack. A shift in the *Tundra Wolf*'s stance, or the malice that bred in Torrent's voice the longer they talked. At the last moment he ducked Jove to the right, protecting the shattered side of his cockpit's transparent shield, and leaned forward into the brunt of the assault.

Missiles chewed away at his legs, cracking apart welded seams and clawing through for myomer muscles and control circuitry.

The *Tundra Wolf*'s large laser cut at one arm, splashing armor into a dark, molten mist, and a trio of smaller lasers stabbed into his chest and left shoulder.

Only Jove's impressive armor had kept Raul alive for so long, allowing him to wade through some of the heaviest fighting of the day, protecting him while he learned both the subtle and not-so-subtle nuances of fighting such a massive war avatar. It protected him again now, although the wire-frame darkened to black in several areas, warning Raul of thinning reserves.

Kicking the *Jupiter* into an unsteady walk, Raul shied away from the raising platform and drew Torrent after him. His PPCs answered the star colonel's missiles. Where Torrent relied on lasers, Raul chopped back with his two fifty-mil autocannon.

His heat scale rose steadily as the fusion reactor pumped out joules of energy to drive the BattleMech and power all weapons. As it edged into the red band, a fresh scent of ozone and scorched insulation wafted through the cockpit and Raul breathed with difficulty. Sweat poured off his brow, beaded and ran on his bared legs and arms. On his right, the runnels of sweat mixed with blood, thinned it, and spread the stain further down his arm.

Alternating his PPCs now, Raul blasted more armor away from Torrent's chest. Deep inside one rent sparked the golden fury of a BattleMech's fusion fire. Dark, dry smoke roiled out of the wound.

Torrent ignored it, shaving more plating from Jove's already-weak legs and lower torso.

On the MechWarrior's HUD, his computer painted several new icons. Over the *Tundra Wolf*'s shoulder, Raul saw machines rise above the surface of the landing field: WorkMechs, a half-dozen of them, loaders, mostly, and one ConstructionMech. They displayed no targeting emissions or other evidence of military modifications. These were regular machines, gathered up by Customs Officer Palos Montgomery and urged into battle for Achernar.

"Target practice," Torrent said. "You think I do not see them, Ortega? They will be little else but a nuisance against my Steel Wolves."

A new flight of tactical missiles slammed a heavy fist into Raul's gyro housing, cracking through armor and supports to throw a terrible, grinding into the stabilizer gearing. The *Jupiter* shuddered, swayed. Blinking through the burning haze of sweat-stung eyes, Raul ducked forward and shifted the BattleMech's feet into a wider stance. If he went over now, it was finished. There would be no getting back up, and Torrent's *Tundra Wolf* would tear through the IndustrialMechs without mercy.

This time he kept to his feet.

"You will never have your chance—at—them," Raul said, gritting his teeth against the heat waves and punctuating each of the last three words with weapons fire. PPC. Autocannon. PPC. One of the *Tundra Wolf*'s arms fell to the ground, severed by a particle beam mid-humerus.

Left arm. Torrent's quad of medium-grade lasers.

Throttling into a forward walk, Raul now marched straight into the teeth of the Steel Wolf commander. "You are *through* on Achernar." Another particle cannon. This one carved a huge swath of blackened destruction across the other BattleMech's hip.

Raul gasped for breath in the scorching air.

Tactical missiles and large lasers smashed at the *Jupiter*. A long branch of pressure-cracked ferroglass squealed across the front face shield. Raul leaned forward again, his face within a meter of the worried shield, forcing Jove onward. Torrent cut loose with LRMs but misjudged his angle for a point-blank assault. Most of the missiles stuttered into the ground at the *Jupiter*'s feet, geysering up blackened ferrocrete and throwing a veil of smoke over the lower half of the assault 'Mech.

Raul kicked his way through the broken ground, drew flashing crosshairs over the *Tundra Wolf*'s left shoulder. The heat-addled circuitry could do no better than a partial lock. He clenched back both primary triggers regardless.

"No more," he whispered.

One of his PPCs gashed wide the *Tundra Wolf*'s chest. Flames licked out and up the broad torso, wreathed the cockpit shield in a halo of fire.

Slapping at the shutdown override, Raul stomped to a halt bare meters from the staggered *Tundra Wolf*. No other part of the battle registered, HUD forgotten. Nothing mattered but the 'Mech and MechWarrior in front of him. Stretching his arms forward, Raul set the autocannon barrels up against the chest of the *Tundra Wolf*. "Stand down, Star Colonel." It was over, and Raul breathed a quick exhale of relief. There was no compromise left in his voice, only a promise. Torrent surely heard it.

Heard it, but did not care.

The Steel Wolf commander, reaching for the brass ring right up until the end, shifted the *Tundra Wolf*'s left arm over, planted it into the *Jupiter*'s gut, and destroyed his own arm by firing his tactical missile system with the launcher in actual contact against Raul's gyroscope housing.

The force of nine simultaneous detonations squeezed in between two BattleMechs actually lifted the hundred-ton assault 'Mech off the ground. No balancing act would save Raul from gravity's clutches this time. Hauling back on both control sticks, fingers tight on his triggers, Raul surrendered to the fall while pumping two hot streams of high-velocity metal into the *Tundra Wolf*'s chest.

The fall likely saved Raul's life.

With feedback damage already spiking through the *Tundra Wolf*'s power systems, Raul's fifty-millimeter autocannons tore through the last of the physical shielding and blasted apart the fusion engine's safeguard systems as well. Dampening fields cut out completely, releasing the fires that burned so powerfully at the heart of every BattleMech.

The fusion reaction expanded, gobbled up myomer, armor, and titanium skeletal structure as fuel. A column of golden fire burned up and through the cockpit. Then the engine burst free completely in a violent explosion of golden fire, flattening a nearby LoaderMech, picking up a Scimitar and throwing it through the air like a child's plaything.

The force grabbed at Raul's *Jupiter,* twisted it about on the ground, but otherwise washed over it in a wave of destructive fire that did little more than finish flash-burning the paint from Jove's front.

Then silence descended.

Silence, or Raul had gone deaf with the titanic thunderclap. Inventorying his limbs and checking his teeth with a rough-coated tongue, the MechWarrior rolled his 'Mech onto its side and then to its chest, propping himself up with one arm to better see the stunned field.

And looked into the wide-bore port of an SM1's assault cannon.

The battle did continue in several isolated patches. The Swordsworn still fought a holding action at the city's edge, protecting themselves from a small cordon of Steel Wolf treaded tanks and advancing infantry. Palos Montgomery and a trio of LoaderMechs shuffled into a loose circle around a Demon, hydraulic pincers grabbing and tearing. Diago was still alive and fighting as well, matching off in the distance with a Steel Wolf catapult.

But near Raul and the metal carcass that had been the Steel Wolf commander's BattleMech, everyone waited to see what would happen now between the *Jupiter* and the Destroyer.

"If you are going to shoot," Raul croaked, his voice breaking on almost every word, "do it now or quit wasting my time."

Several painful heartbeats passed before an answer came. "I am Star Captain Nikola Demos. I claim you as bondsman."

"No," Raul told her, shocked that she would even think of such a thing after losing her commander. "You've won nothing here."

"The Steel Wolves . . . my . . . *my* Steel Wolves still control the spaceport."

"Keep it," Raul told her. "Run the damn thing if you want. But there will be no occupation of River's End and there is no HPG station to fight over any longer." He coughed, trying to ease the burning itch at the back of his throat. "Pick up your dead and injured, and allow us to do the same, and tomorrow we can do this all over again or maybe—maybe—we can bargain for an honorable withdrawal."

Remembering how Tassa Kay and Kyle Powers had both argued for the important part such concerns played in Steel Wolf reasoning, he figured it couldn't hurt to appeal to her warrior's nature. "Or do you really want Star Colonel Torrent's cast-offs?" he asked derisively, with all the strength he had left.

Raul never heard the order passed but, first singly and then in large packs, the Steel Wolves broke away from the fighting and fell back toward their waiting DropShips. Blaire ordered all retreating forces to be left alone. On the far side of the field, Erik Sandoval knew enough to also let the Steel Wolves withdraw.

"We will consider our position," the SM1 commander told him. "Tomorrow we bargain."

Then the Destroyer spun around in place and raced away, cutting close to several IndustrialMechs but never targeting them, unafraid that they would dare touch her.

"Tomorrow we bargain," Raul agreed, but with less enthusiasm than before. With adrenaline bleeding away along with his life's blood, a heavy weariness crept up. Rolling the injured BattleMech onto its back again, Raul stretched it out in the best possible posture for loading. "I could use a recovery vehicle here," he said, closing his eyes.

In the darkness, he felt his shoulder throb. "And a medic."

Lying back into his seat, he let exhaustion claim him.

28

Reunion

M.A.S.H. Truck Bravo-Four
Achernar
18 March 3133

Raul fought his way back to consciousness through dark cobwebs, peeling away one sticky layer at a time. Bit by bit, he remembered the battle.

Tassa Kay's fighting retreat and eventual dodge back into the city.

Star Colonel Torrent's death in a blazing, acrid pyre.

The dark exhaustion that had claimed him.

Trying to coax some life back into his body, Raul focused all his strength into one arm, lifting it to his face where he hoped to rub the last of the cobwebs from his eyes. Someone caught his hand, held it. A warm, soft touch.

"Jessica?" Was that too much to hope for? In his waking state, Raul did not want to believe so.

"Is it over?" Jessica Searcy asked.

The battle. The fighting. Raul had no doubt that that was what she meant.

"I think so. I hope so." But because he had learned more in the last few weeks than he had ever wanted to with regard to war, he told her, "For now."

He forced his gummy eyes open. Jess sat beside his wall-mounted cot, still wearing the paramilitary uniform, although now it was spattered with blood and smudged dark in several places.

"I told you to stay safe," she said.

He blinked, then glanced down at his bare chest and heavily bandaged shoulder. "Just a small scar," he reminded her. He had a double I.V. stuck into his arm, slowly rebuilding his fluid and blood loss. He started to rise, but felt too tired to put much effort into it and so slowly settled back. "Just for you."

"Get some sleep, Raul." Already her voice sounded distant. "You've earned a rest."

He shook his head. "Not today. Not yet. One more thing to do, Jess." He closed his eyes. "Then we'll see." See about the two of them. That was what he'd meant to say. Had he said it?

She seemed to know, regardless.

"Is it over?" she asked. And he knew what she meant as well.

"I hope not, Jess. I hope not."

And he drifted back off, his hand still warm in hers.

29

Strength and Honor

DropShip **Lupus**
Achernar
19 March 3133

Achernar's sun had barely cleared the spaceport's administration buildings when Star Captain Nikola Demos arrived at the head of the *Lupus*'s main ramp, dressed down in a field uniform and a Needle pistol strapped against the side of her leg.

Shielding her eyes with one hand, the Steel Wolves' ranking officer surveyed the distant edge of spaceport grounds where her salvage crews continued to work over the site of yesterday's battle. Early-morning winds had dispersed a great deal of the battle's dark pallor, but a gray haze still hung over the city and spaceport, and a breeze brought to her the acrid stench of scorched metal. Nikola Demos swiped at her nose, peered into the distance to watch her technicians stripping useful parts from the wreckage of so many vehicles and 'Mechs, hauling back entire bodies when useful.

Good enough, she decided. It was a new day, and time for a new leader.

She wouldn't know until later just how prophetic that thought had been.

The Republic party waited near the ramp's foot, their jeep parked nearby with a uniformed soldier behind the wheel and a blonde-haired medic standing next to the vehicle, repeatedly shifting her weight from one foot to the other. Their extra presence was not welcome, but Nikola let that go as she turned her attention to the waiting trio.

Three warriors, as arranged, one with his arm in a sling. No weapons on their persons that she could see, although no provision had excluded arms. Nikola checked the position of her Elemental sentries—one at each edge of the upper ramp. She didn't expect treachery—new treachery—but like her predecessor, she had learned to plan for it.

Not everyone played by the same rules as the Steel Wolves. Not many could, she supposed, and still be able to compete against the genetically engineered warriors.

Nikola's *guests* talked amongst themselves while watching her people's activities with interest. Two of them did, at least. She was halfway down the ramp before she finally recognized the third as Star Commander Yulri. He wore a white bondcord around his wrist and hovered off the shoulder of the female MechWarrior—this Tassa Kay—like an obedient guard dog.

Rather pathetic, she thought then, seeing how low one of Torrent's handpicked warriors had fallen. Could fall. There was another warning in that.

"If you will all follow me," she said in clipped tones, spending courtesy with a miser's grip, "I will take you somewhere we can sit."

"Just the two of us will be accompanying you," Tassa Kay said, nodding for herself and Yulri. "Captain Ortega has another obligation this morning."

Nikola Demos nodded. "I see. You are not an officer of The Republic, MechWarrior Kay. You can batchall on their behalf?" Batchall was the formal term for a bargaining of forces for battle. Nikola wasn't certain it would come to that, but saw no reason to waste time if it did.

"We can discuss it inside," the other woman said.

Turning to Raul Ortega then, oblivious of the star captain's presence, Tassa stepped half a pace closer to The Republic captain. Nikola found herself appraising him with a woman's eye. He did not have the size or inherent presence of a man such as Star Colonel Torrent, but there was a hardness—a confidence—in his dark eyes that spoke of an inner strength. And he had bested Torrent in battle. Good genes, Nikola judged.

"You're certain?" Raul asked. Nikola's appraisal dropped one notch with his lazy use of contractions. "I can hold this off until tomorrow."

"To each his own." Tassa reached into a pocket, slipped out a folded piece of verifaxed paper and handed it over. "To your Exarch, with my compliments. I will not be needing it anymore."

Ortega caught up Tassa Kay's hand, tensed a moment as if caught in the act of something shameful, and then plunged on ahead. He lifted her hand up and kissed its back. "With the gratitude of Achernar."

Tassa Kay laughed. Her voice was rich and full of life. "You are Republic all right." Grabbing up a handful of his uniform front, she pulled him in for a brief, hard kiss on the mouth. "Save the courtly love for knights and ladies. And make certain my *Ryoken* is brought out here at once, or the next smack you get might loosen a tooth."

"I will miss you, too." With a sad smile, Ortega traded casual salutes with Tassa Kay and then left without a backward glance.

"That sounded quite a bit like a good-bye." Nikola Demos leveled a hard gaze at the other woman. "Going somewhere?"

Tassa ignored her, stepped around the star captain and preceded her up the ramp. "Aren't you coming?" she asked, the curt question tossed over her shoulder as if she didn't care one way or the other whether Nikola did or not.

Nikola placed a hand into the middle of Yulri's chest, stopping him from following and thereby also preceding her. With a hard mask set over her face, she jogged up to Tassa Kay and escorted the MechWarrior into the DropShip's main bay and then through to officer's country and a series of ladders that took them up to Star Colonel Torrent's former office—now hers.

Torrent had preferred dim lighting. Nikola Demos did not. With so many hours logged inside cramped and dimly lit tanks, she reveled in brightly lit open spaces. The wall panels washed the Spartan room in sterile light, emphasizing the absence of any wall decorations or personal touches. Those would come later, when and if Prefect Kal Radick confirmed Nikola as Torrent's successor.

"Bare, but functional," was Tassa's opinion. She slid into a seat on the near side of the desk. Star Commander Yulri waited back at the door, standing honor guard to one side of the entry. "I will not challenge you for it, so long as you provide me with good quarters and a place inside the main BattleMech bay for my *Ryoken*."

"You," Nikola said, hovering over her own chair, disbelief certainly showing on her face, "will not . . . challenge?"

"Not so long as all three DropShips are off Achernar by midnight, local time. That is the deal I bargained with the militia on the Steel Wolves' behalf. If there is no JumpShip due from Tigress soon, we will take the next available commercial transport from this system."

Sitting down into her own chair with a stiff, military bearing, Nikola Demos stared daggers at the woman who presumed to dictate terms to her. She was no representative of The Republic—was not even an officer except for an honorary title they had awarded her for piloting a BattleMech. Her idea of a uniform, in fact, was nothing more than hip-hugging leather pants and a leather jacket with stainless steel buckles for fastening. Beneath the jacket, she wore nothing more official than a black T-shirt emblazoned with a red hourglass. Casual. Irreverent.

Familiar . . . ?

"If The Republic believes that they can dictate terms

so easily to the Steel Wolves, we can show them the error of their ways. The HPG station may indeed be out of commission, but Achernar might still be pressed to serve as a staging ground for future operations. Who do you think you are to come in here and—"

Tassa did not allow her to build further momentum, interrupting with a hand slapped down flat and loud on the desk.

"I'm the woman who put that HPG station out of commission because it would get your attention, and I knew that we did not want the Swordsworn to keep possession of it. I'm the woman who is also telling you that Achernar is off limits. First, you have no good reason to remain here. Second, if you should try, I promise you that I will split your force strength in half, or worse, and ensure your defeat."

Nikola scoffed. "You would do that how?"

"By challenging you for command in a Trial of Position."

"You cannot. You have no standing here." She paused, hedged. "Unless . . ." Only one thing might back up such a claim: unless Tassa Kay was Clan, and a Wolf.

A fact Tassa proved by reaching up to pull her necklace charm out from her shirt: a clear, faceted data crystal, banded with golden trim.

The star captain grounded herself back in the conversation, putting together an earlier comment by Tassa Kay with her recent orders. "You plan to accompany us back to Tigress." It was not a question; almost coming out as an accusation. Her resolve hardened. "You believe Kal Radick will support you so easily?"

With a quick yank Tassa broke the chain, then tossed the military codex to Nikola. "You will find your answers in there."

It took a single moment to power up the computer built into Torrent's office desk—her office desk!—and slip the faceted data crystal into a small slot along one edge of the spotless surface. The holographic emitter charged to life, throwing up a white screen over which scrolled two-dimensional pages of text, dates and a directory of video reports. Tassa Kay's military history, dating back from Achernar, through a military operation on Dieron and before that on the Republic world of Marfik.

And more. Tassa's original Trial of Position as a MechWarrior and Star Colonel. Also her full genetic history, and a note of her victory in winning a Bloodname from the House of—

"You are . . . " Nikola began, then swallowed dryly to coax greater strength out of her voice. "That is, we have another . . ."

Tassa shook back her mane of dark, red hair and awarded Nikola Demos a poisonous smile.

"The name you are looking for," Tassa said with a generous helping of serious humor, "is Kerensky."

Epilog

Blackout

ComStar HPG Station: Stryker-A7
Achernar
19 March 3133

Helping Raul over the larger piles of rubble and through the twisted wreckage that had once been the HPG station's front entry, Jessica Searcy worked to keep her opinions from showing. There was still too much left to work out between Raul and herself, but she had hope for the first time in days, and she didn't care for the way he pushed himself only one day after so much dehydration and blood loss. He was, if nothing else, a patient. He was also a man she had cared for—did care for—deeply.

The compound looked better from the outside, Jessica decided, getting her first look at the ruined interior. Fire-blackened walls and a missile-scarred street was all that remained to tell of the recent battle, that and a scorched superstructure running up one side of the support tower into a twisted framework on the back of the mammoth dish.

The interior destruction was far worse, striking her like a heavy slap in the face.

Consoles sat darkened at every customer service desk. Some monitors had blown outward, as if from a massive power surge. Dark, greasy smoke stains blackened the ceiling overhead. The acrid, ozone smell of an electrical fire hung thick and cloying in the air.

Glass slivers littered the floor and stuck into seat backs as if shot there from a gun. The damage reminded Jessica of the various shards and splinters she had removed from Raul's neck and shoulder, once the corpsmen dragged him out of the *Jupiter*'s cockpit: twelve deep lacerations, counting the shard he had pulled from his own shoulder. Yes, he'd have a good scar by which to remember the day. And why did she feel guilty about that?

She hadn't actually meant for him to get hurt.

Well, she also believed—truly believed—that Raul hadn't meant for her to get hurt either. But was she ready to stop making him feel guilty about it?

"What the blazes is *he* doing here?" Raul asked, tensing beneath her touch.

Erik Sandoval-Groell picked his way over a collapsed portion of the wire-hung ceiling, dusting chalky residue from his hands and glaring daggers at Raul. The young lord had a smudge of charcoal over one ear where he shaved up his hairline. His topknot had seen better times, sweat-matted and streaked with plaster.

A burly infantryman—their driver and courtesy guard—stepped between the two men until Raul waved him aside. Erik somehow managed to look down his nose at the taller soldier, but afforded Raul something akin to respect. Not of equals, certainly, but better than he awarded the average man.

"Do not worry. Your Governor Haidall allowed Legate Stempres and I the courtesy of twenty-four hours before liftoff. Stempres is still packing. I thought I'd use the time to make certain the HPG was down."

Raul nodded, as if expecting no less. "What about your toady, Michael Eus? Any sign of him?" The Governor's expulsion edict, arranged the previous night and which Jessica had read about this morning, had not stopped with Erik Sandoval and Brion Stempres. All Swordsworn military forces and quite a few civilian managers of companies with economic ties to the Sandovals were joining them. All but Michael Eus, who had gone to ground.

"I'm certain he will turn up," Erik promised darkly.

At the most inopportune time, Jessica felt certain. She watched Raul survey the room, and nod at a nearby ComStar manager who left his technicians and joined the small group. "Quite the mess," he greeted Raul, trading a handshake that belonged more in a mahogany-trimmed boardroom than a ruined station. Raul introduced him as Hanson Doles, chief operations manager for Stryker Productions. "I never thought I'd see the day I'd be glad to be out of business."

"We'll have you running again as soon as we can spare enough engineers and material to patch up the dish," Raul told him.

Doles slumped a bit. "From our own early evaluations, that may prove to be optimistic. We were fortunate enough to be spared when the net went down, but whatever gave us immunity, well, the blackout looks to have a hold of us now. We get no test return from Ronel, or out of Genoa."

Jessica had been wondering about that. The interior of the compound looked bad, true, but in a superficial way, like a scalp wound that bleeds worse than its actual severity.

"You can move the dish?" Jessica asked, and felt Raul tighten under her touch.

"The dish was locked onto a strong signal from Ronel when it went down," Doles told her. "Our margin of error allows us to still try and use it, at least for another four days. Once per day we swing through a good position for Ronel and for Genoa. But so far, no return. We may be down for good."

Erik appeared cheered by the news, though he frowned again at Raul's easy shrug. "Of all the scenarios I ran through in my mind," Erik said, "that you would force the charges to detonate was not one of them. Even after I chased you—Tassa Kay, whoever was in that *Leigonnaire*—from the city, I didn't see it coming."

"That's called détente." Raul glanced around the open room. "With the HPG out of our way, there's nothing left to fight over."

The nobleman smiled, thin and cold. "You win your world back, and I go home to Tikonov as a hero of the people. Of *my* people." He caught Jessica's look of confusion, and politely addressed himself to her. "My orders were to deny this station to the Steel Wolves. It was the reason I thought the Swordsworn and Republic could work together."

"Not a mistake you will make again," Jessica said frostily.

"No. Not again," Erik agreed. "Still, it was my foresight that prevented a loss of the compound to Torrent's Steel Wolves, and our arrival at the spaceport which turned the battle. A modest victory, considering the forces I had to work with. In Caesar's Game, I believe that should be worth some kind of prize. A promotion, and perhaps a barony."

Of course, he left out the part about being forced into that battle. From necessity, Jessica decided. It was easier to play up his action in a positive light.

"When Devlin Stone returns," Raul said, "your uncle will be lucky to keep a summer home inside the Republic."

"I'll give him your message." Erik gave Doles a nasty grin. "Since no one else around here can."

"Do that." Raul shrugged aside Jessica's helping hand. "Let him know that the Republic will stand no matter how badly small men try to tear it down. The next time one of you comes for Achernar, you will find us ready."

Laughing, Erik waved Raul's warning aside as if it carried no weight with him at all. "What you don't understand, Ortega, is that without your working HPG, Achernar is not worth anything at all. Not to the Swordsworn, *or* to The Republic." Erik left the two of them on that note, rubbing grit out of his hair as he made his way toward the ruined entry.

"All the damage, all the deaths you can lay at their

feet," Jessica said. "Stempres and Sandoval. And both walk away. It doesn't seem fair."

"No," Raul agreed, "but that's the province of nobility. The noble courts might be able to deal with them, eventually, once the Republic can reassert some control." He shifted his weight during the awkward pause. "He was right, you know. Without the HPG, we'll have trouble keeping the Republic's attention long enough to do something about rebuilding." But there was hope in his voice when he said it.

"You don't sound too worried."

"We'll make do," Raul promised. "One way or another."

Hanson Doles tore his gaze away from Sandoval's back. His eyes could have been lasers for all the fire Erik's parting comments had raised in them. "In the meantime," Doles said, "how would you like to be our first return customer? One thing our computer work *has* managed to do is reconstruct your general delivery message, Mr. Ortega. You will need to use my office system, but you can finally view the full recording." He moved toward a nearby closed door.

Raul nodded. "This shouldn't take a minute," he promised Jessica, stepped away and then paused. "Would you like to come?" he asked her.

"Show it to me later," she said. "I'll see what I can do to help out here, then we should go by the hospital." She reached up to rub a finger over the golden caduceus, still pinned to her collar. "As long as I'm still wearing this, I should earn it."

Raul leaned forward and kissed her on the cheek. "You earned it." When he left, it was with greater strength than he had shown before, walking unassisted and with the hint of a smile on his lips.

Jessica waited until Hanson Doles had let Raul into the office, and then caught up with him as he directed a clean-up crew. "Is there anything you need here in the way of medical attention?" she asked.

"Medical attention? No, I don't believe so."

"Good." Jessica smiled. "Everyone already taken care of then. Are they in River's End General? I'd be happy to look them over personally, this afternoon."

"No," Hanson said again. "That is, no one was injured."

"At all?"

Hanson shook his head slowly, and with no little amount of regret. Then he found something else to do and excused himself.

Jessica walked over again to a nearby station, counting the glass shards longer than her finger, and looking at the shredded cloth on the back of the seat. And another one. And one over there. Some splinters looked as if they had been hurled a dozen meters or better.

"And no one was injured?" she asked herself again, and reached up to rub at the caduceus.

"That Tassa Kay chose to return with the Steel Wolves to Tigress is not a comforting fact," Lady Janella Lakewood told Raul. "It bodes ill for The Republic. You trust her to keep quiet?"

Sitting in Hanson Doles' chair, letting the day's fatigue drain down through his legs and into the station's tiled floor, Raul nodded. "I do. Her role was a necessary part in the deception, and her only concern was to keep the Swordsworn from retaining control over the facility and Achernar."

So while Tassa kept Sandoval busy, her infantry had moved into position planting dummy charges and stripping away the sabotaging devices. Then the big show of fire and smoke—or smoke and mirrors, Raul thought with a grim smile—to convince them all of the illusion that the HPG had been damaged.

Lady Janella Lakewood looked more composed this time than during their last conversation, contacting Raul through the Ronel station itself rather than from a field relay. "A worthy gamble," she said. "One I would be tempted to use on Ronel, except that two factions here couldn't care less—so far—for the advantage of the

HPG. An old enmity," she explained, "between Sandoval's Swordsworn and the Dragon's Fury."

"All enmities seem to be old ones, these days." Raul shook his head. "Sometimes I wonder if Devlin Stone did not leave us a legacy of chaos. Does that make me a poor citizen?" he asked.

"It makes you human, Raul. Devlin Stone left us with a lot of unanswered questions. He also left us the hope of a better future, but it still comes down to personal choice. Your choices have been exemplary."

Raul shook his head, feeling a sharp stab of guilt. He heard the door open back behind him, and then close. He knew it would not be Hanson Doles, and the facility manager had instructions from Raul to allow only one person to follow him, but he still said exactly what had been on his mind. "No, Lady Lakewood. I have made mistakes that have cost people their lives, and some their trust." He buried his darker memories of Charal DePriest, and Jessica. "I didn't do so well."

Janella Lakewood smiled sadly. "We rarely do, in the beginning, but we learn and we endure. Along the way, we can find absolution. You did not shirk your duty to Achernar or The Republic. You persevered in the face of personal loss and injury. What more do you expect of yourself?"

"Better." Raul laughed at himself. "I expect better."

"Good, because I am going to give you that chance." Janella Lakewood's blue eyes radiated a new confidence. "It will be good for myself, and others, to know we have hands in the area that we can trust implicitly. I'd like to name you a Knight-Errant of the Sphere, Raul. Subject to confirmation by Exarch Redburn, of course."

A cold thrill spiked through Raul's backbone at the offer. A Knight of the Sphere! Not only was such a position beyond Raul's original dreams, the responsibilities rose up and threatened to roll over him like Juggernaut's carriage. "I never thought . . ." he began, then cleared his throat. "I did not want . . ."

Behind him, a new voice trumped his own. "That is Raul's way of saying that he accepts, Lady."

Raul had hoped that Jessica would change her mind and follow him, though he had not figured on her hearing—or accepting for him!—such an offer.

On the flat-screen monitor, Lady Lakewood stiffened with surprise as Raul stood and moved the chair aside, allowing Jessica to join him in the real-time conversation. "You have a strange way of keeping secrets, Mr. Ortega." Her voice was a noticeably bit colder than before.

"It's not his fault," Jessica said. "Not *entirely* his fault. When I found out that no one had been injured here, despite the explosions and fires and collapsed walls, I knew that a majority of the damage had been staged." She offered the other woman a discreet smile as her hand crept over to take Raul's in a clasp. "I can fix some documents at the hospital. A death or two in the public records should help."

"Besides," Raul added, feeling the warmth of Jessica's hand in his, "if I cannot decide who I can place *my* trust in, what good is my judgment to you?"

Janella Lakewood considered this, and nodded, reluctantly. "Then you do accept?"

Raul turned Jessica to him. "I still think it's my duty to stand up for the Republic," he told her, "but I have to admit, I don't want this as much as I once would have."

"I'll feel better knowing that some of the luster has worn off the dream. Maybe you will stay safer that way." She hesitated, then, "I don't know how much stock I'm putting into the Republic yet, Raul, but I've definitely decided to stand for Achernar. You can do the same, only more so, as a Knight."

He remembered another of her old arguments. "In my duties, I might be called away from Achernar."

"It might be good for me to not see your face some times." Jessica smiled. "So long as you come back."

"I think this is a yes," Raul said. "I accept, Lady."

"Then I commend Achernar into your hands," she told him. "It may take some time to pass your Knighthood through proper channels, but I'll get something to your world governor on the next possible JumpShip. In the meantime, maintain the Blackout—this charade of a Blackout—while I see how things develop on Ronel. And do your level best to prepare for anything."

Raul couldn't help smiling at the suggestion—at once sobering and amusing. "I'll learn quickly," he promised her.

"That is good," Lady Janella Lakewood said. "Because I'm not certain how much time The Republic has."